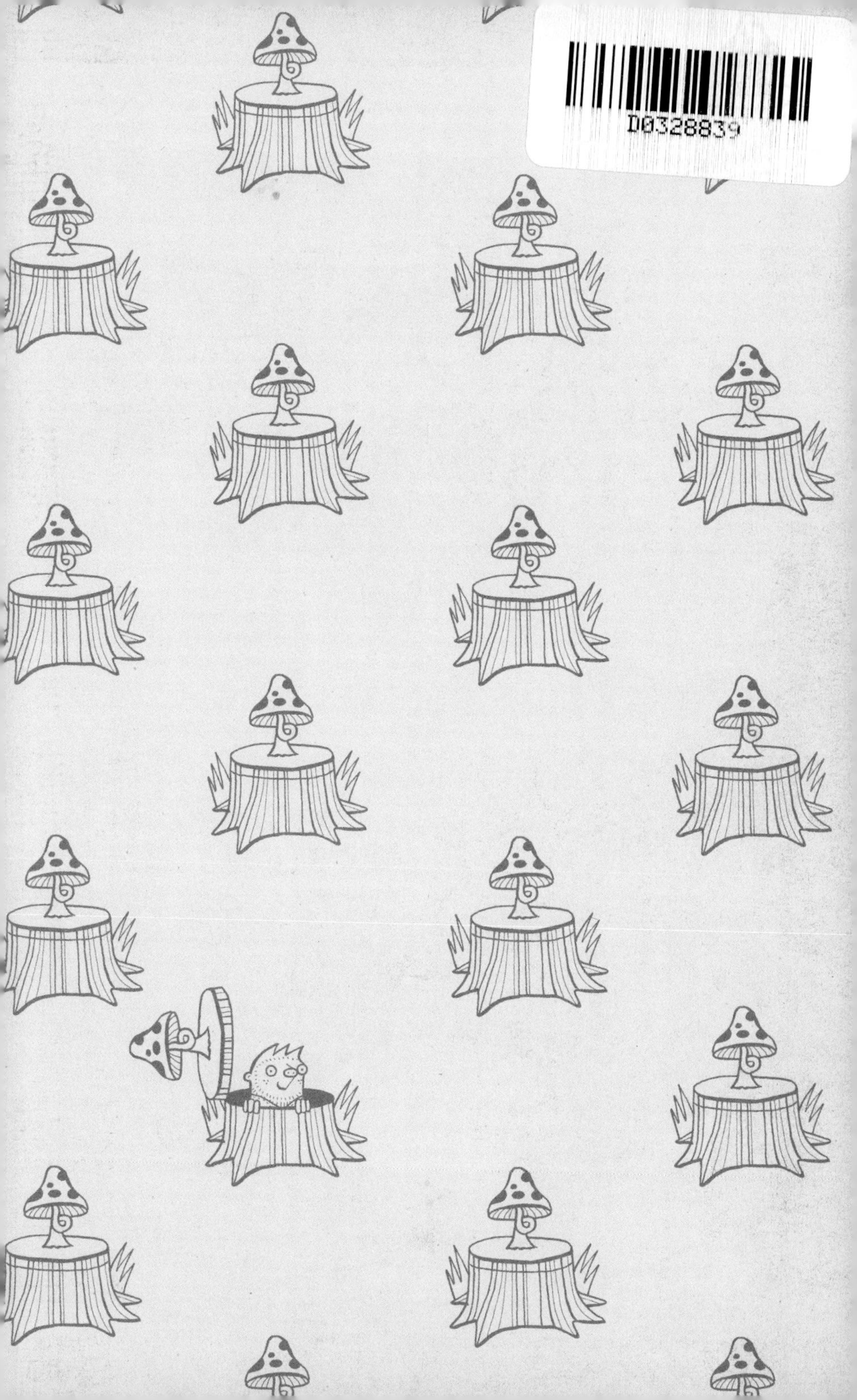

READ ALL THE PACEY PACKER BOOKS!

1

PACEY PACKER, UNICORN TRACKER

2

PACEY PACKER, UNICORN TRACKER:
♦ HORN SLAYER ♦

I can hardly wait.

PACEY 2 PACKER
UNICORN TRACKER

• HORN SLAYER •

J. C. PHILLIPPS

RANDOM HOUSE 🏠 NEW YORK

Copyright © 2021 by J. C. Phillipps
All rights reserved. Published in the United States by Random House Children's Books,
a division of Penguin Random House LLC, New York.

Random House and the colophon are registered trademarks of Penguin Random House LLC.

RH Graphic with the book design is a trademark of Penguin Random House LLC.

Visit us on the Web! rhcbooks.com

Educators and librarians, for a variety of teaching tools,
visit us at RHTeachersLibrarians.com

Library of Congress Cataloging-in-Publication Data
Names: Phillipps, J. C. (Julie C.), author.
Title: Horn slayer / J. C. Phillipps.
Description: First edition. | New York: Random House Children's Books, [2021] |
Series: Pacey Packer, unicorn tracker; 2
Summary: "After slicing the horn off of the Evil Alpha Unicorn and becoming a legend, Pacey Packer
returns to Rundalyn to free the statue children she left behind"—Provided by publisher.
Identifiers: LCCN 2020037417 | ISBN 978-1-9848-5057-7 (hardcover) |
ISBN 978-1-9848-5058-4 (library binding) | ISBN 978-1-9848-5059-1 (ebook)
Subjects: LCSH: Graphic novels. | CYAC: Graphic novels. | Adventure and adventurers—Fiction. |
Toys—Fiction. | Unicorns—Fiction. | Sisters—Fiction.
Classification: LCC PZ7.7.P5213 Hor 2021 | DDC [Fic]—dc23

MANUFACTURED IN CHINA
10 9 8 7 6 5 4 3 2 1
First Edition

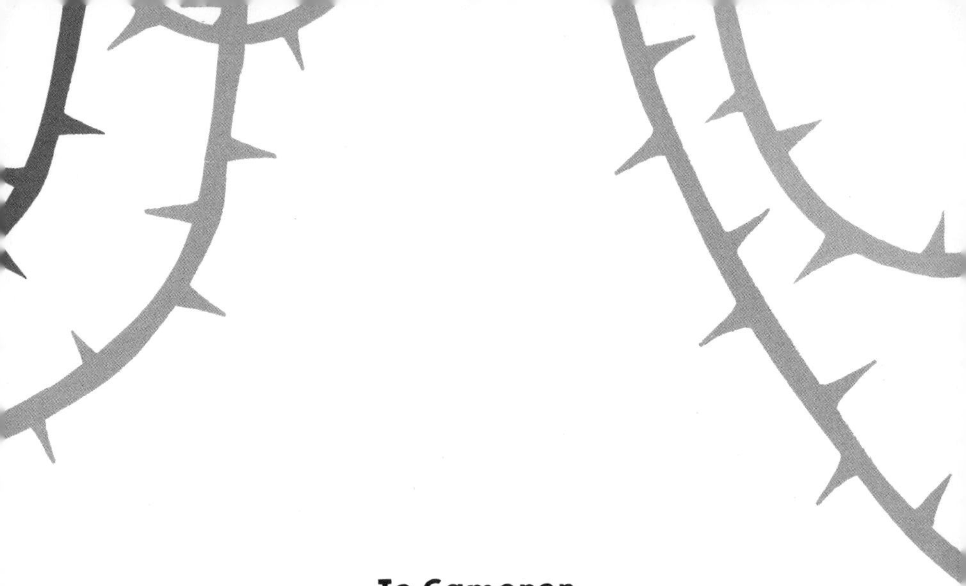

To Cameron.
Kittens need their mother;
then they don't.

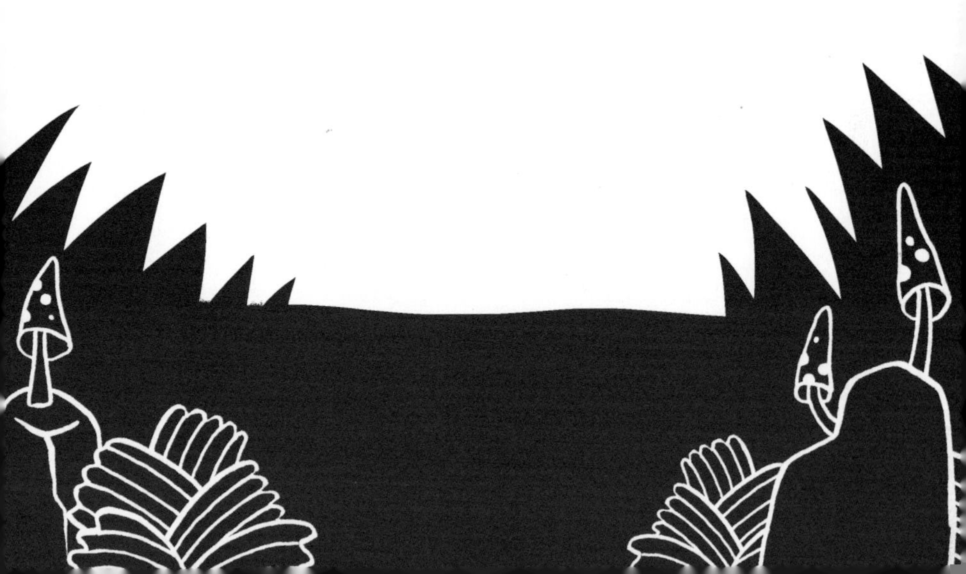

LEGEND OF THE HORN SLAYER

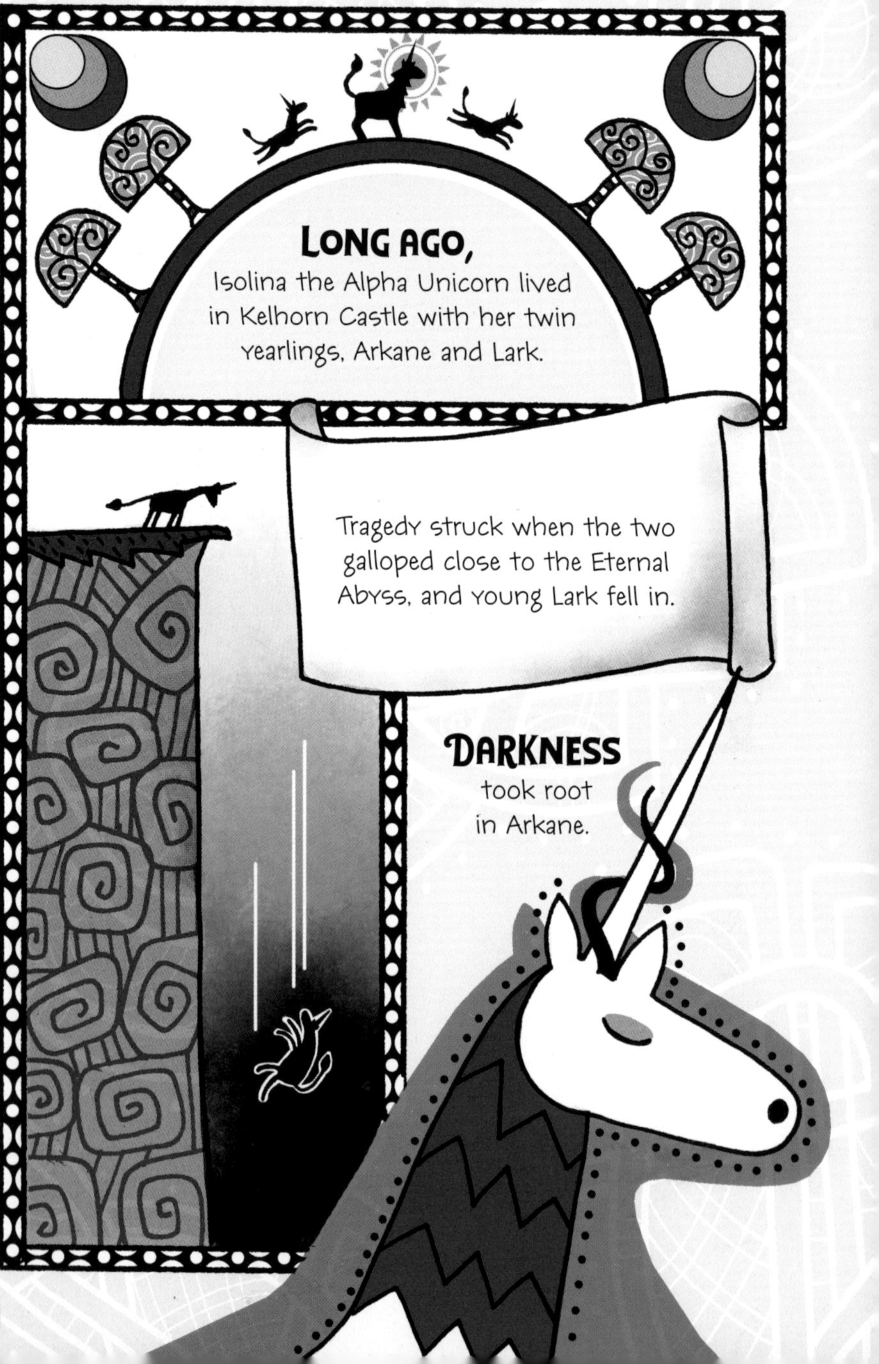
LONG AGO,
Isolina the Alpha Unicorn lived in Kelhorn Castle with her twin yearlings, Arkane and Lark.
Tragedy struck when the two galloped close to the Eternal Abyss, and young Lark fell in.
DARKNESS
took root in Arkane.

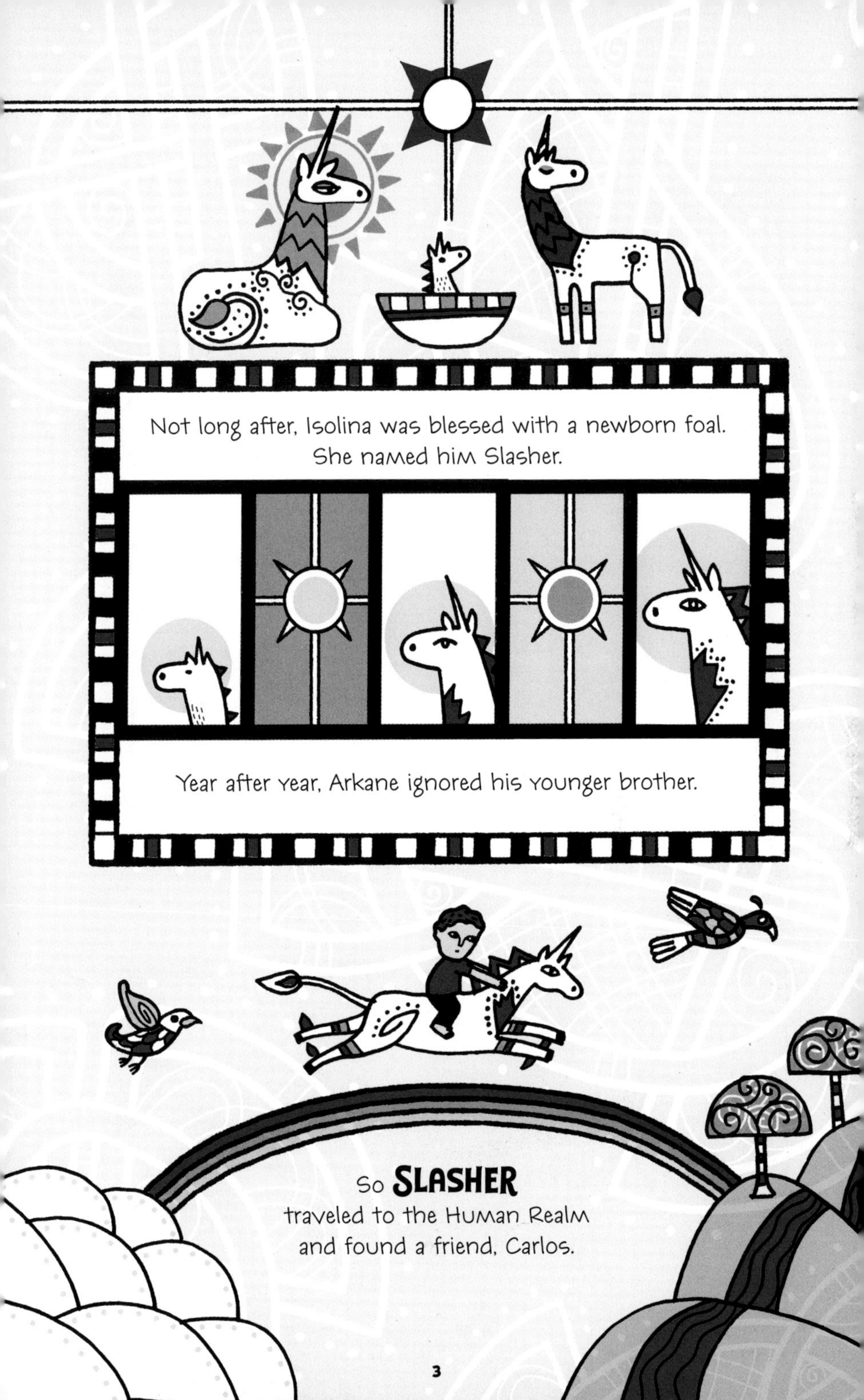
Not long after, Isolina was blessed with a newborn foal. She named him Slasher.
Year after year, Arkane ignored his younger brother.
So **SLASHER** traveled to the Human Realm and found a friend, Carlos.

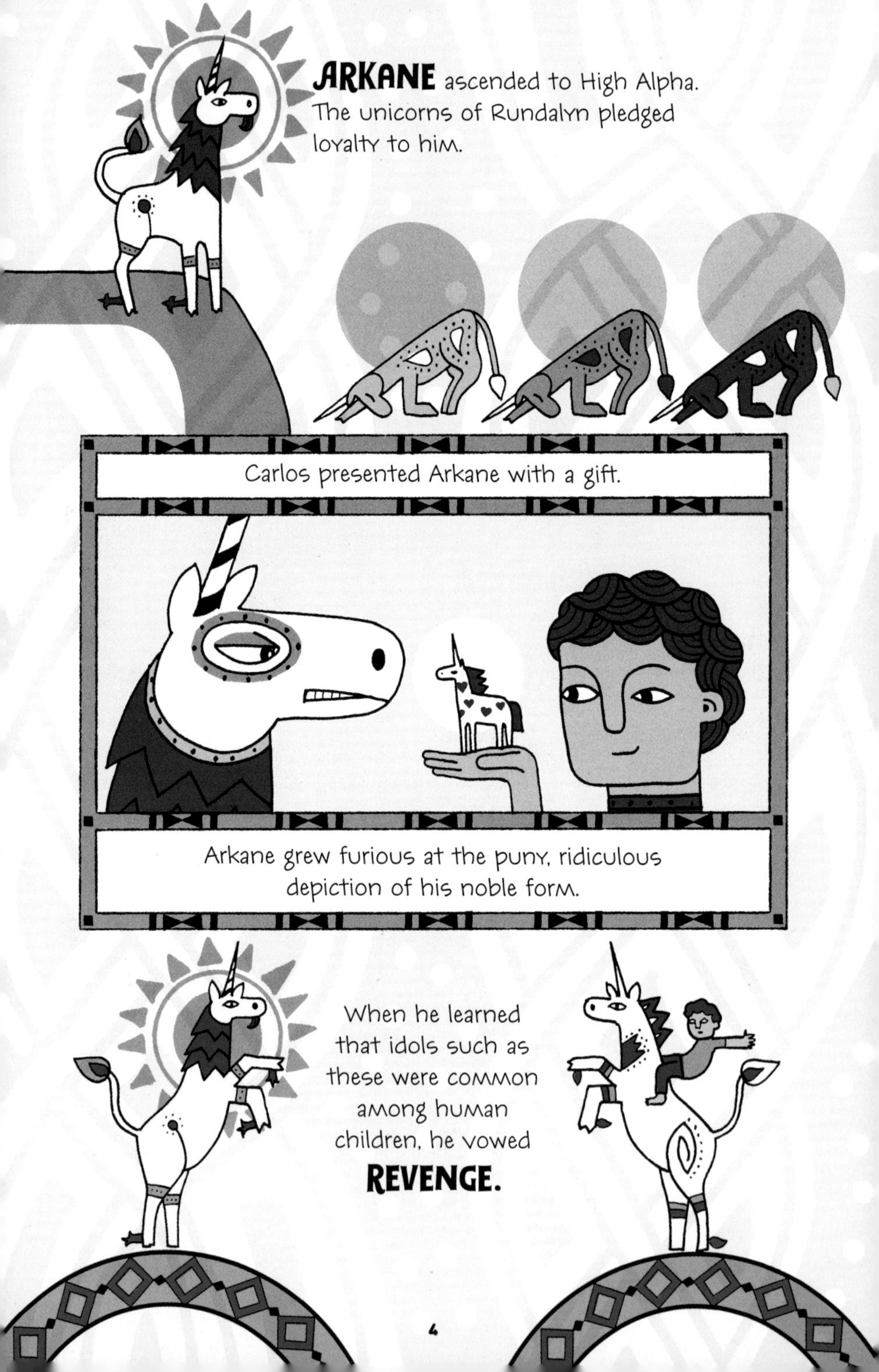
ARKANE ascended to High Alpha. The unicorns of Rundalyn pledged loyalty to him.
Carlos presented Arkane with a gift.
Arkane grew furious at the puny, ridiculous depiction of his noble form.
When he learned that idols such as these were common among human children, he vowed REVENGE.

Arkane used his
DARK POWER
to transform his brother,
Slasher, into a lesser being.

He banished Slasher to the
Human Realm and turned
Carlos into stone.

He lured other **YOUNG HUMANS** to his castle,

then turned them into statues as well.

ONE DAY, Slasher returned with a pair of human sisters, **MINA AND PACEY.**

ARKANE turned Mina into a statue, but Pacey fought back.

She sliced Arkane's horn from his head, thus becoming . . .

THE HORN SLAYER

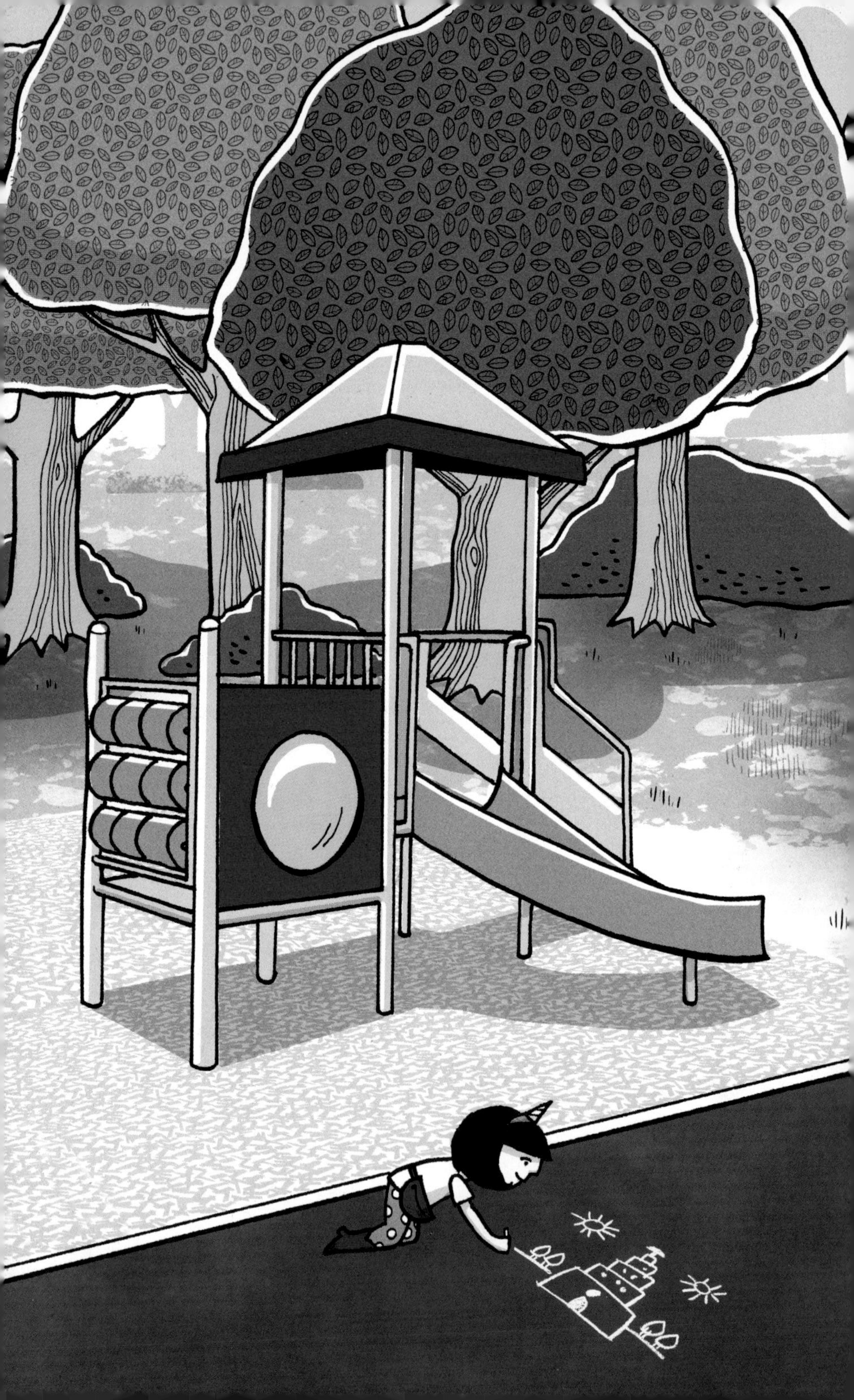

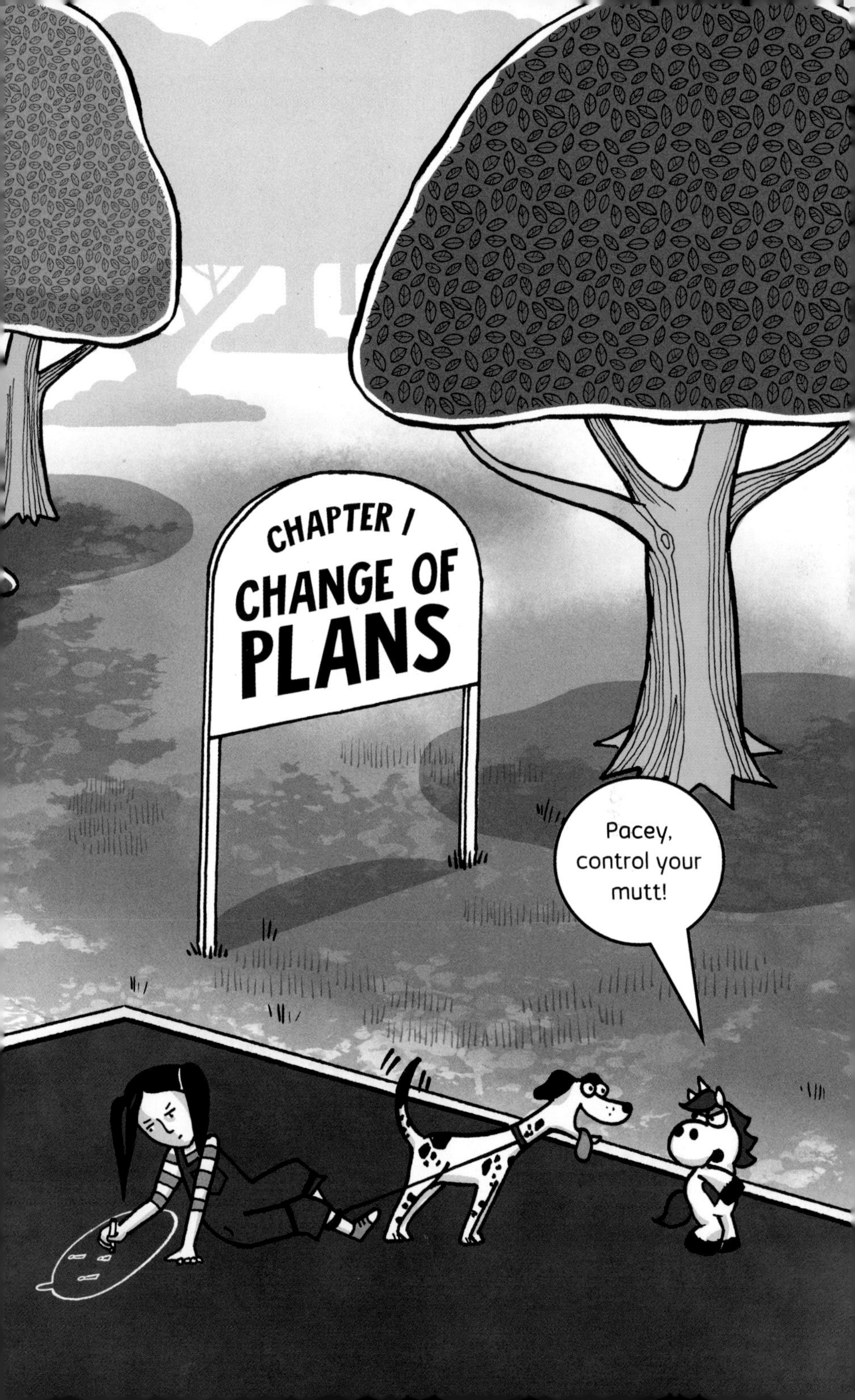
CHAPTER 1
CHANGE OF PLANS
Pacey, control your mutt!

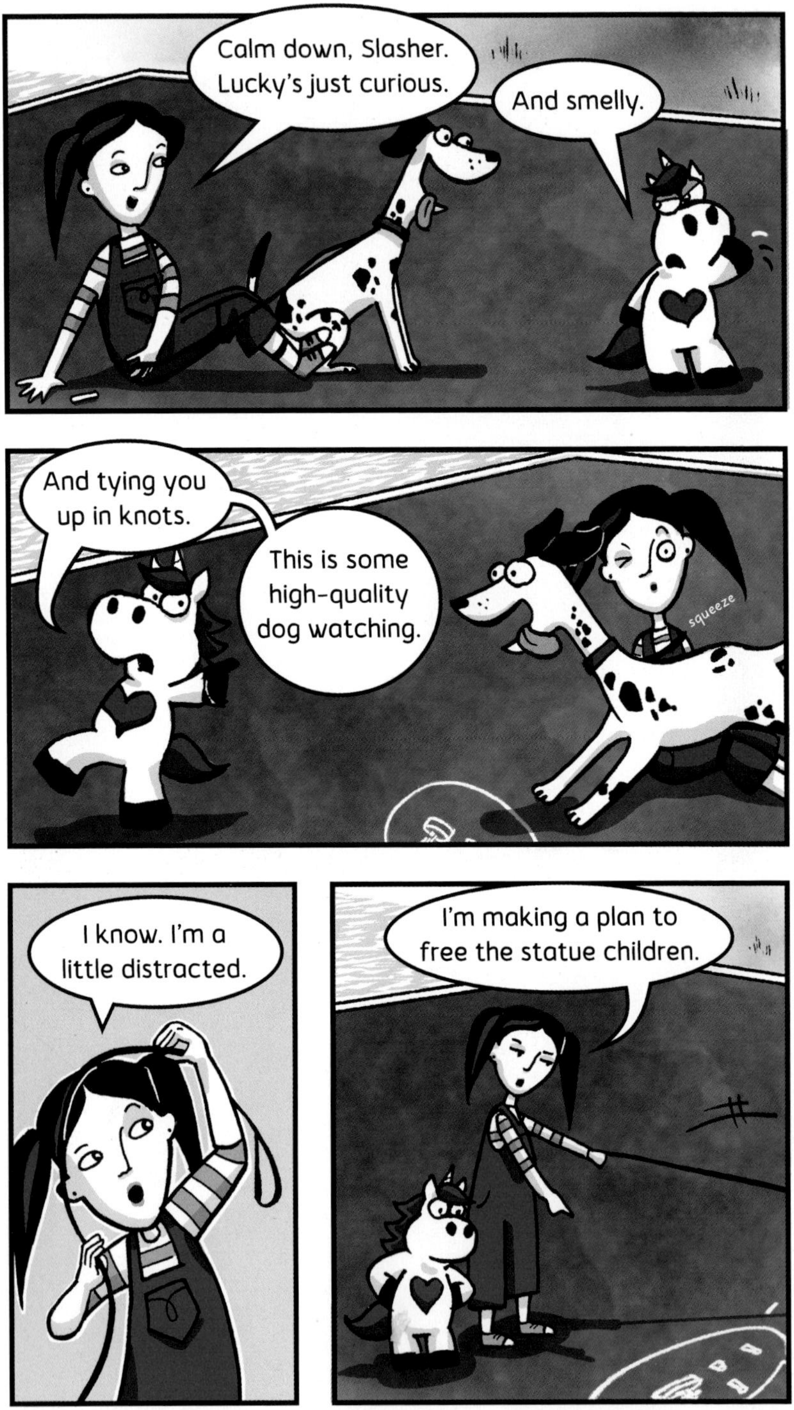

Calm down, Slasher. Lucky's just curious.
And smelly.
And tying you up in knots.
This is some high-quality dog watching.
squeeze
I know. I'm a little distracted.
I'm making a plan to free the statue children.

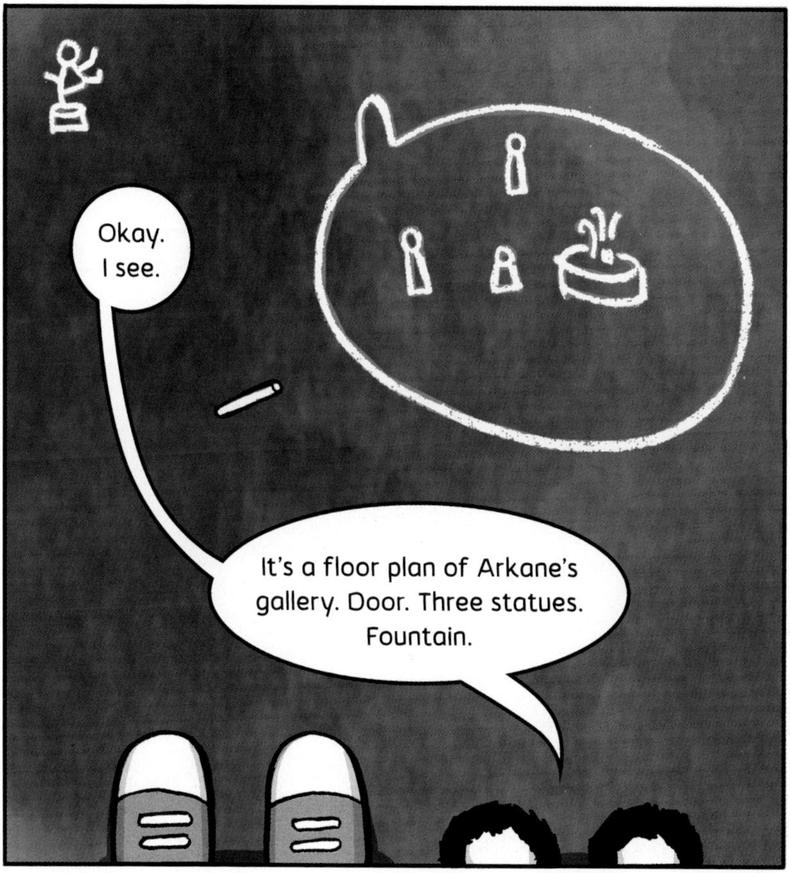
Okay.
I see.
It's a floor plan of Arkane's gallery. Door. Three statues. Fountain.

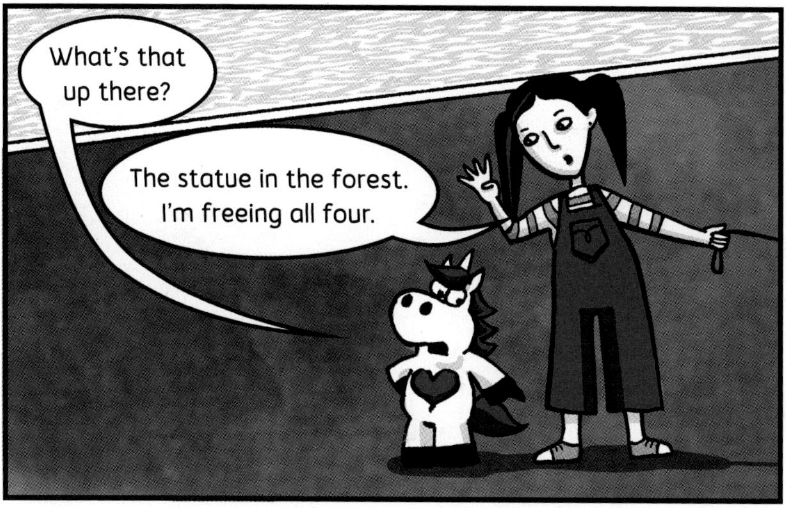
What's that up there?
The statue in the forest. I'm freeing all four.

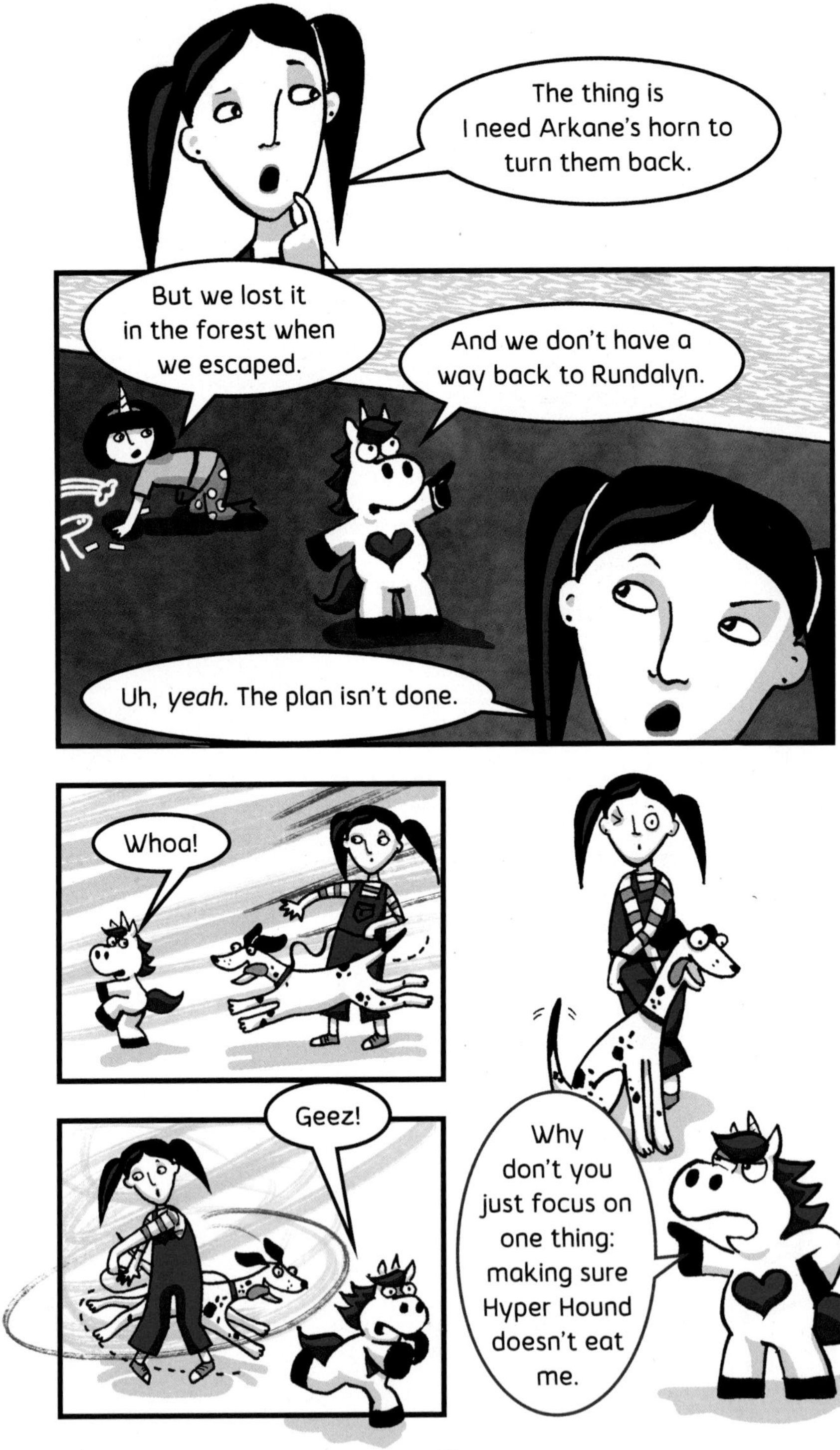
The thing is
I need Arkane's horn to
turn them back.
But we lost it in the forest when we escaped.
And we don't have a way back to Rundalyn.
Uh, *yeah.* The plan isn't done.
Whoa!
Geez!
Why don't you just focus on one thing: making sure Hyper Hound doesn't eat me.

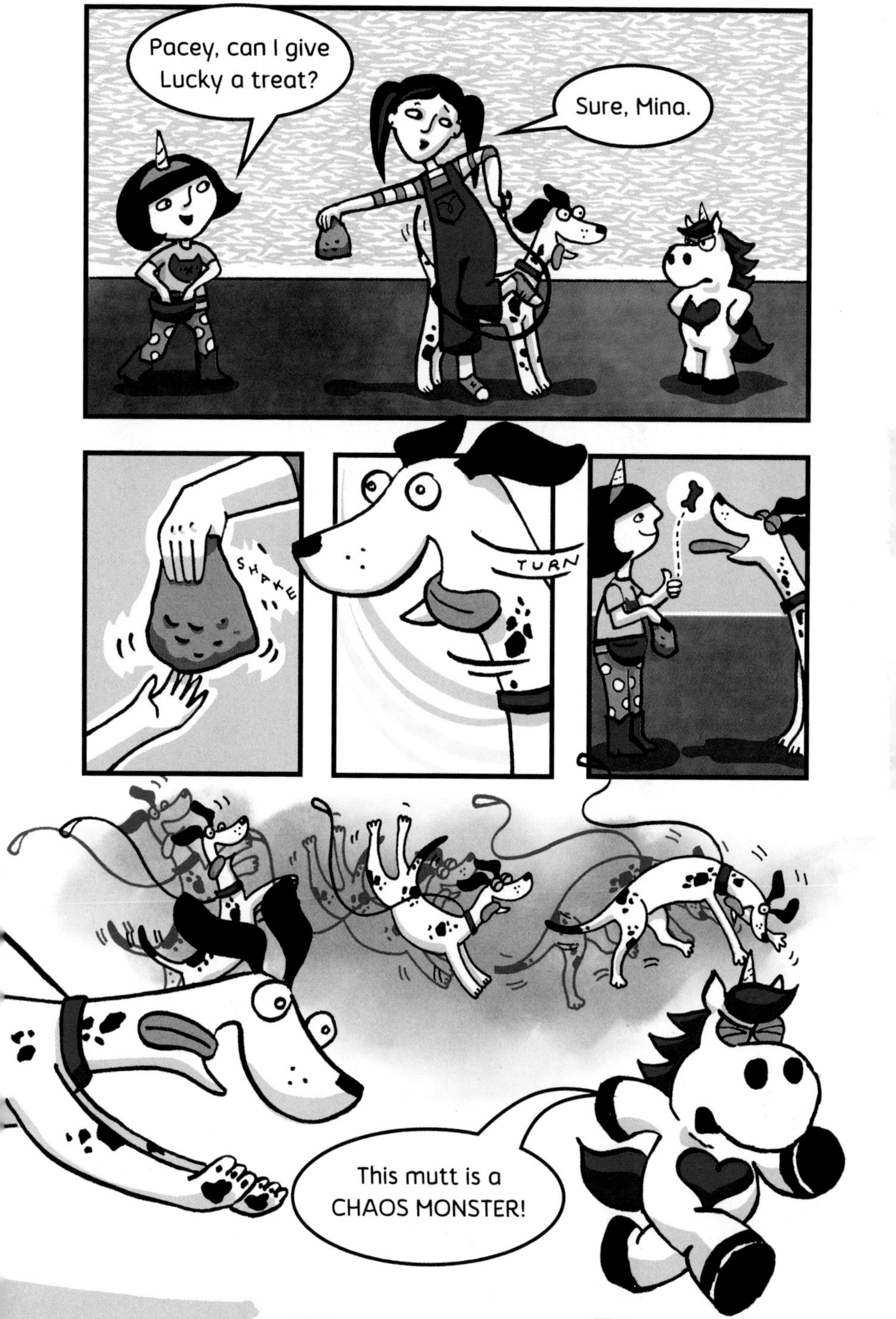
Pacey, can I give Lucky a treat?
Sure, Mina.
SHAKE
TURN
This mutt is a CHAOS MONSTER!

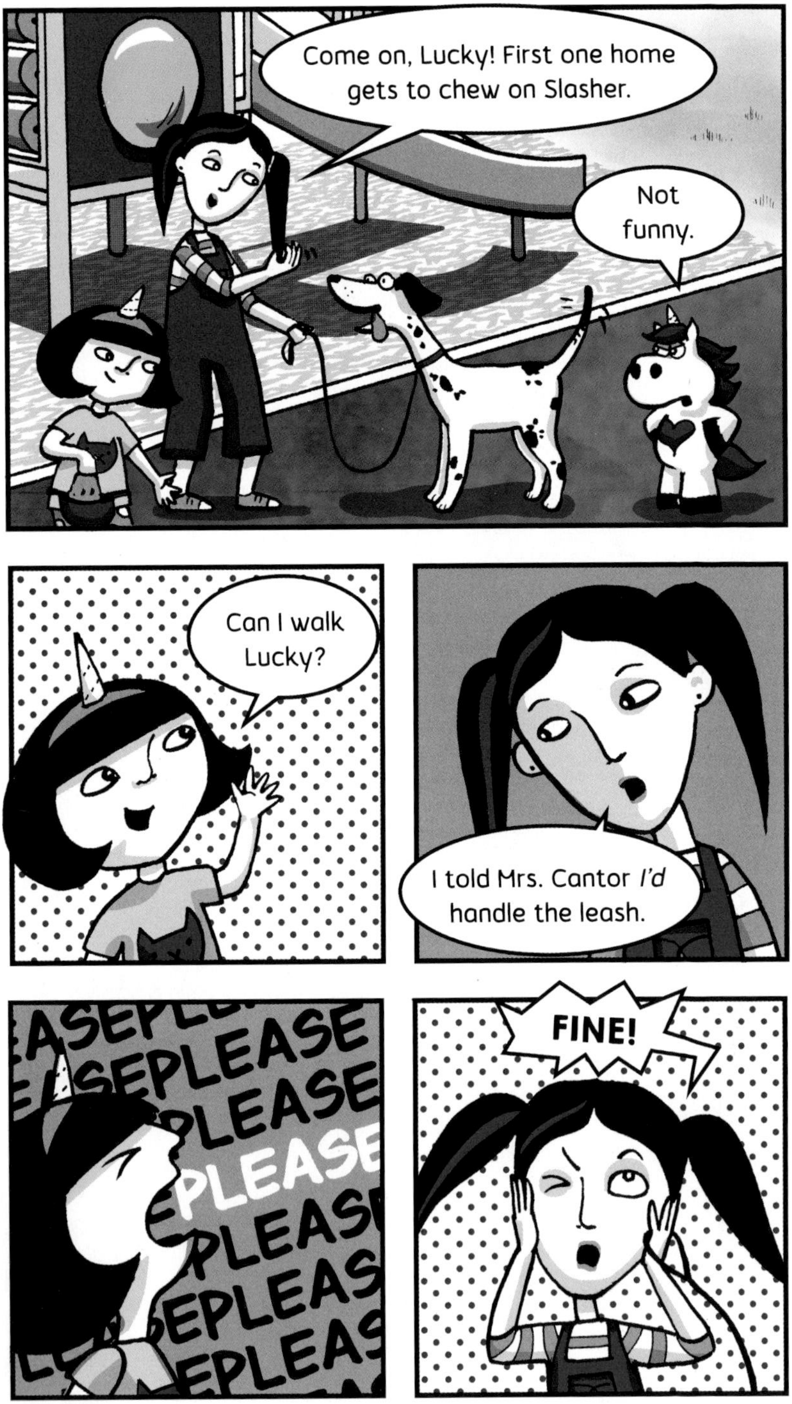
Come on, Lucky! First one home gets to chew on Slasher.
Not funny.
Can I walk Lucky?
I told Mrs. Cantor *I'd* handle the leash.
PLEASE
PLEASE
PLEASE
FINE!

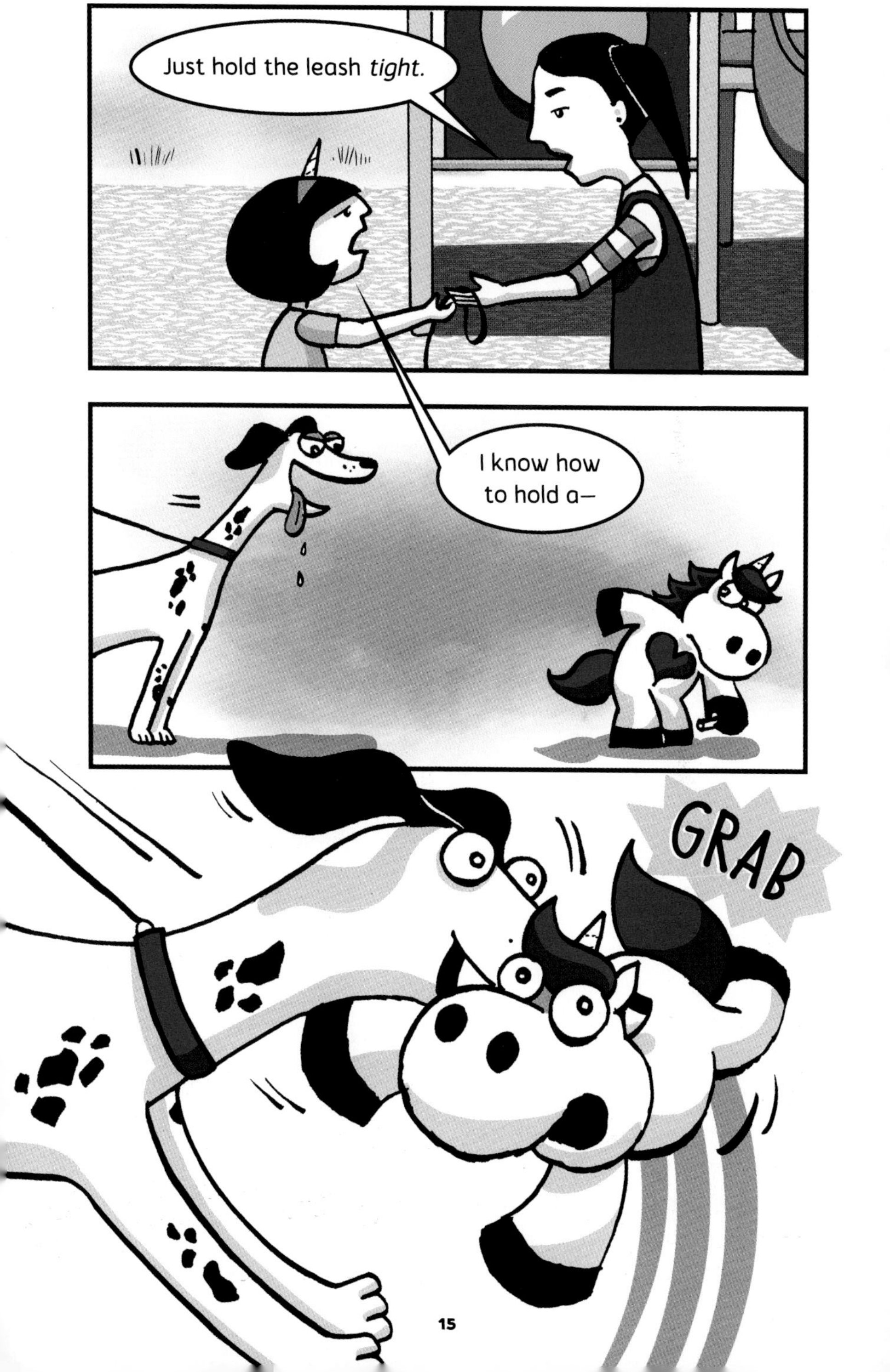
Just hold the leash *tight*.
I know how to hold a—
GRAB

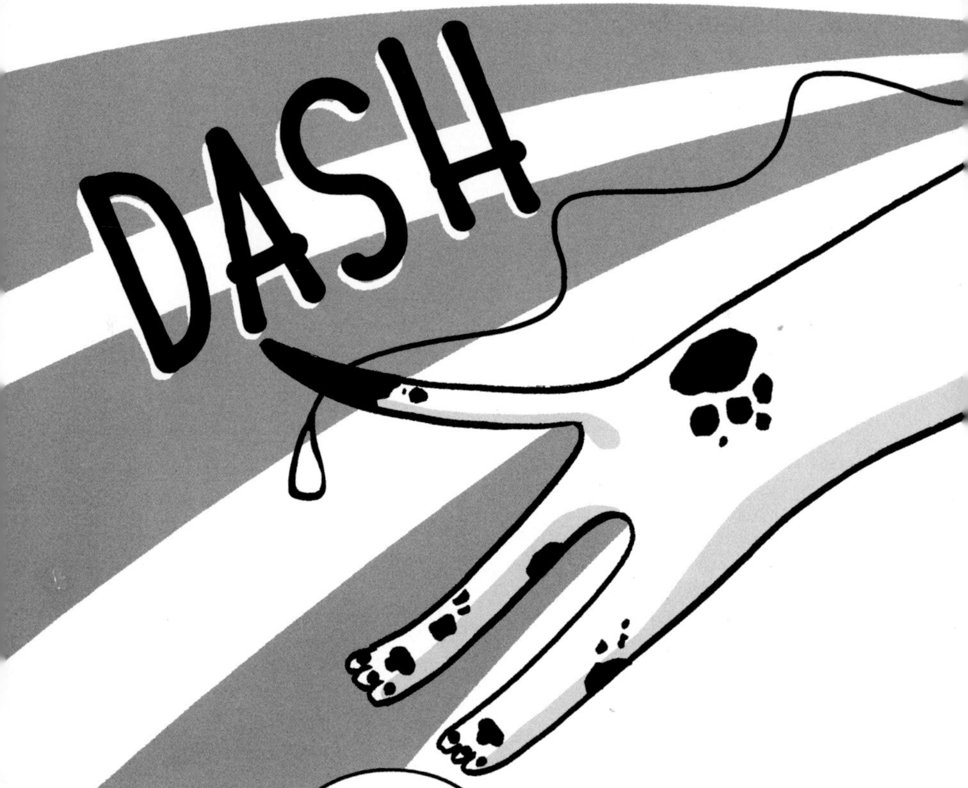
DASH

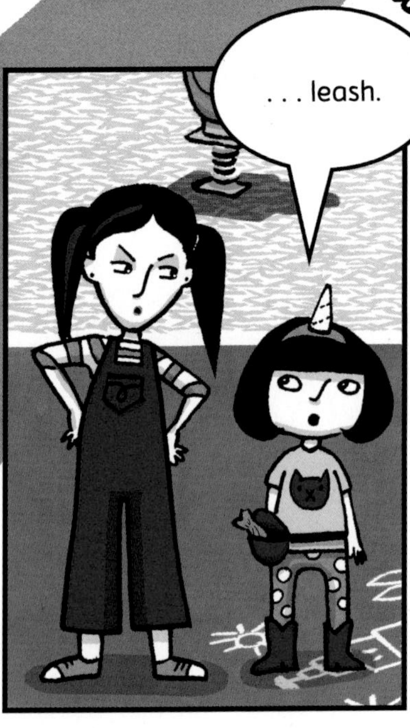
. . . leash.

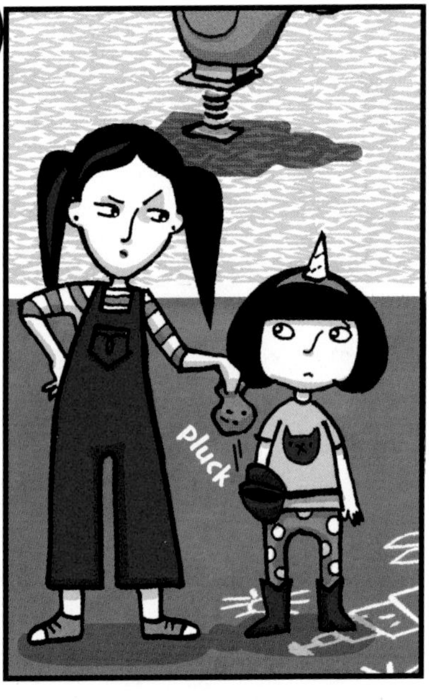
pluck

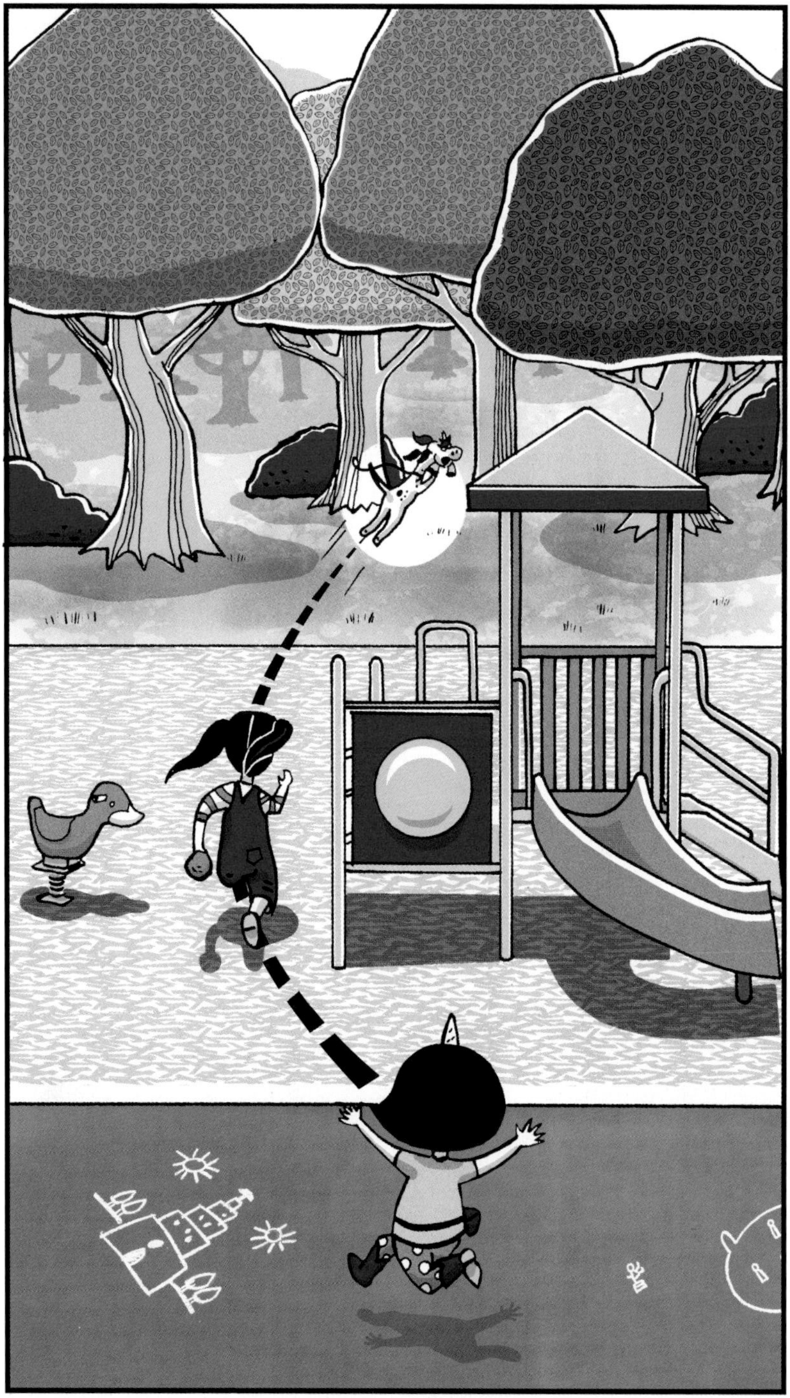

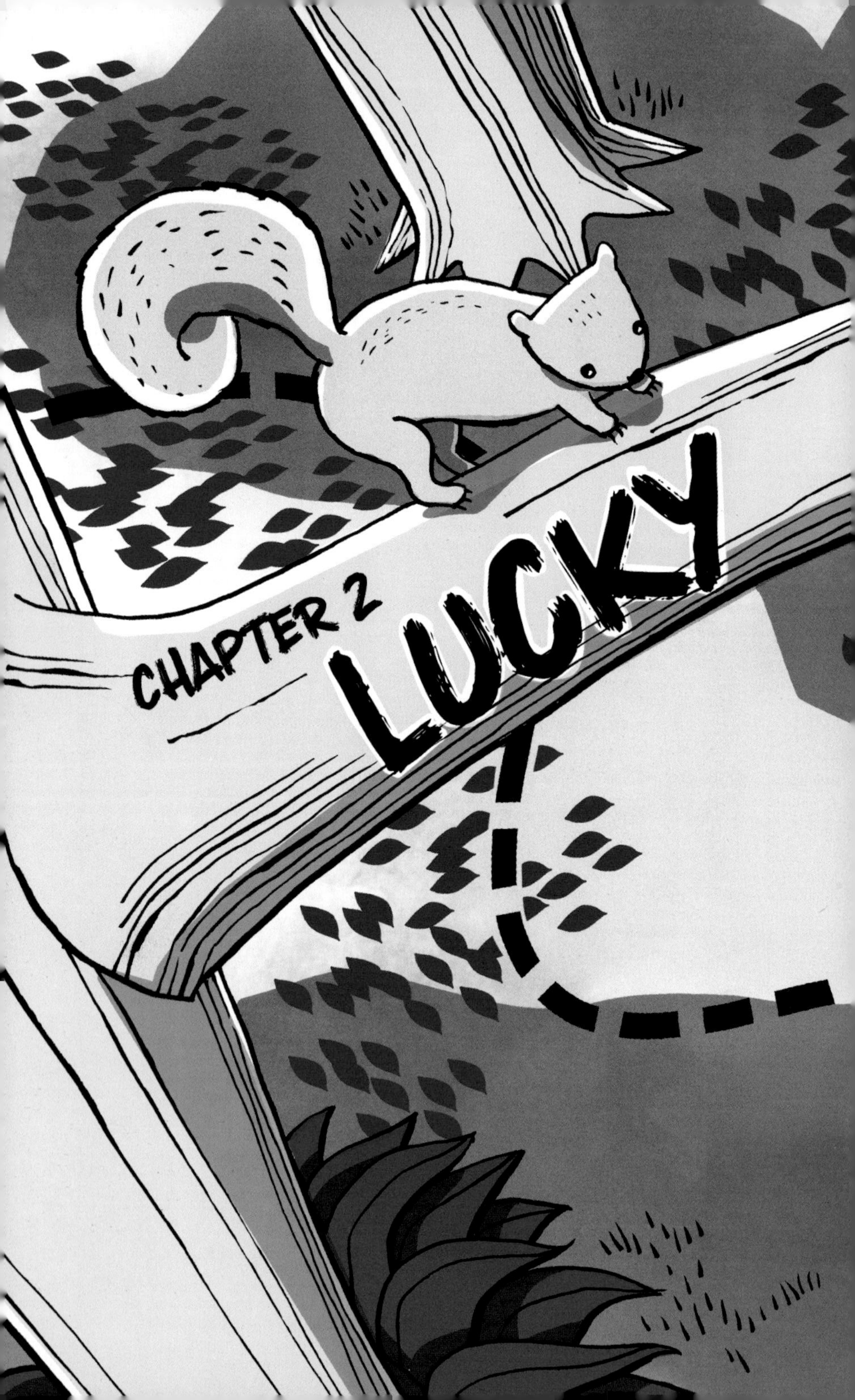
CHAPTER 2
LUCKY

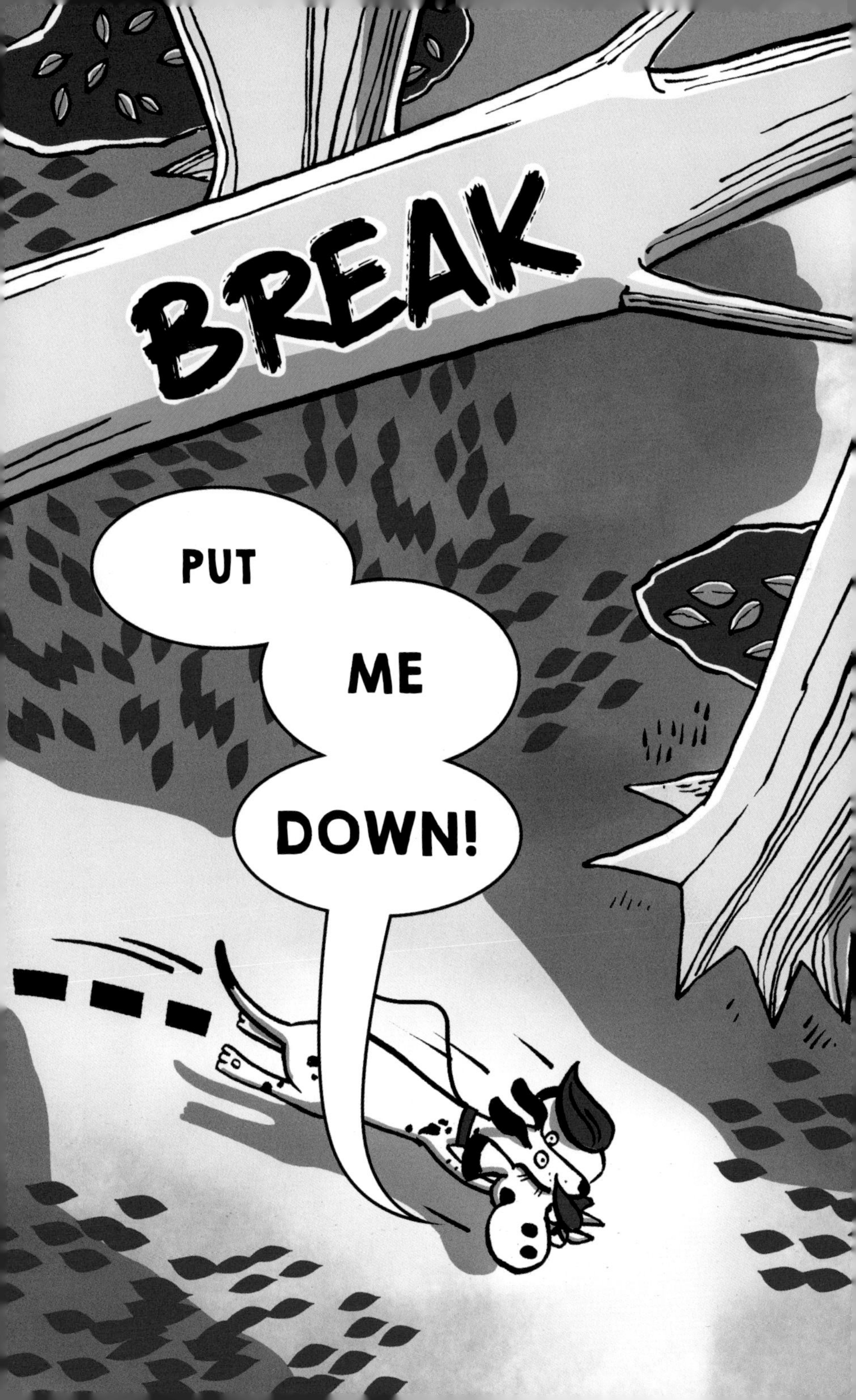
BREAK
PUT ME DOWN!

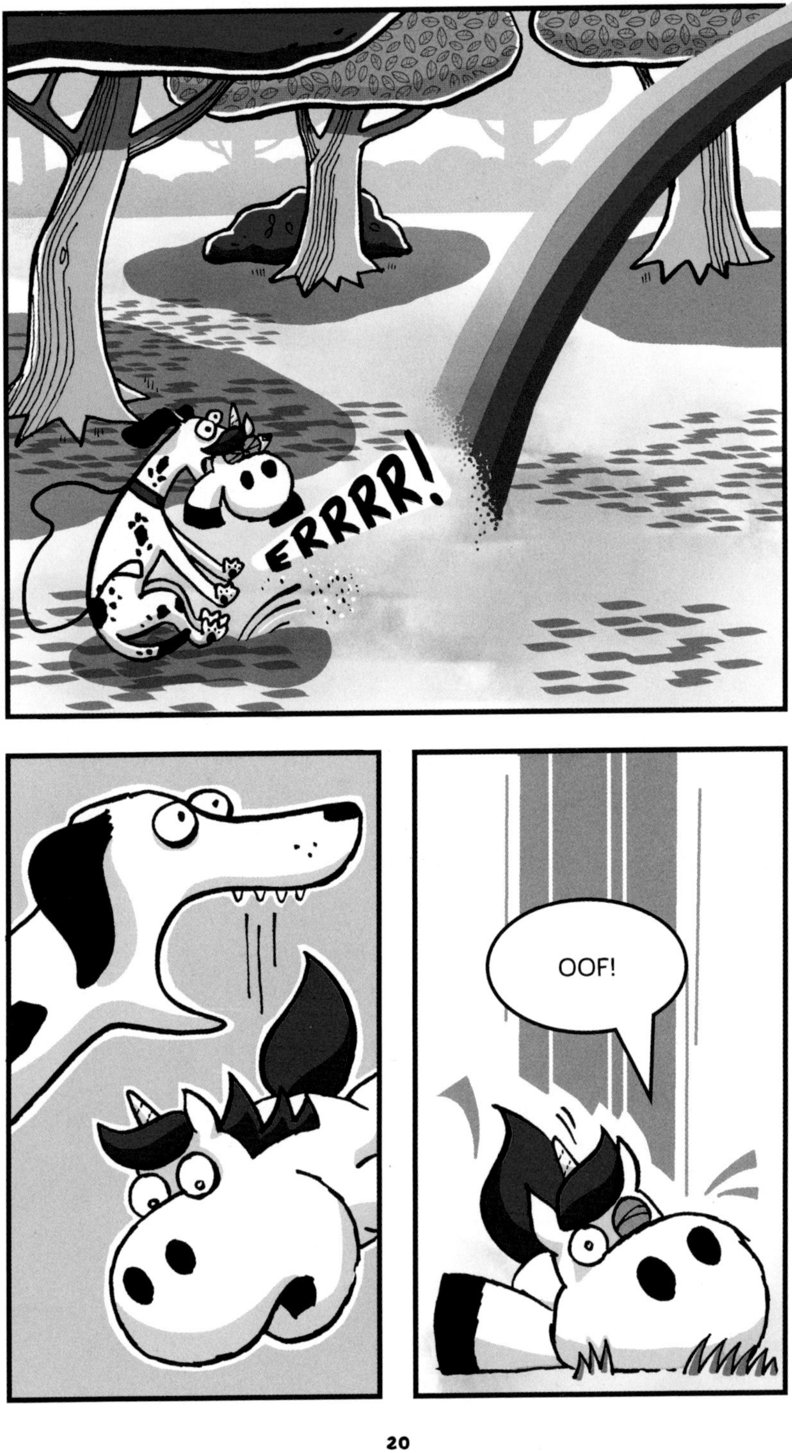
ERRRR!
OOF!

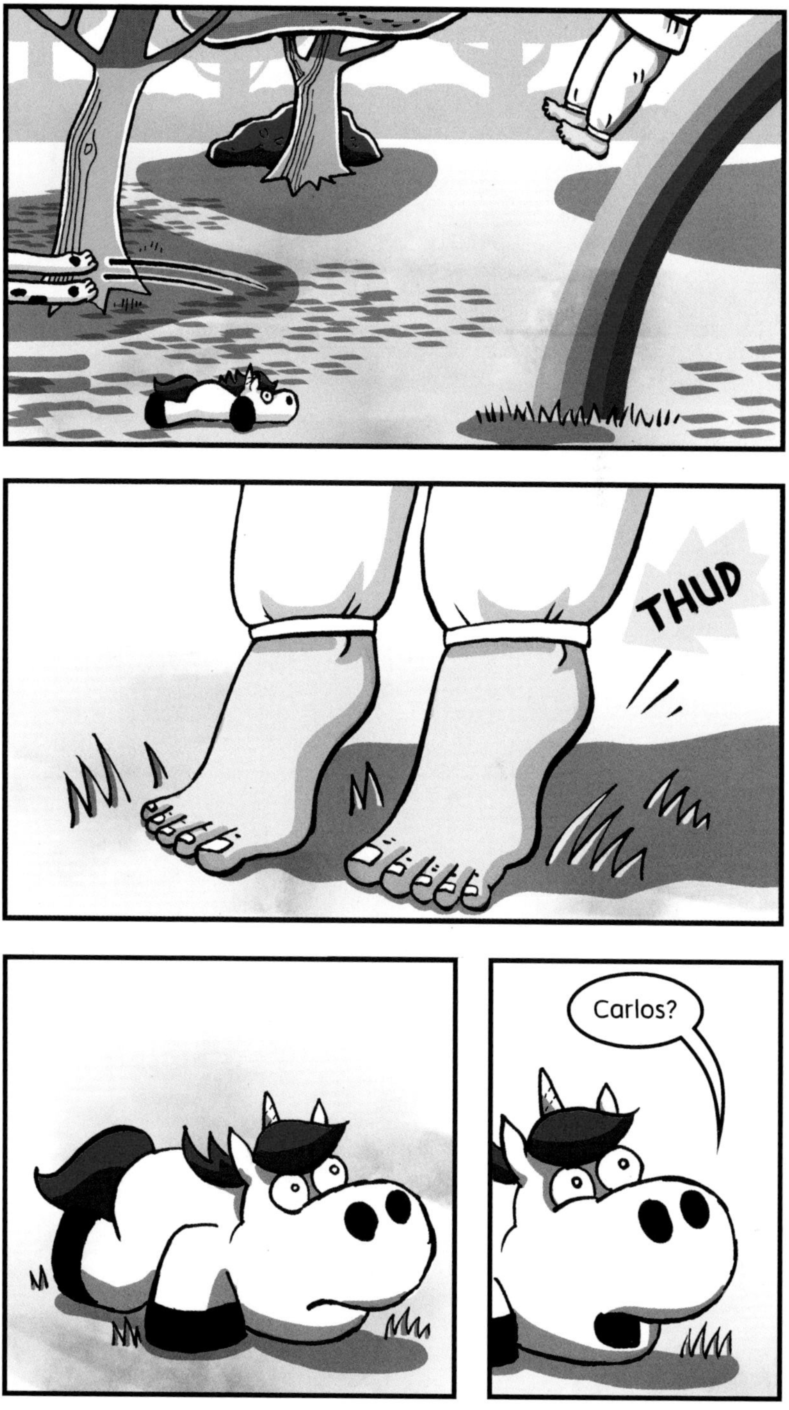
THUD
Carlos?

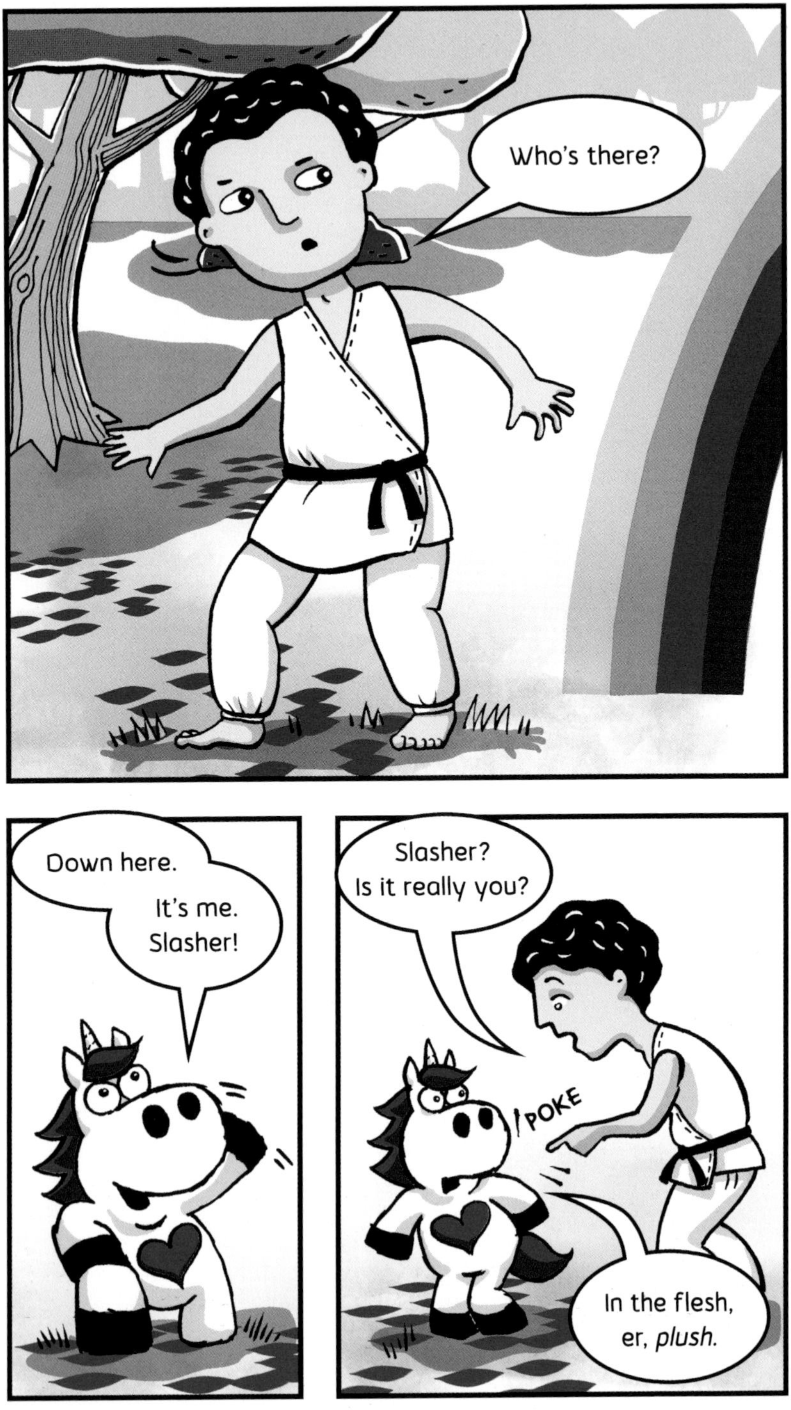
Who's there?
Down here.
It's me. Slasher!
Slasher? Is it really you?
POKE
In the flesh, er, *plush.*

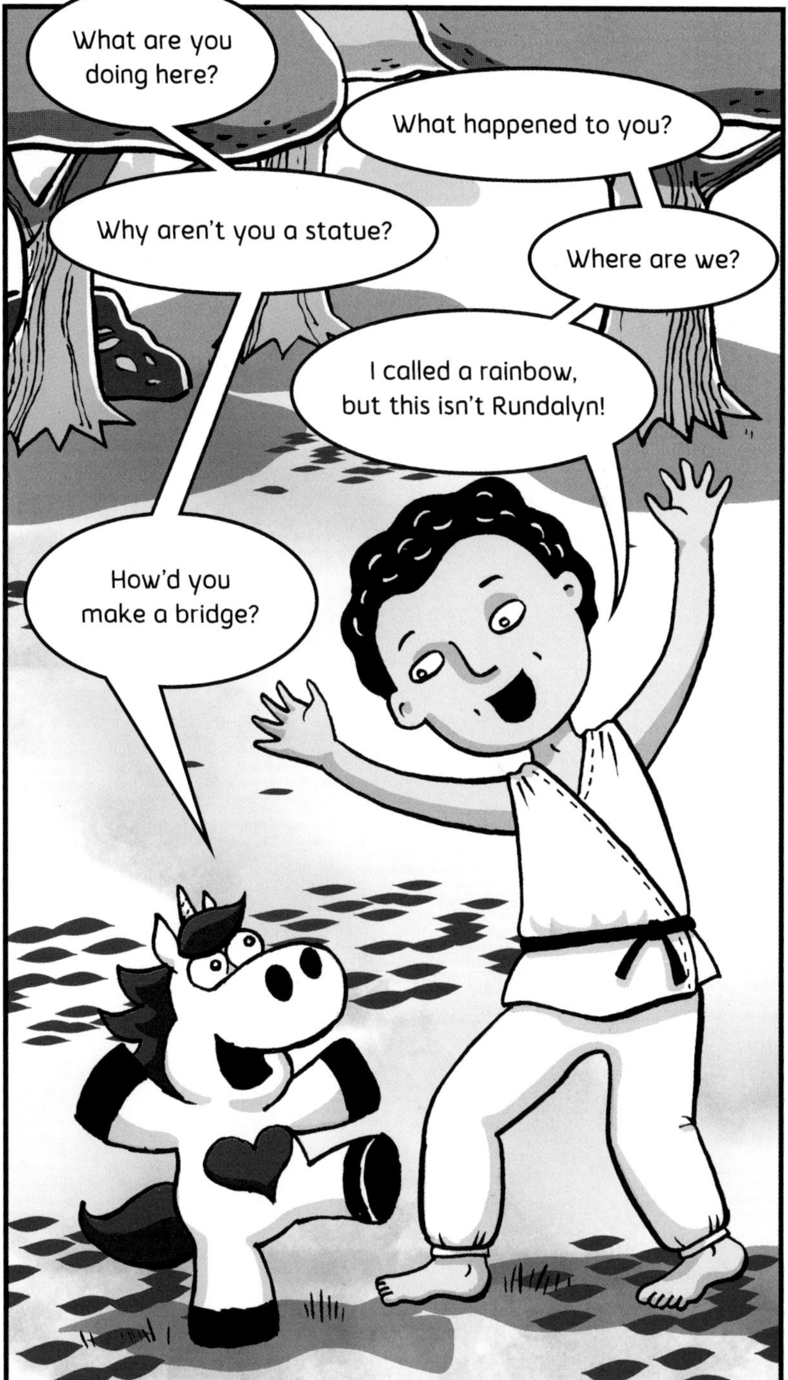
What are you doing here?
What happened to you?
Why aren't you a statue?
Where are we?
I called a rainbow, but this isn't Rundalyn!
How'd you make a bridge?

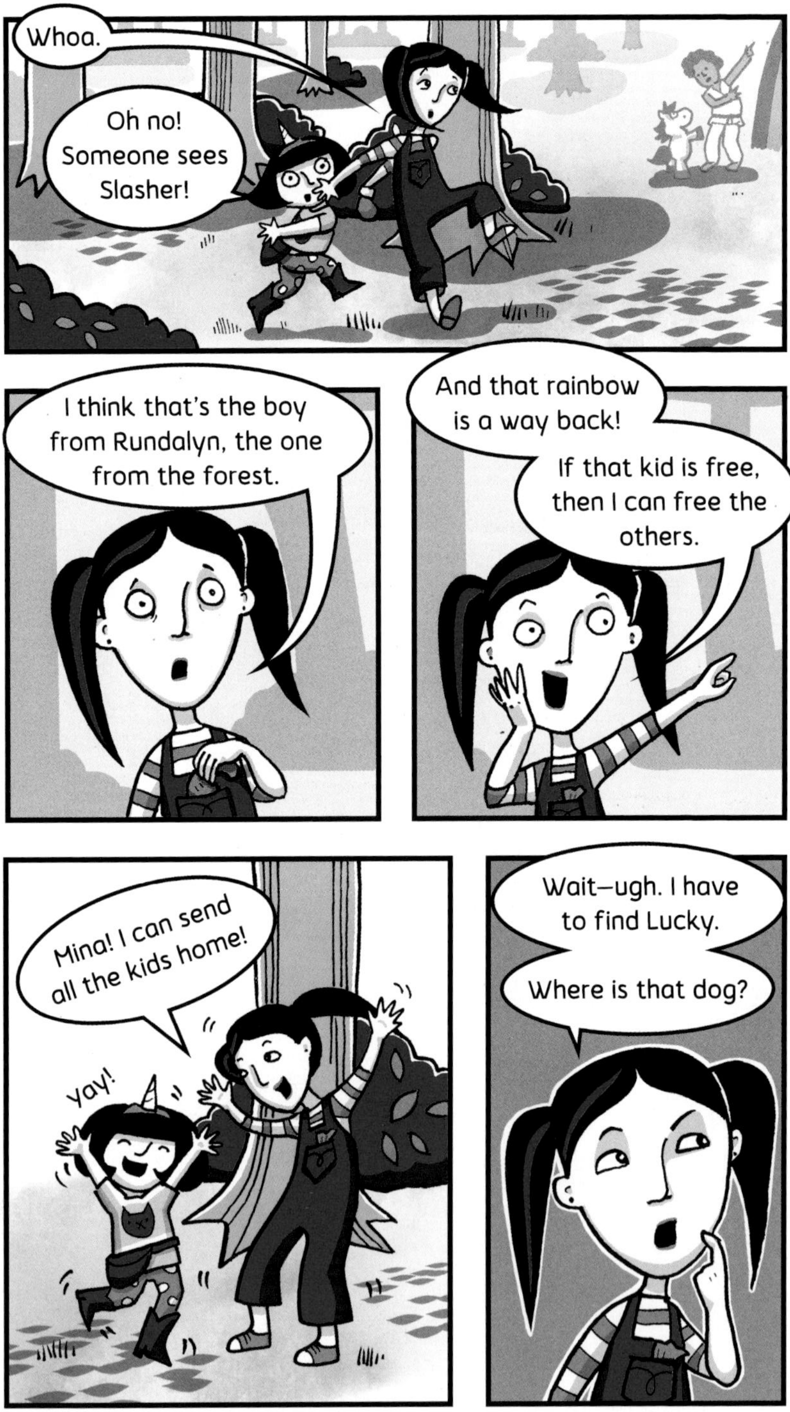
Whoa.
Oh no! Someone sees Slasher!
I think that's the boy from Rundalyn, the one from the forest.
And that rainbow is a way back!
If that kid is free, then I can free the others.
Mina! I can send all the kids home!
Yay!
Wait—ugh. I have to find Lucky.
Where is that dog?

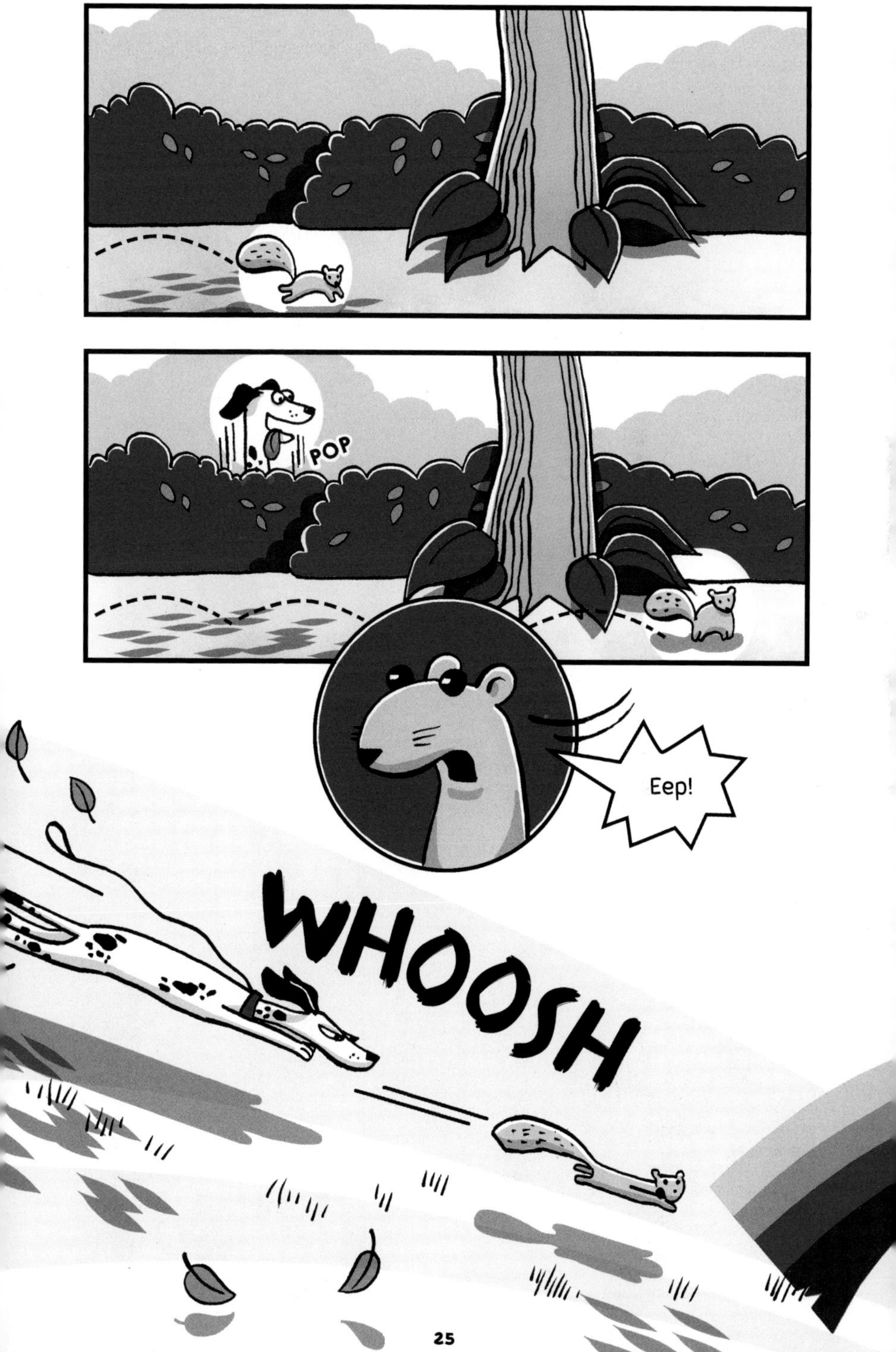
POP
Eep!
WHOOSH

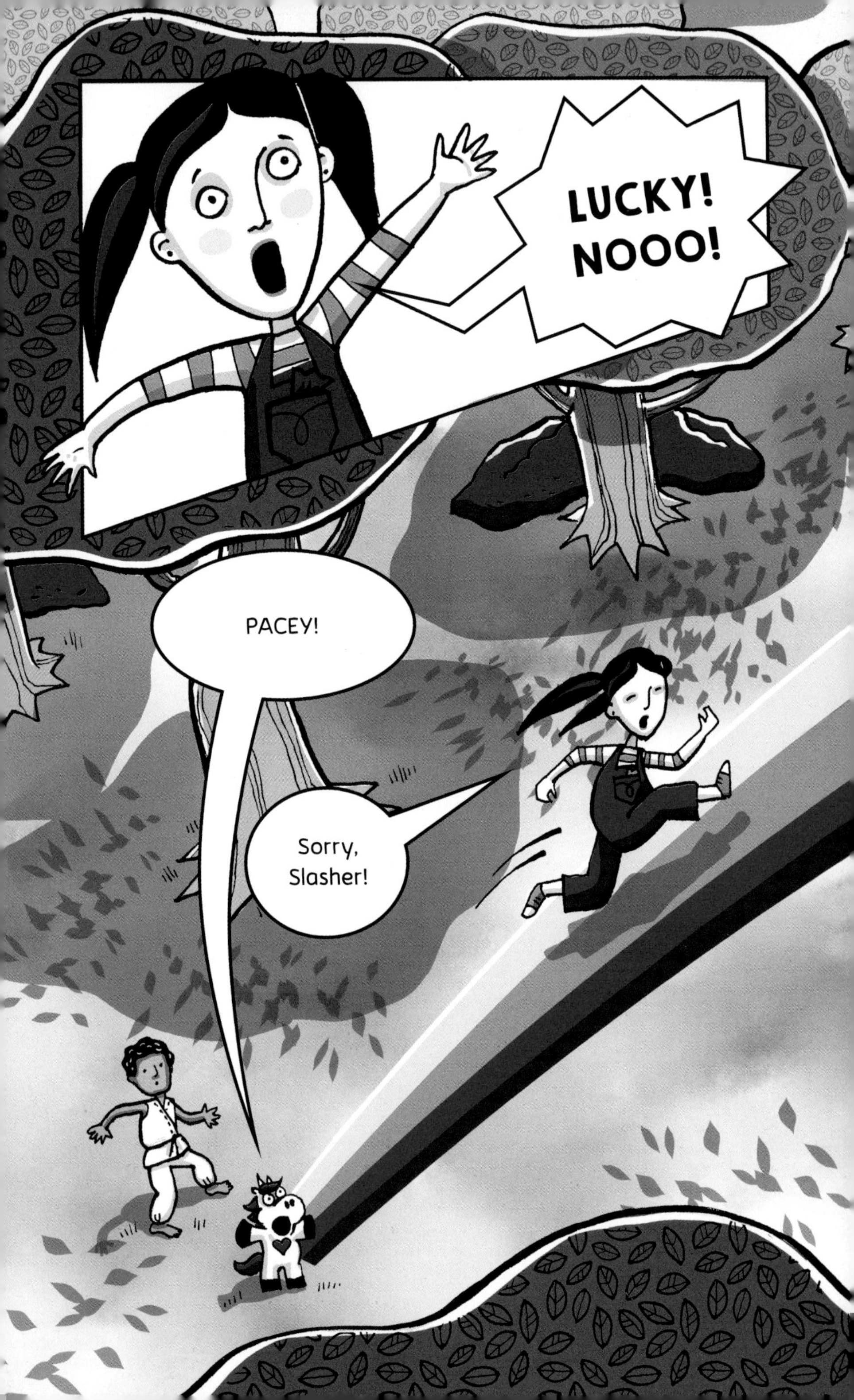
LUCKY! NOOO!
PACEY!
Sorry, Slasher!

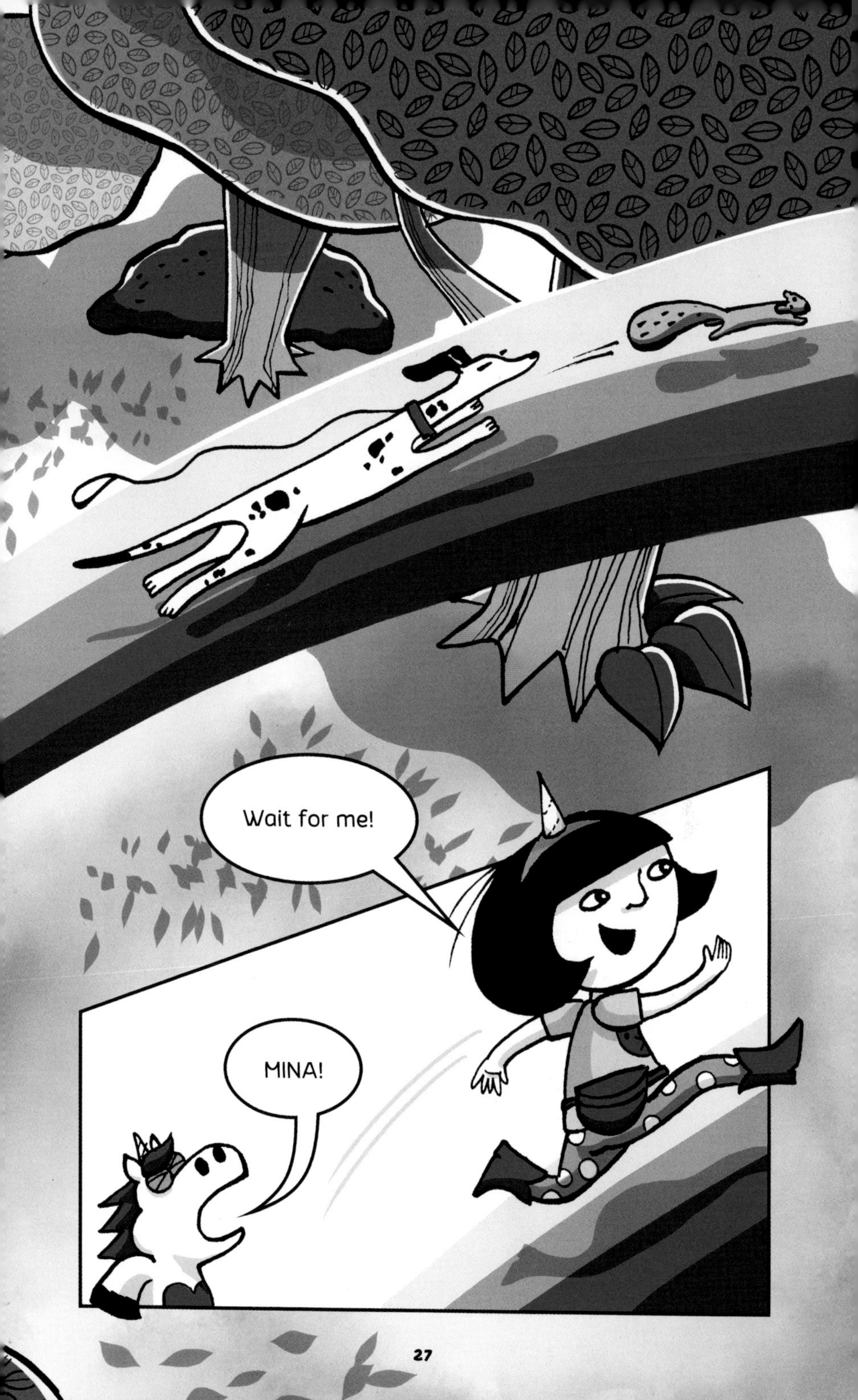
Wait for me!
MINA!

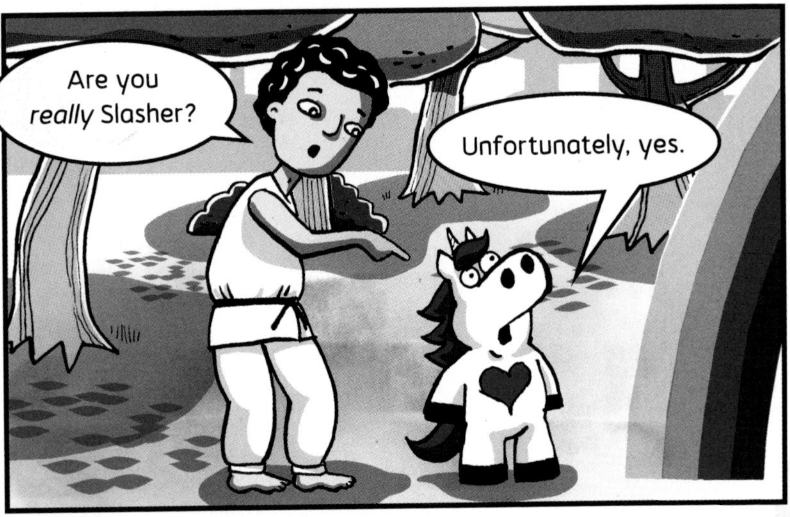
Are you *really* Slasher?
Unfortunately, yes.

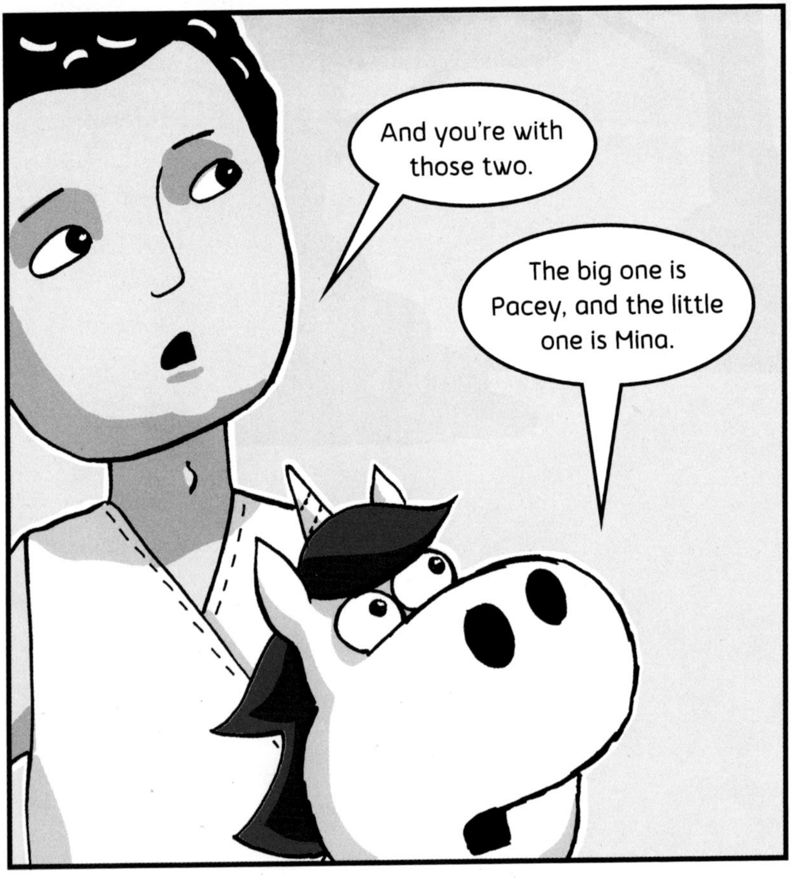
And you're with those two.
The big one is Pacey, and the little one is Mina.

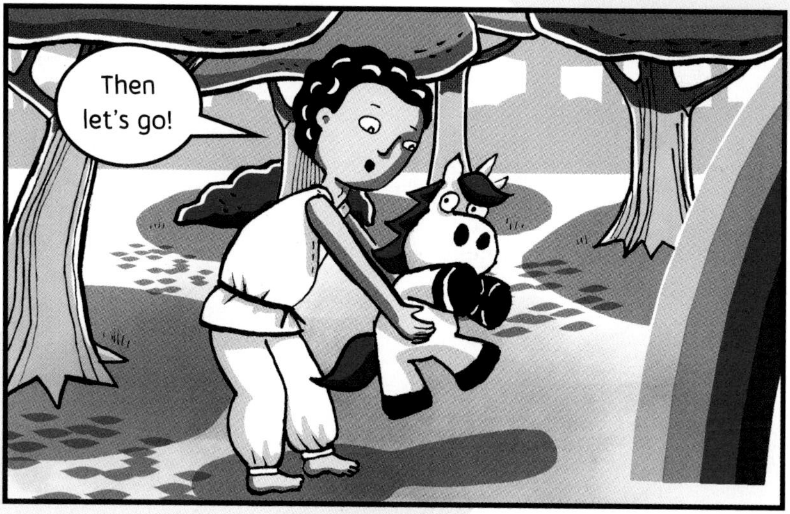
Then let's go!

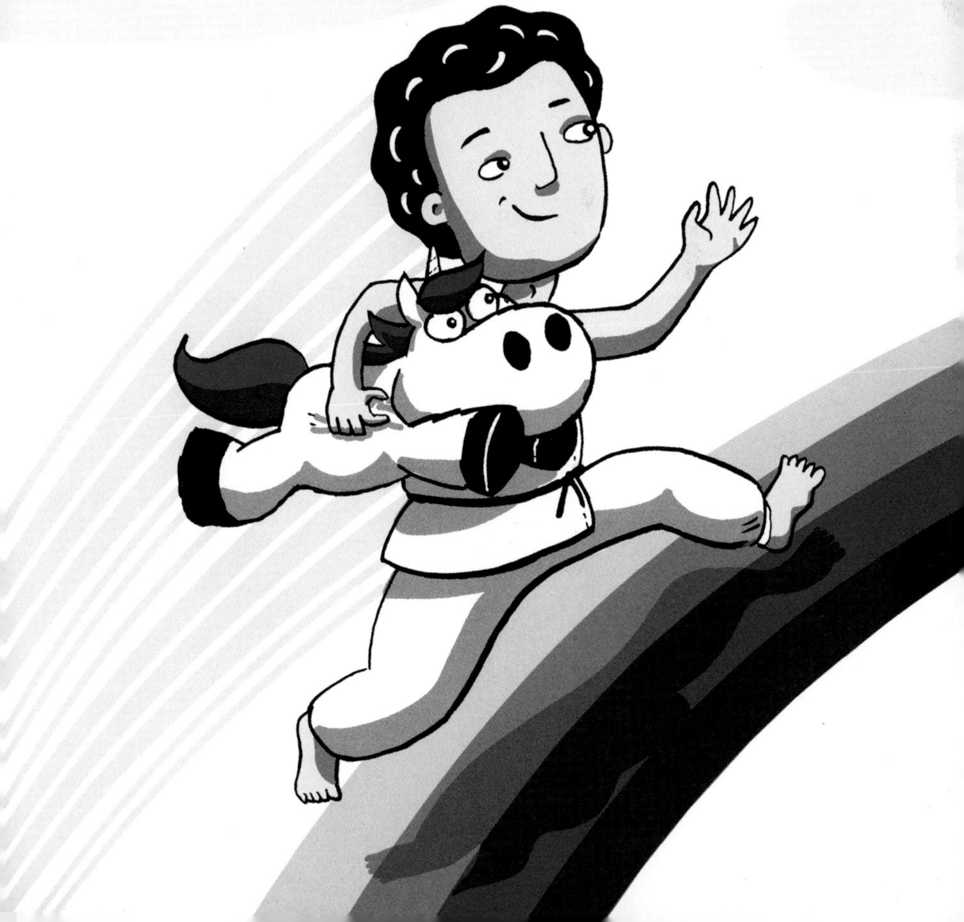

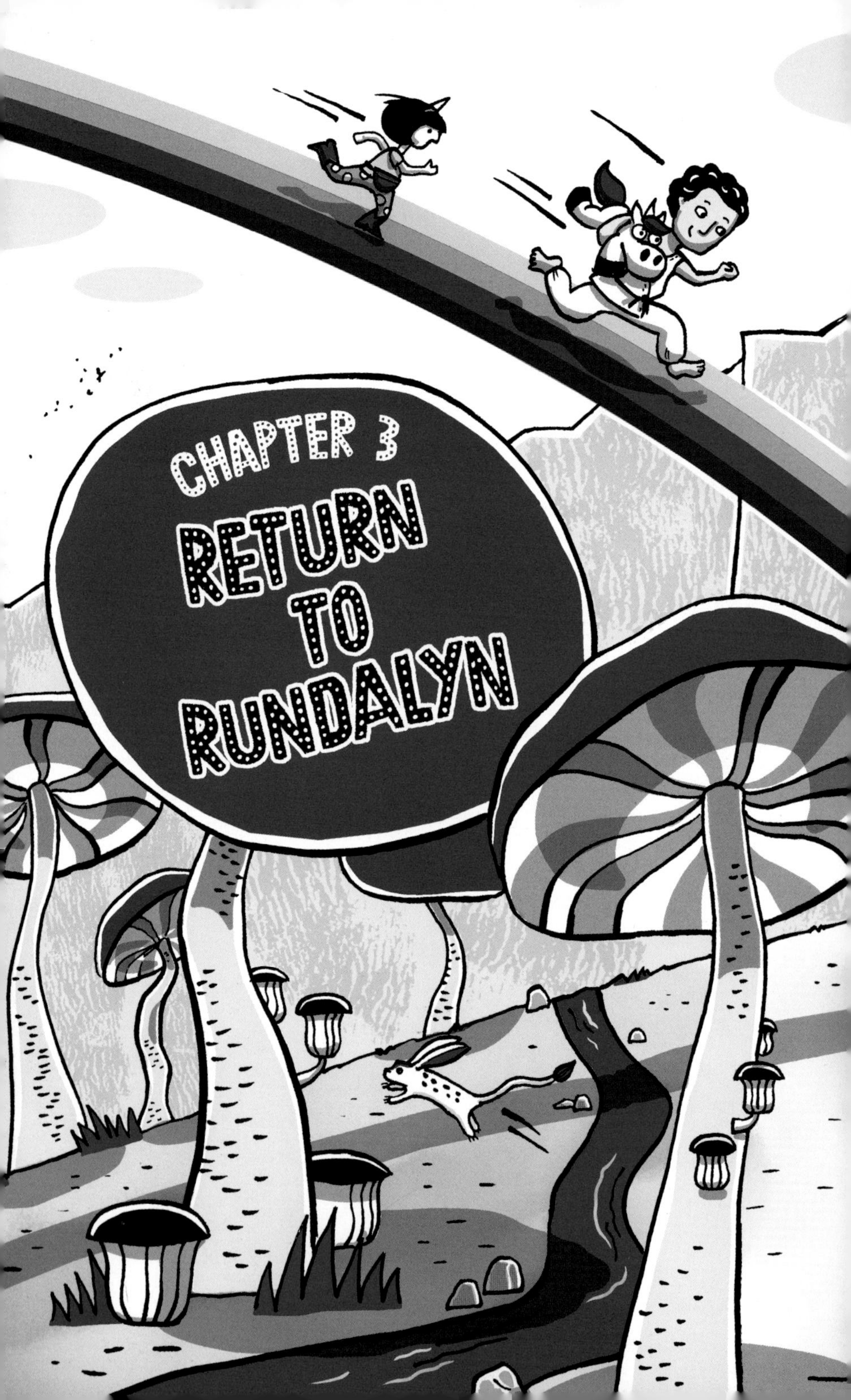
CHAPTER 3
RETURN TO RUNDALYN

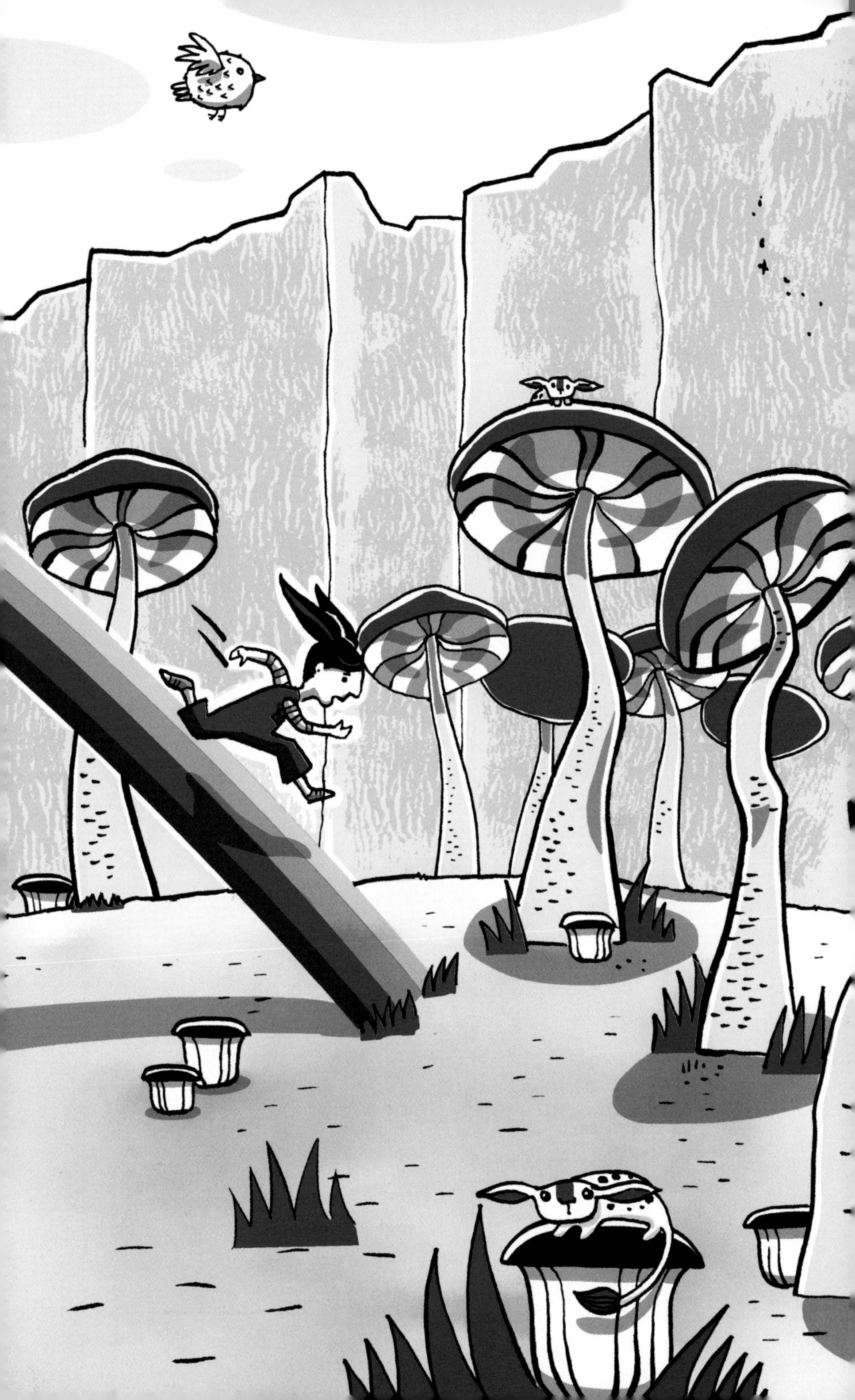

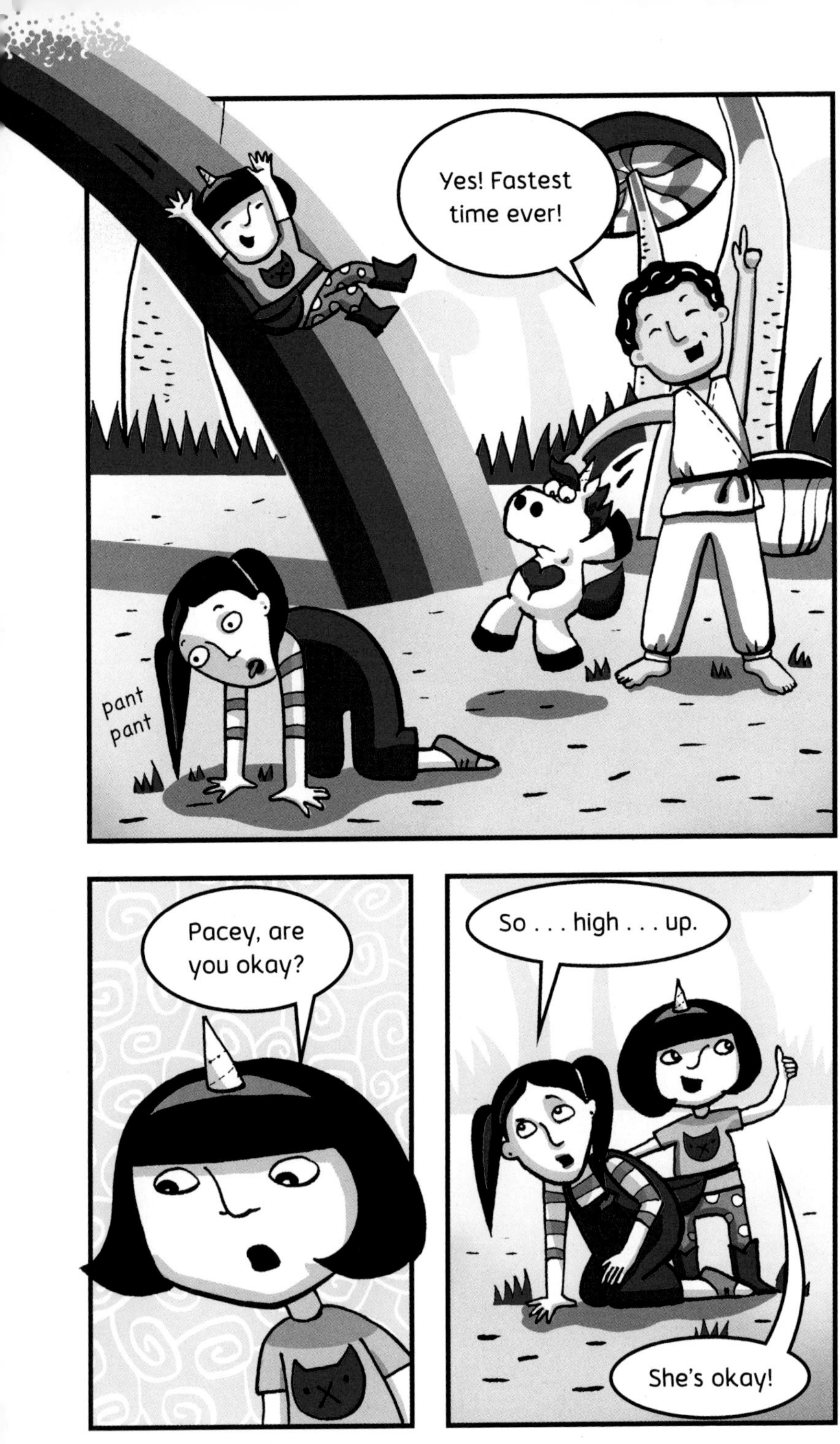
Yes! Fastest time ever!
pant pant
Pacey, are you okay?
So . . . high . . . up.
She's okay!

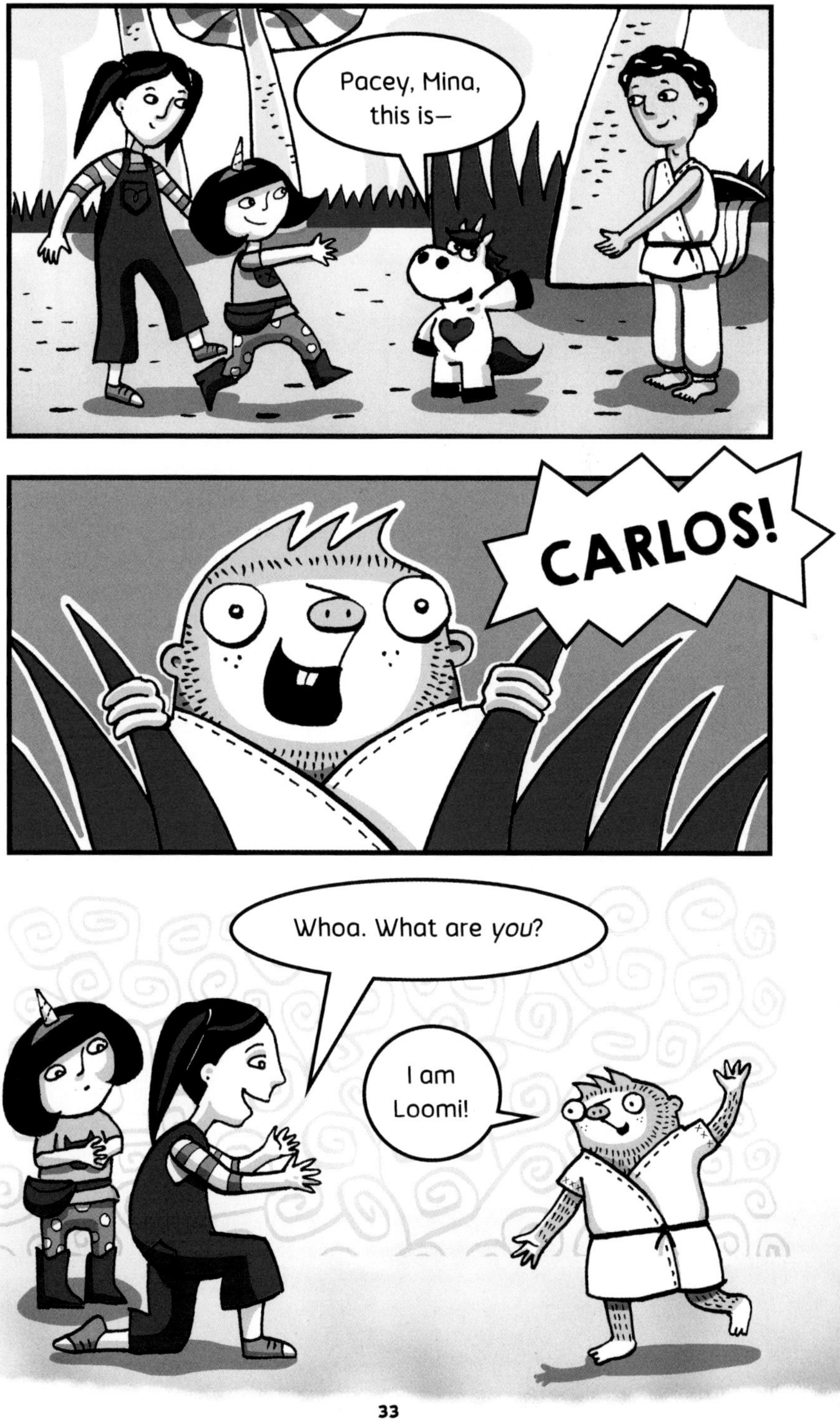
Pacey, Mina, this is—
CARLOS!
Whoa. What are *you*?
I am Loomi!

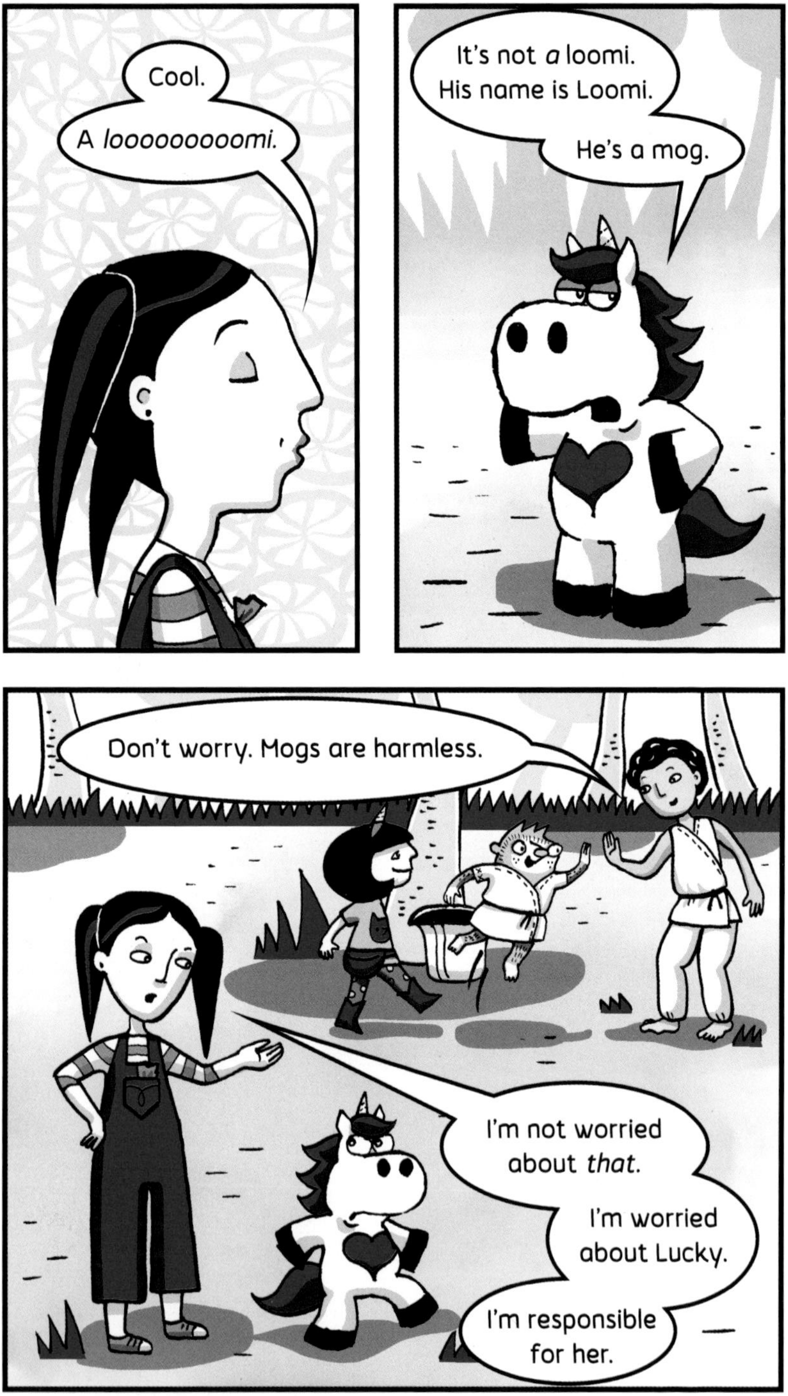
Cool.
A *looooooooomi.*
It's not *a* loomi.
His name is Loomi.
He's a mog.
Don't worry. Mogs are harmless.
I'm not worried about *that.*
I'm worried about Lucky.
I'm responsible for her.

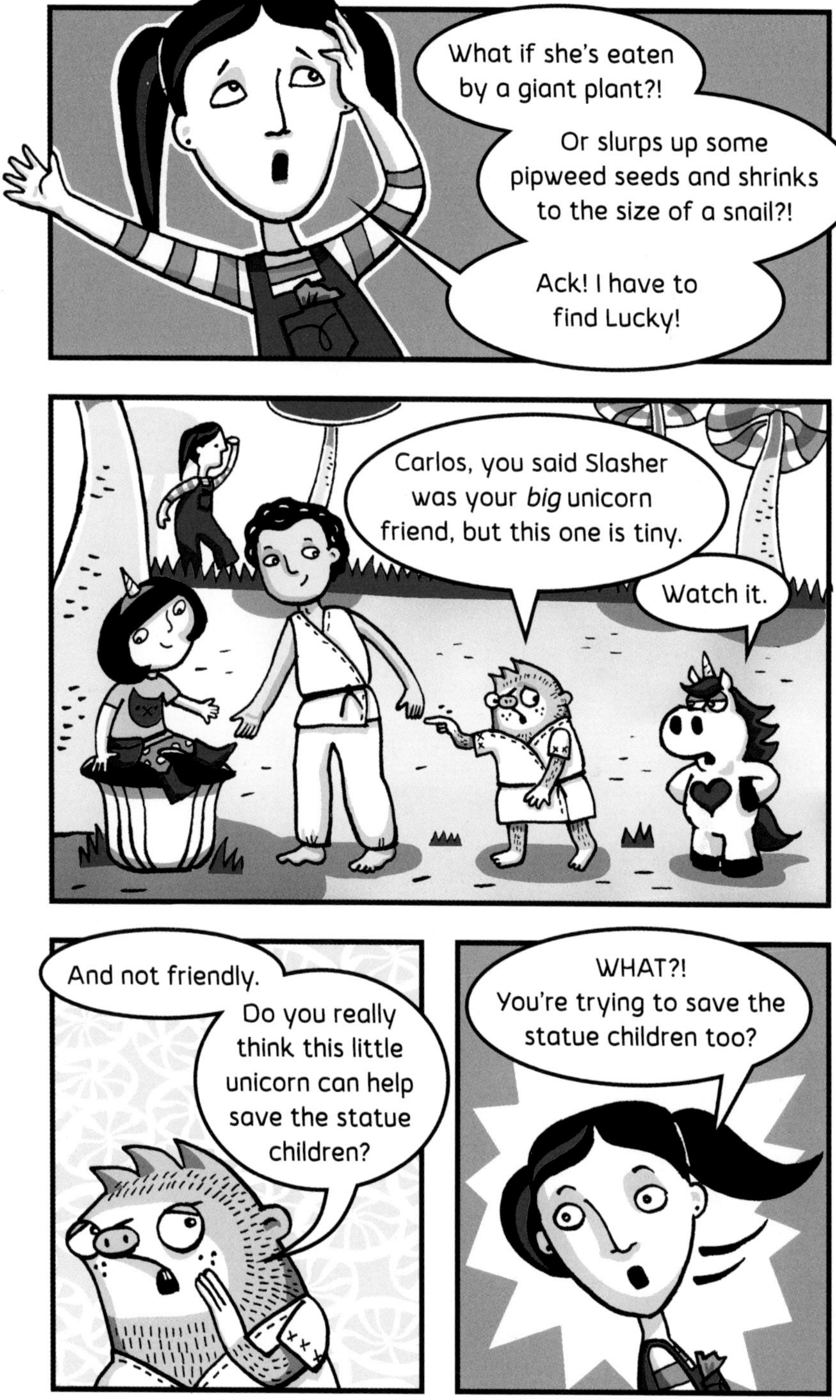
What if she's eaten by a giant plant?!
Or slurps up some pipweed seeds and shrinks to the size of a snail?!
Ack! I have to find Lucky!
Carlos, you said Slasher was your *big* unicorn friend, but this one is tiny.
Watch it.
And not friendly.
Do you really think this little unicorn can help save the statue children?
WHAT?! You're trying to save the statue children too?

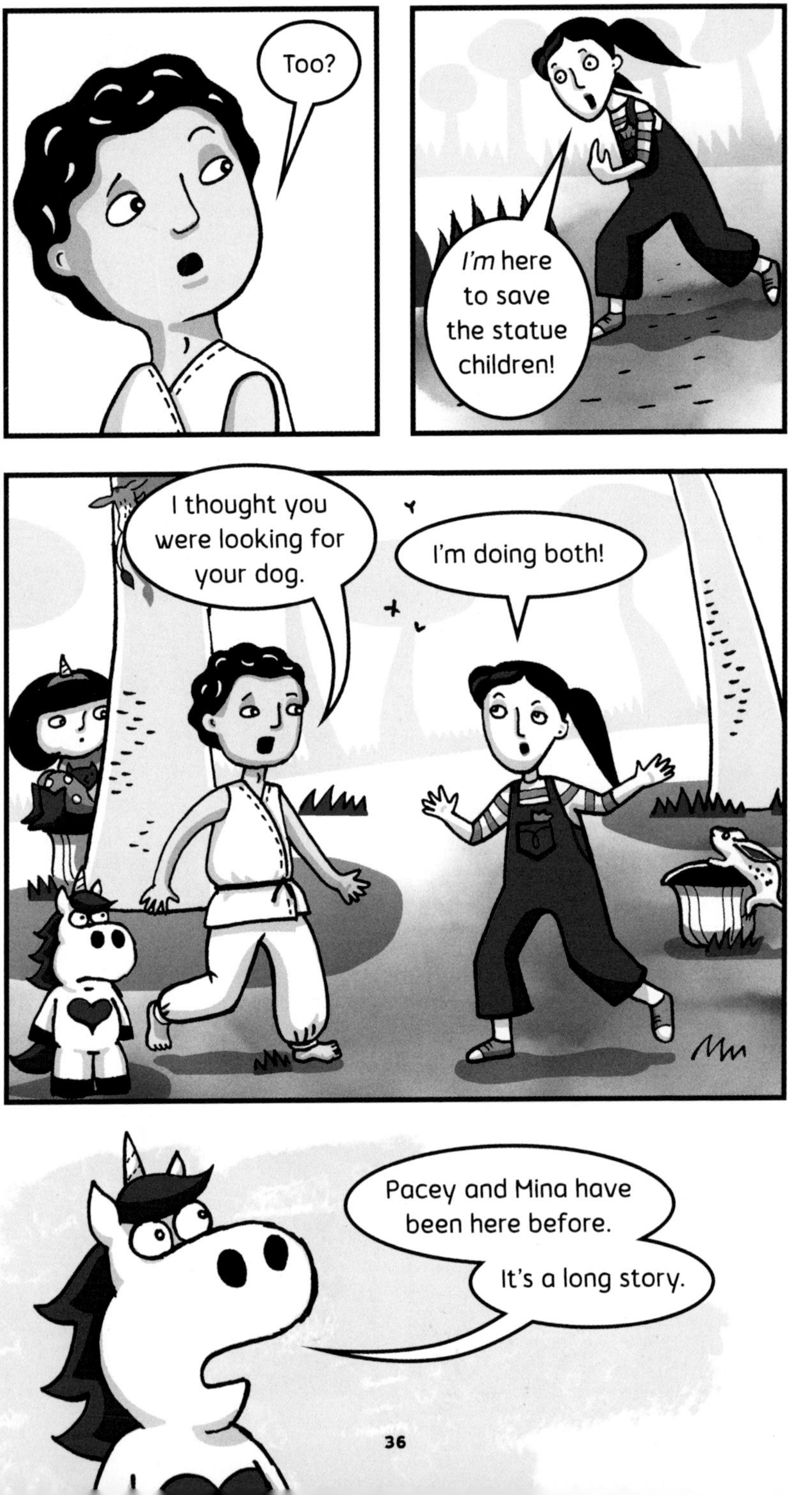
Too?
I'm here to save the statue children!
I thought you were looking for your dog.
I'm doing both!
Pacey and Mina have been here before.
It's a long story.

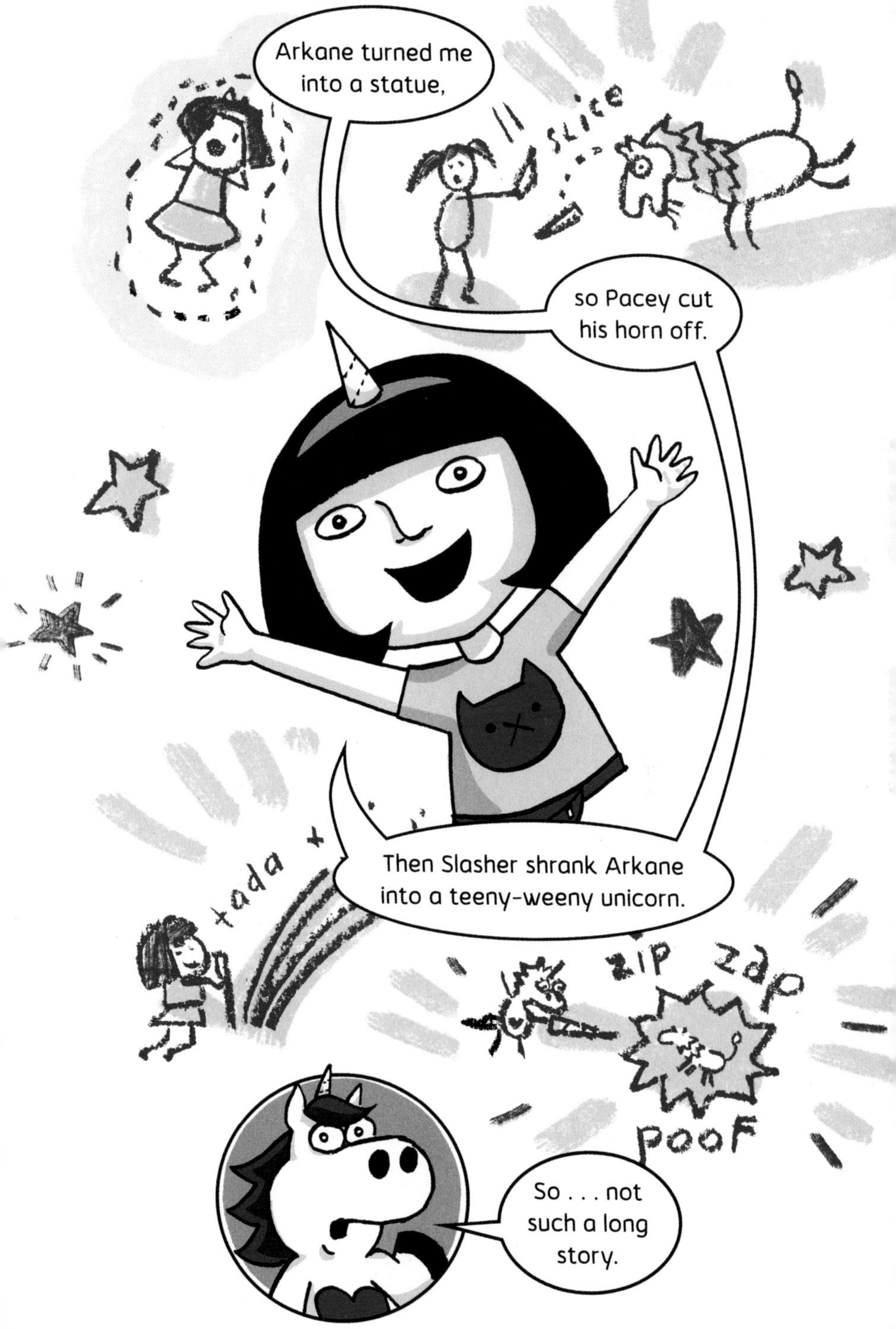
Arkane turned me into a statue,
SLICE
so Pacey cut his horn off.
tada
Then Slasher shrank Arkane into a teeny-weeny unicorn.
zip zap
POOF
So . . . not such a long story.

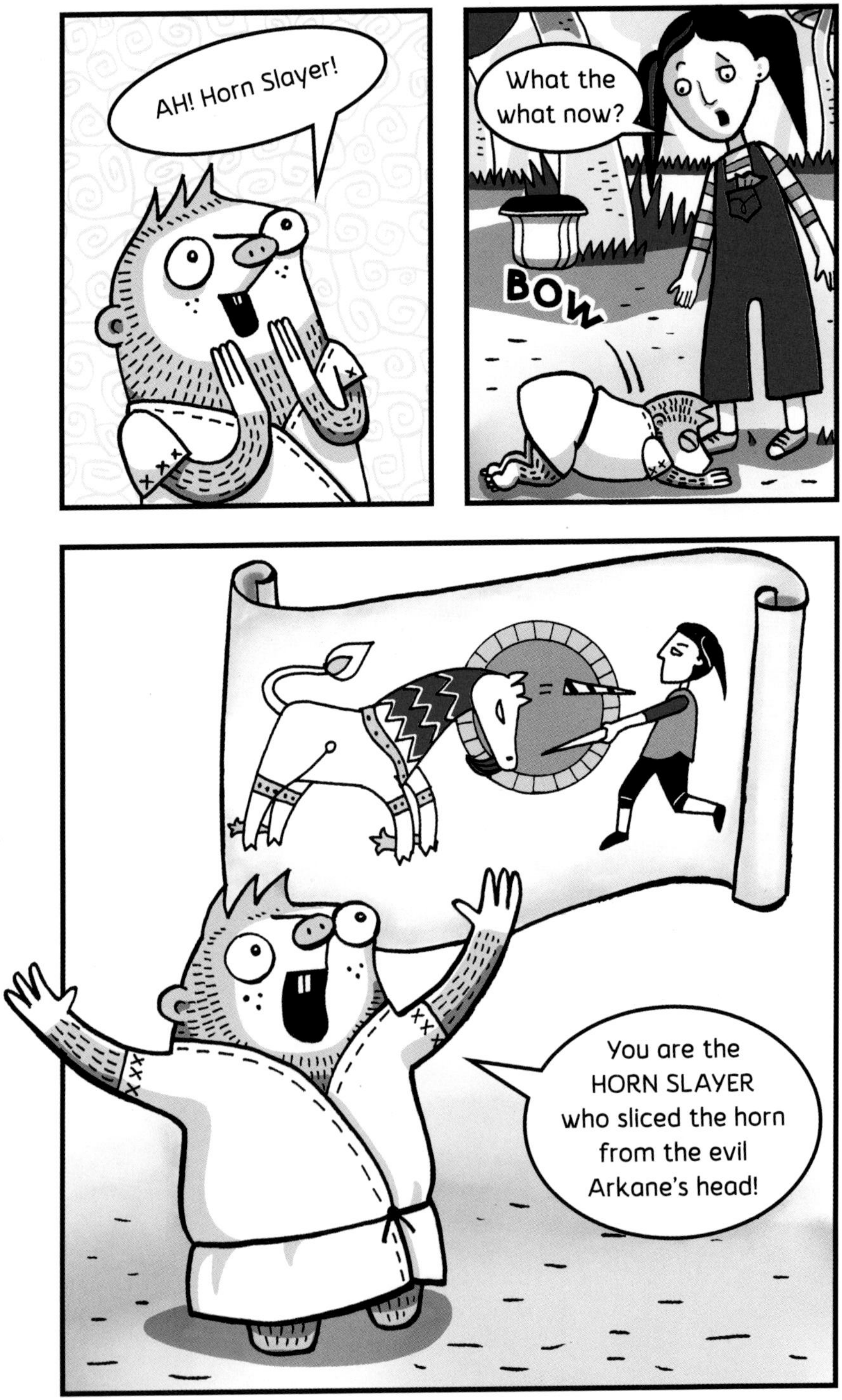
AH! Horn Slayer!
What the what now?
BOW
You are the HORN SLAYER who sliced the horn from the evil Arkane's head!

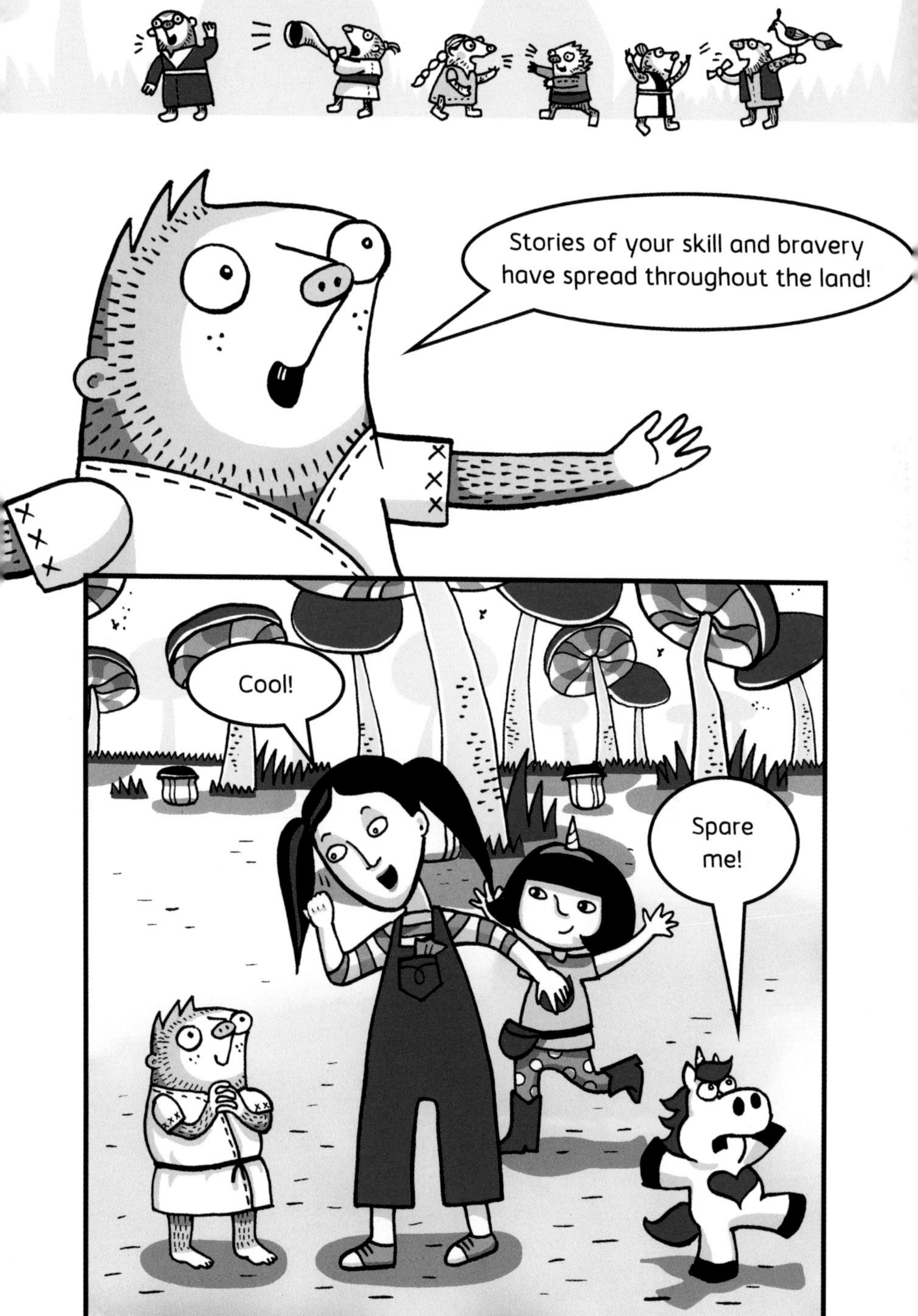
Stories of your skill and bravery have spread throughout the land!
Cool!
Spare me!

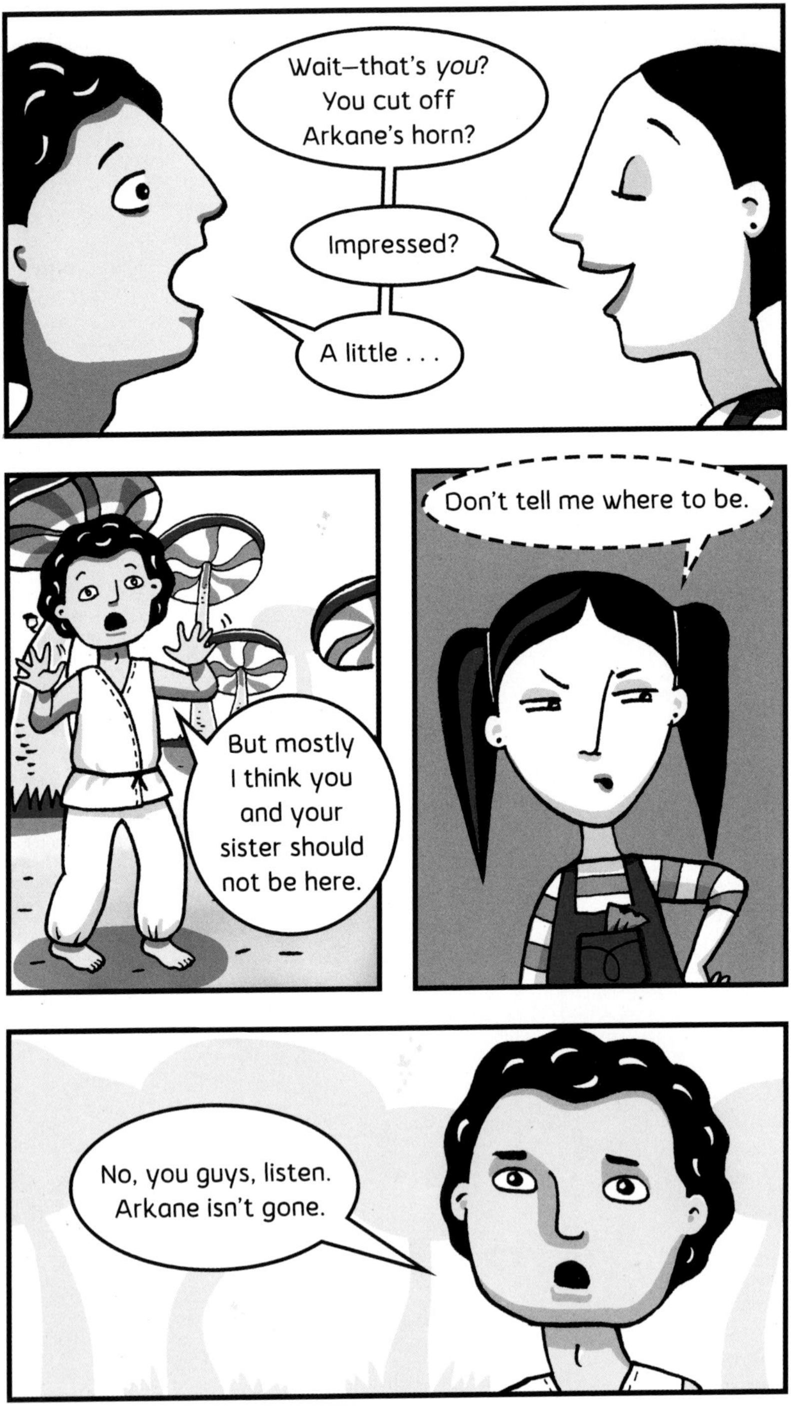
Wait—that's *you*? You cut off Arkane's horn?
Impressed?
A little . . .
But mostly I think you and your sister should not be here.
Don't tell me where to be.
No, you guys, listen. Arkane isn't gone.

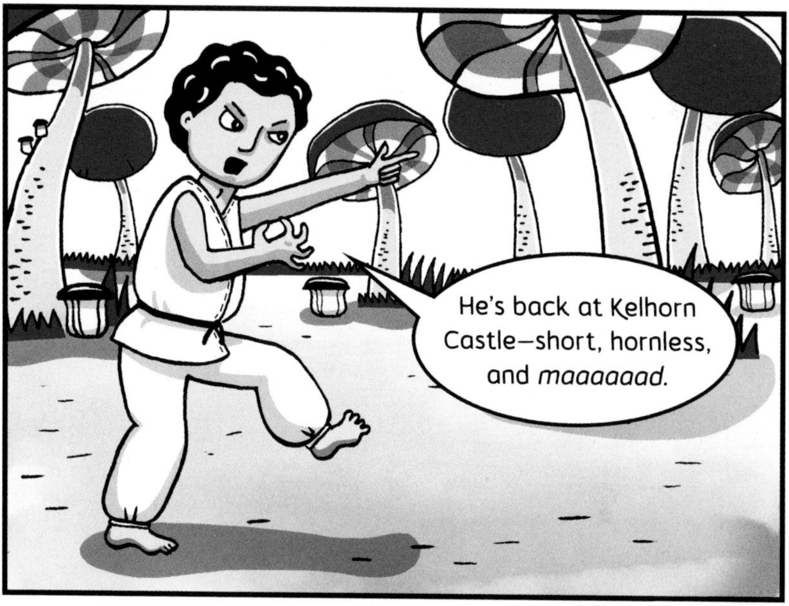
He's back at Kelhorn Castle—short, hornless, and *maaaaaad.*

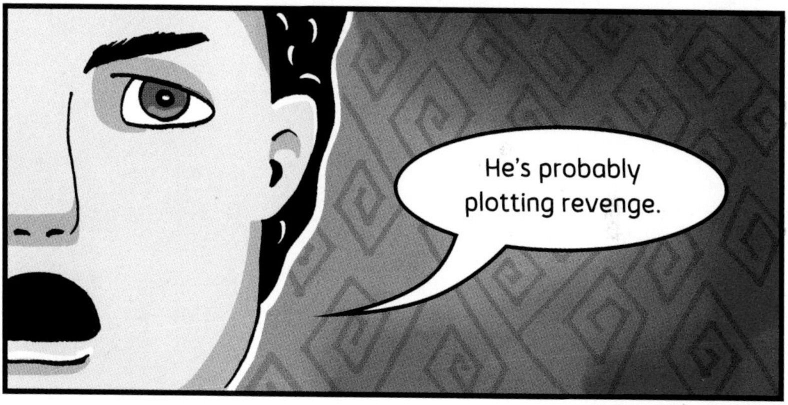
He's probably plotting revenge.

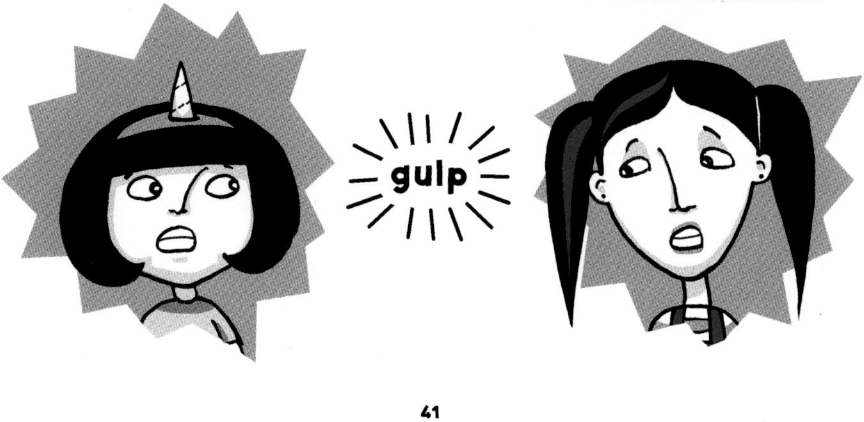
gulp

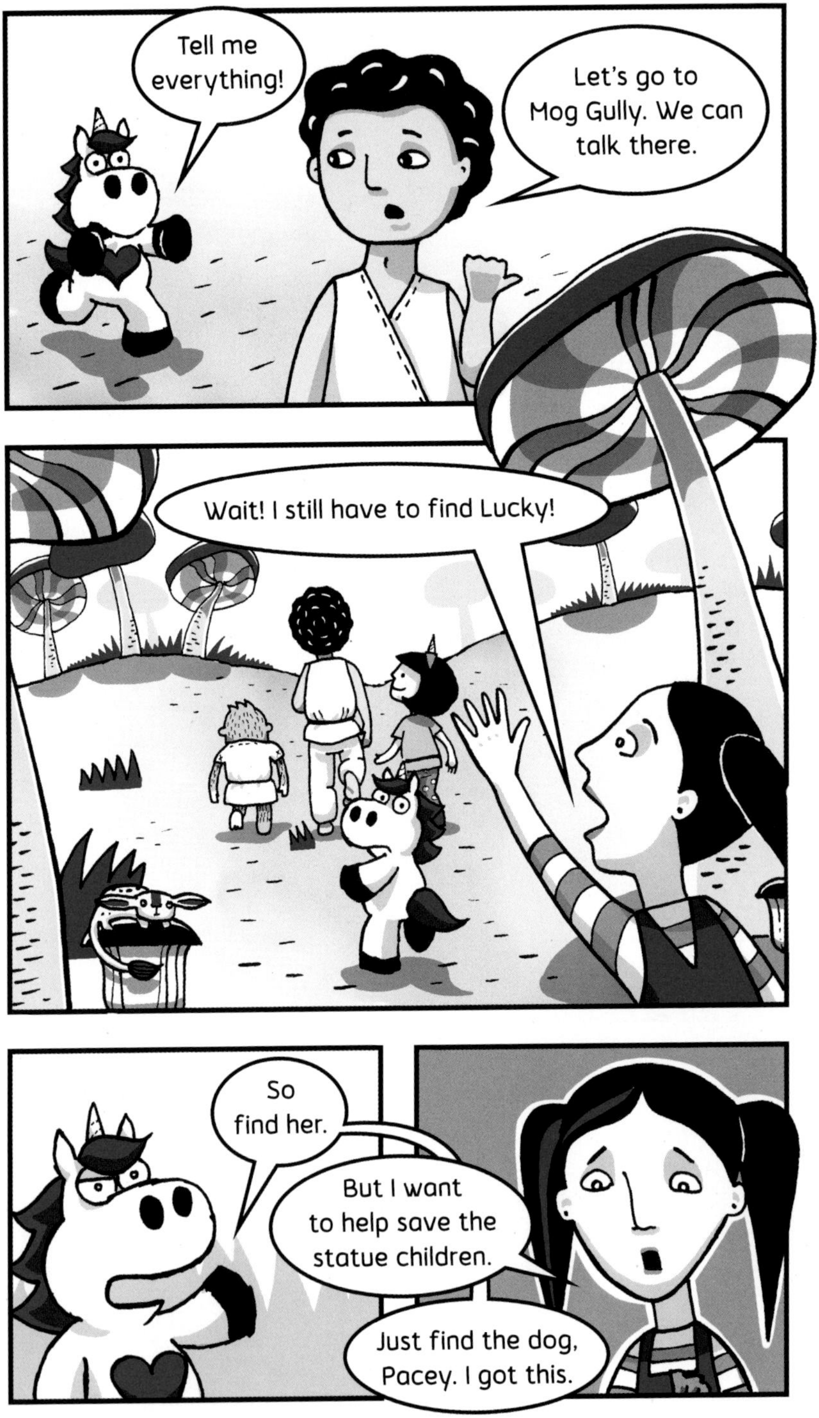
Tell me everything!
Let's go to Mog Gully. We can talk there.
Wait! I still have to find Lucky!
So find her.
But I want to help save the statue children.
Just find the dog, Pacey. I got this.

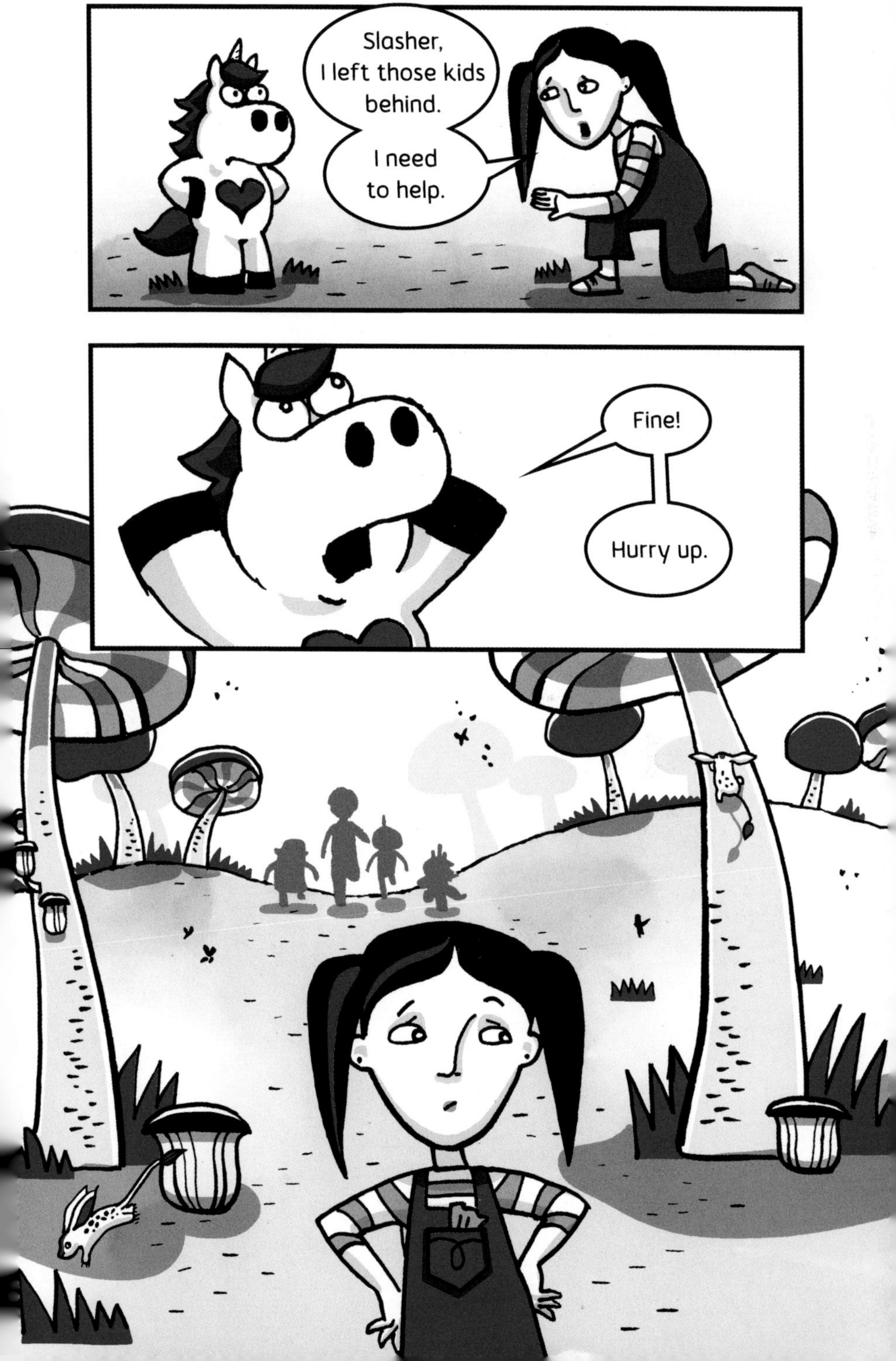
Slasher, I left those kids behind.
I need to help.
Fine!
Hurry up.

CHAPTER 4

SHAKE IT UP

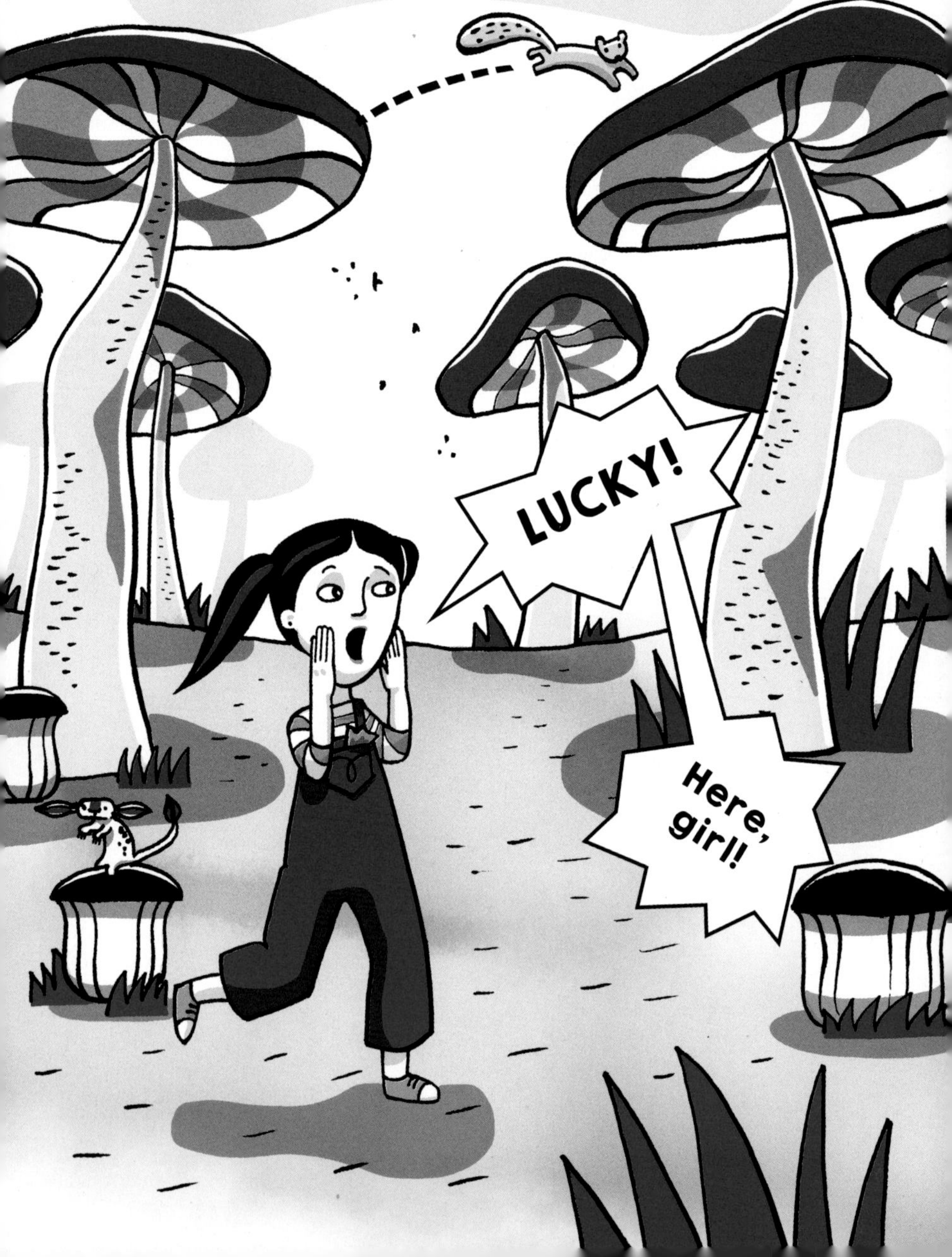
LUCKY!
Here, girl!

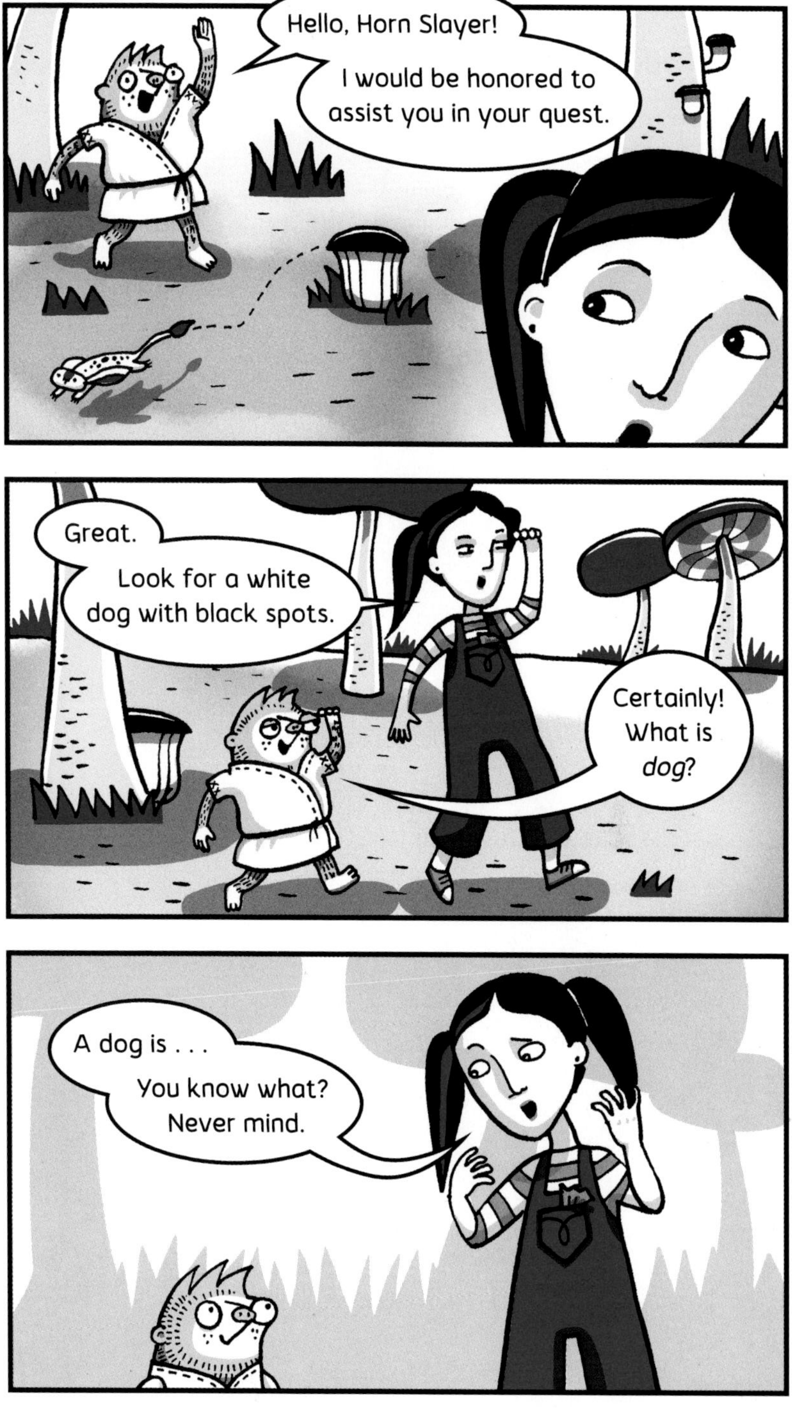
Hello, Horn Slayer!
I would be honored to assist you in your quest.
Great.
Look for a white dog with black spots.
Certainly! What is *dog*?
A dog is . . .
You know what? Never mind.

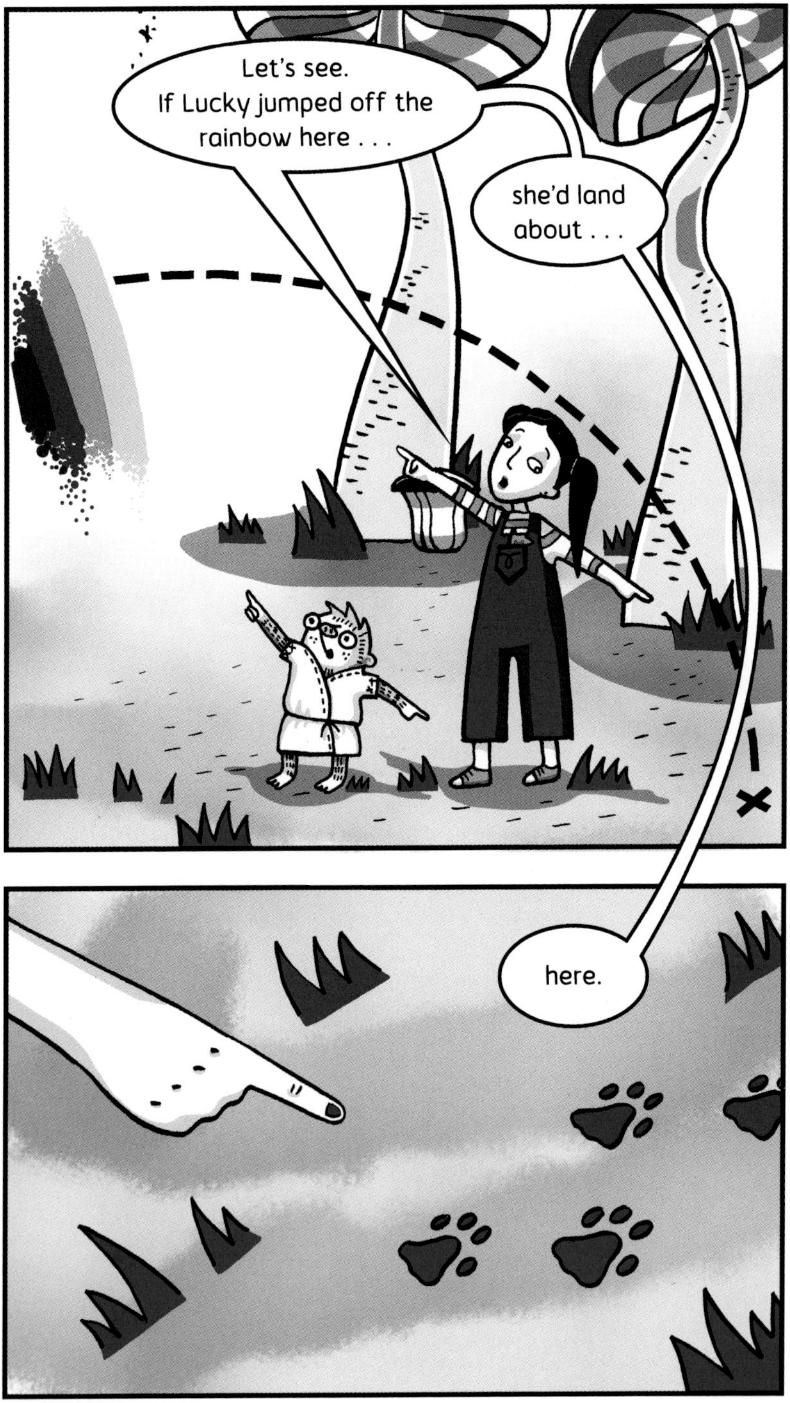
Let's see.
If Lucky jumped off the rainbow here . . .
she'd land about . . .
here.

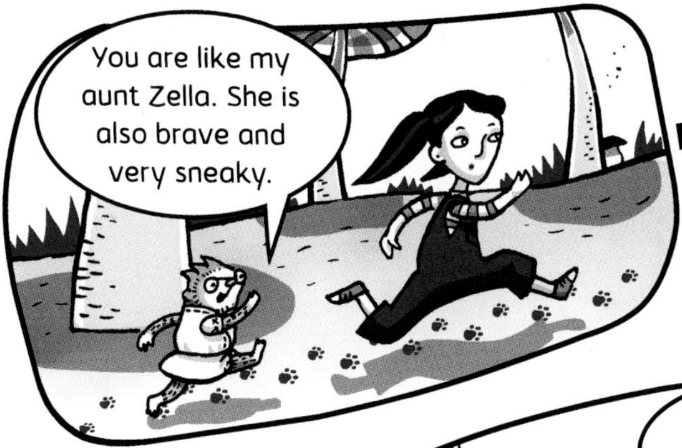
You are like my aunt Zella. She is also brave and very sneaky.

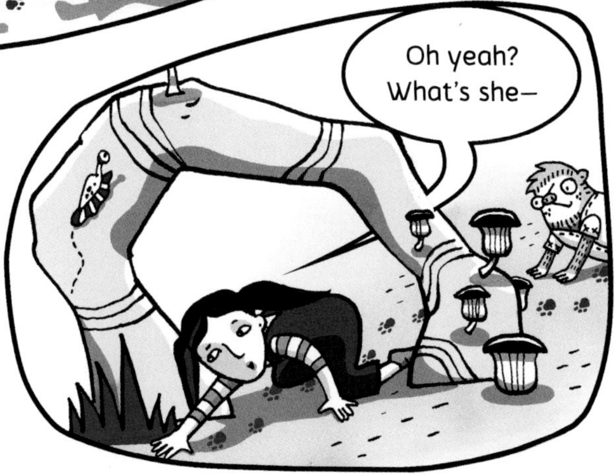
Oh yeah? What's she–

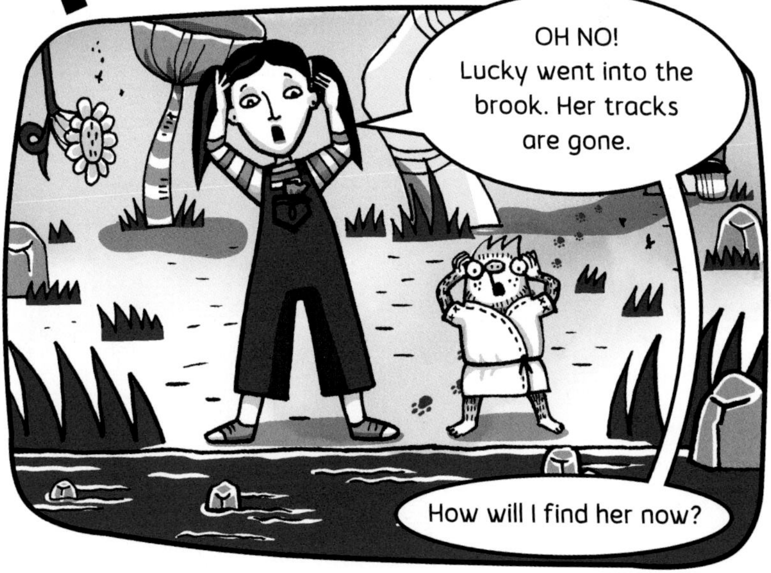
OH NO! Lucky went into the brook. Her tracks are gone.
How will I find her now?

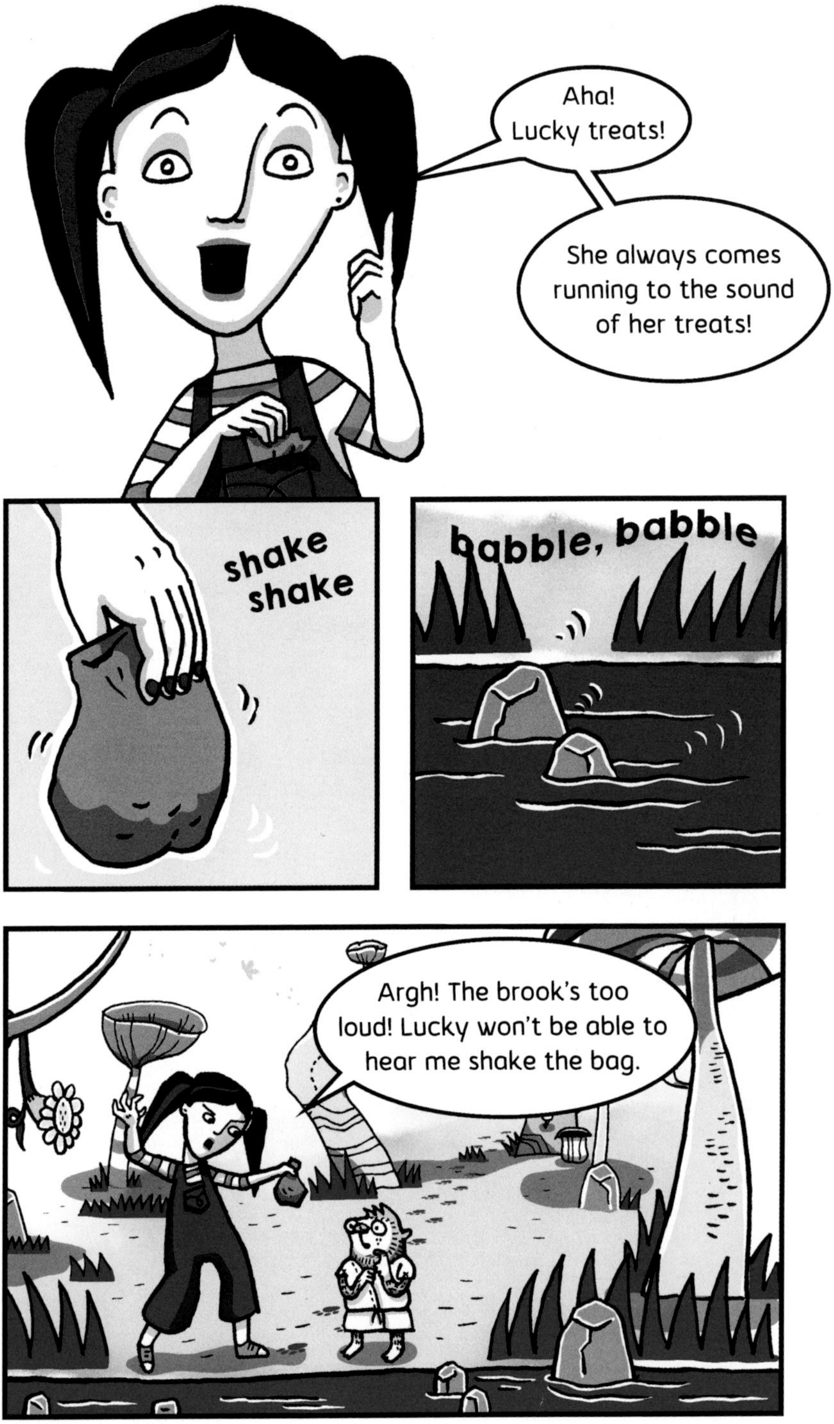
Aha! Lucky treats!
She always comes running to the sound of her treats!
shake shake
babble, babble
Argh! The brook's too loud! Lucky won't be able to hear me shake the bag.

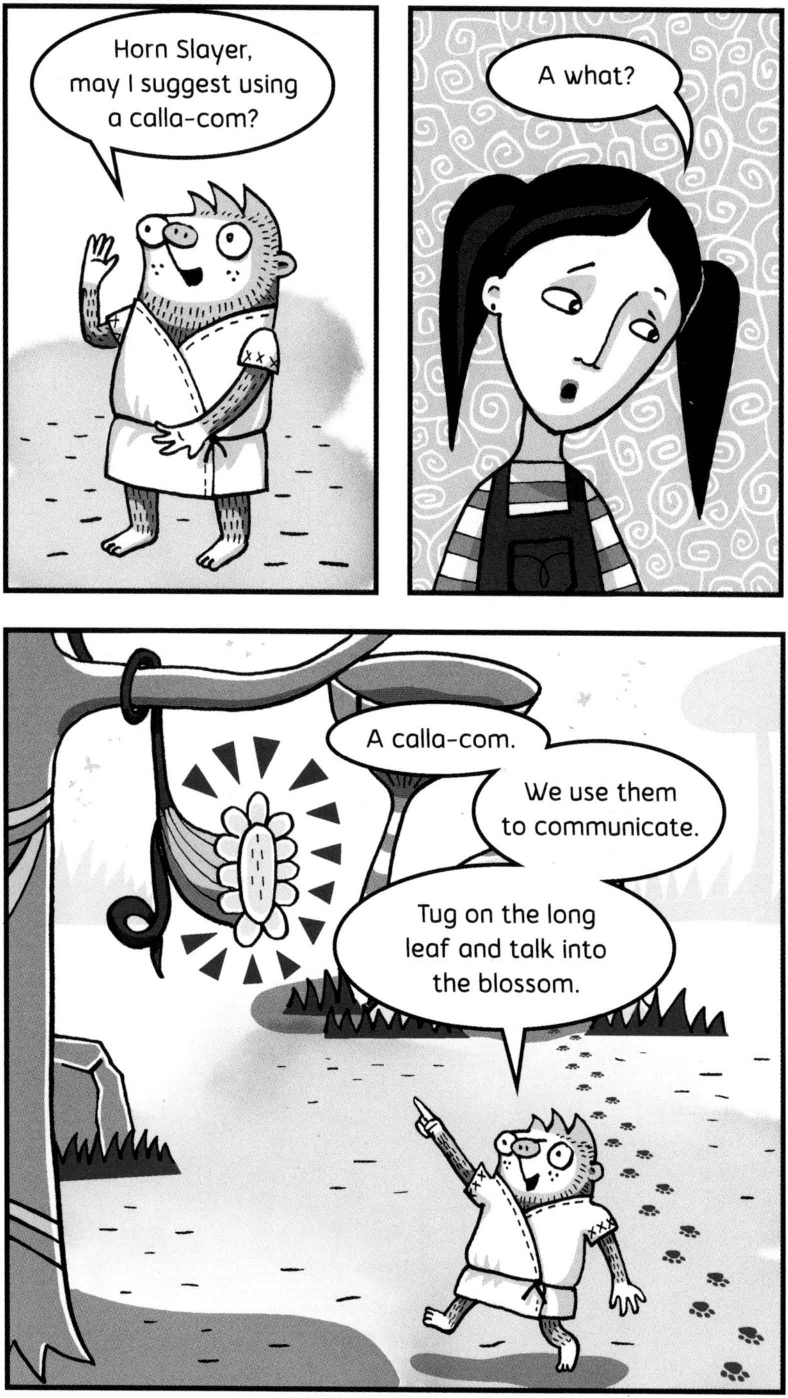
Horn Slayer, may I suggest using a calla-com?
A what?
A calla-com.
We use them to communicate.
Tug on the long leaf and talk into the blossom.

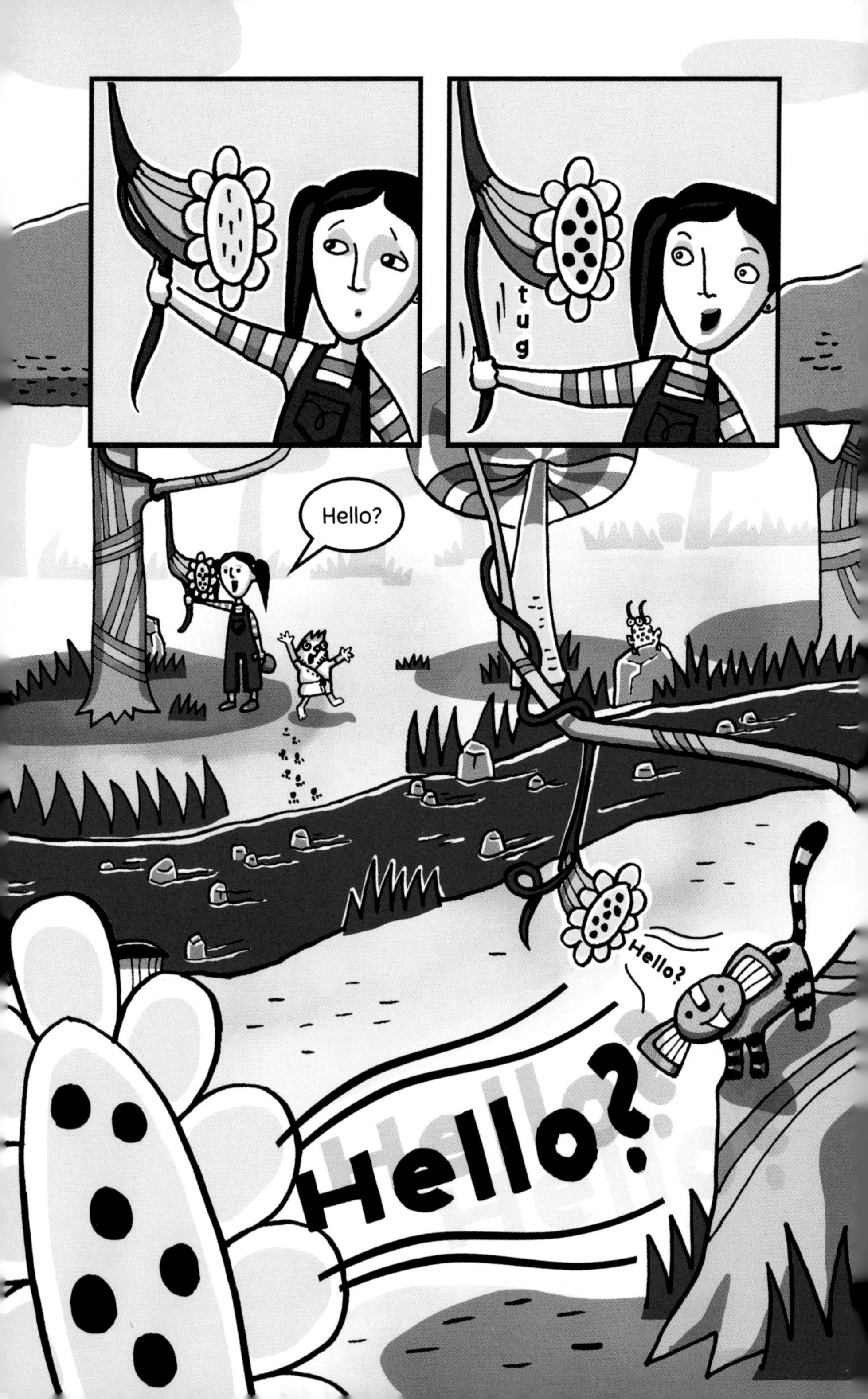
tug
Hello?
Hello?
Hello?

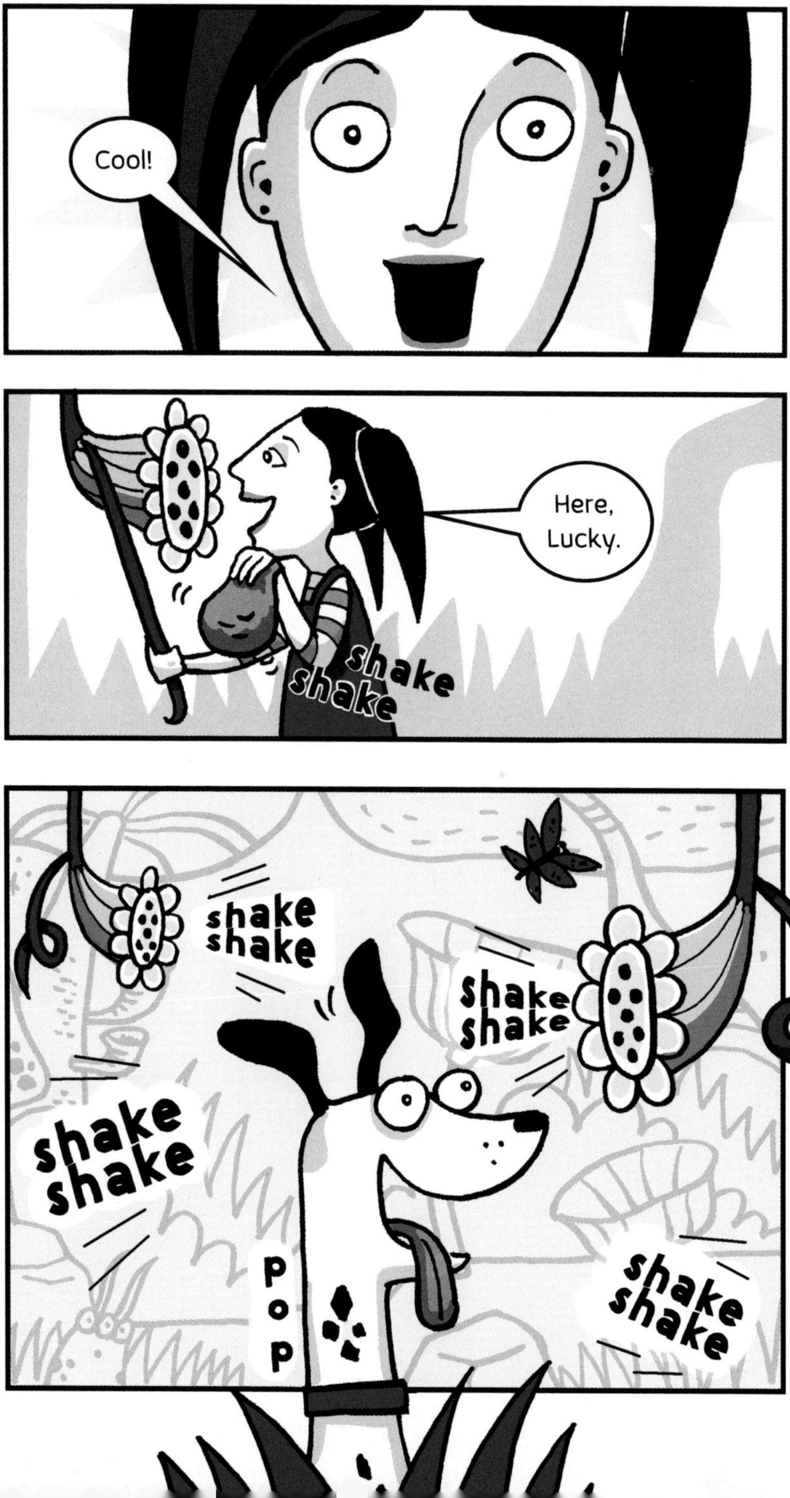
Cool!
Here, Lucky.
shake shake
shake shake
shake shake
shake shake
pop
shake shake

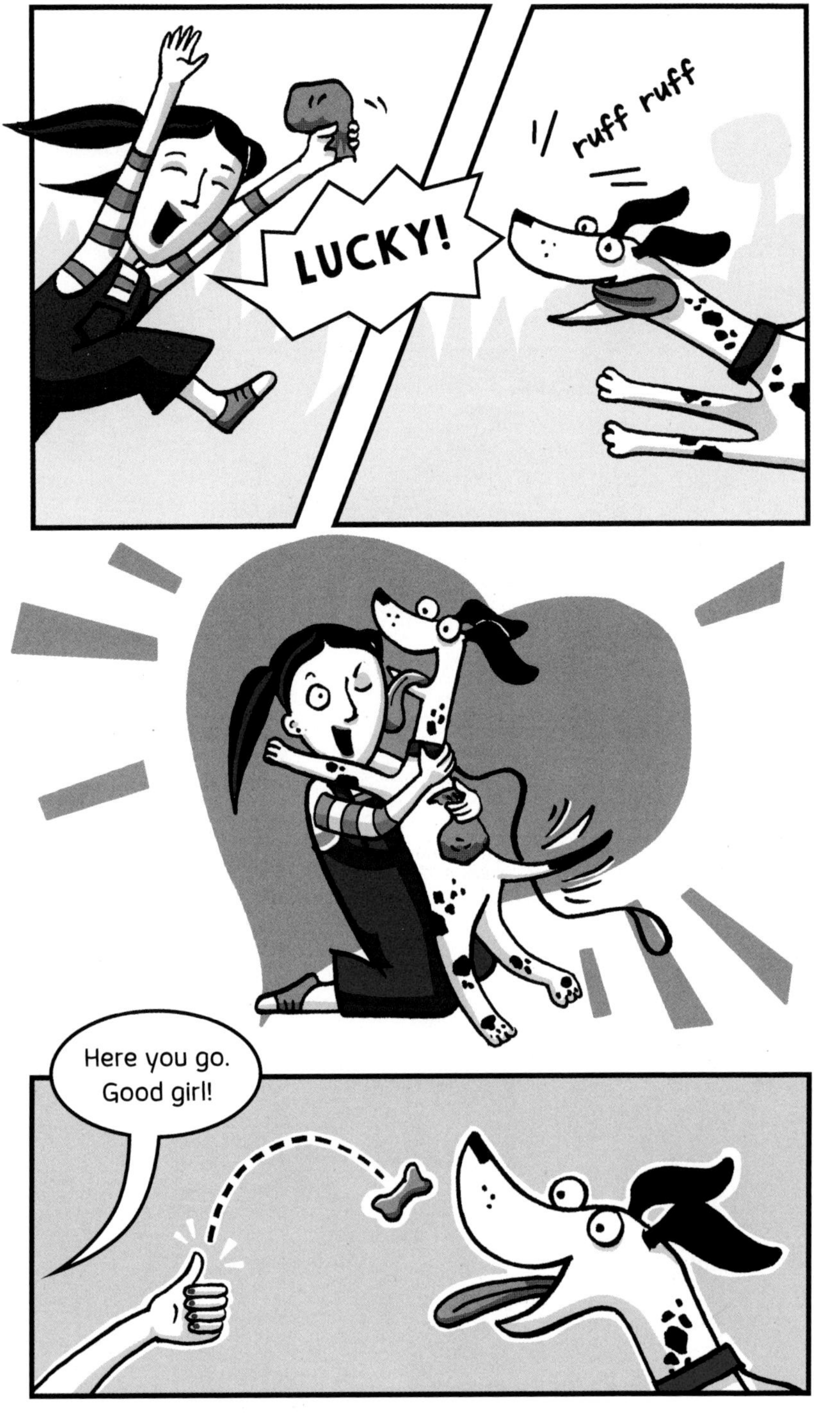
LUCKY!
ruff ruff
Here you go.
Good girl!

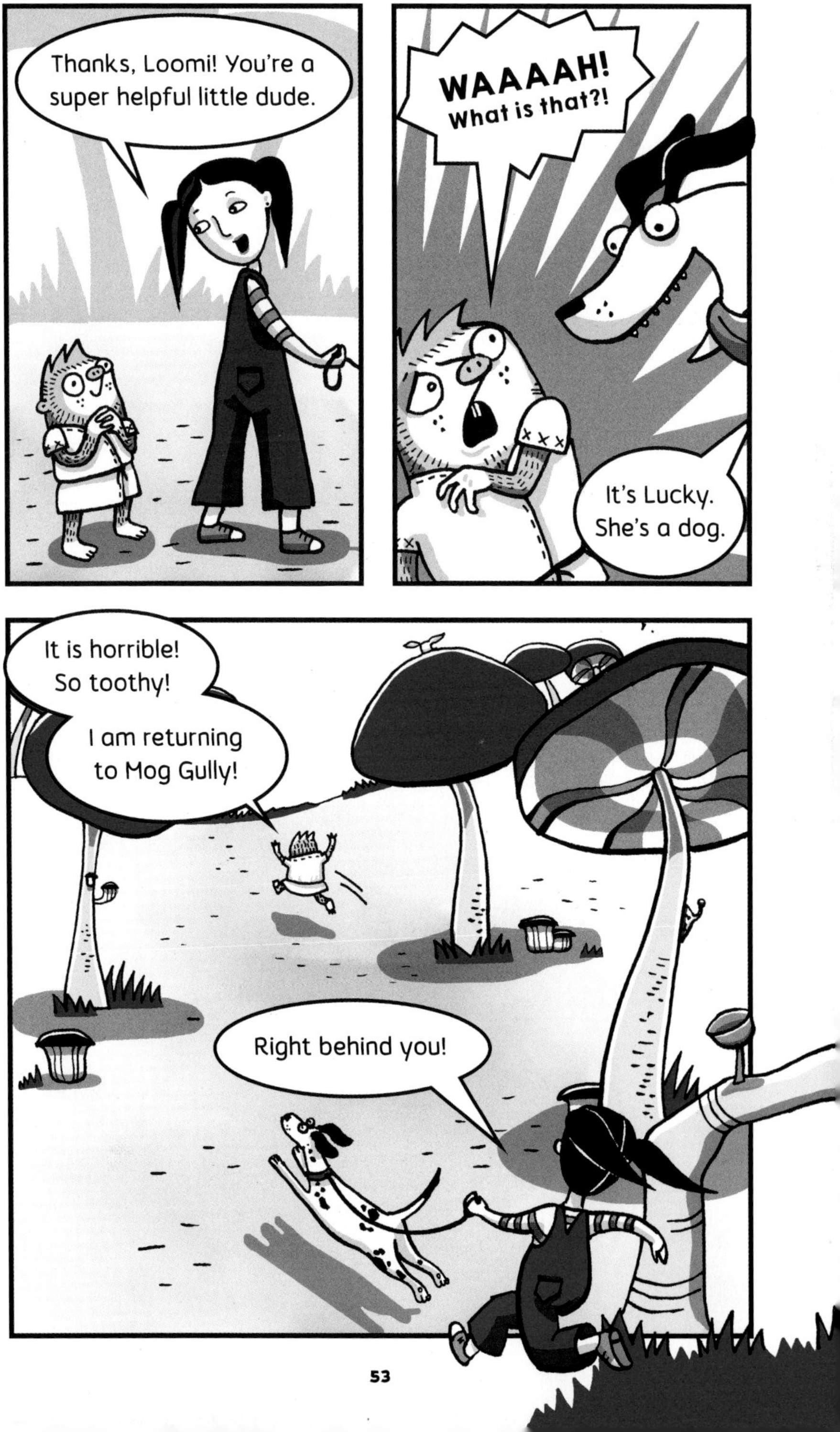
Thanks, Loomi! You're a super helpful little dude.
WAAAAH! What is that?!
It's Lucky. She's a dog.
It is horrible! So toothy!
I am returning to Mog Gully!
Right behind you!

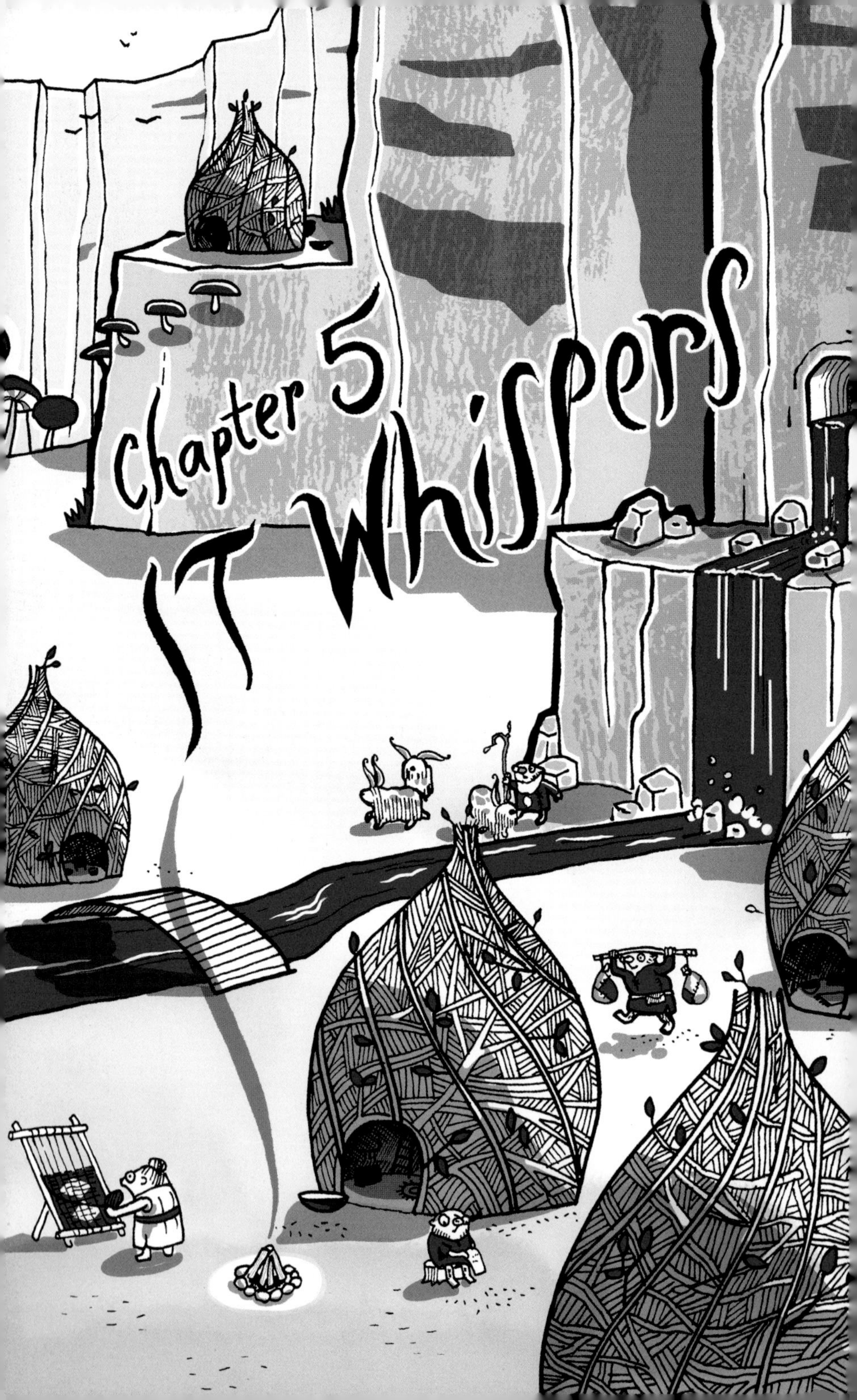
Chapter 5
IT Whispers

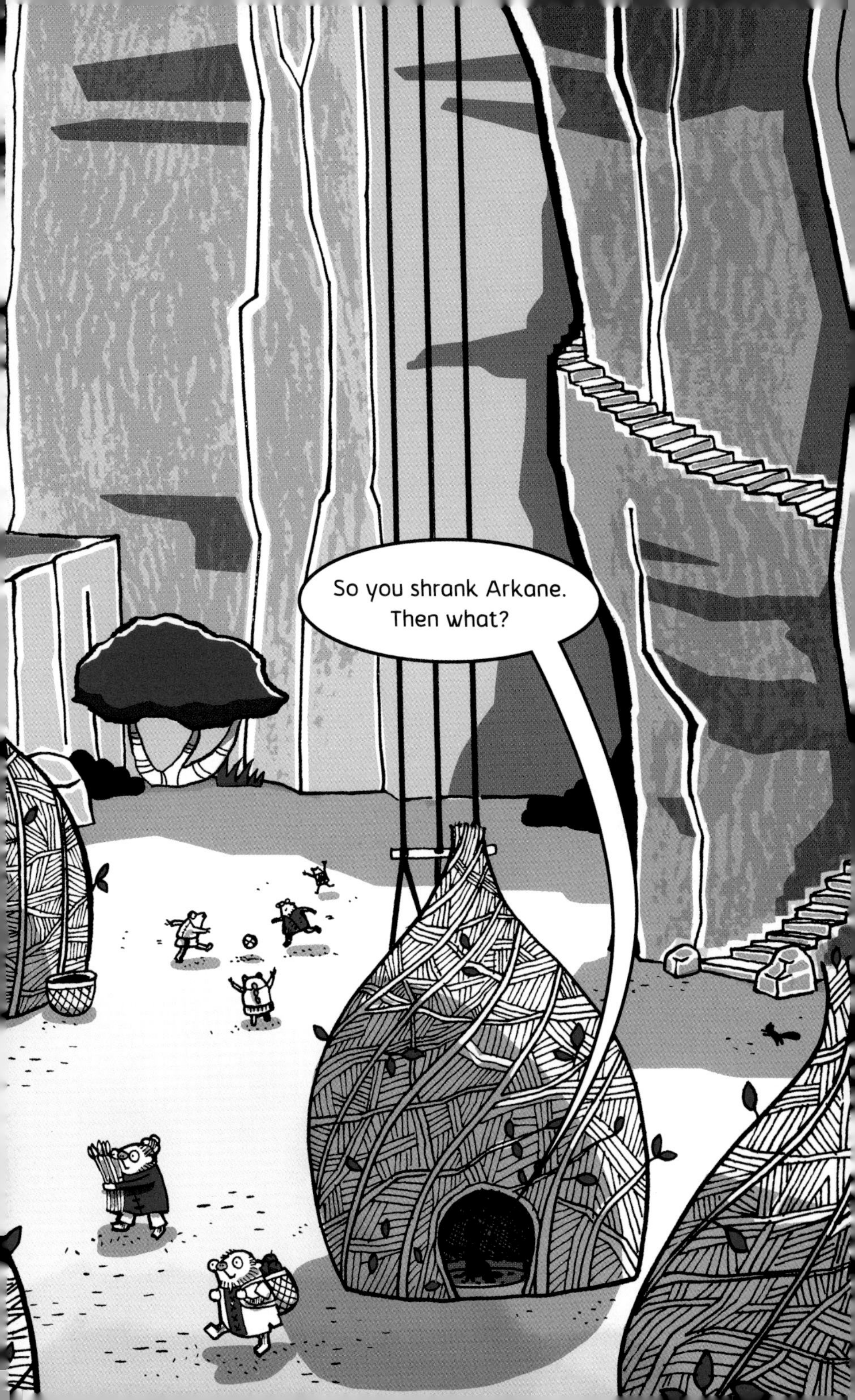
So you shrank Arkane. Then what?

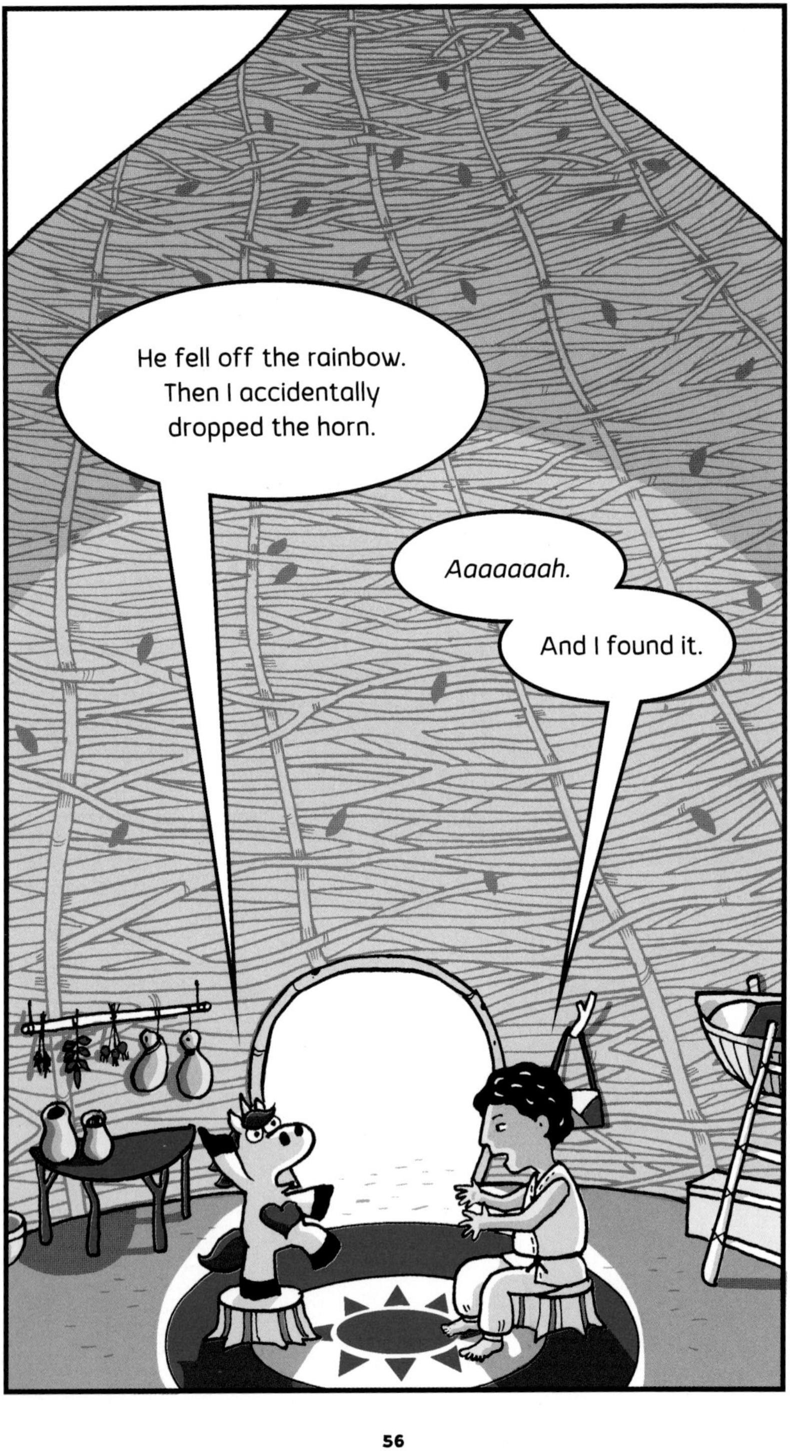
He fell off the rainbow. Then I accidentally dropped the horn.
Aaaaaaah.
And I found it.

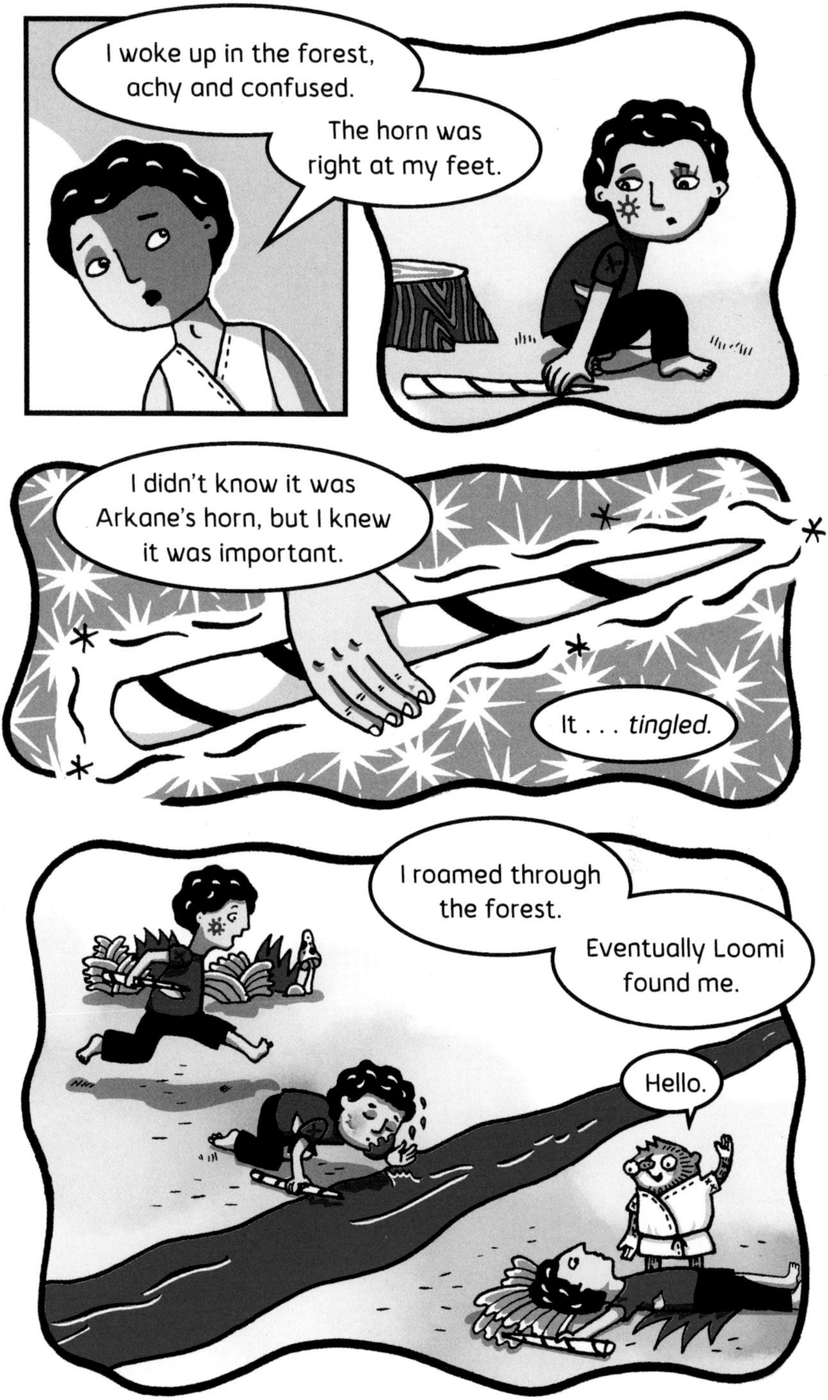
I woke up in the forest, achy and confused.
The horn was right at my feet.
I didn't know it was Arkane's horn, but I knew it was important.
It . . . *tingled.*
I roamed through the forest.
Eventually Loomi found me.
Hello.

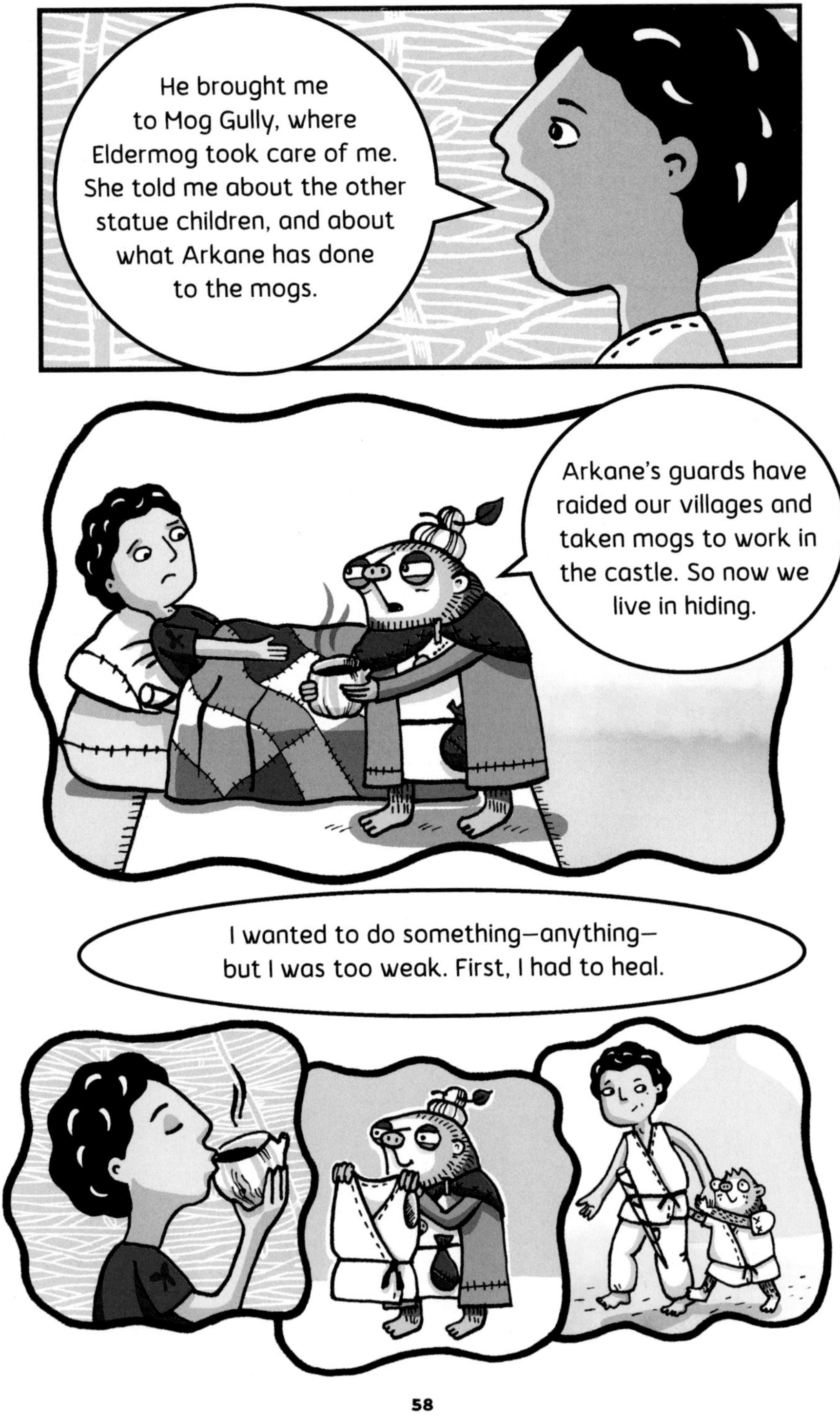
He brought me to Mog Gully, where Eldermog took care of me. She told me about the other statue children, and about what Arkane has done to the mogs.
Arkane's guards have raided our villages and taken mogs to work in the castle. So now we live in hiding.
I wanted to do something—anything—but I was too weak. First, I had to heal.

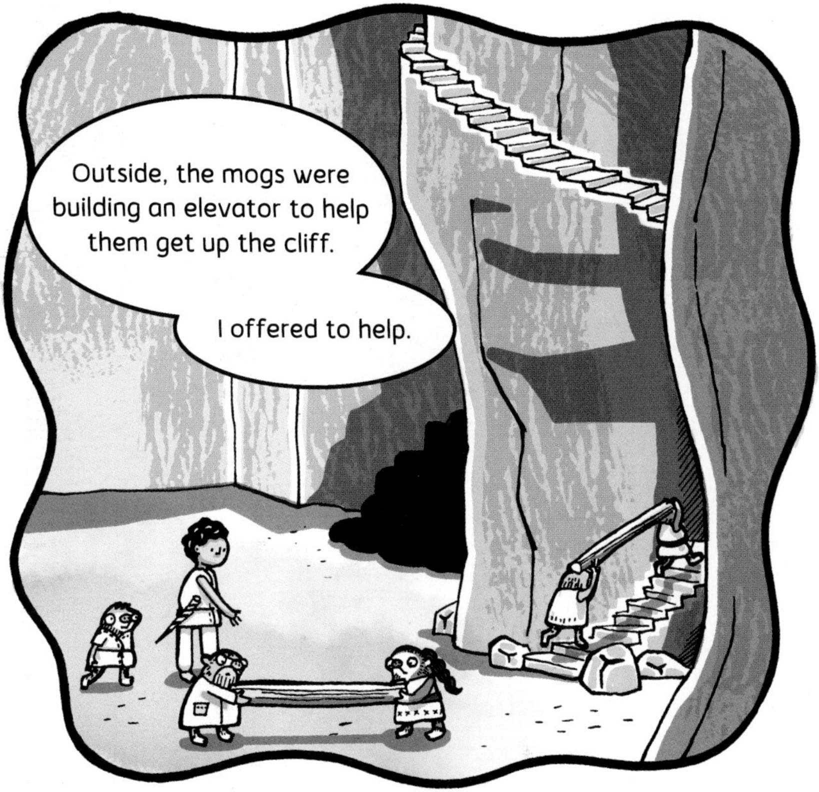
Outside, the mogs were building an elevator to help them get up the cliff.
I offered to help.

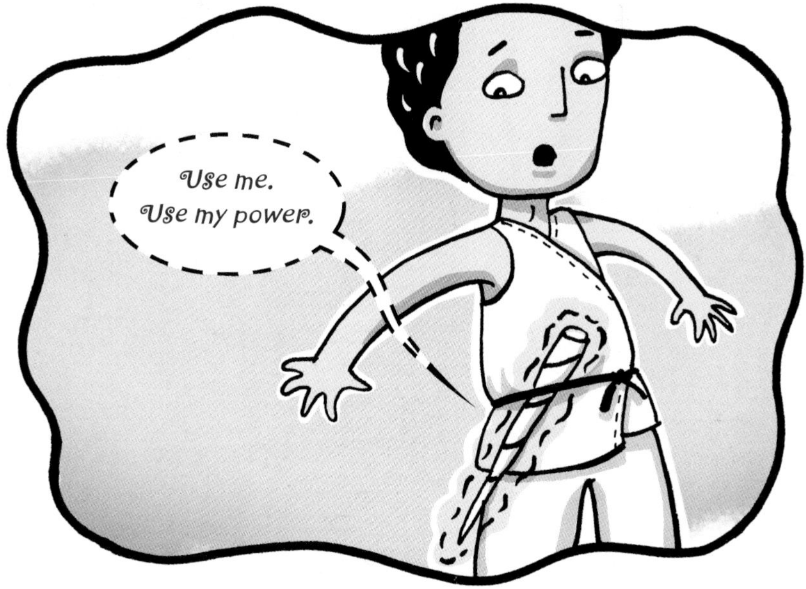
Use me.
Use my power.

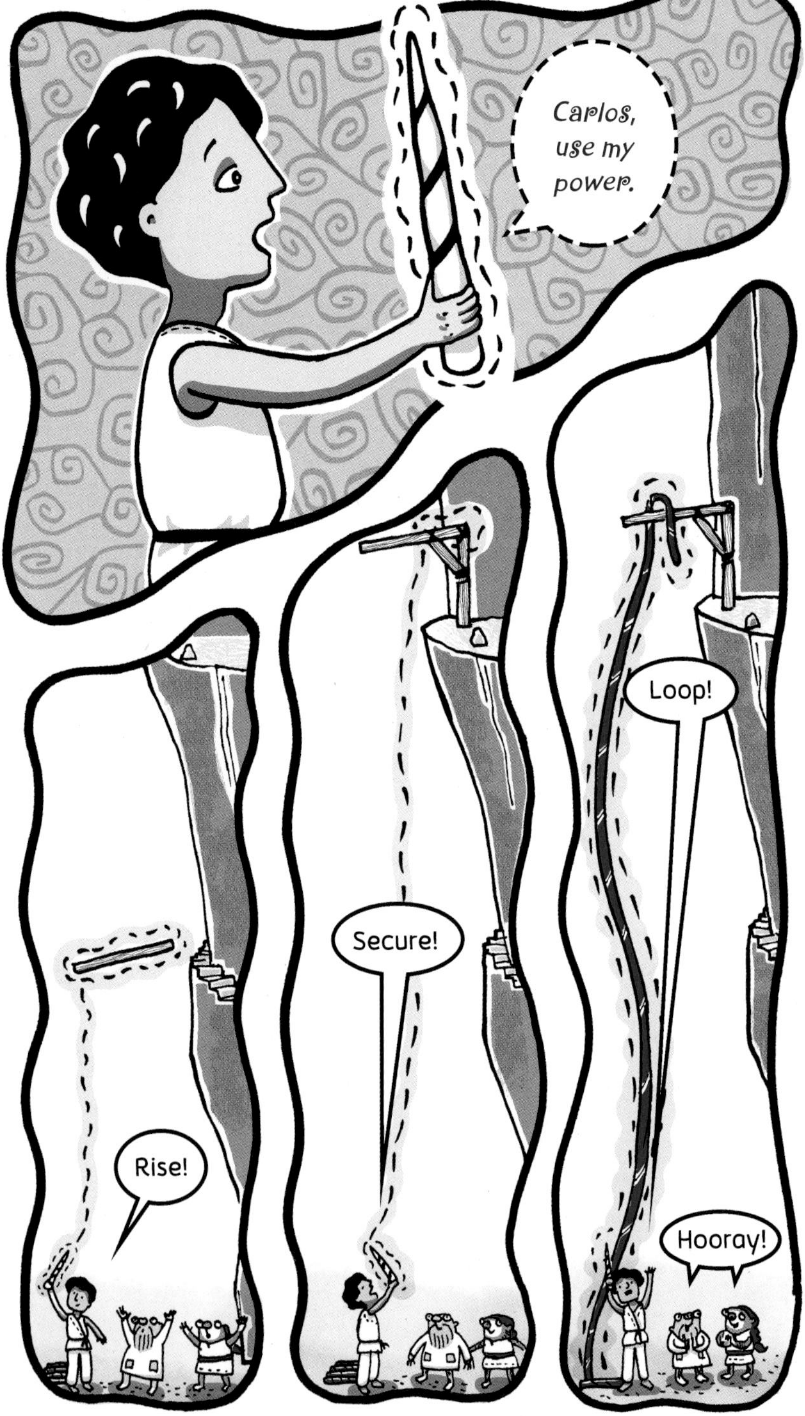
Carlos, use my power.
Rise!
Secure!
Loop!
Hooray!

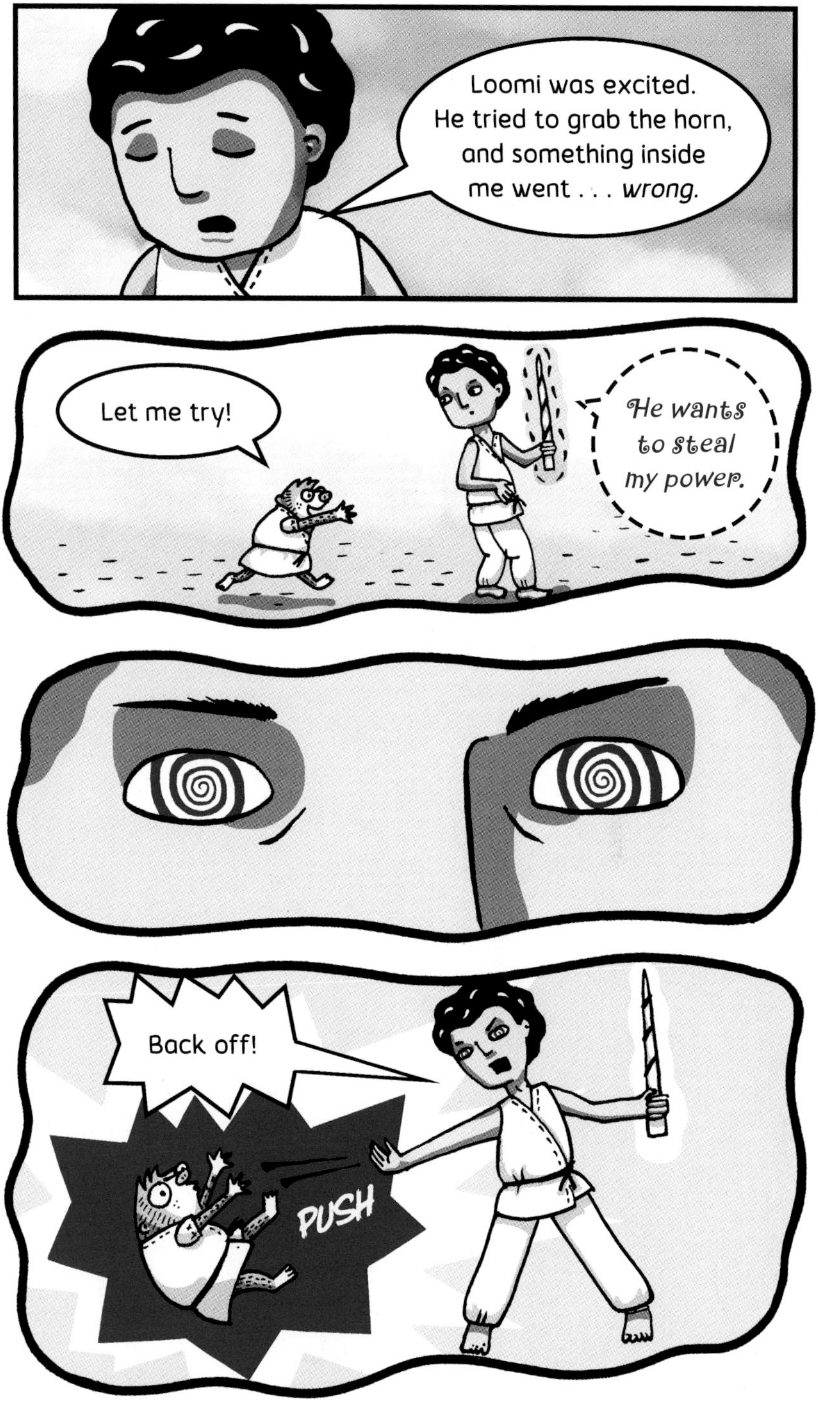
Loomi was excited. He tried to grab the horn, and something inside me went . . . *wrong.*
Let me try!
He wants to steal my power.
Back off!
PUSH

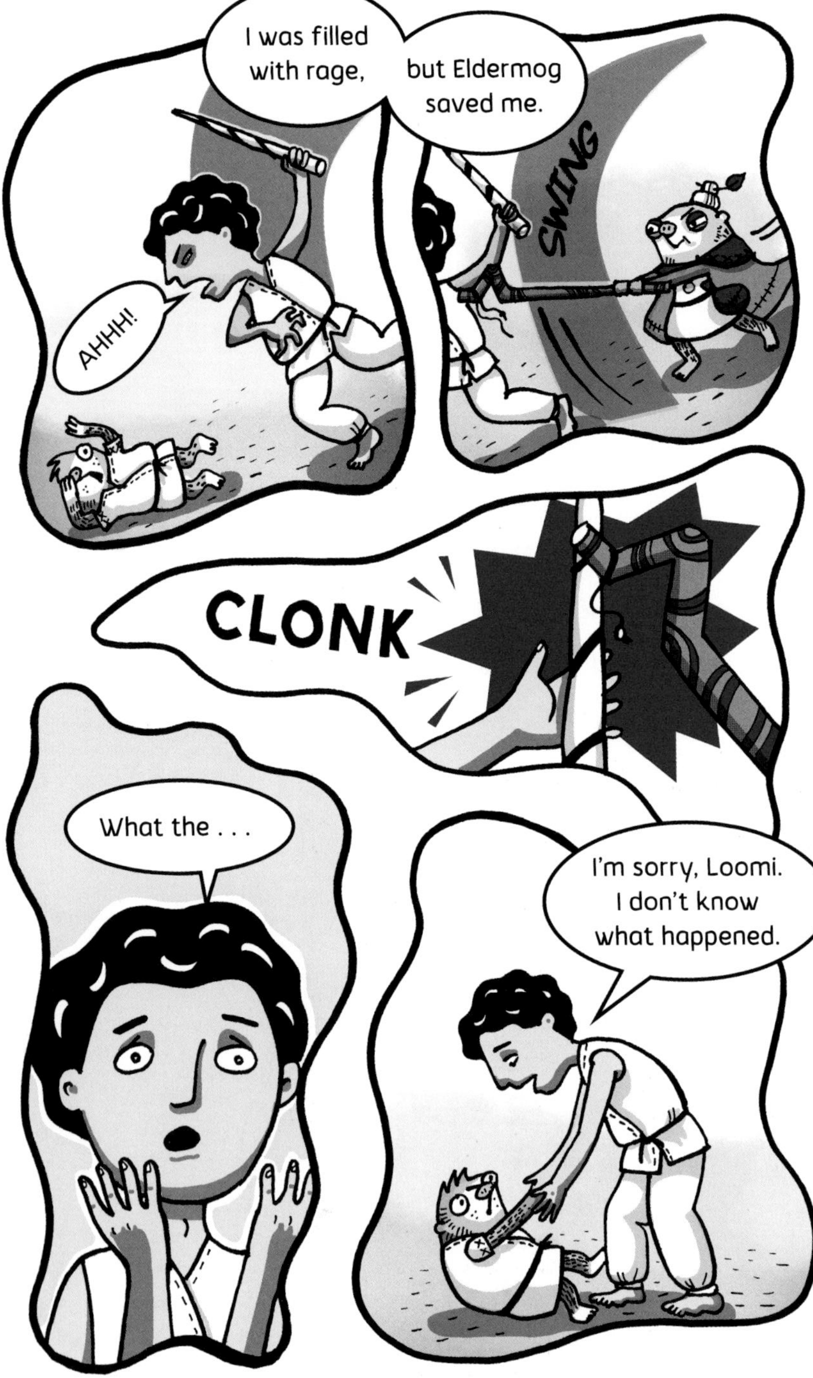
I was filled with rage,
but Eldermog saved me.
AHHH!
SWING
CLONK
What the . . .
I'm sorry, Loomi. I don't know what happened.

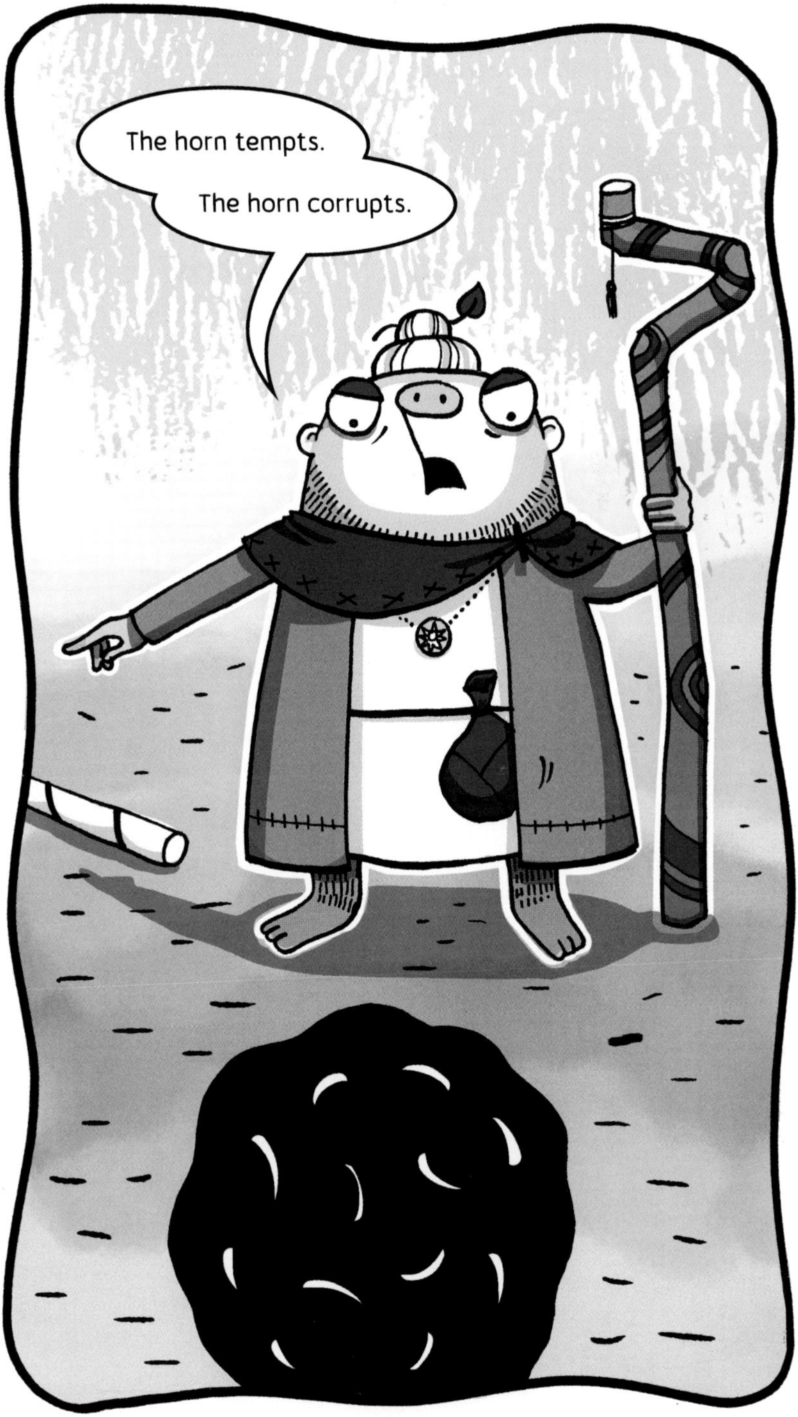
The horn tempts.
The horn corrupts.

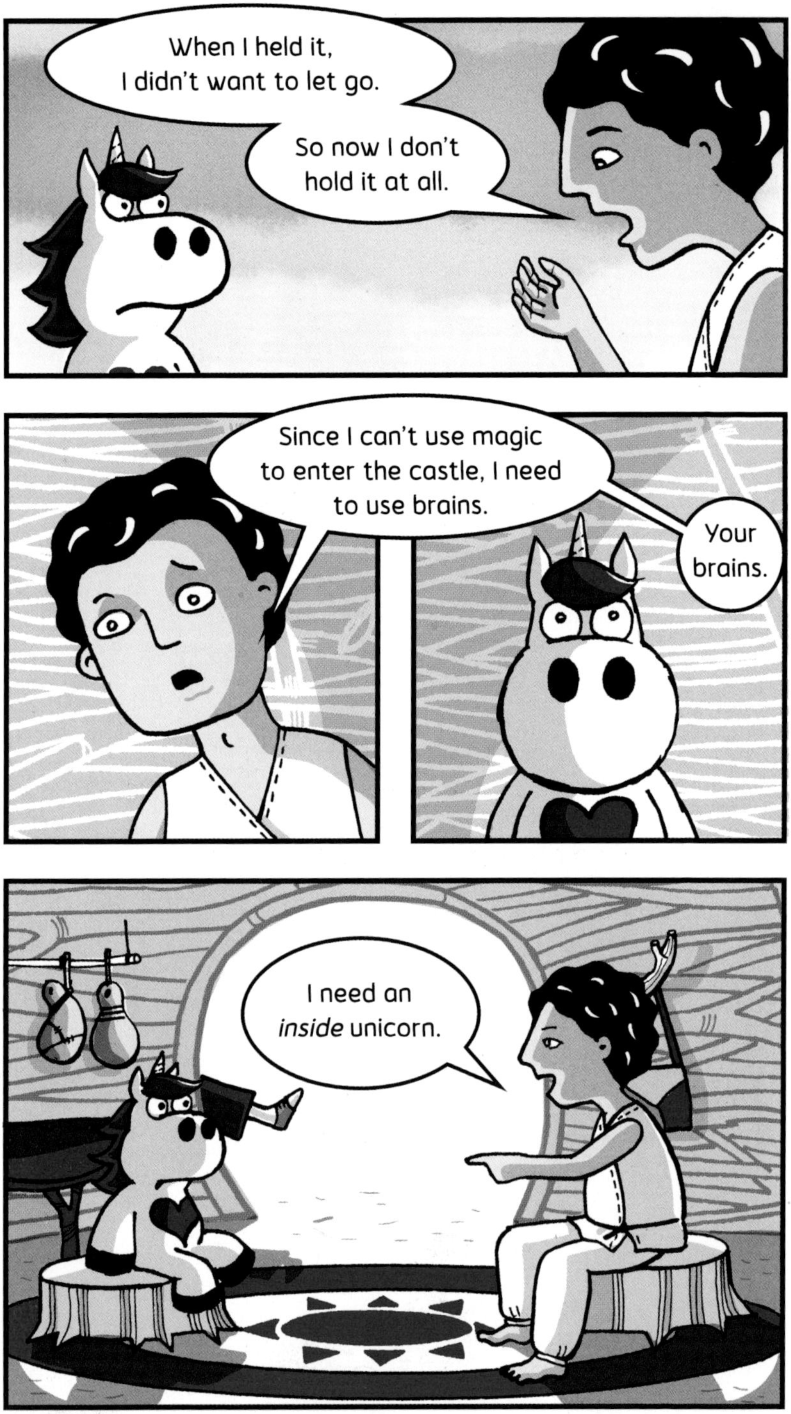
When I held it, I didn't want to let go.
So now I don't hold it at all.
Since I can't use magic to enter the castle, I need to use brains.
Your brains.
I need an *inside* unicorn.

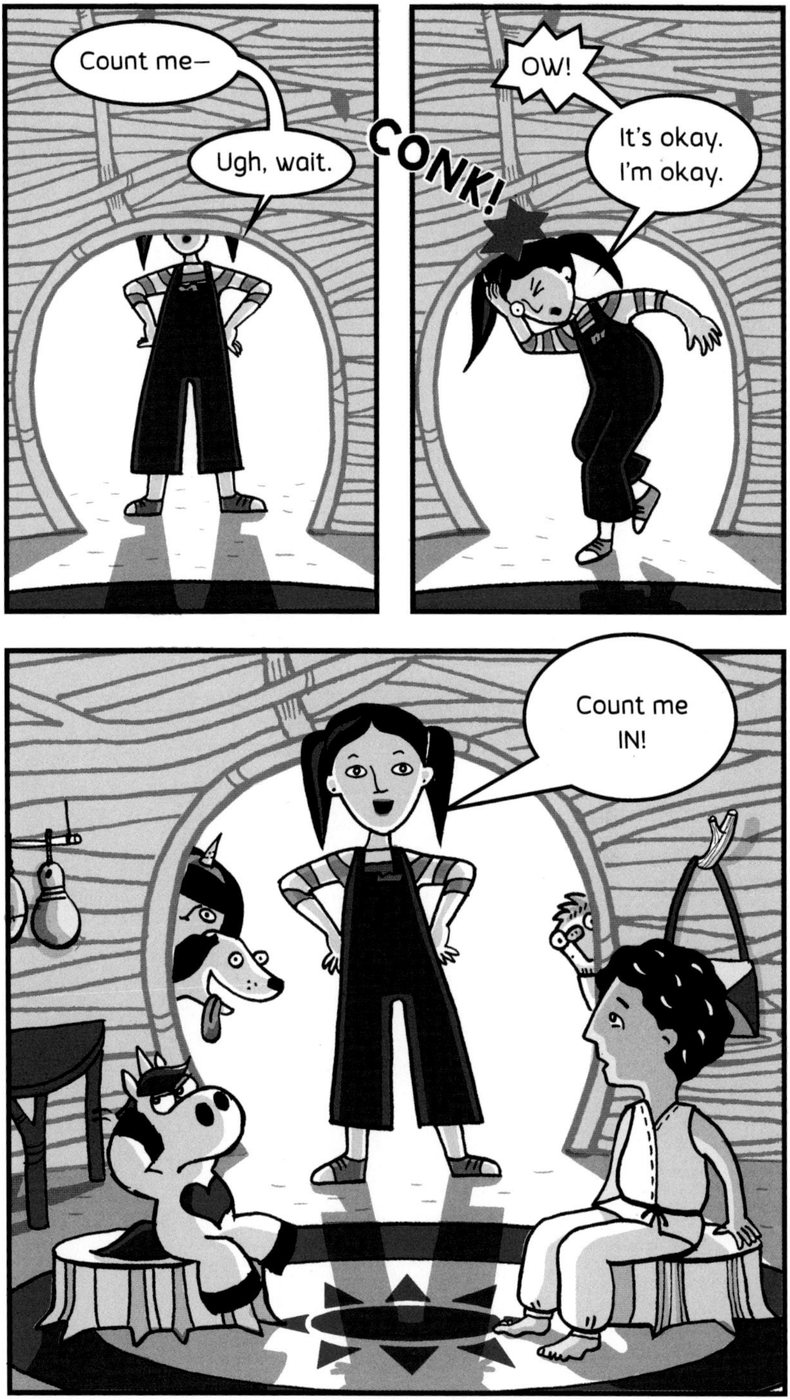

Count me—
Ugh, wait.
CONK!
OW!
It's okay.
I'm okay.
Count me
IN!

Chapter 6

STAND BY YOUR PLAN

Now that's what I call a plan! I'm naming it Operation: Awesome.

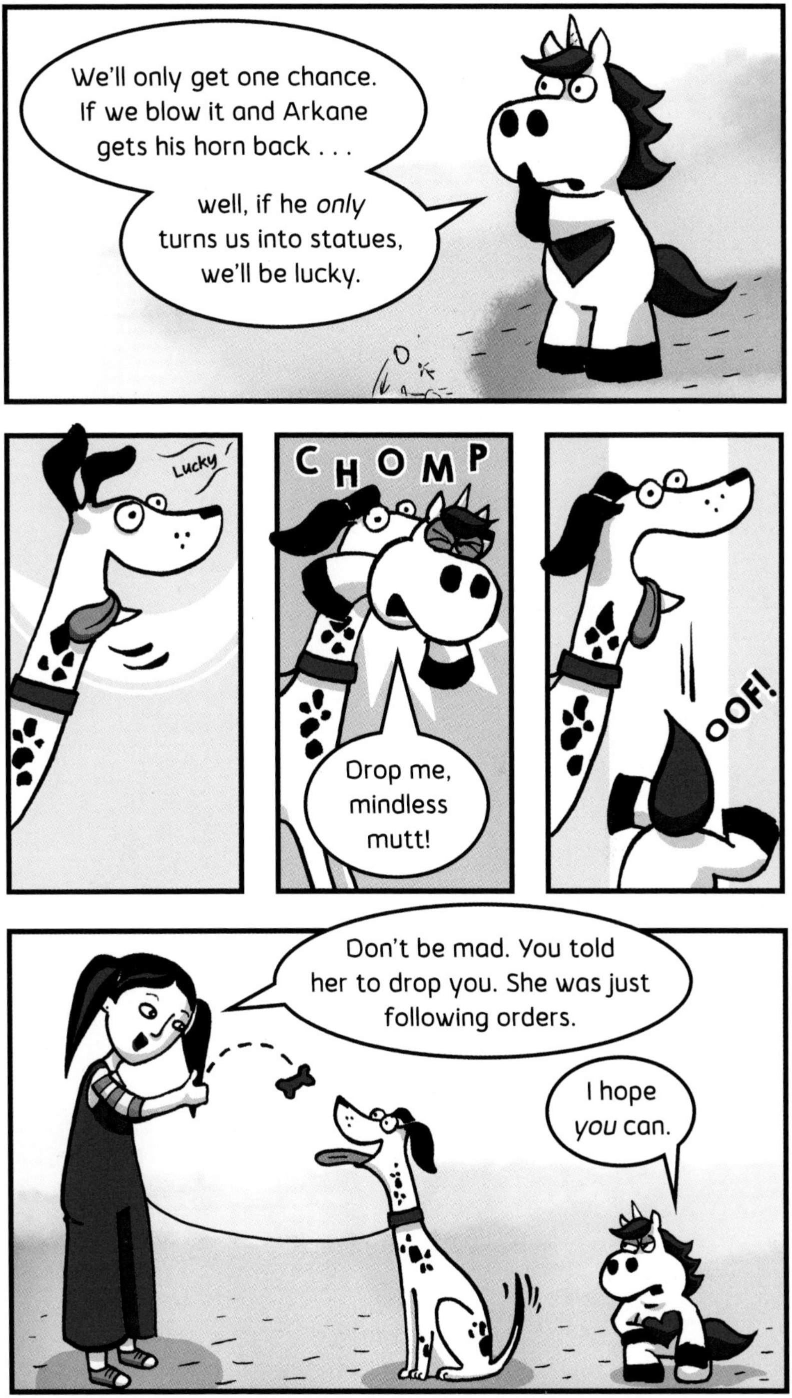
We'll only get one chance. If we blow it and Arkane gets his horn back . . .
well, if he *only* turns us into statues, we'll be lucky.
Lucky
CHOMP
Drop me, mindless mutt!
OOF!
Don't be mad. You told her to drop you. She was just following orders.
I hope *you* can.

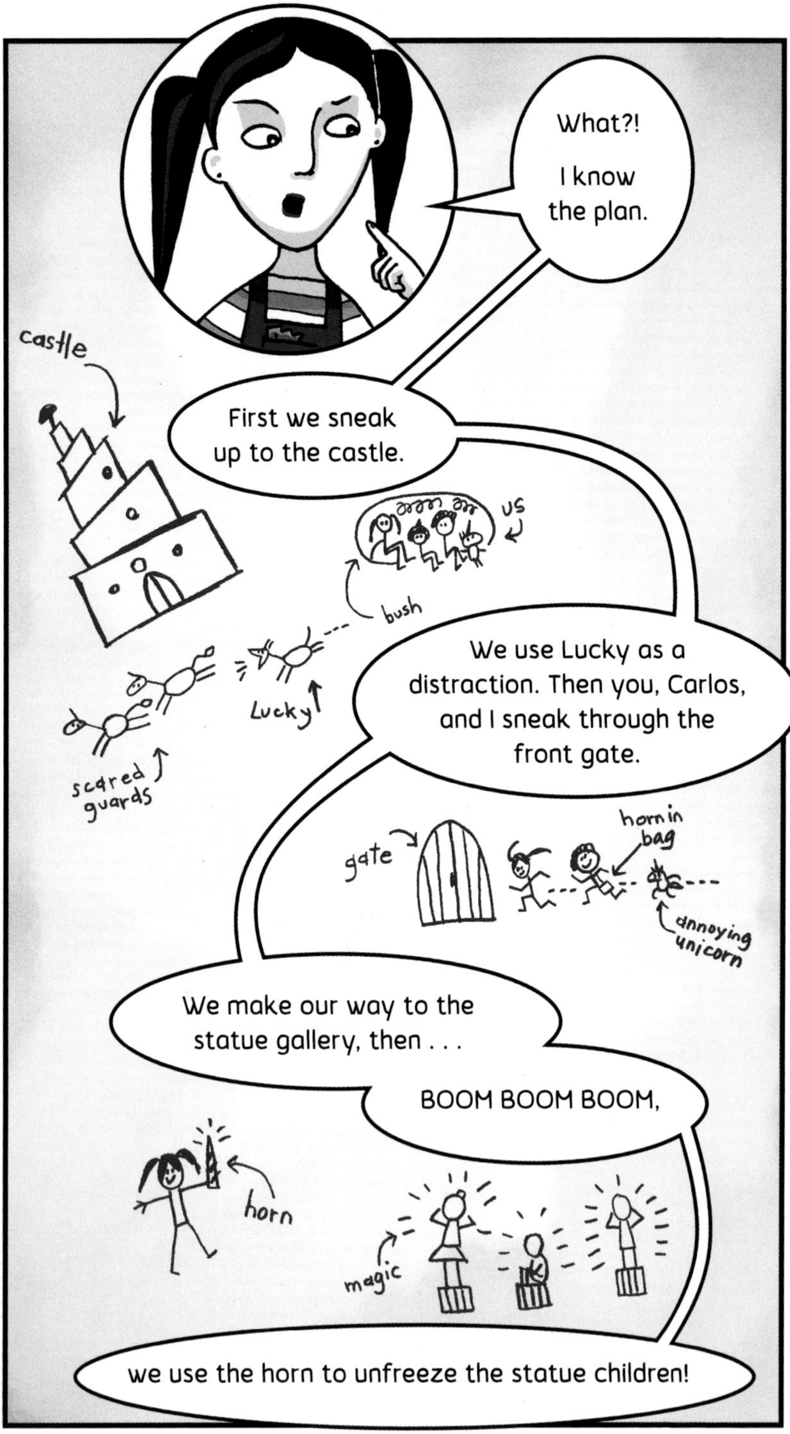
What?!
I know the plan.
First we sneak up to the castle.
castle
us
bush
We use Lucky as a distraction. Then you, Carlos, and I sneak through the front gate.
Lucky
scared guards
gate
horn in bag
annoying unicorn
We make our way to the statue gallery, then . . .
BOOM BOOM BOOM,
horn
magic
we use the horn to unfreeze the statue children!

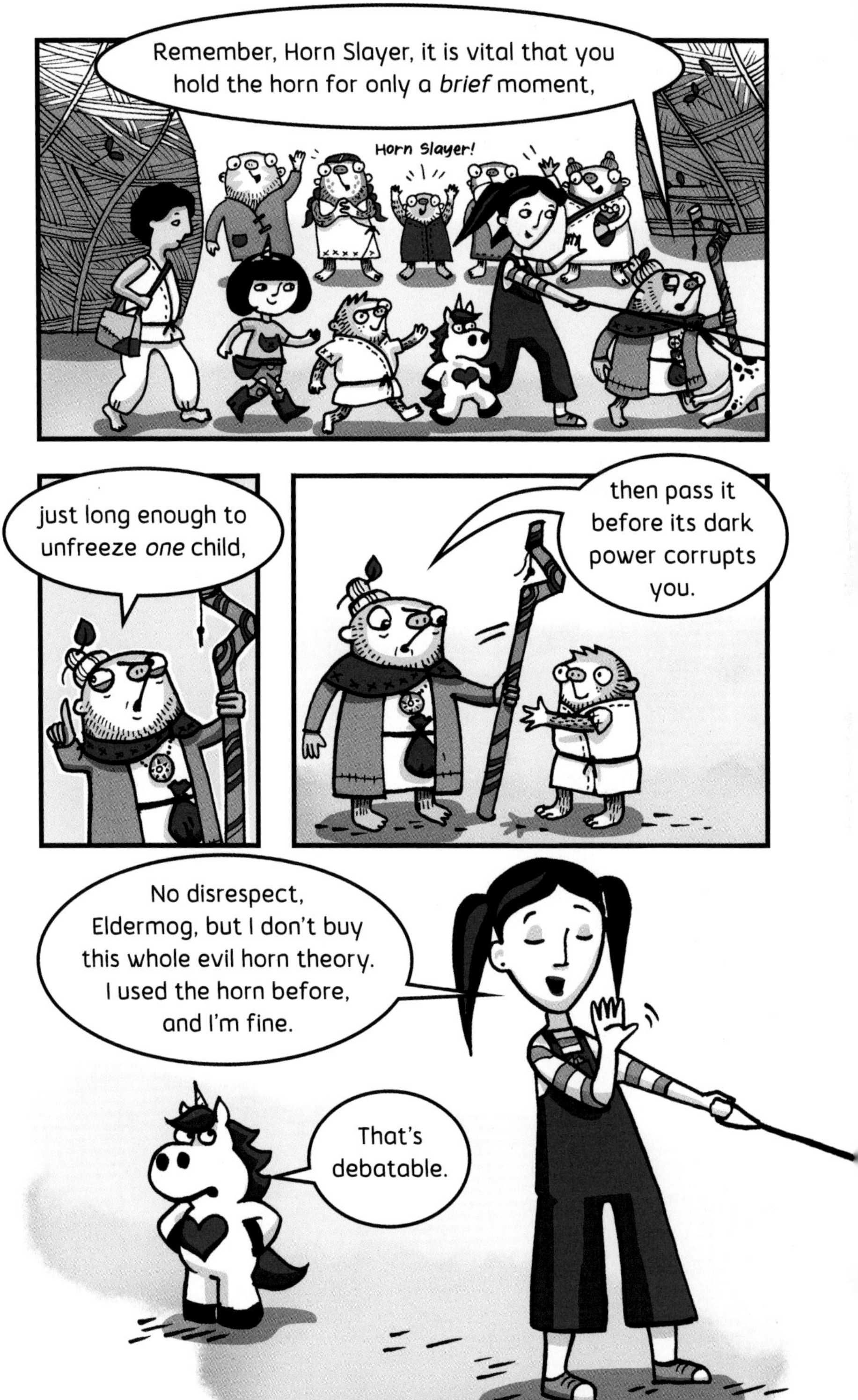
Remember, Horn Slayer, it is vital that you hold the horn for only a *brief* moment,
Horn Slayer!
just long enough to unfreeze *one* child,
then pass it before its dark power corrupts you.
No disrespect, Eldermog, but I don't buy this whole evil horn theory. I used the horn before, and I'm fine.
That's debatable.

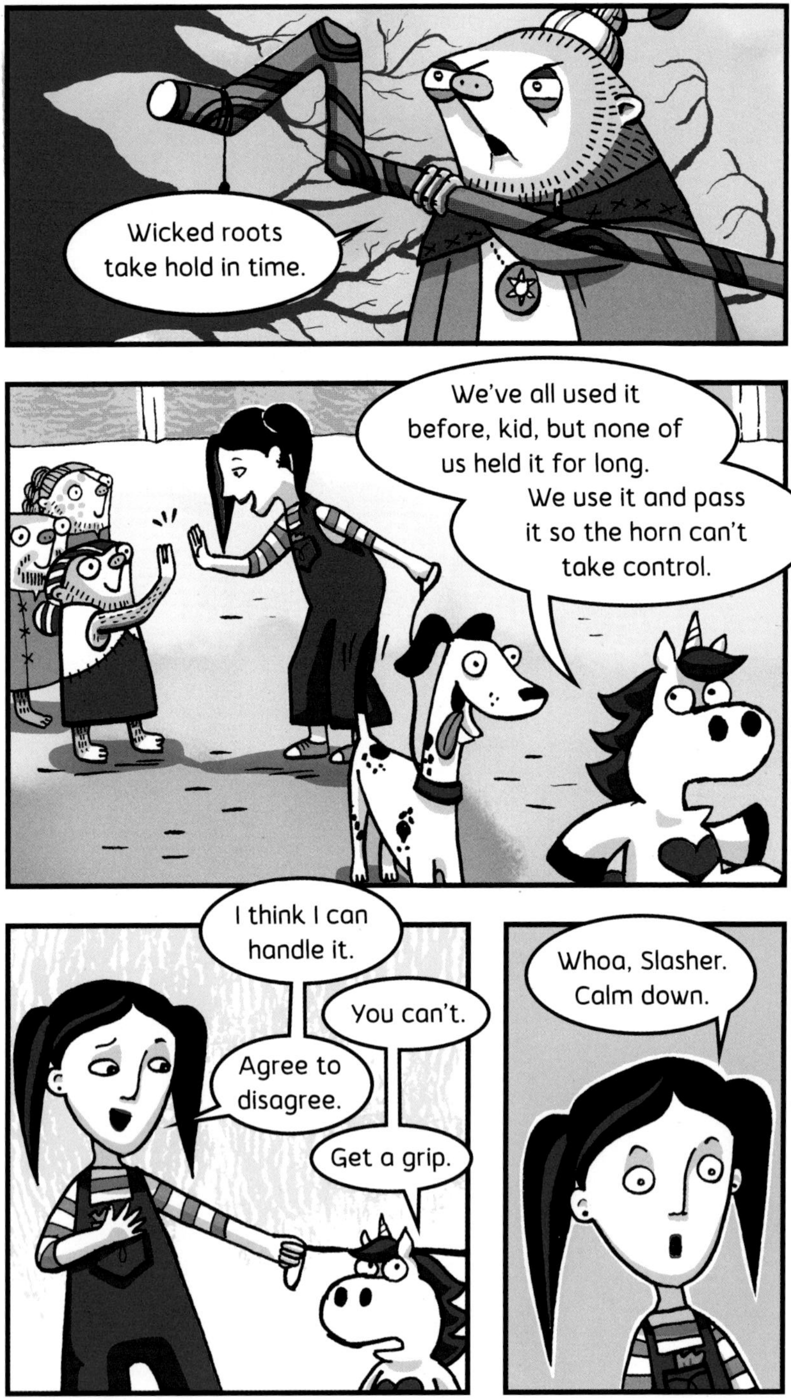

Wicked roots take hold in time.
We've all used it before, kid, but none of us held it for long.
We use it and pass it so the horn can't take control.
I think I can handle it.
You can't.
Agree to disagree.
Get a grip.
Whoa, Slasher. Calm down.

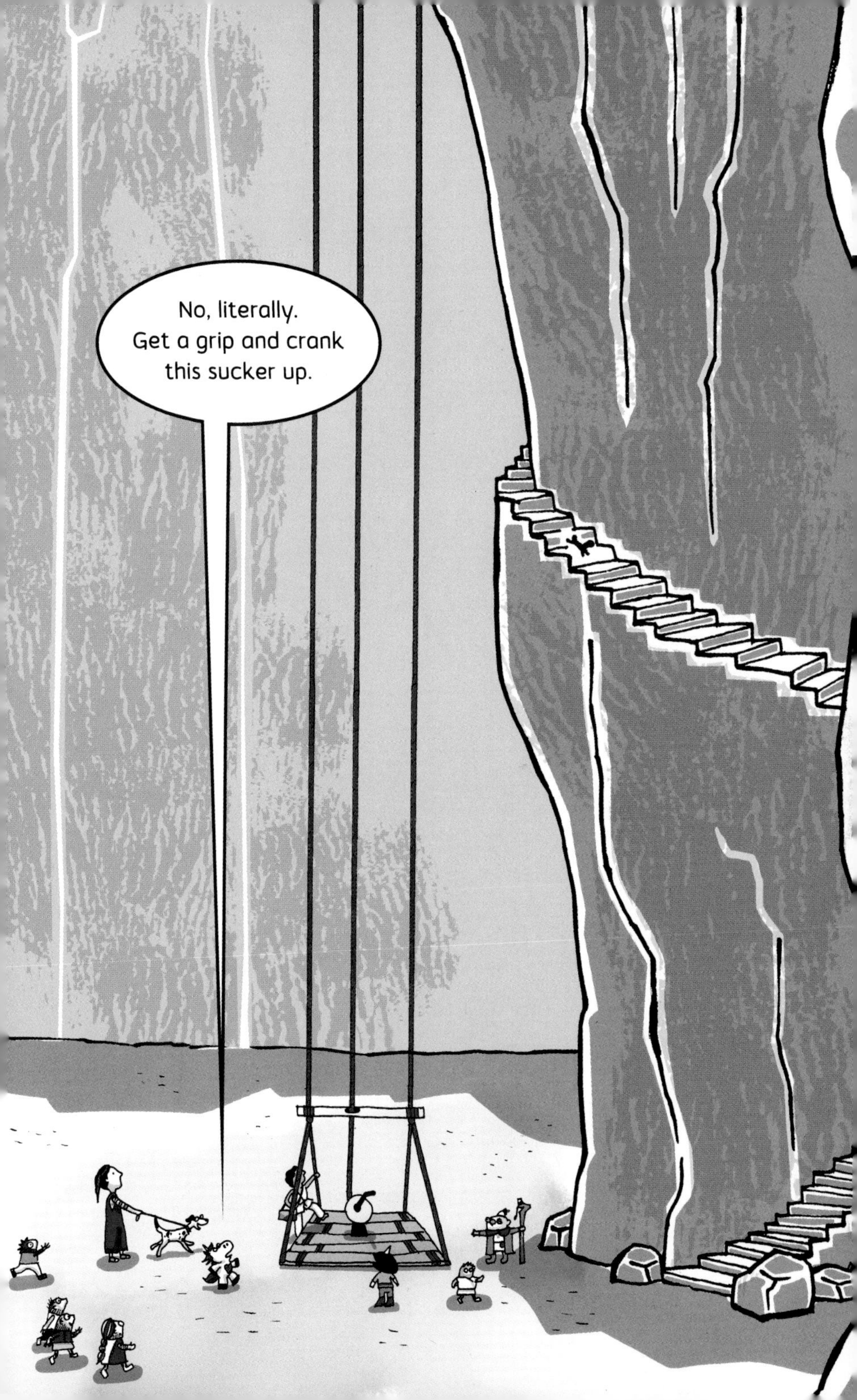
No, literally. Get a grip and crank this sucker up.

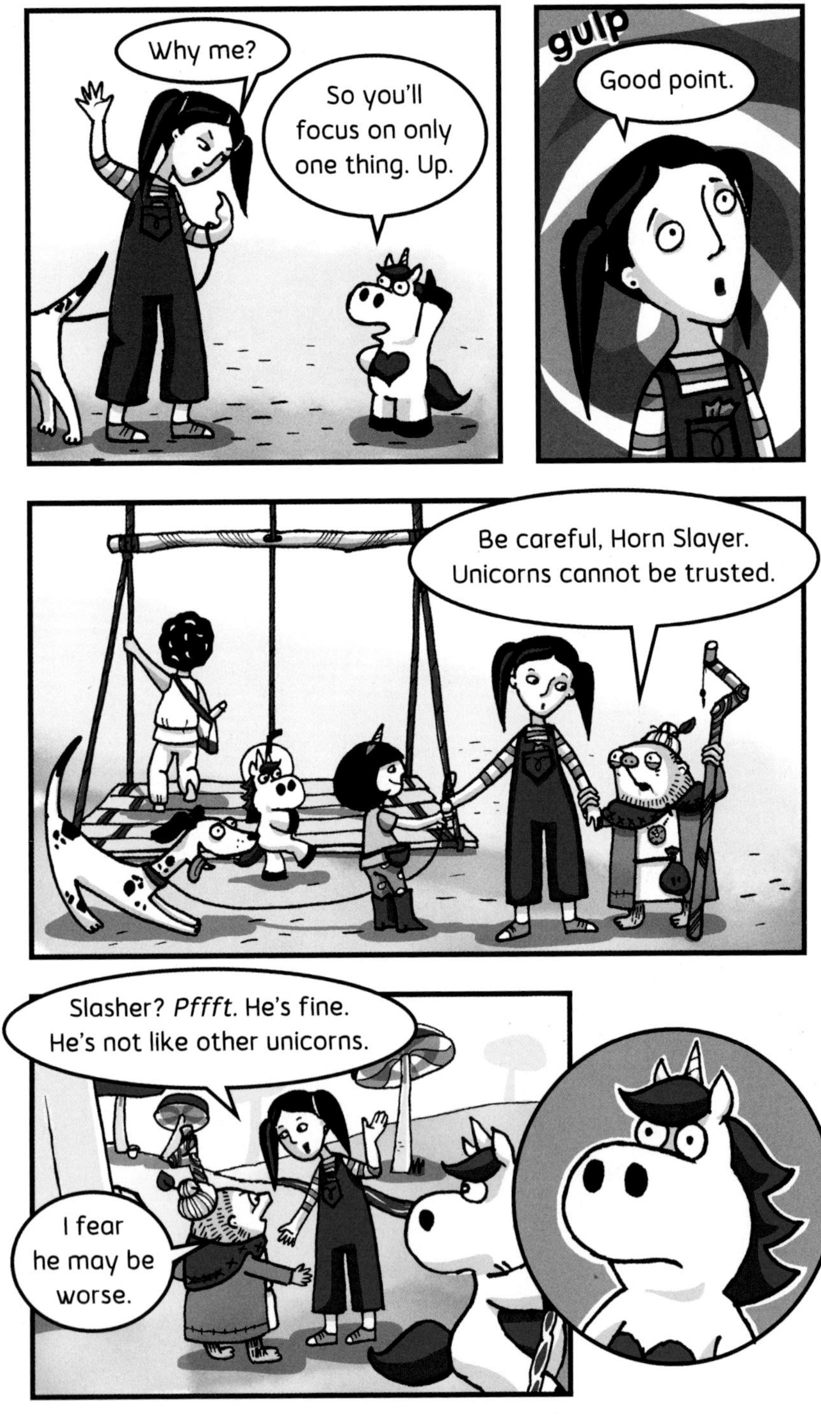
Why me?
So you'll focus on only one thing. Up.
gulp
Good point.
Be careful, Horn Slayer. Unicorns cannot be trusted.
Slasher? *Pffft.* He's fine. He's not like other unicorns.
I fear he may be worse.

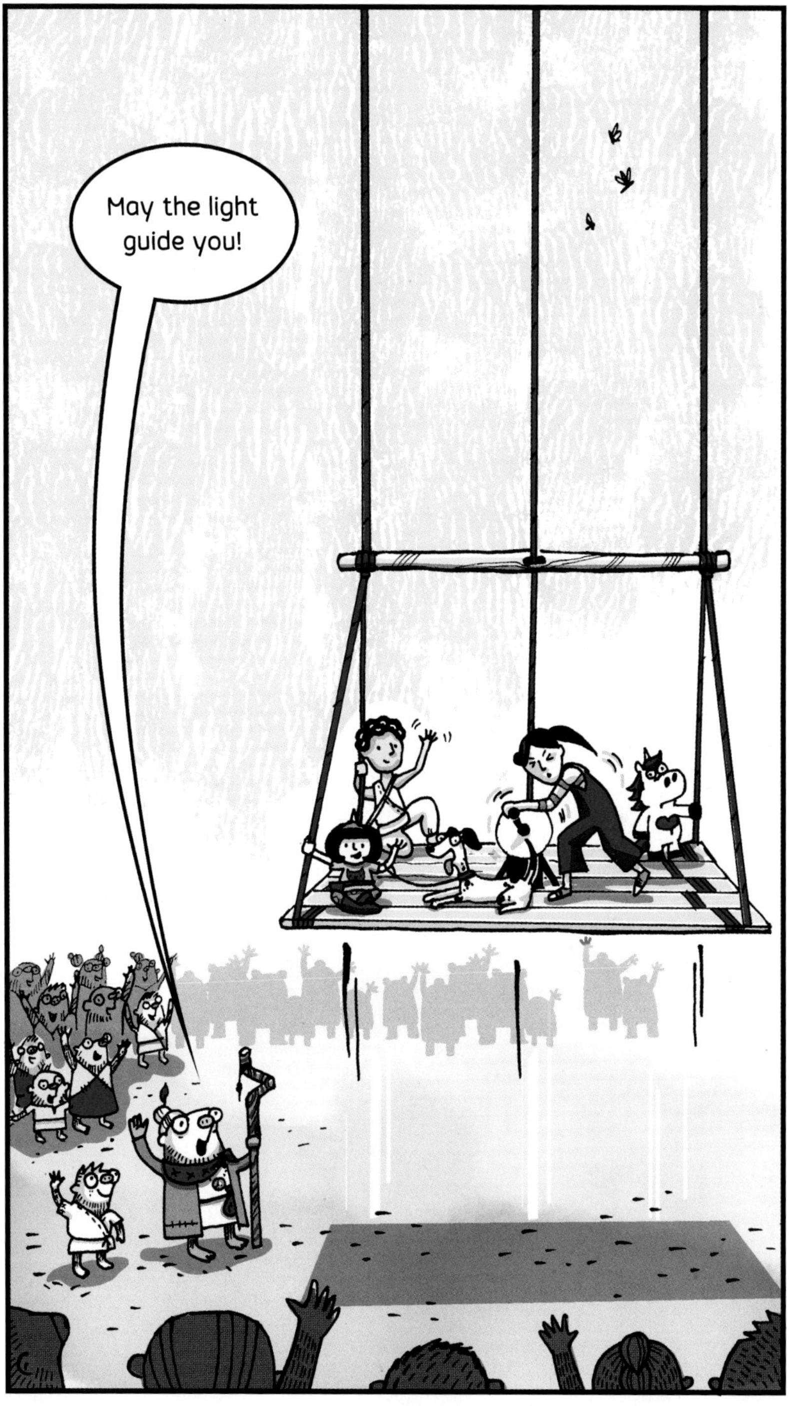
May the light guide you!

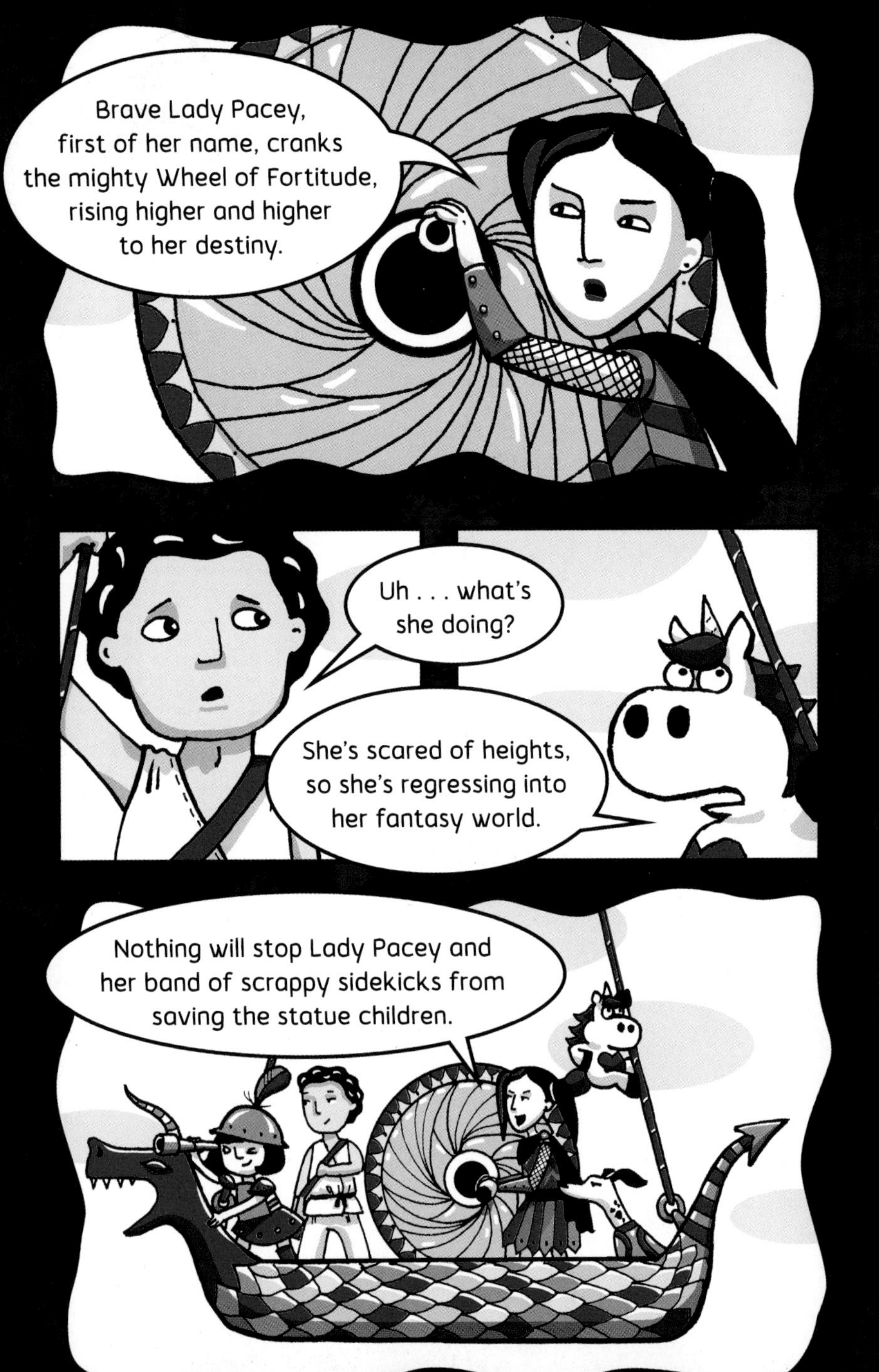
Brave Lady Pacey, first of her name, cranks the mighty Wheel of Fortitude, rising higher and higher to her destiny.
Uh . . . what's she doing?
She's scared of heights, so she's regressing into her fantasy world.
Nothing will stop Lady Pacey and her band of scrappy sidekicks from saving the statue children.

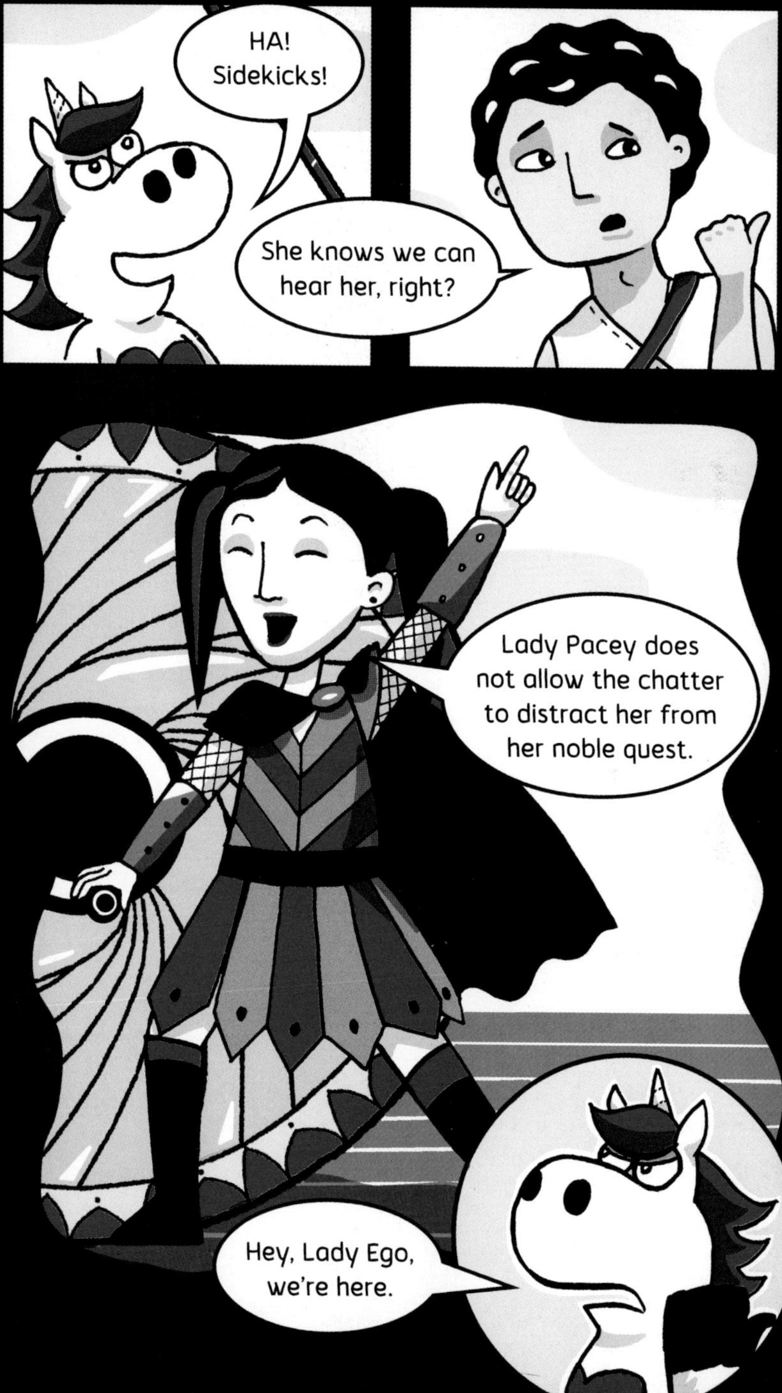
HA! Sidekicks!
She knows we can hear her, right?
Lady Pacey does not allow the chatter to distract her from her noble quest.
Hey, Lady Ego, we're here.

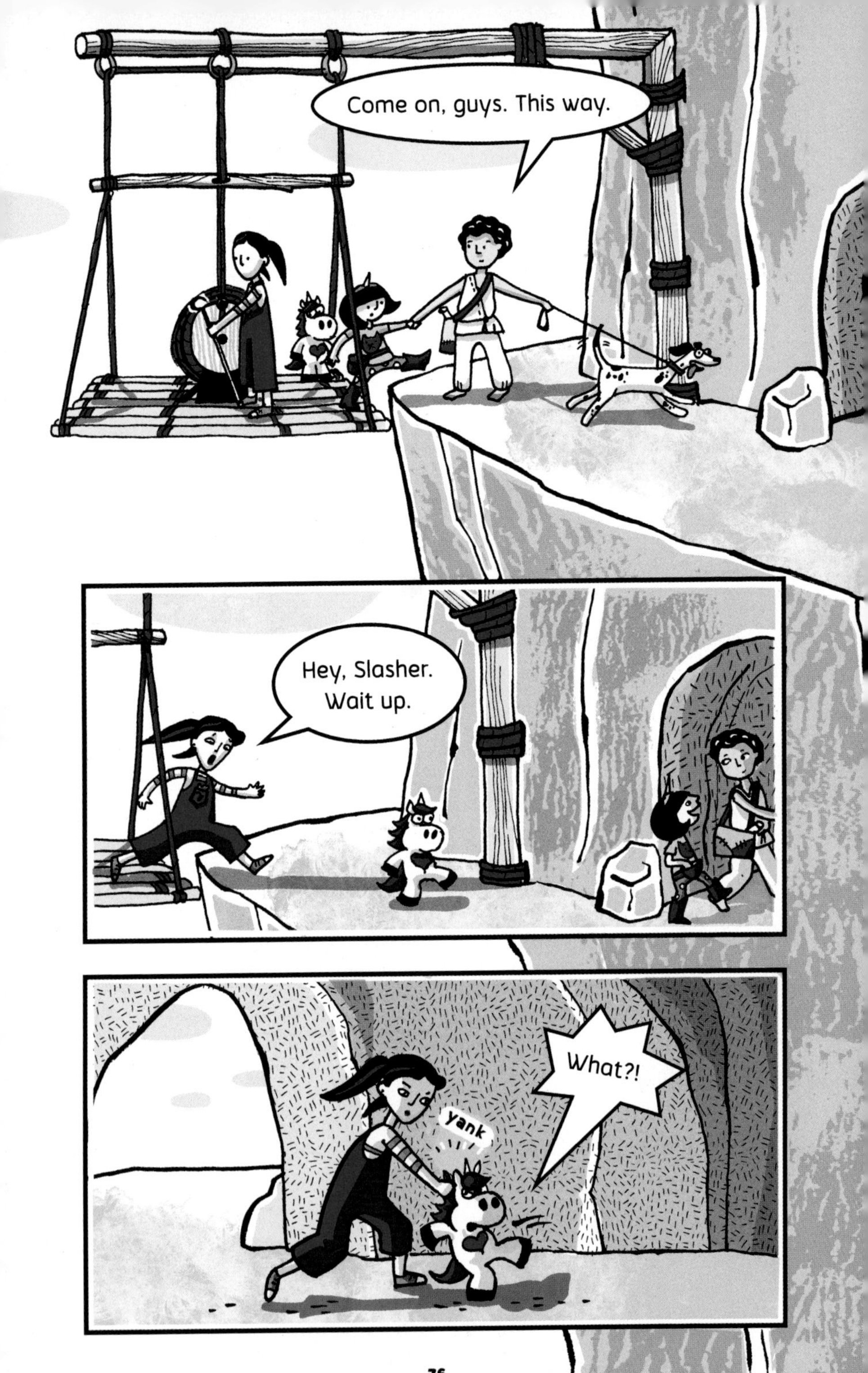
Come on, guys. This way.
Hey, Slasher. Wait up.
What?!
yank

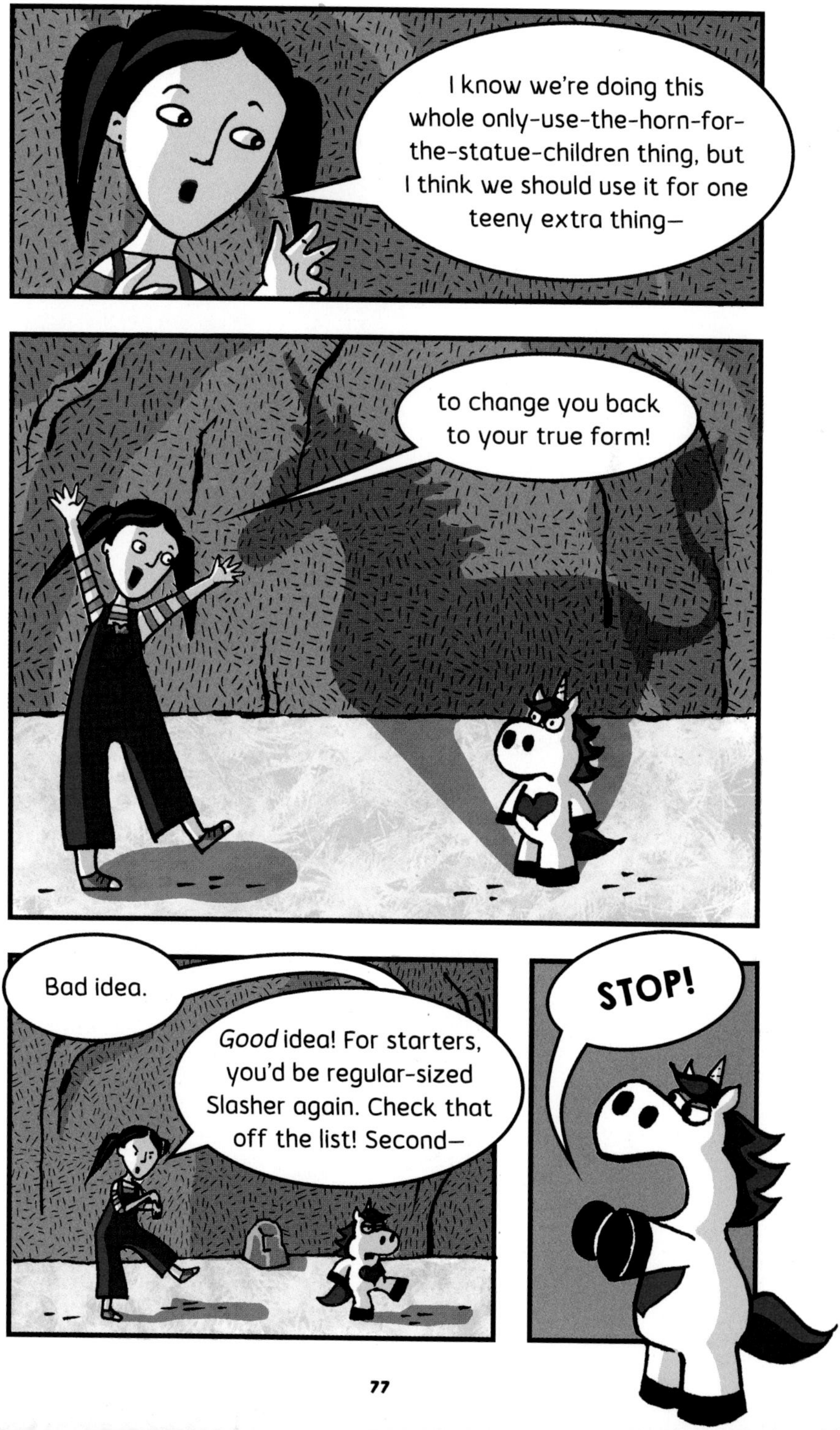
I know we're doing this whole only-use-the-horn-for-the-statue-children thing, but I think we should use it for one teeny extra thing—
to change you back to your true form!
Bad idea.
Good idea! For starters, you'd be regular-sized Slasher again. Check that off the list! Second—
STOP!

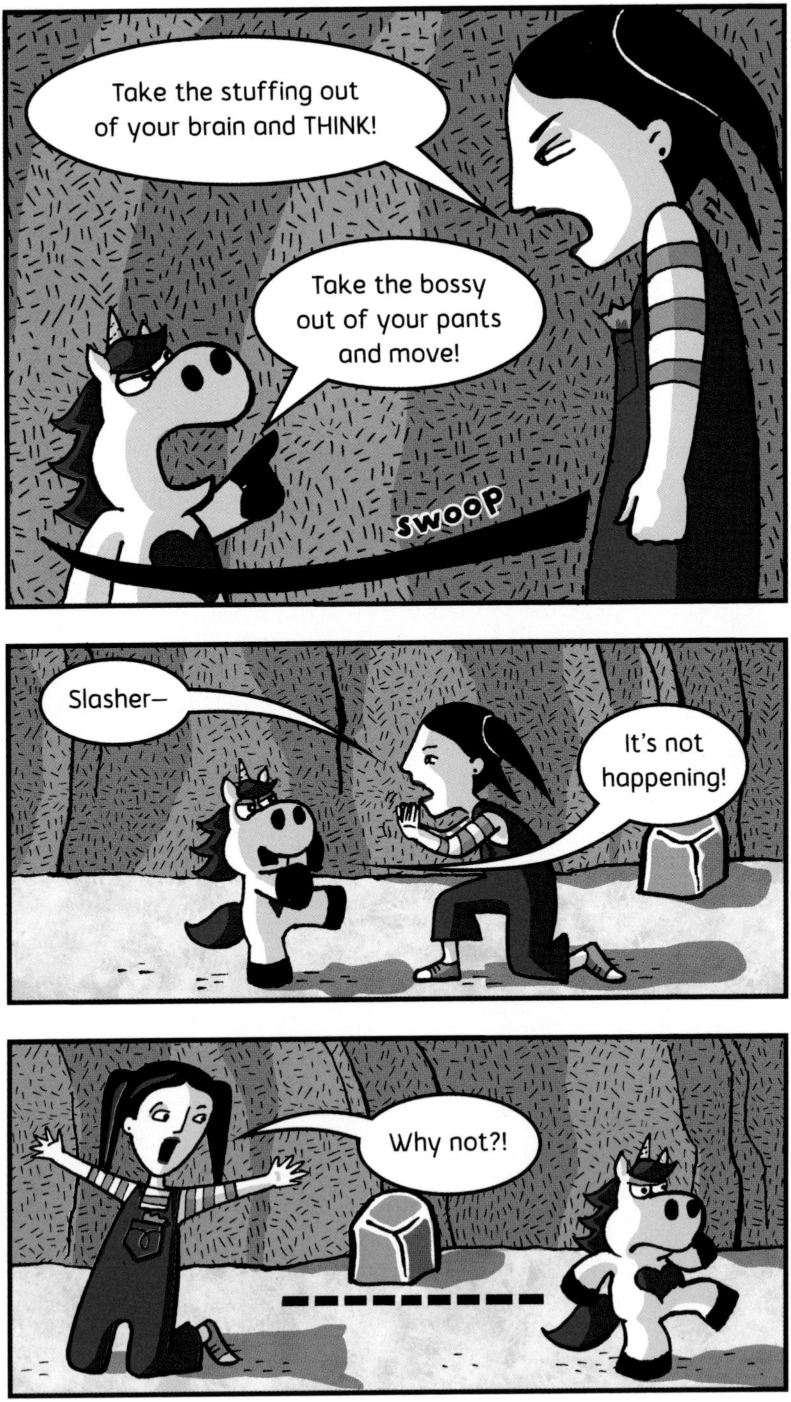
Take the stuffing out of your brain and THINK!
Take the bossy out of your pants and move!
SWOOP
Slasher–
It's not happening!
Why not?!

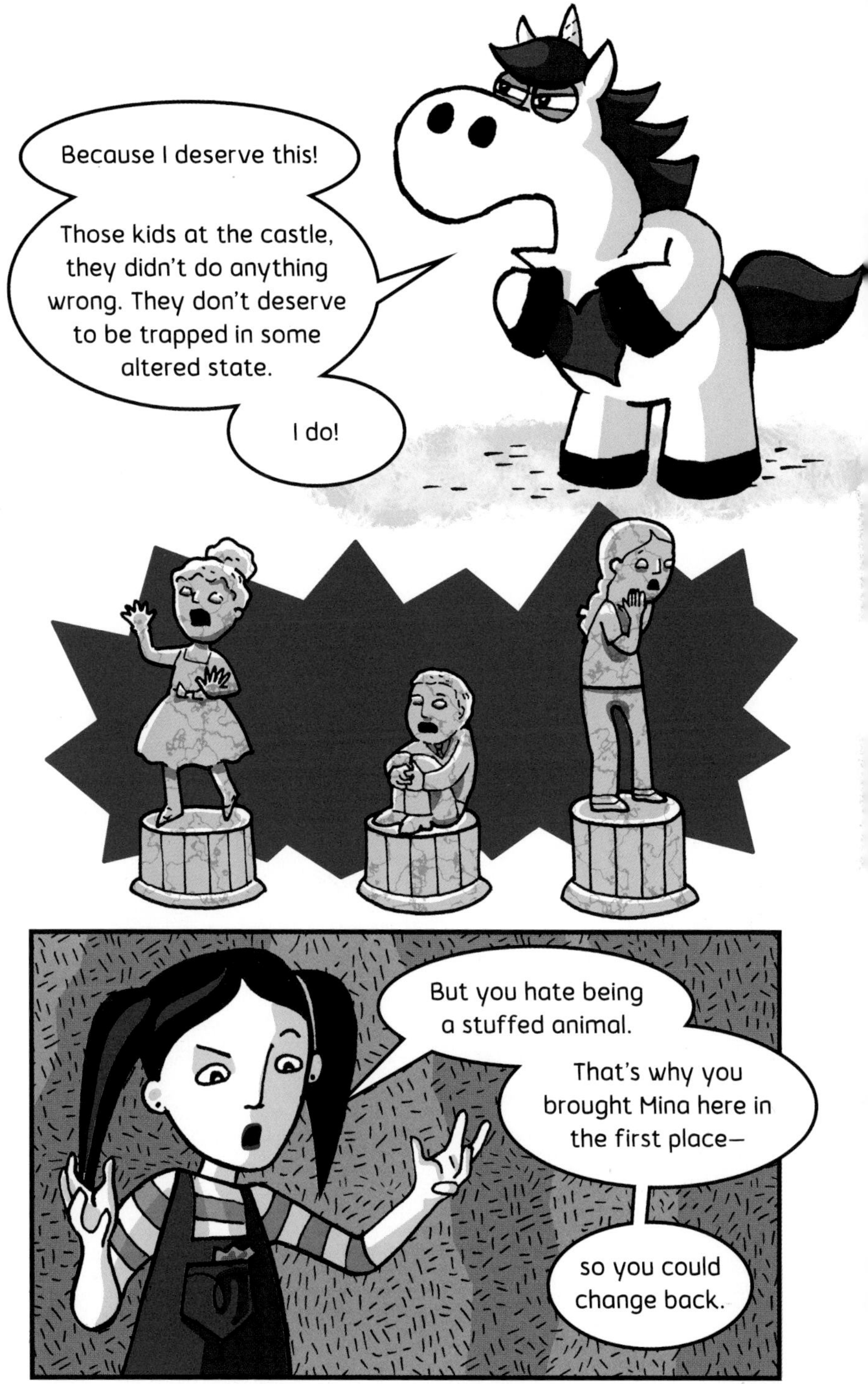
Because I deserve this!
Those kids at the castle, they didn't do anything wrong. They don't deserve to be trapped in some altered state.
I do!
But you hate being a stuffed animal.
That's why you brought Mina here in the first place—
so you could change back.

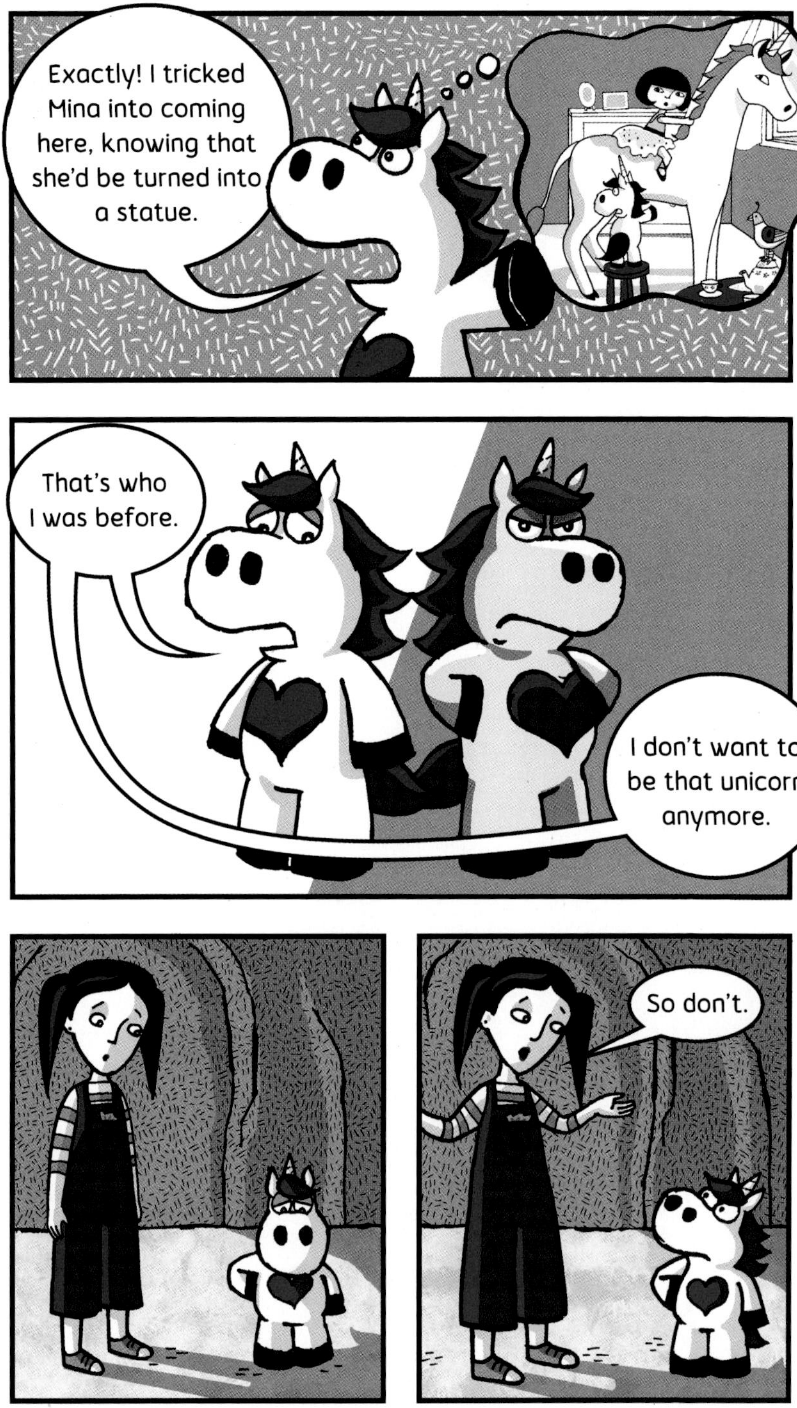

Exactly! I tricked Mina into coming here, knowing that she'd be turned into a statue.
That's who I was before.
I don't want to be that unicorn anymore.
So don't.

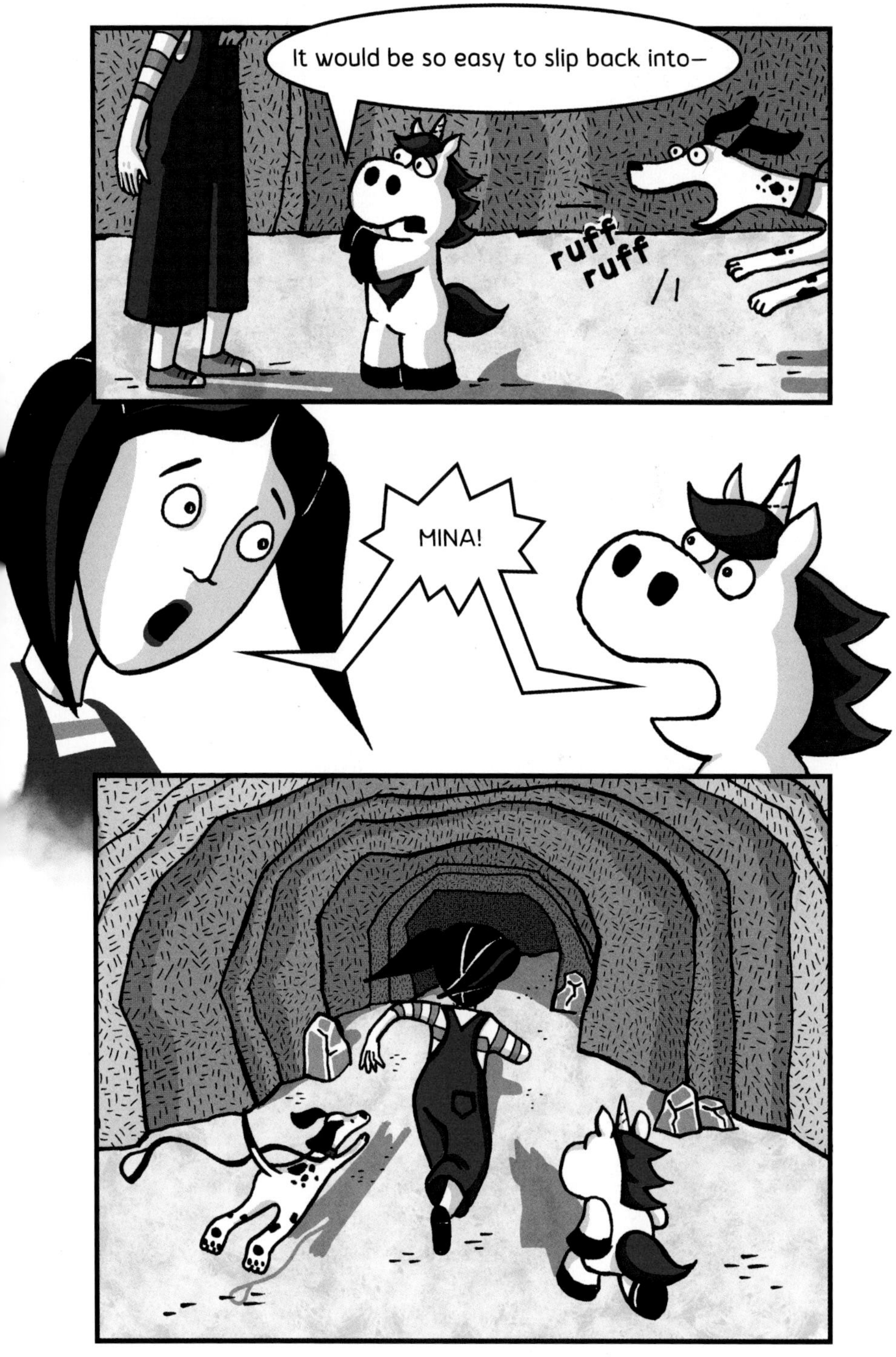
It would be so easy to slip back into—
ruff ruff
MINA!

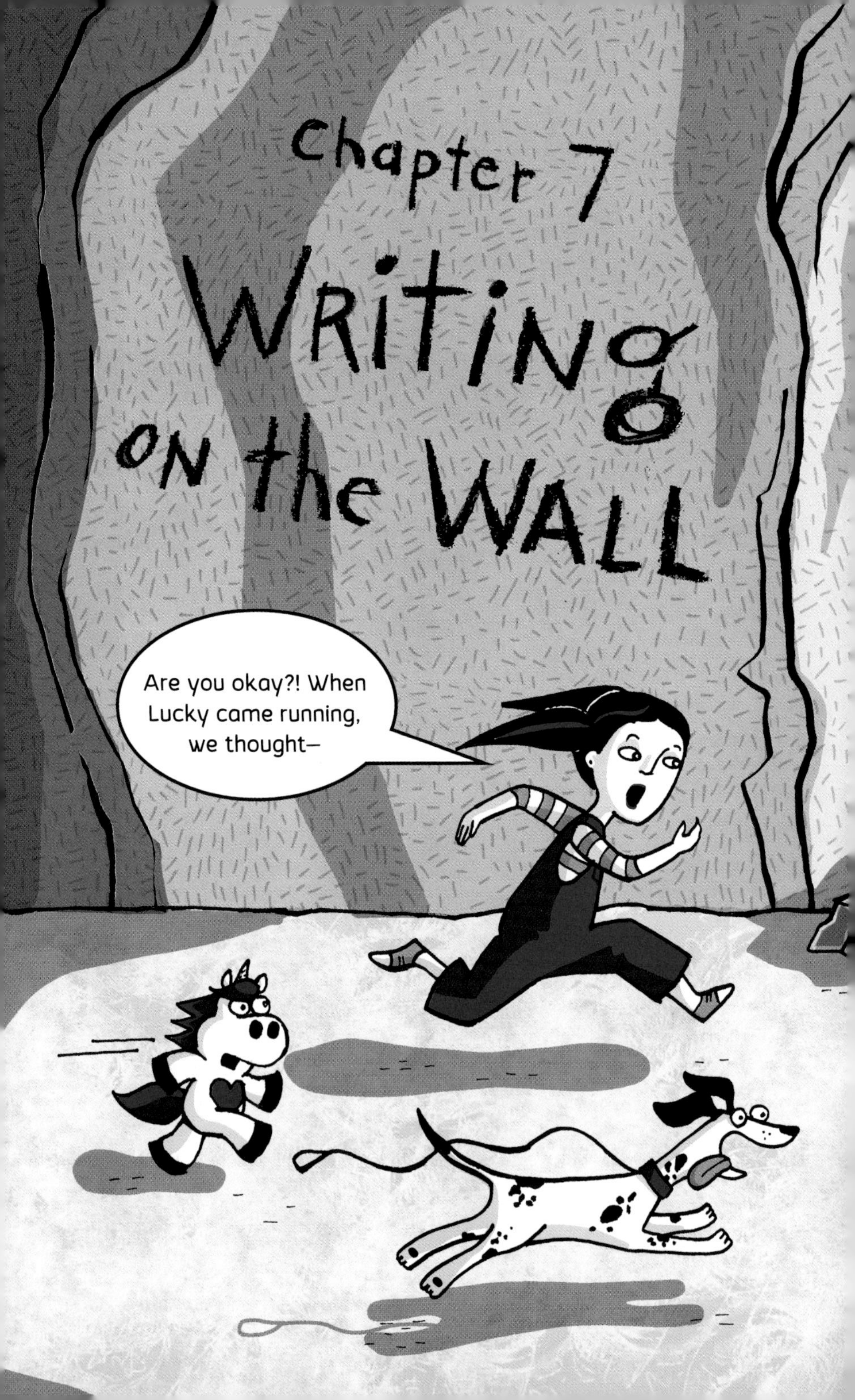
Chapter 7
Writing on the Wall
Are you okay?! When Lucky came running, we thought—

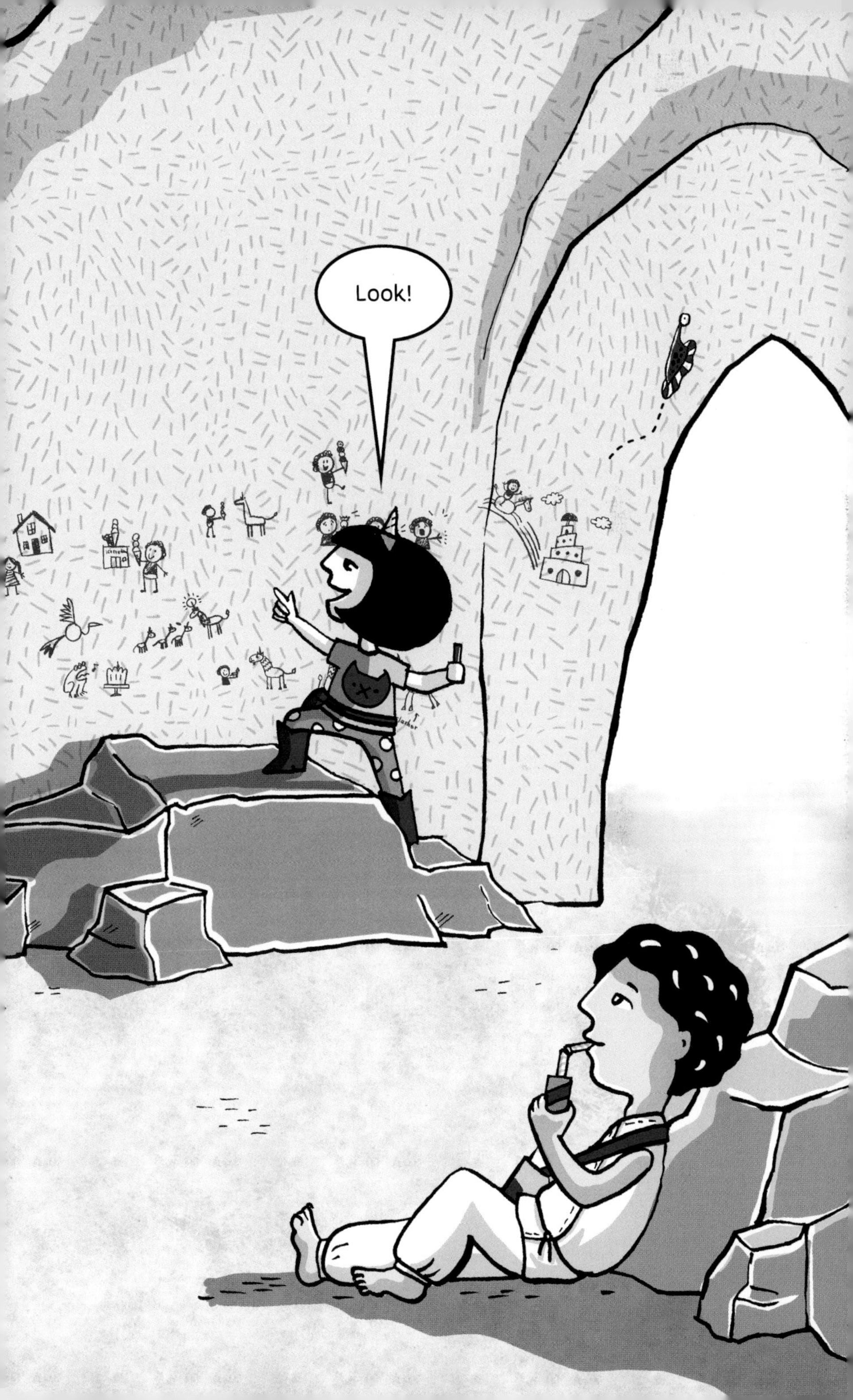
Look!

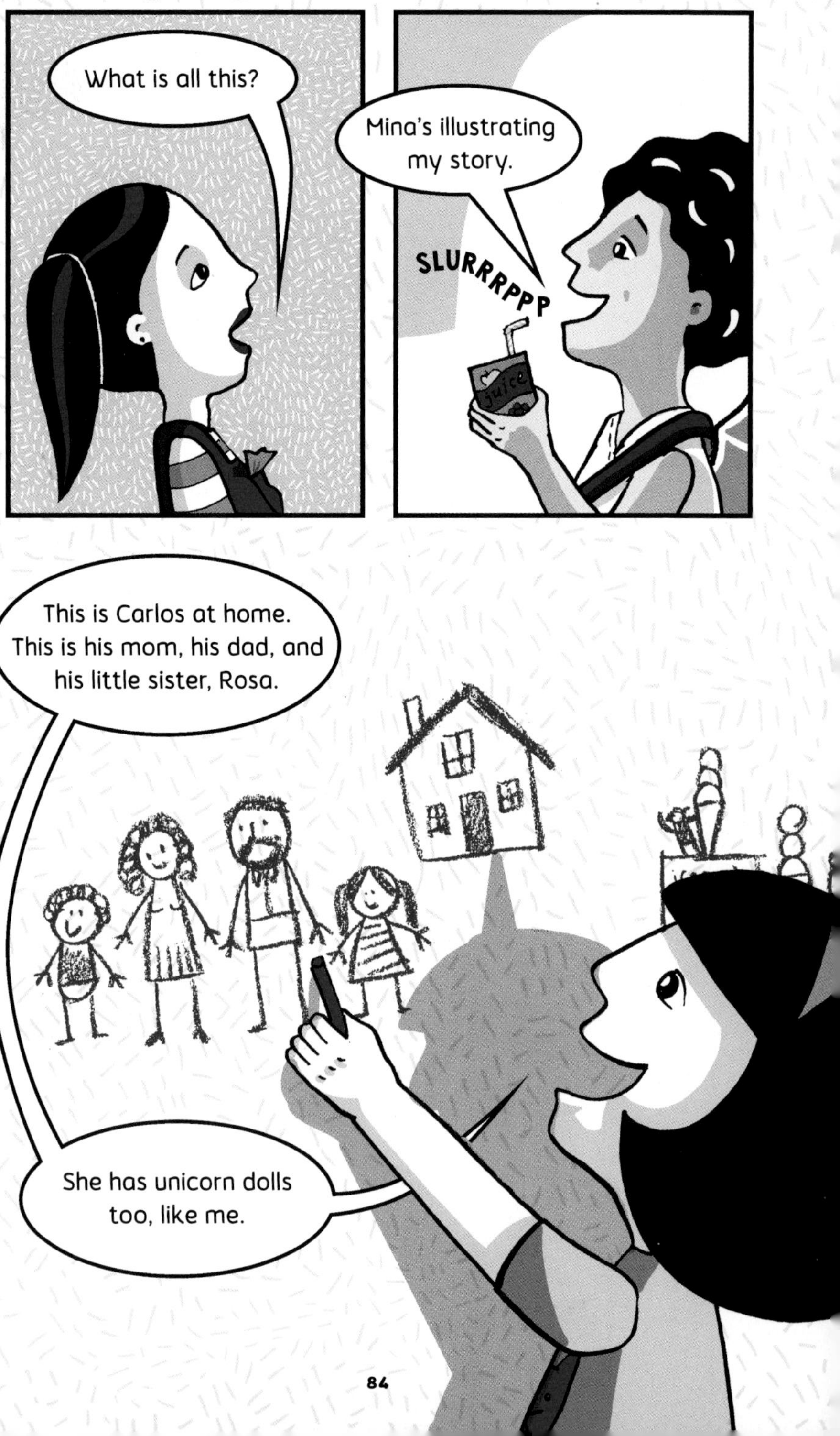
What is all this?
Mina's illustrating my story.
SLURRRPPP
juice
This is Carlos at home. This is his mom, his dad, and his little sister, Rosa.
She has unicorn dolls too, like me.

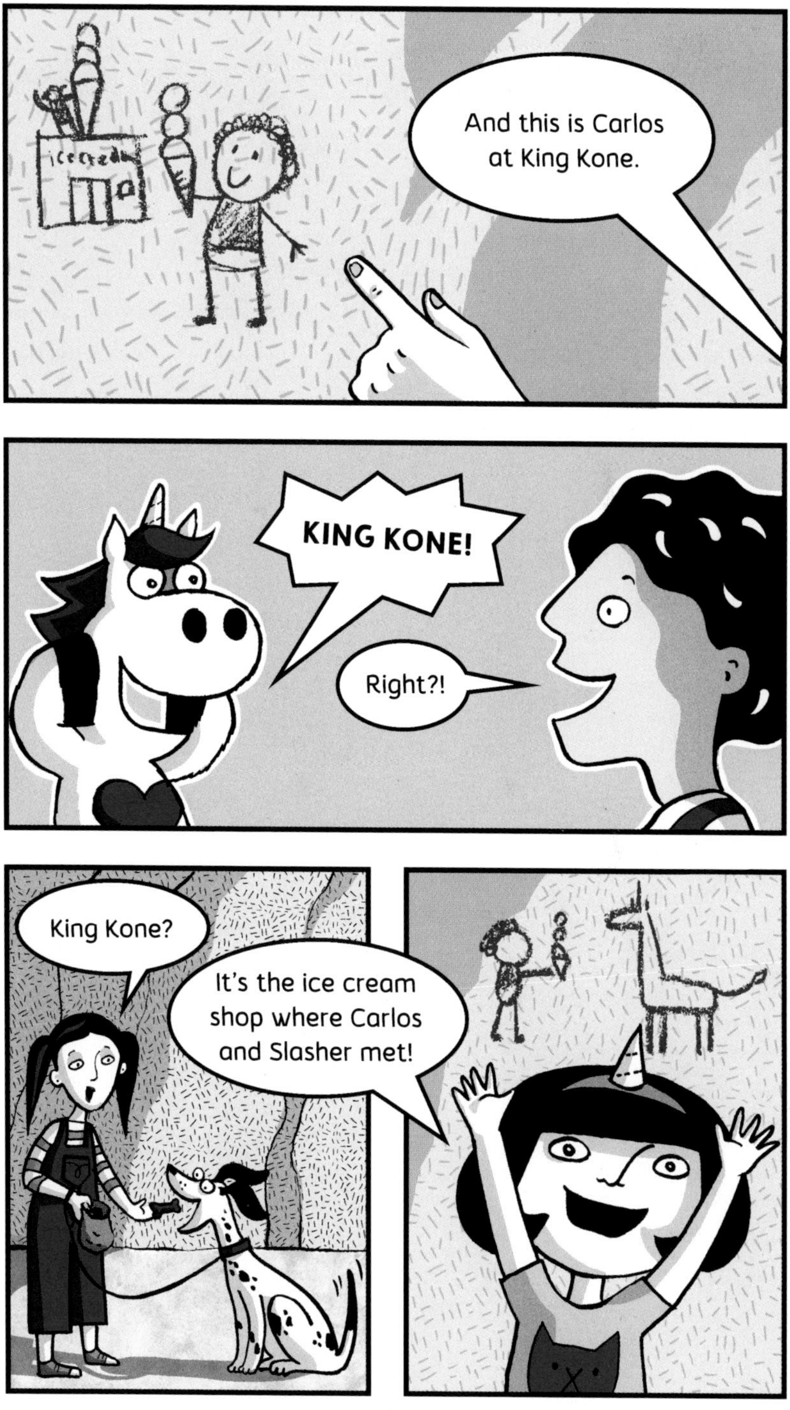
And this is Carlos at King Kone.
KING KONE!
Right?!
King Kone?
It's the ice cream shop where Carlos and Slasher met!

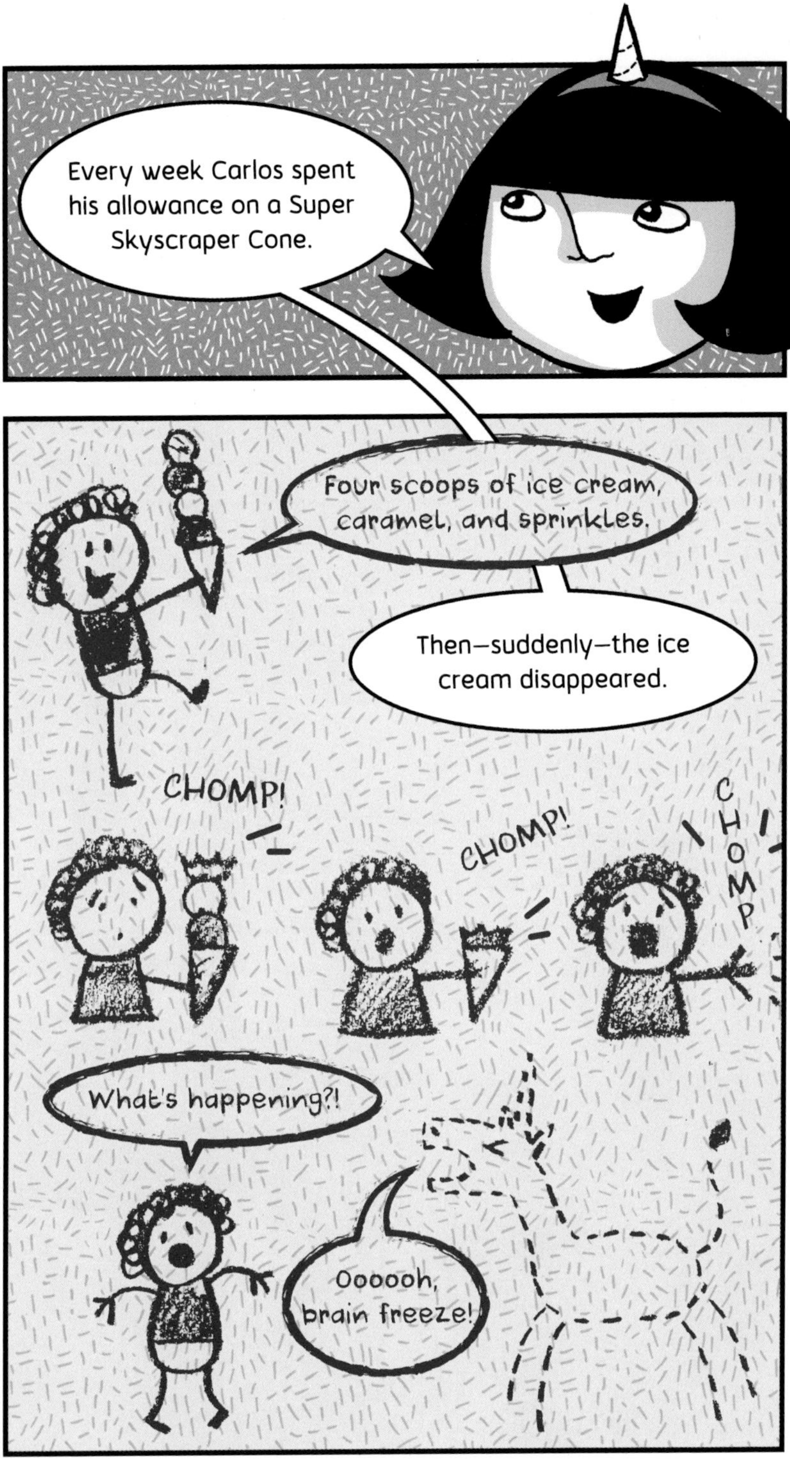
Every week Carlos spent his allowance on a Super Skyscraper Cone.
Four scoops of ice cream, caramel, and sprinkles.
Then—suddenly—the ice cream disappeared.
CHOMP!
CHOMP!
CHOMP
What's happening?!
Oooooh, brain freeze!

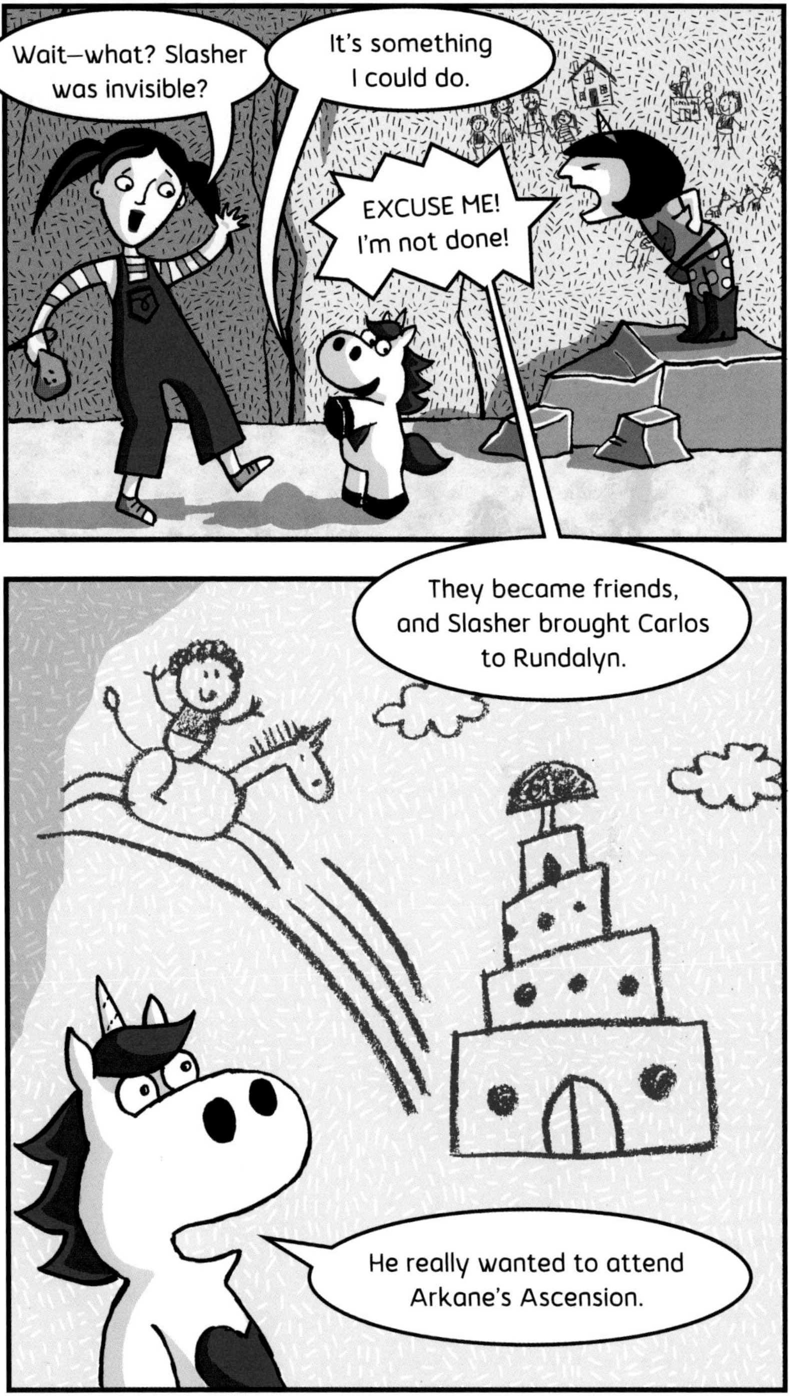
Wait—what? Slasher was invisible?
It's something I could do.
EXCUSE ME! I'm not done!
They became friends, and Slasher brought Carlos to Rundalyn.
He really wanted to attend Arkane's Ascension.

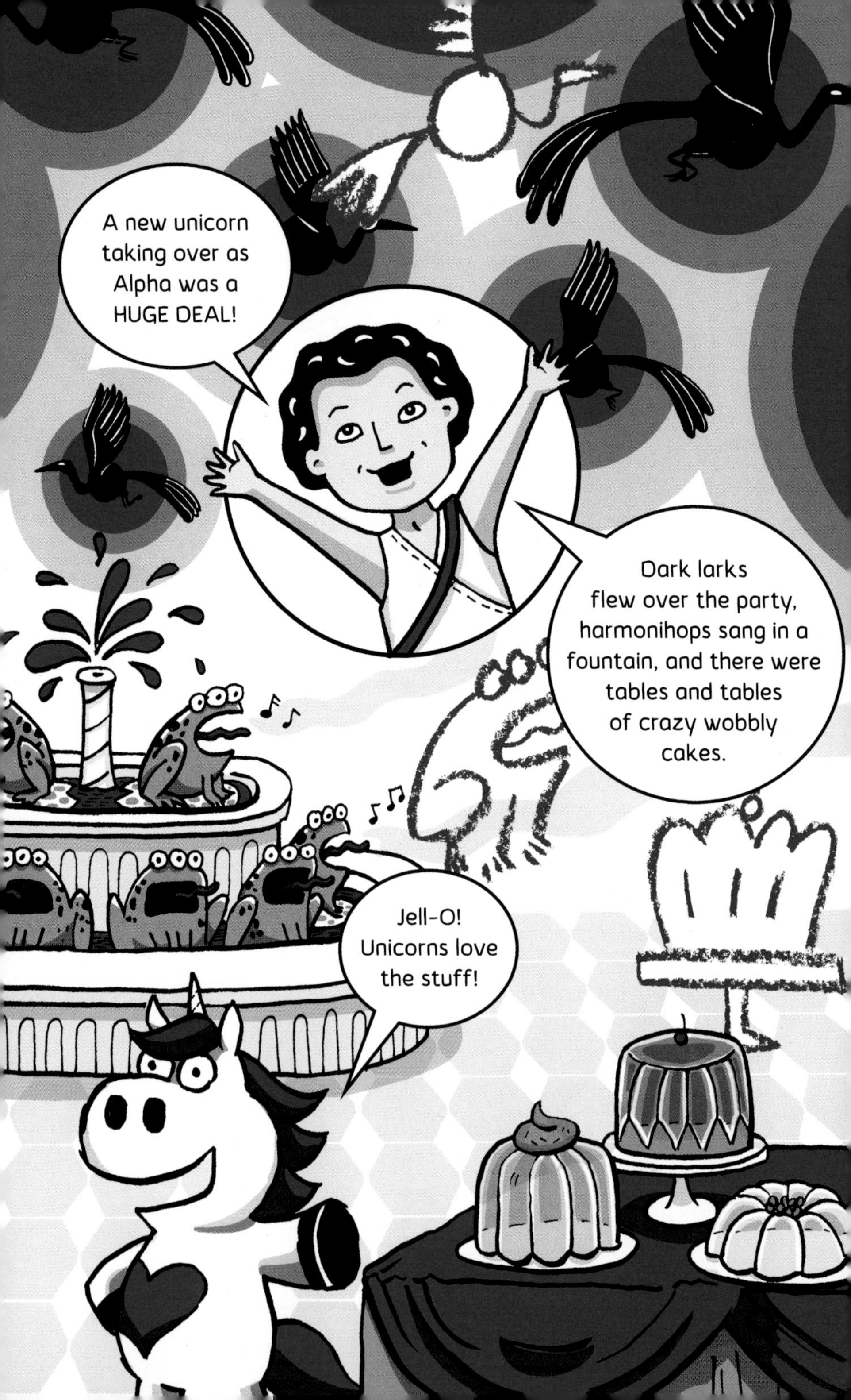
A new unicorn taking over as Alpha was a HUGE DEAL!
Dark larks flew over the party, harmonihops sang in a fountain, and there were tables and tables of crazy wobbly cakes.
Jell-O! Unicorns love the stuff!

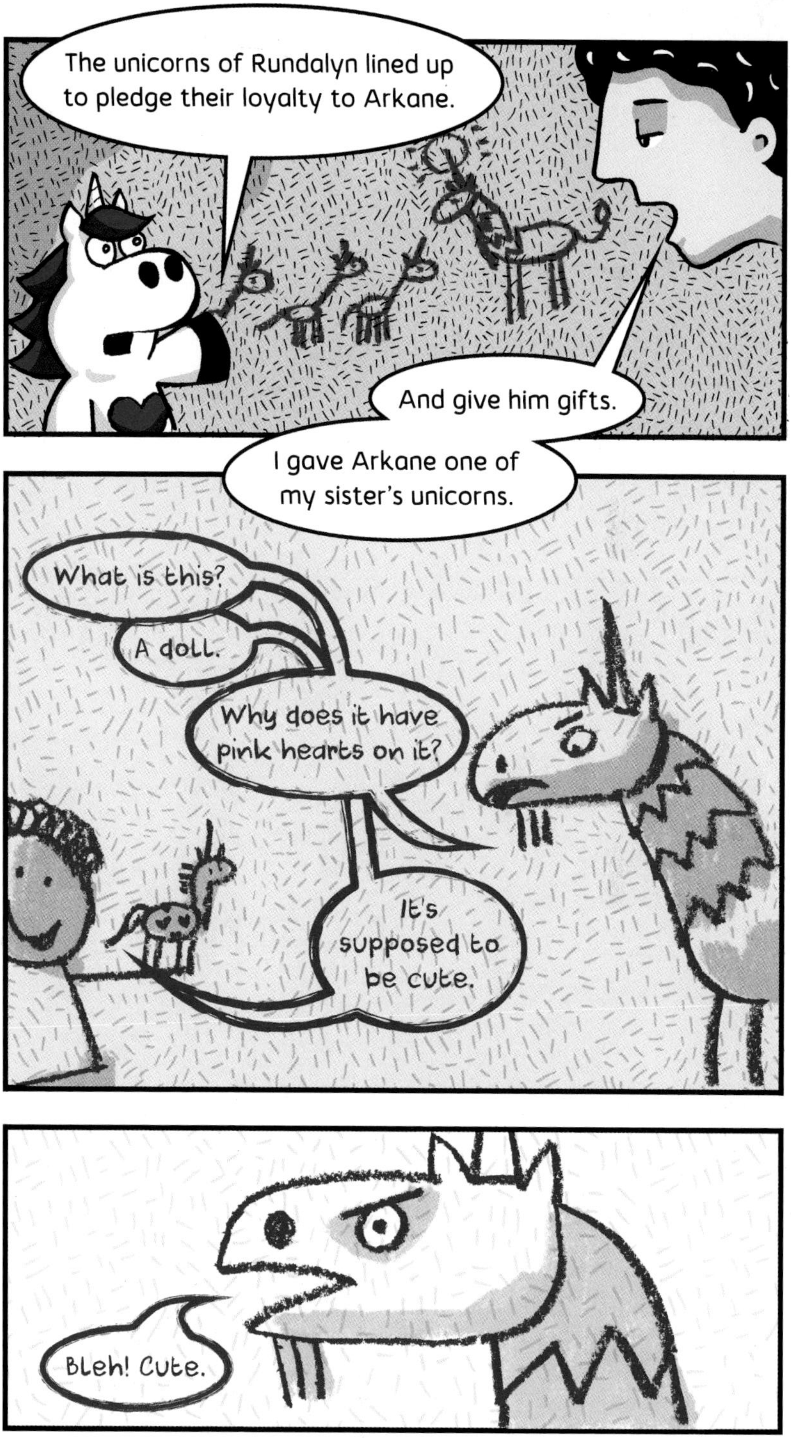
The unicorns of Rundalyn lined up to pledge their loyalty to Arkane.
And give him gifts.
I gave Arkane one of my sister's unicorns.
What is this?
A doll.
Why does it have pink hearts on it?
It's supposed to be cute.
Bleh! Cute.

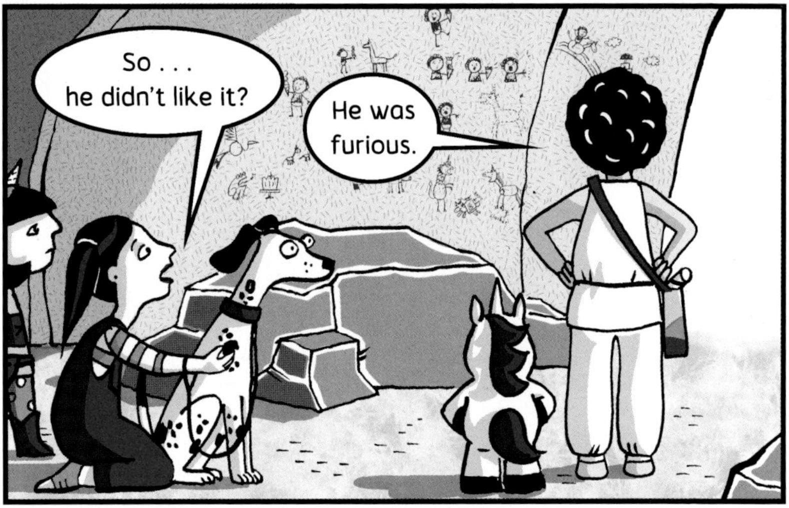
So . . .
he didn't like it?
He was furious.

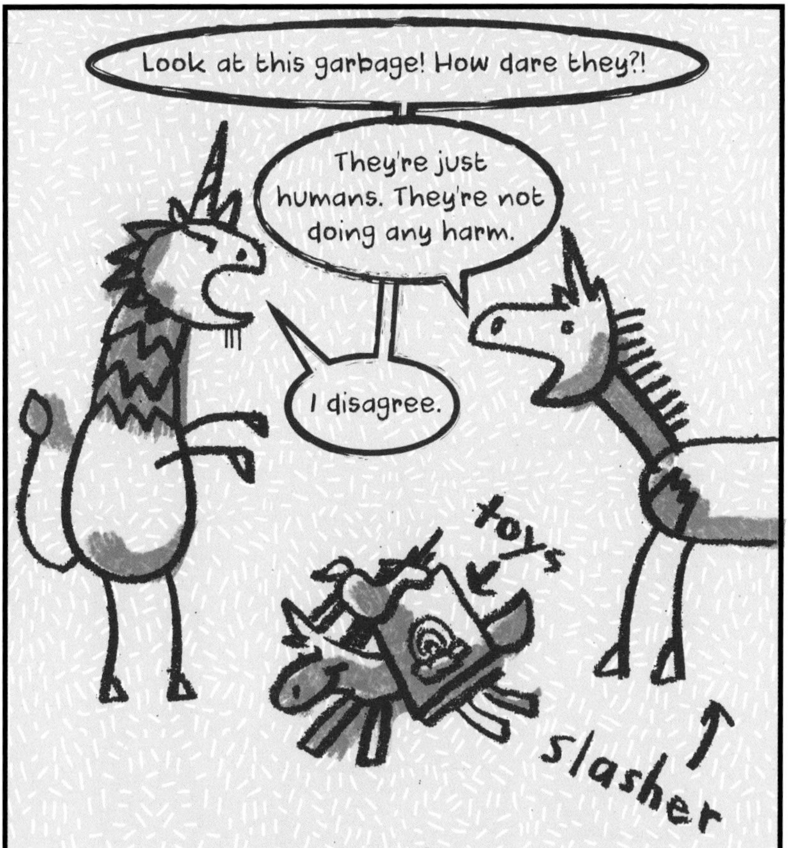
Look at this garbage! How dare they?!
They're just humans. They're not doing any harm.
I disagree.
toys
slasher

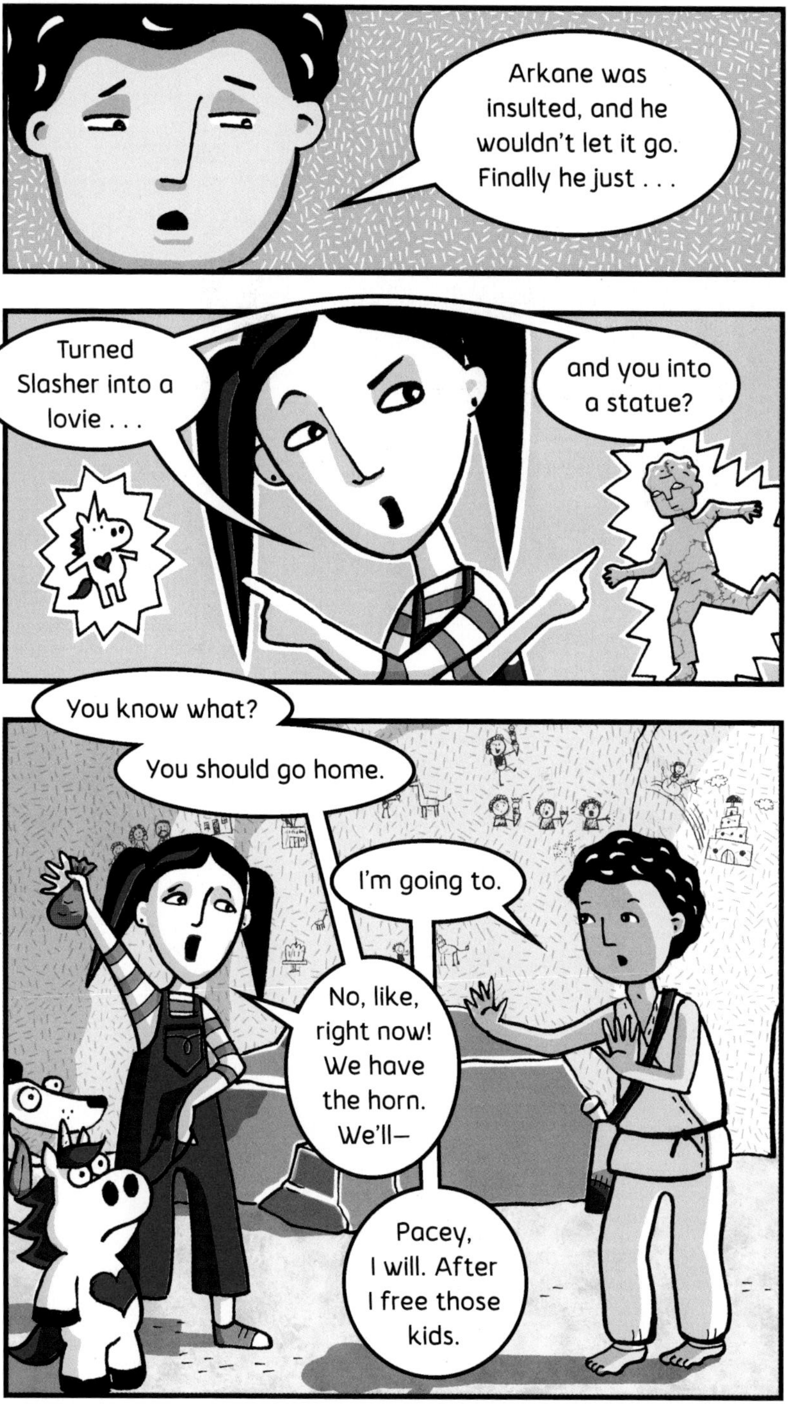
Arkane was insulted, and he wouldn't let it go. Finally he just . . .
Turned Slasher into a lovie . . .
and you into a statue?
You know what?
You should go home.
I'm going to.
No, like, right now! We have the horn. We'll–
Pacey, I will. After I free those kids.

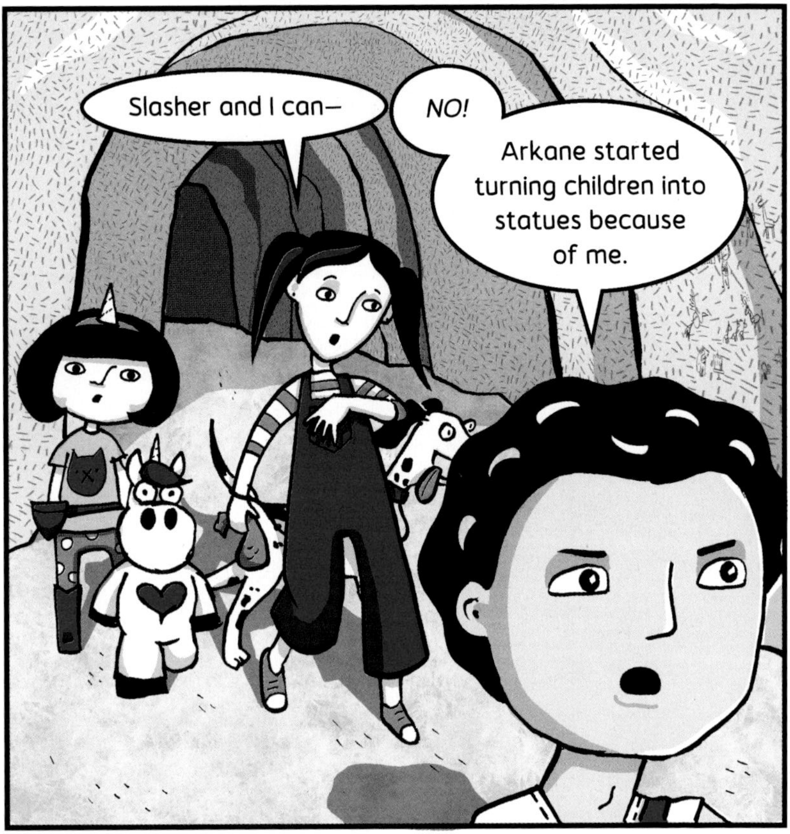
Slasher and I can—
NO!
Arkane started turning children into statues because of me.

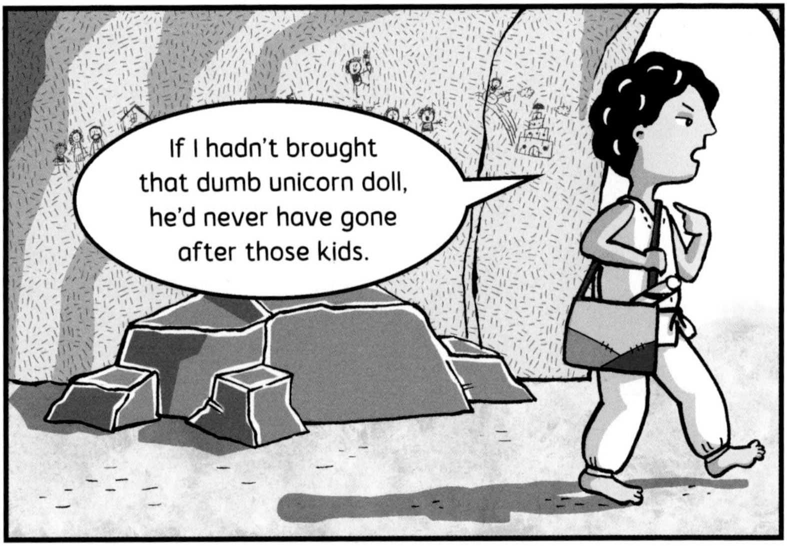
If I hadn't brought that dumb unicorn doll, he'd never have gone after those kids.

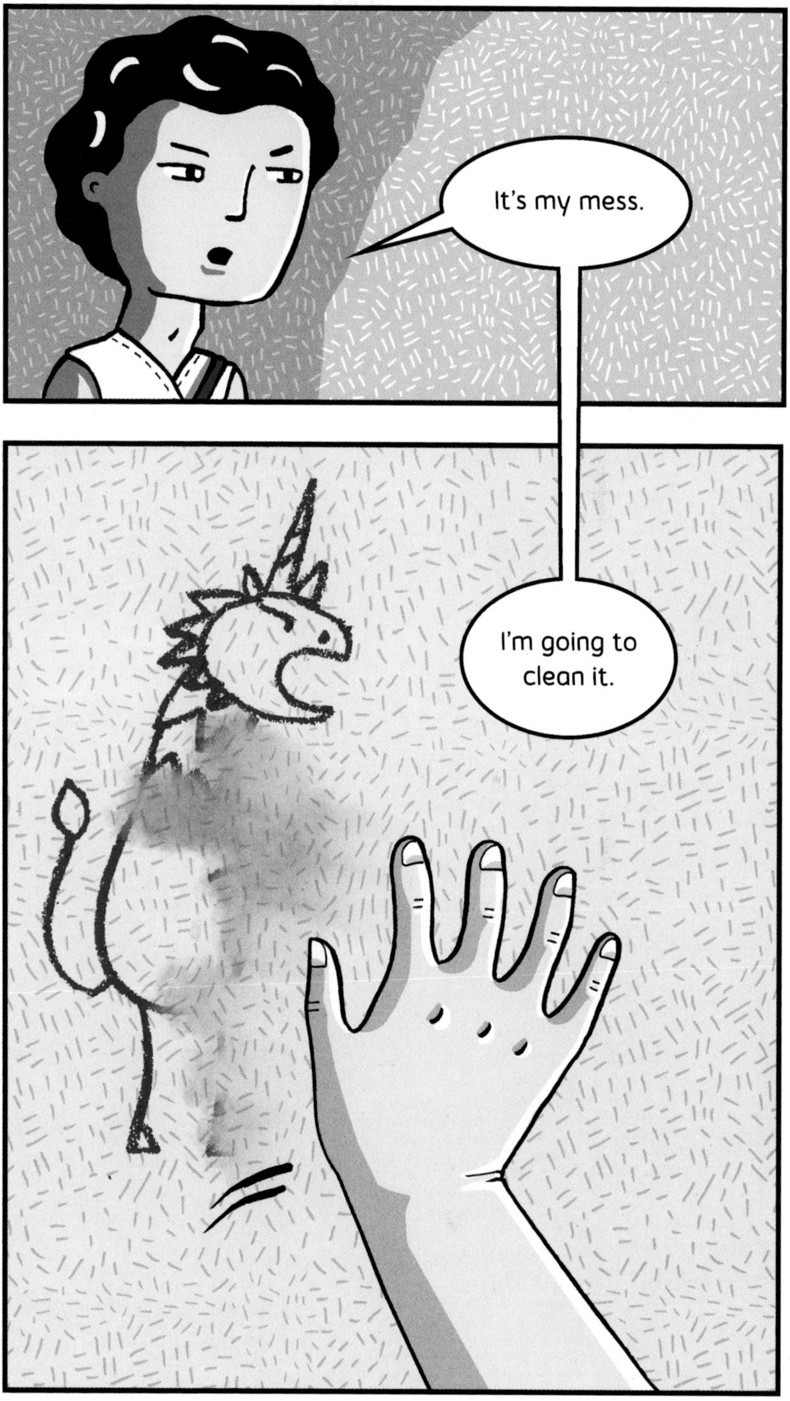
It's my mess.
I'm going to clean it.

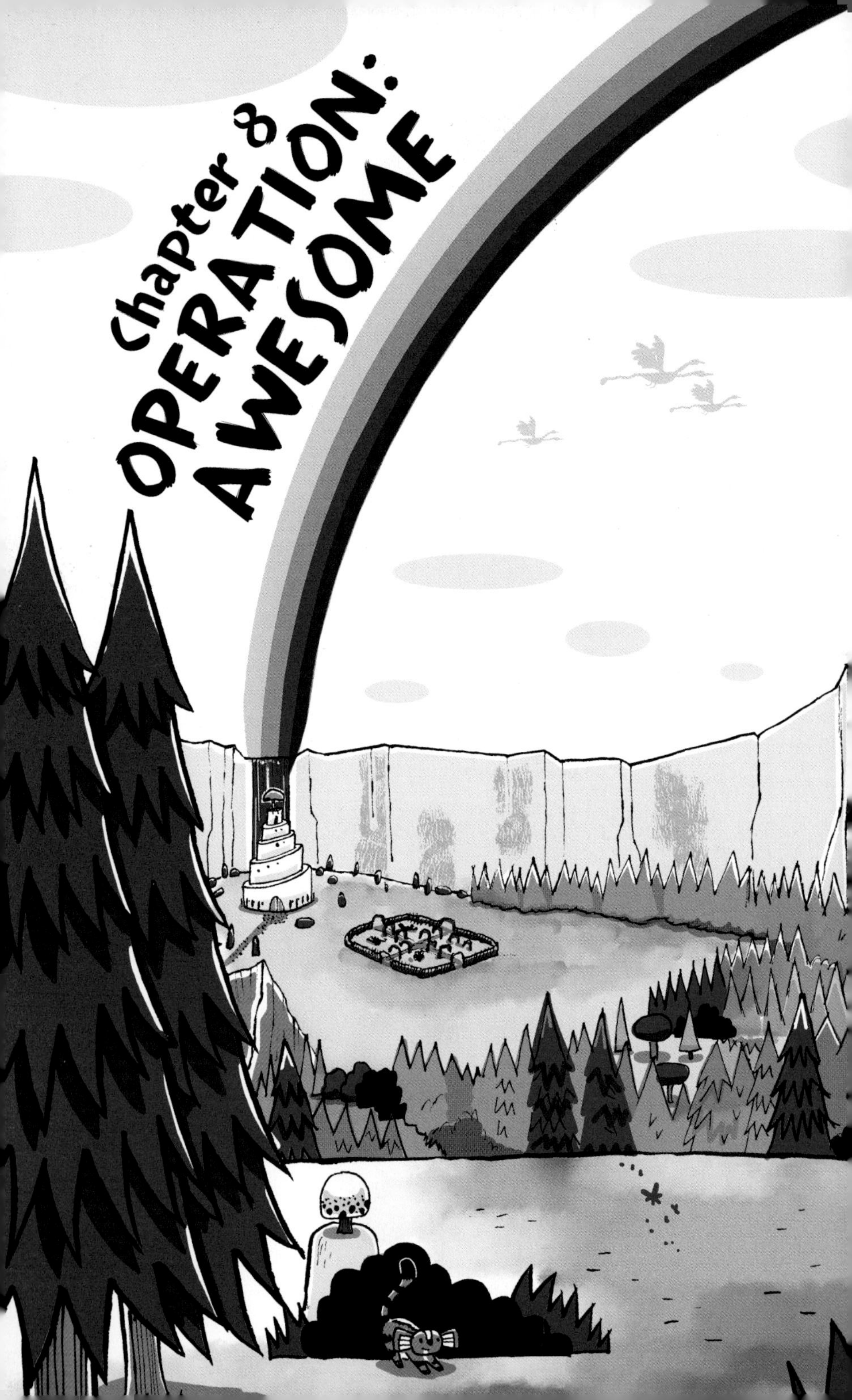
Chapter 8
OPERATION:
AWESOME

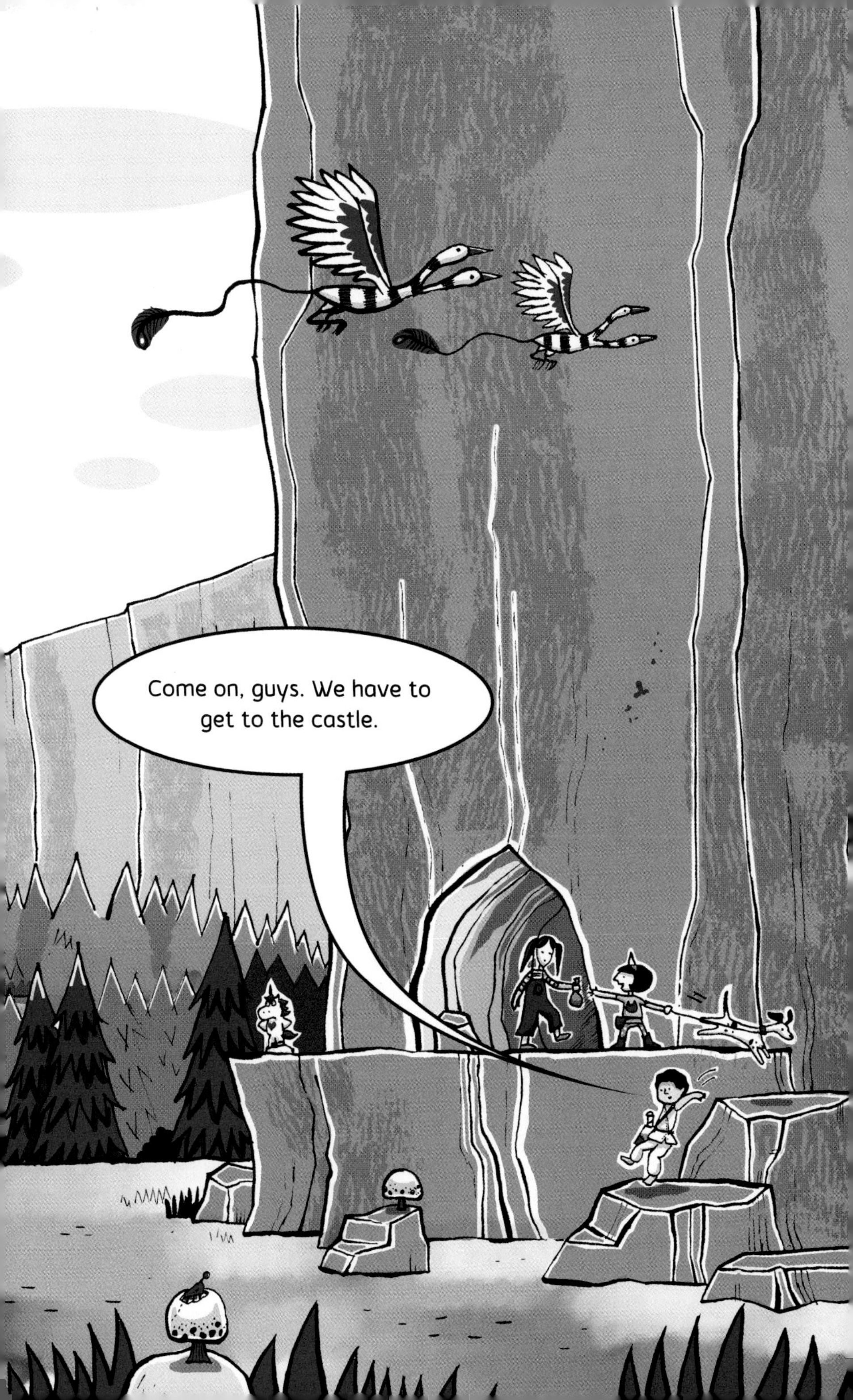
Come on, guys. We have to get to the castle.

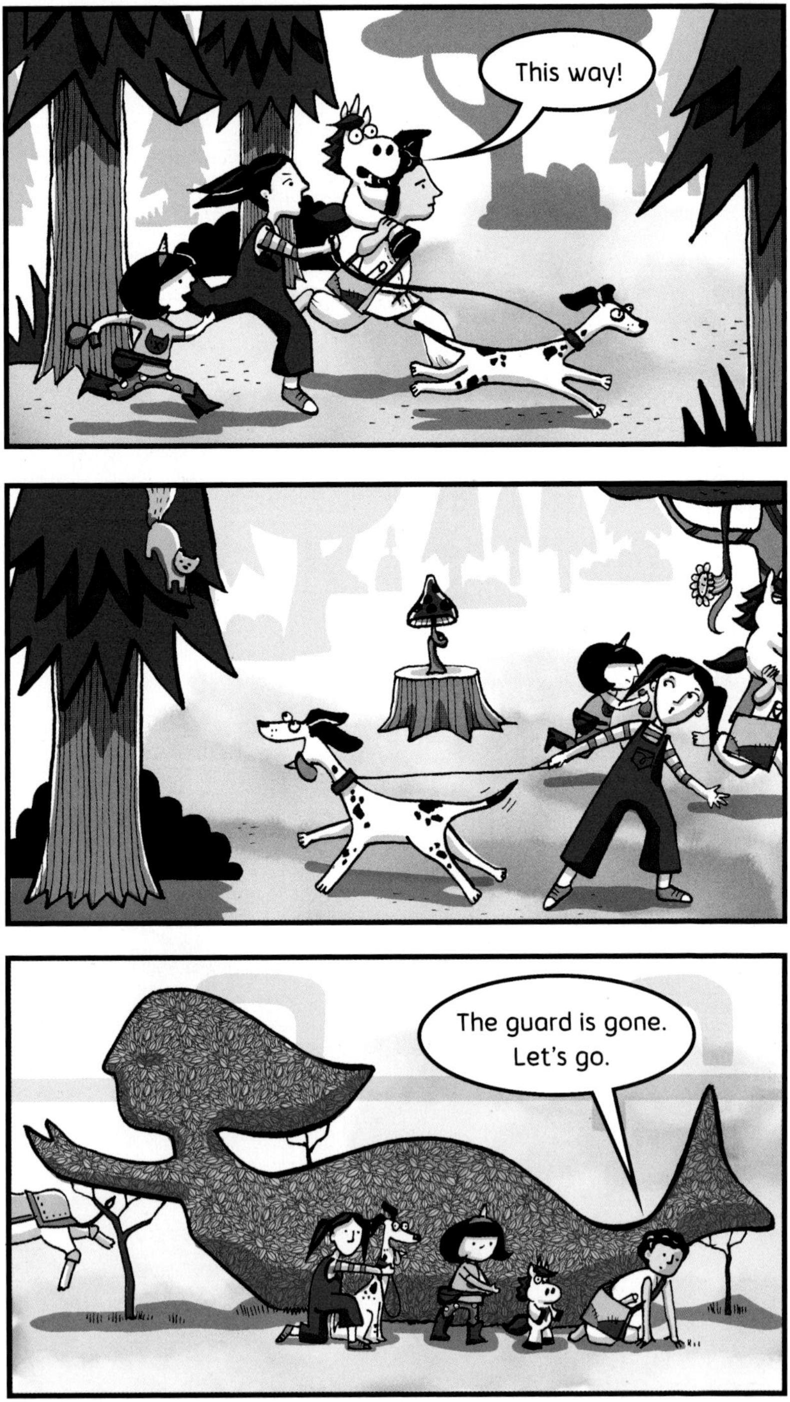
This way!
The guard is gone. Let's go.

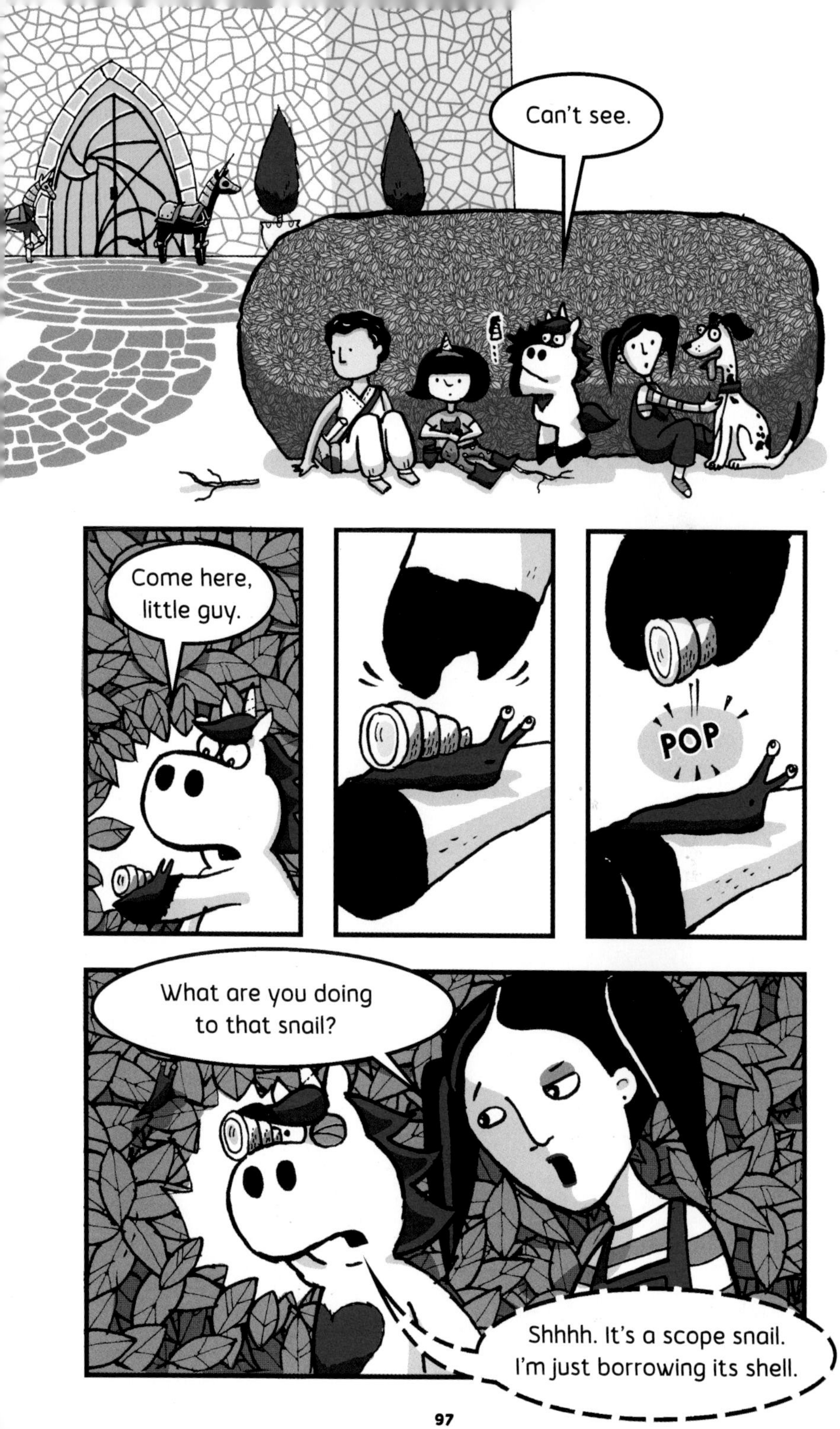
Can't see.
Come here, little guy.
POP
What are you doing to that snail?
Shhhh. It's a scope snail. I'm just borrowing its shell.

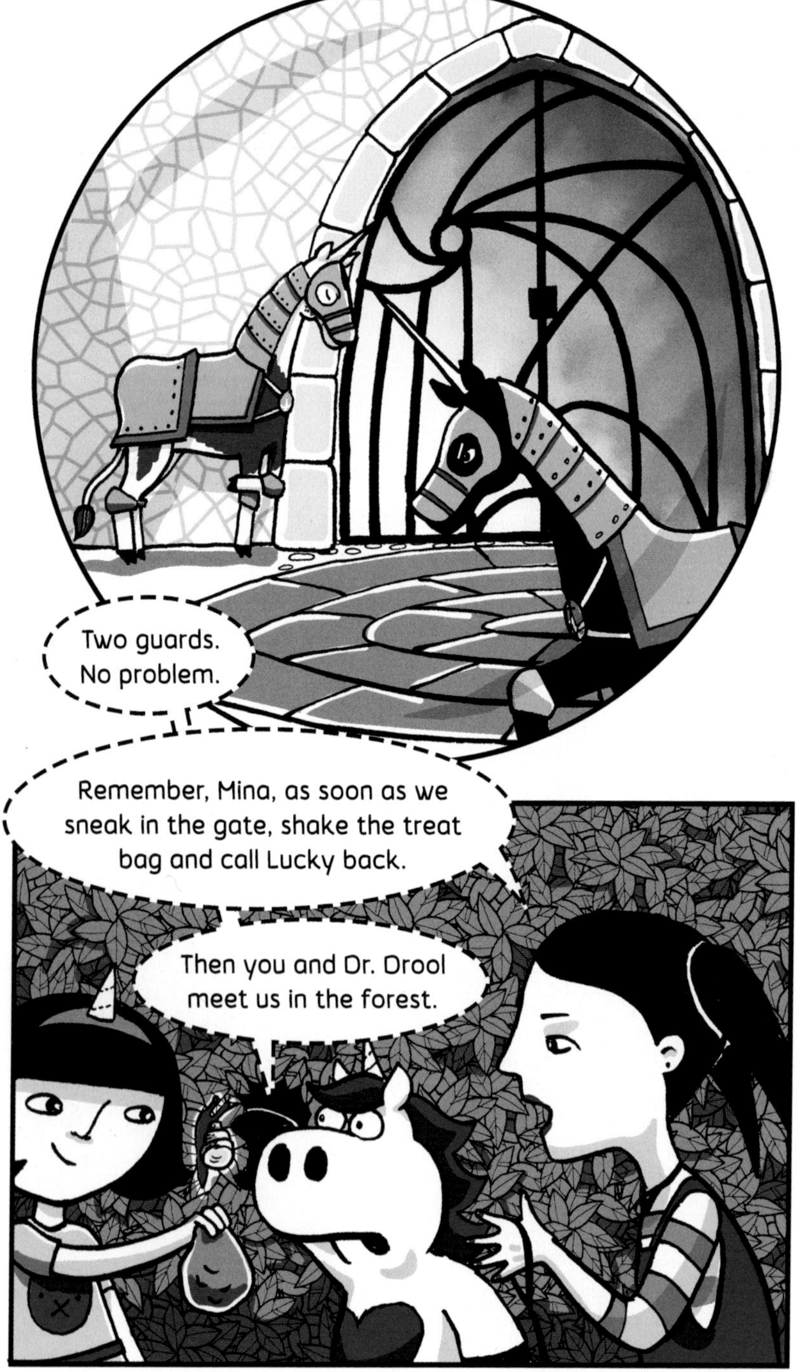
Two guards. No problem.
Remember, Mina, as soon as we sneak in the gate, shake the treat bag and call Lucky back.
Then you and Dr. Drool meet us in the forest.

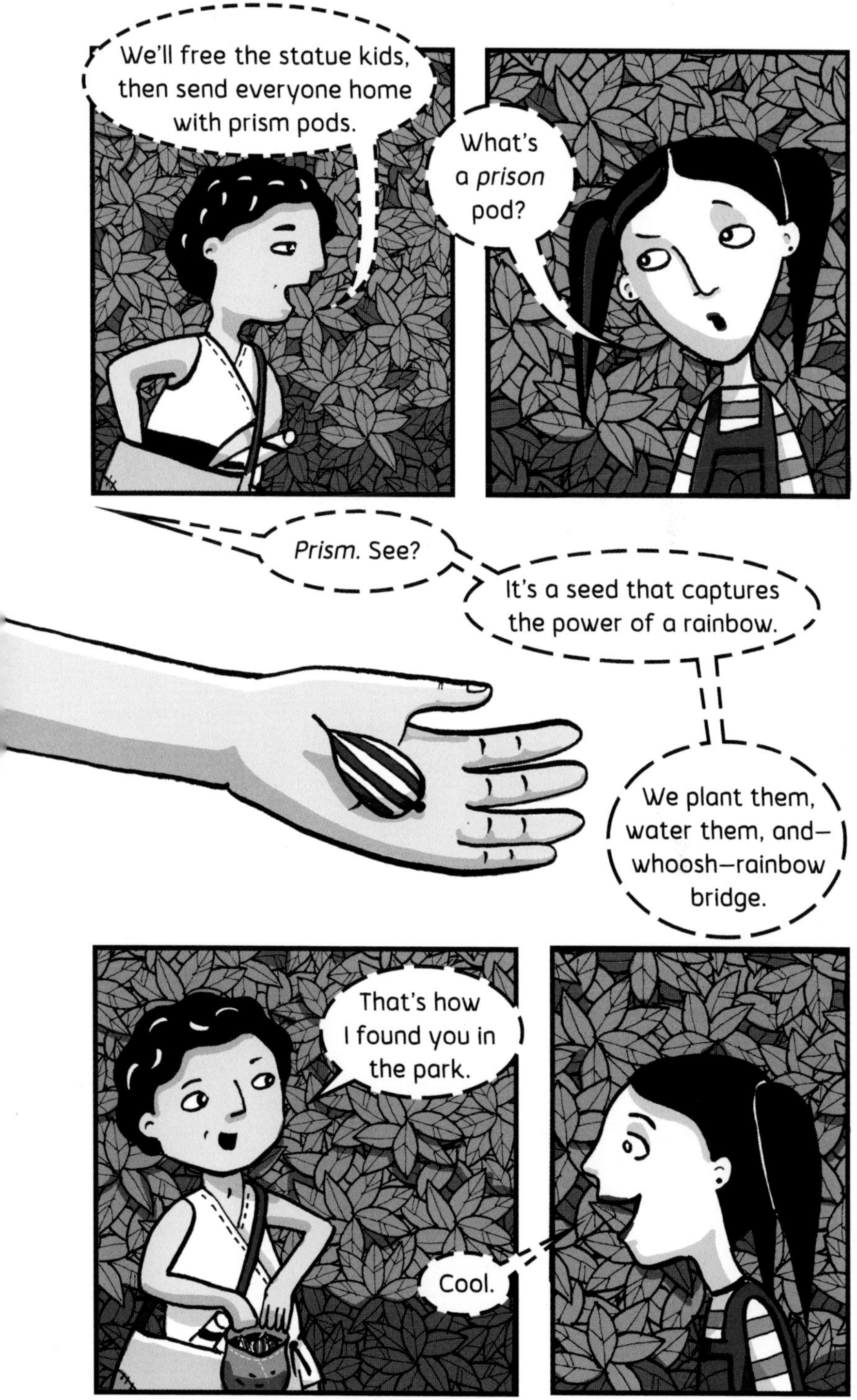
We'll free the statue kids, then send everyone home with prism pods.
What's a *prison* pod?
Prism. See?
It's a seed that captures the power of a rainbow.
We plant them, water them, and—whoosh—rainbow bridge.
That's how I found you in the park.
Cool.

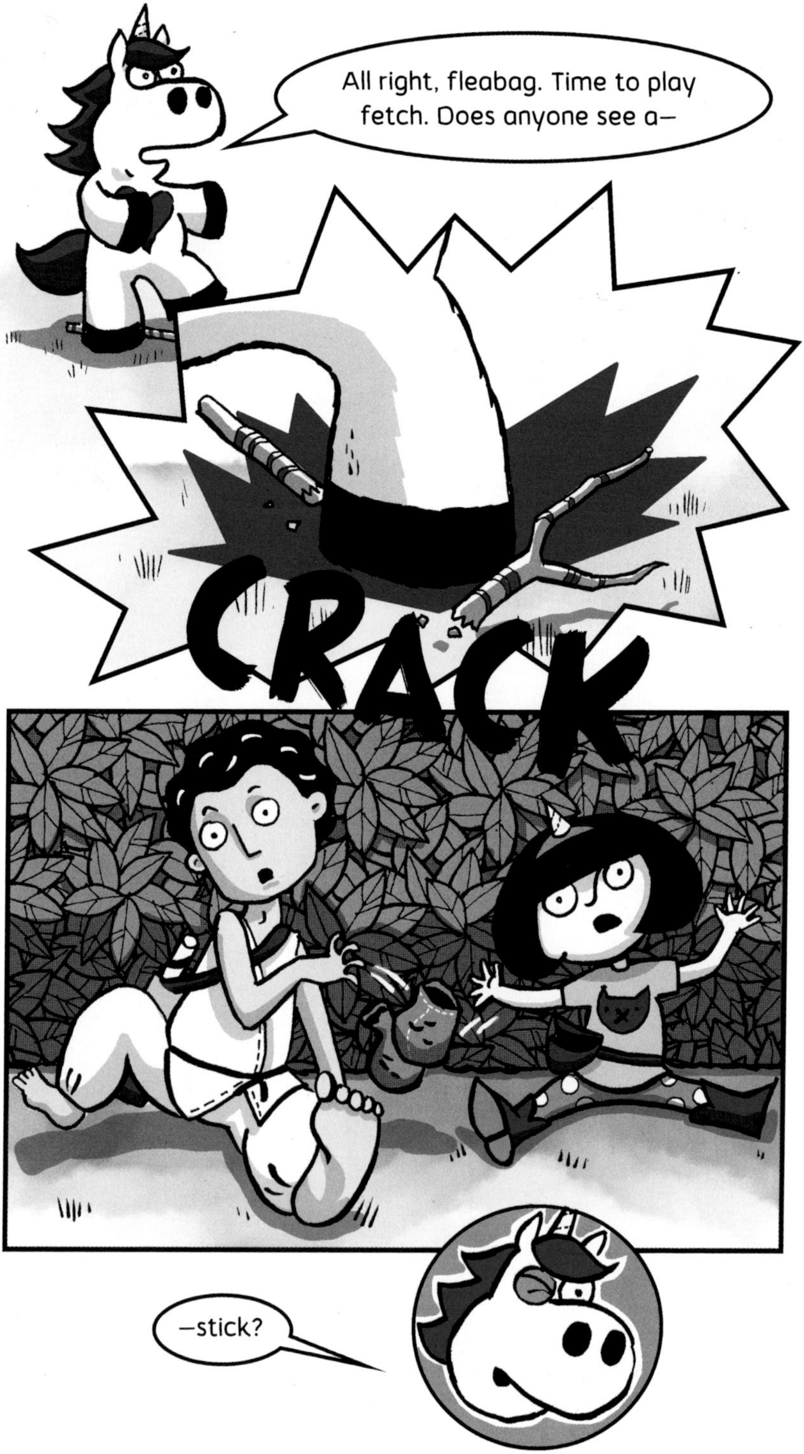
All right, fleabag. Time to play fetch. Does anyone see a—
CRACK
—stick?

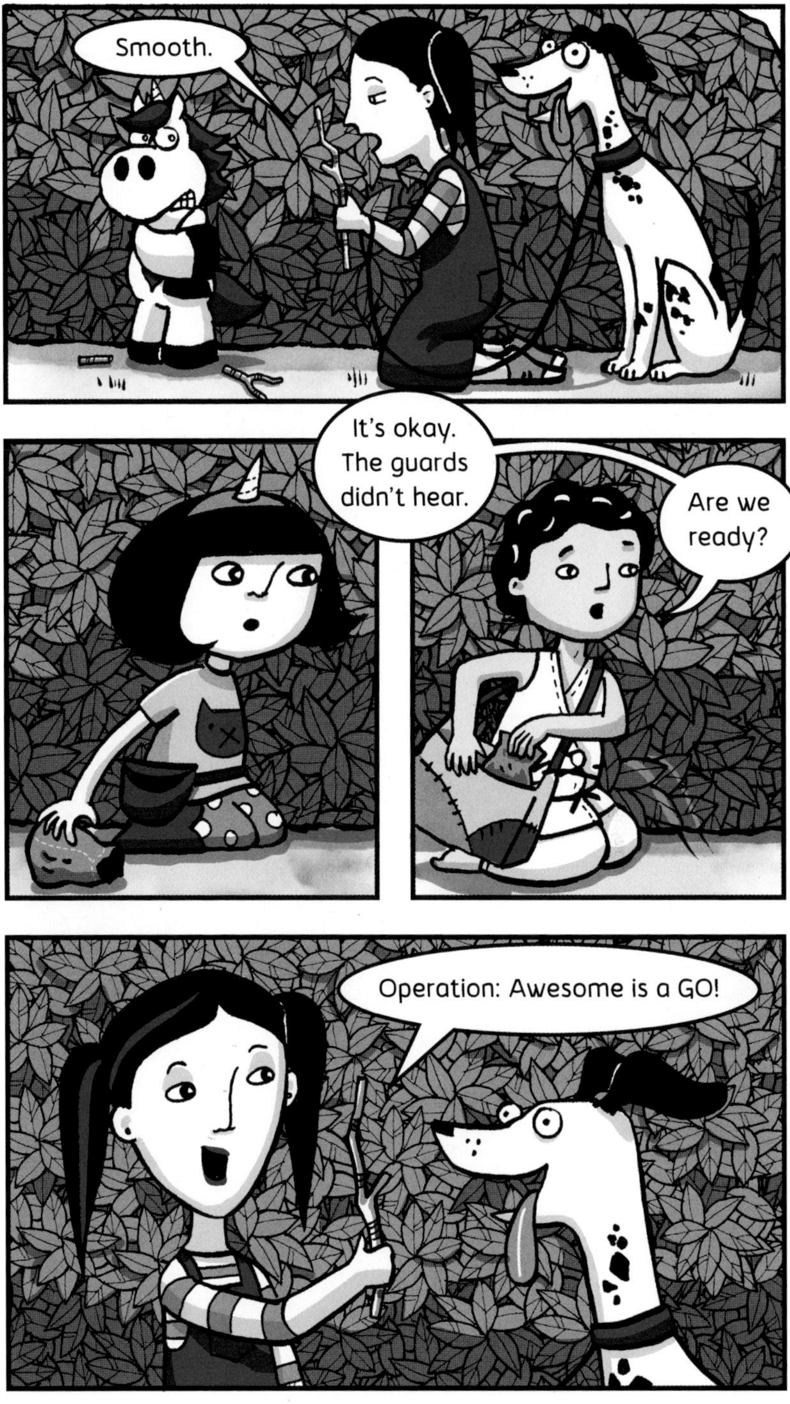
Smooth.
It's okay. The guards didn't hear.
Are we ready?
Operation: Awesome is a GO!

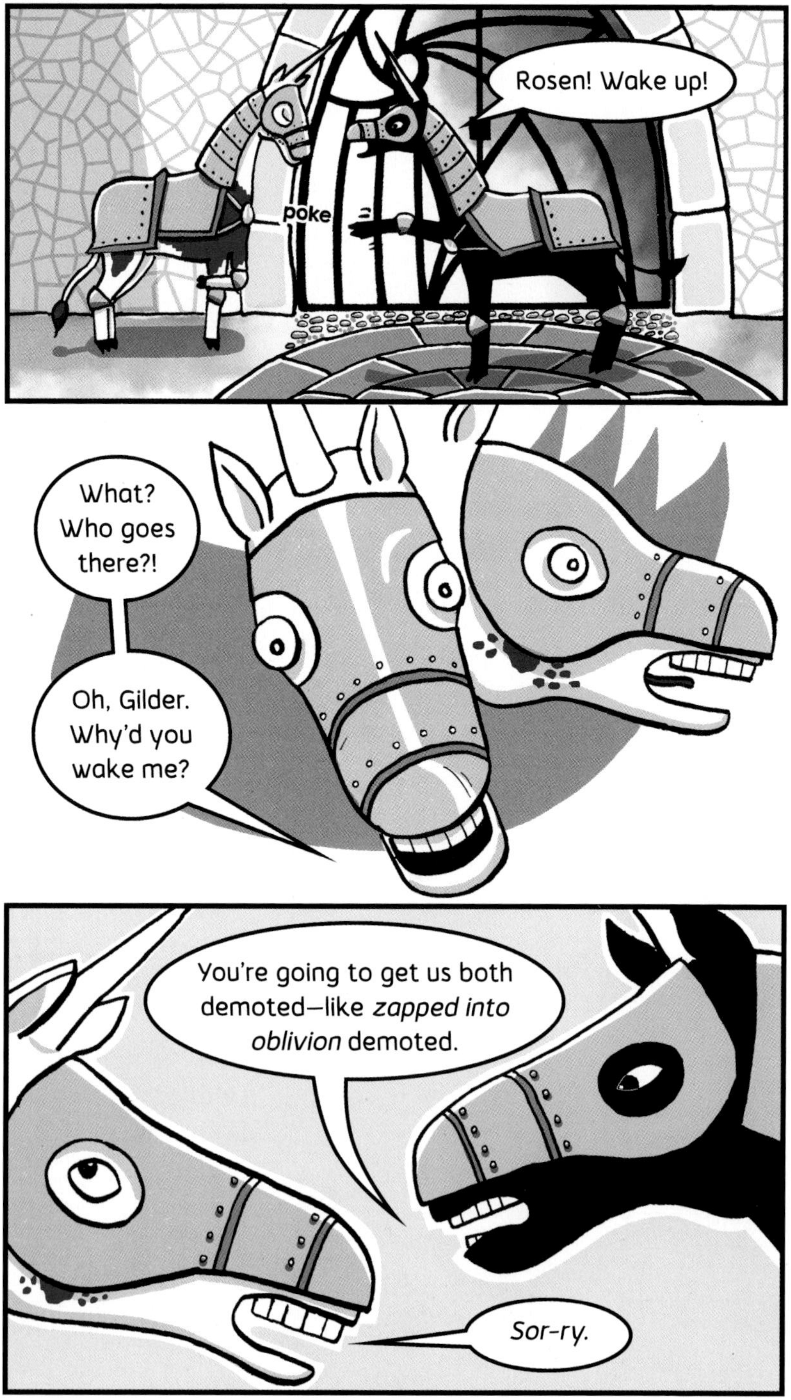
Rosen! Wake up!
poke
What? Who goes there?!
Oh, Gilder. Why'd you wake me?
You're going to get us both demoted—like *zapped into oblivion* demoted.
Sor-ry.

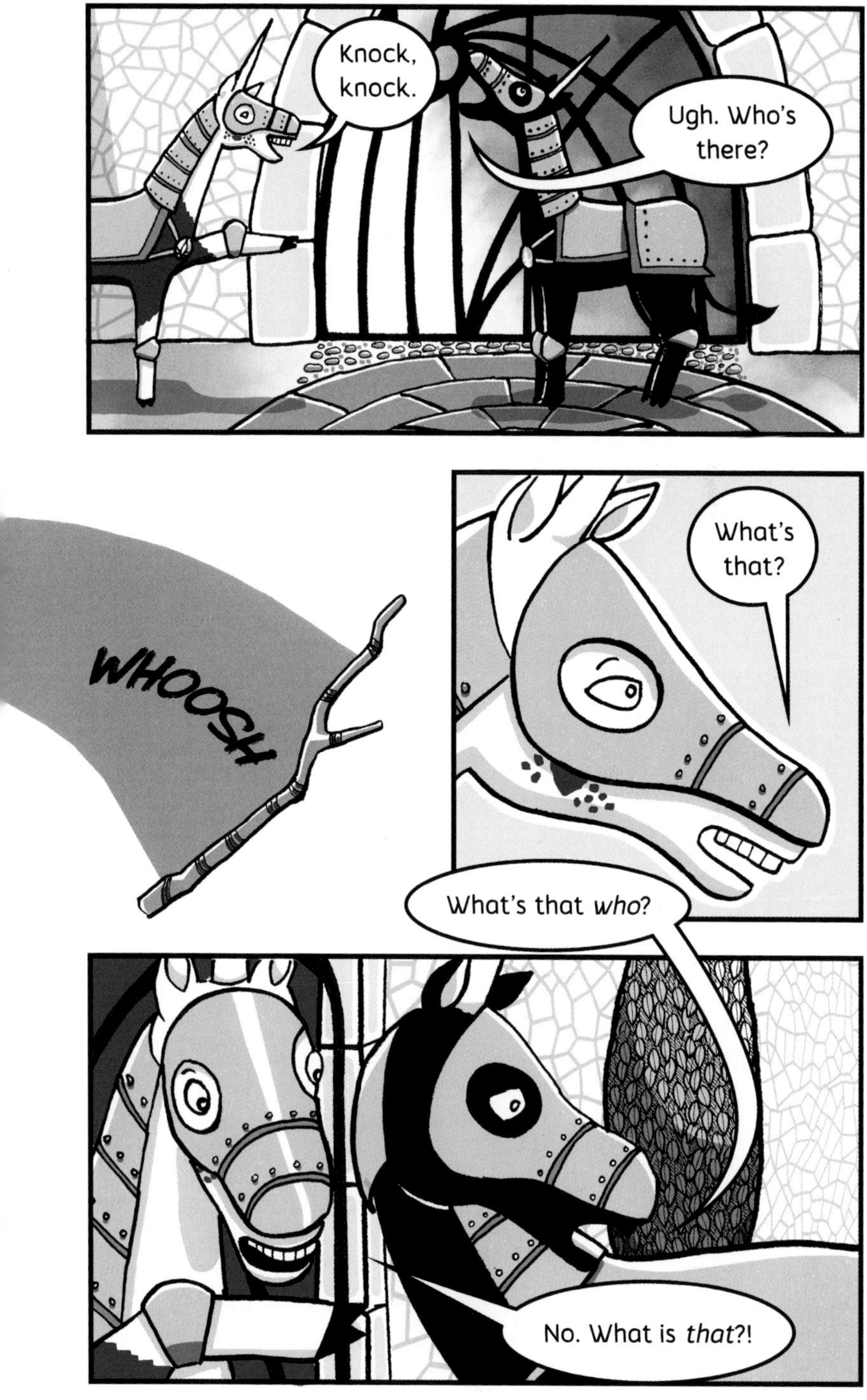
Knock, knock.
Ugh. Who's there?
WHOOSH
What's that?
What's that *who*?
No. What is *that*?!

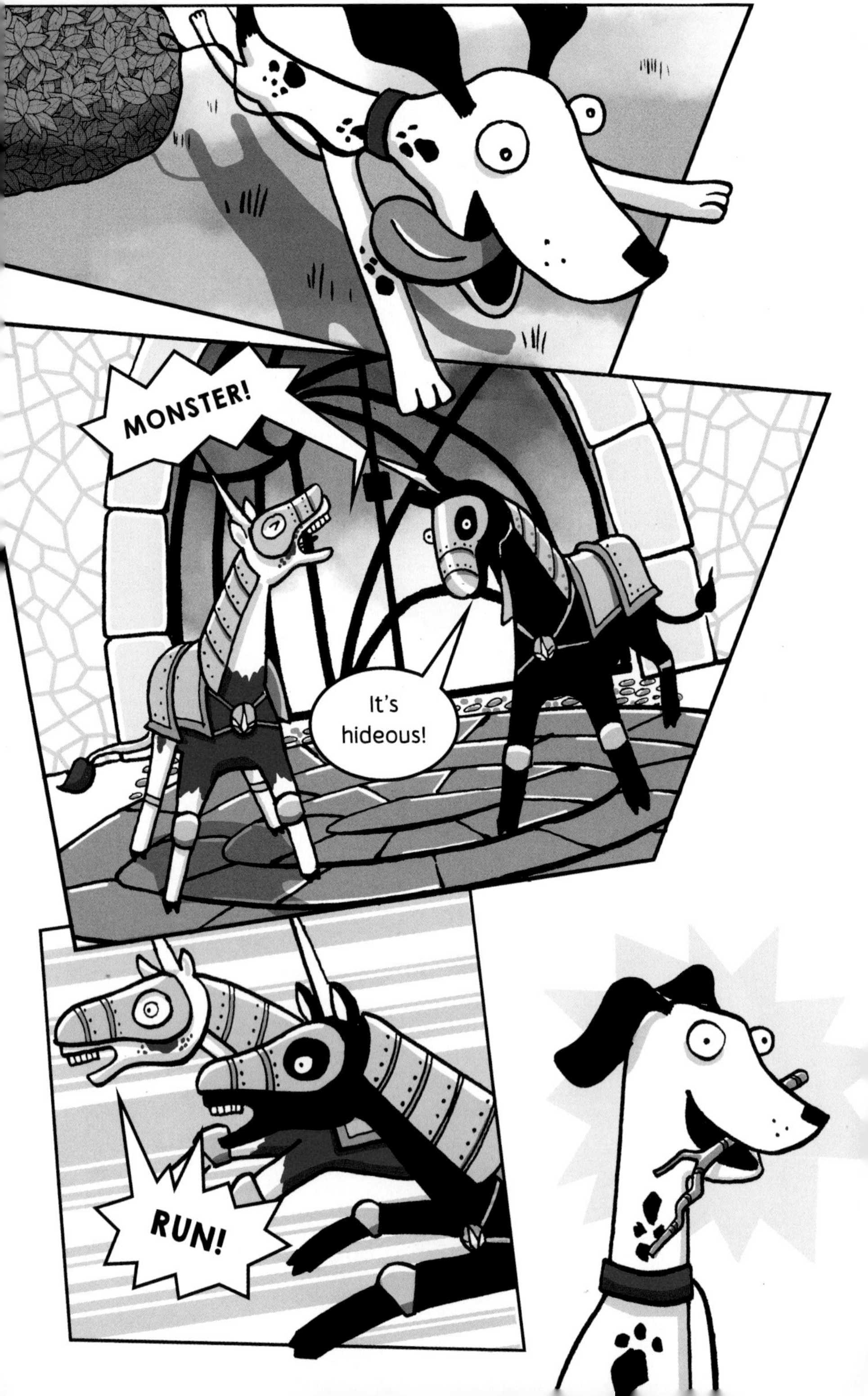
MONSTER!
It's hideous!
RUN!

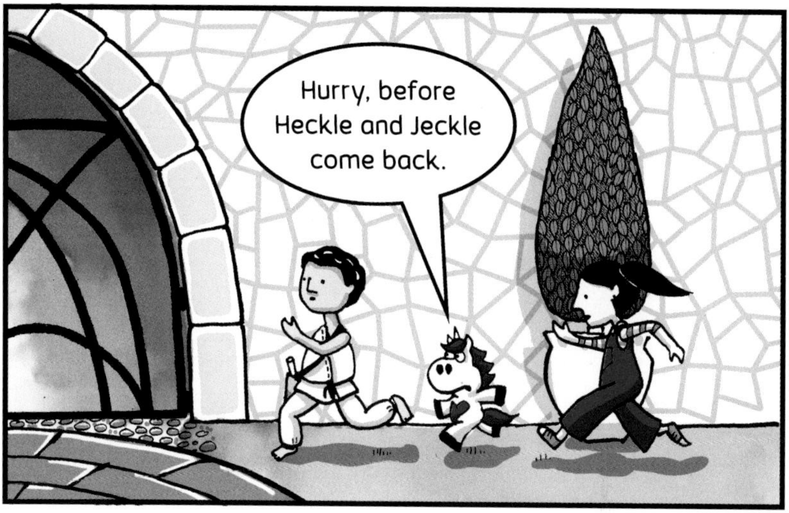
Hurry, before Heckle and Jeckle come back.

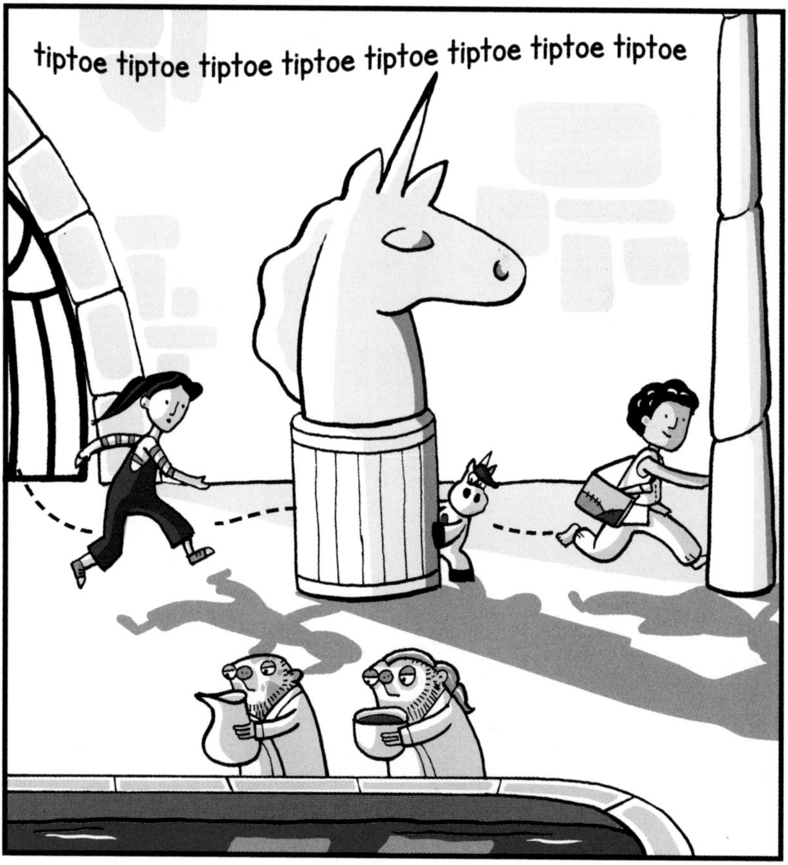
tiptoe tiptoe tiptoe tiptoe tiptoe tiptoe tiptoe tiptoe

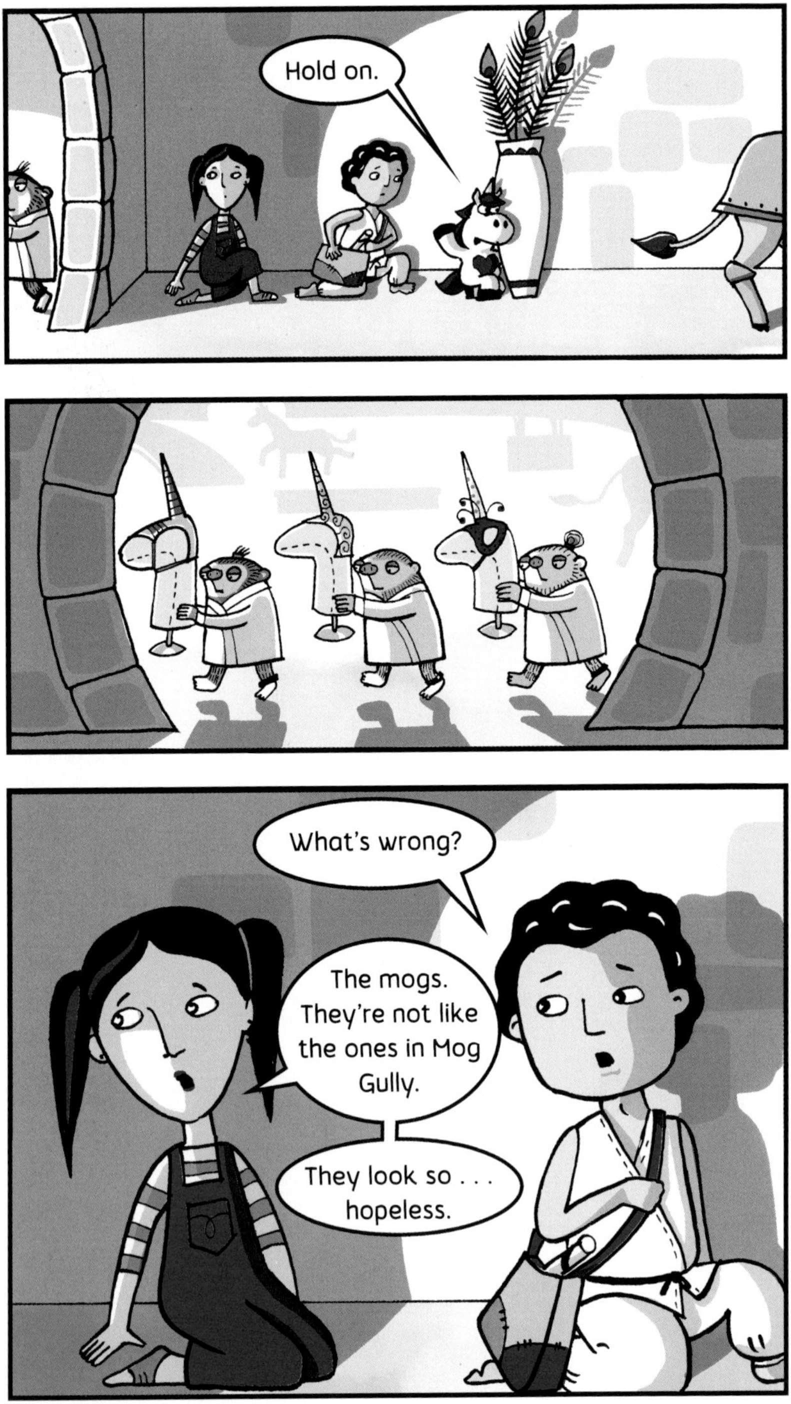
Hold on.
What's wrong?
The mogs. They're not like the ones in Mog Gully.
They look so . . . hopeless.

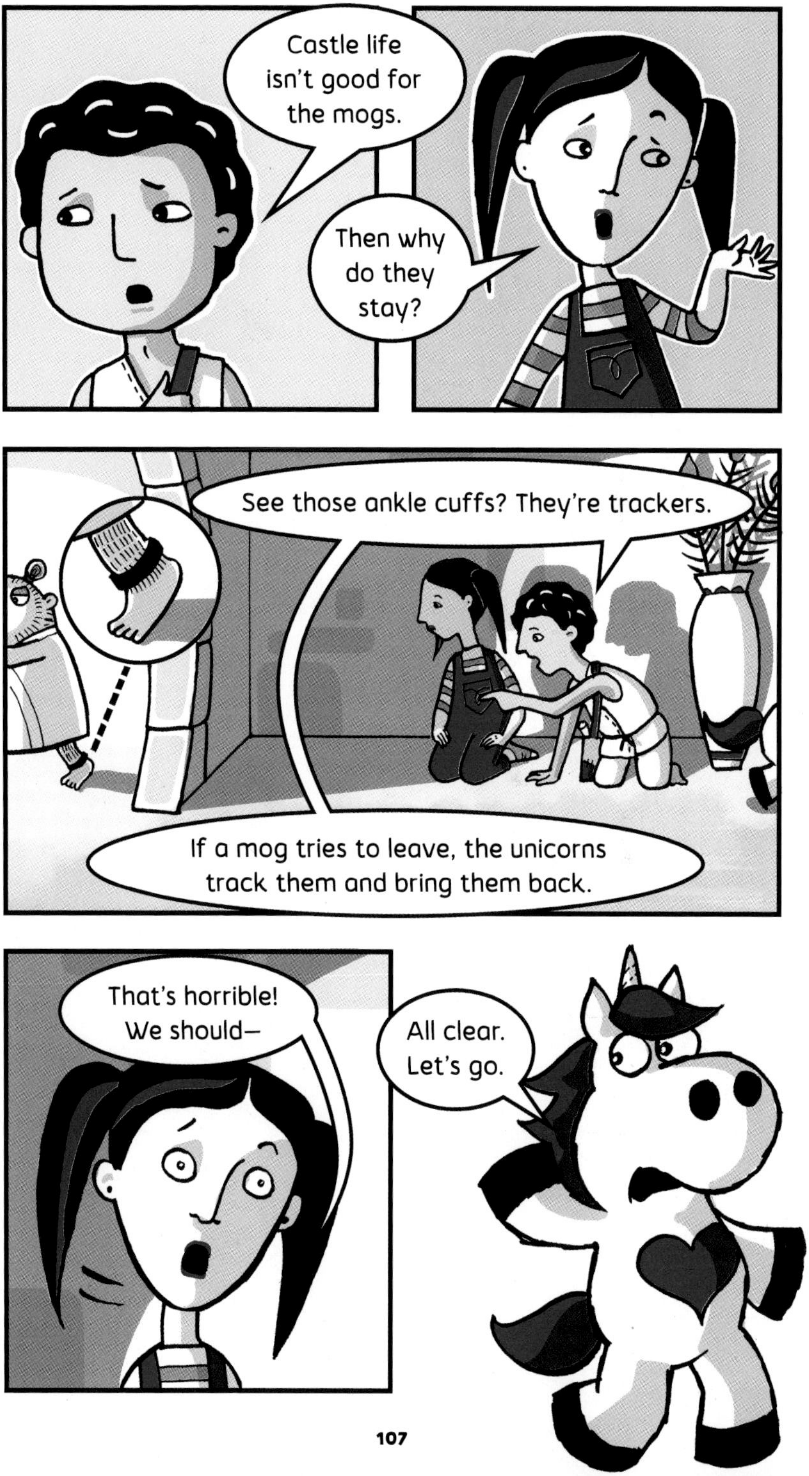
Castle life isn't good for the mogs.
Then why do they stay?
See those ankle cuffs? They're trackers.
If a mog tries to leave, the unicorns track them and bring them back.
That's horrible! We should—
All clear. Let's go.

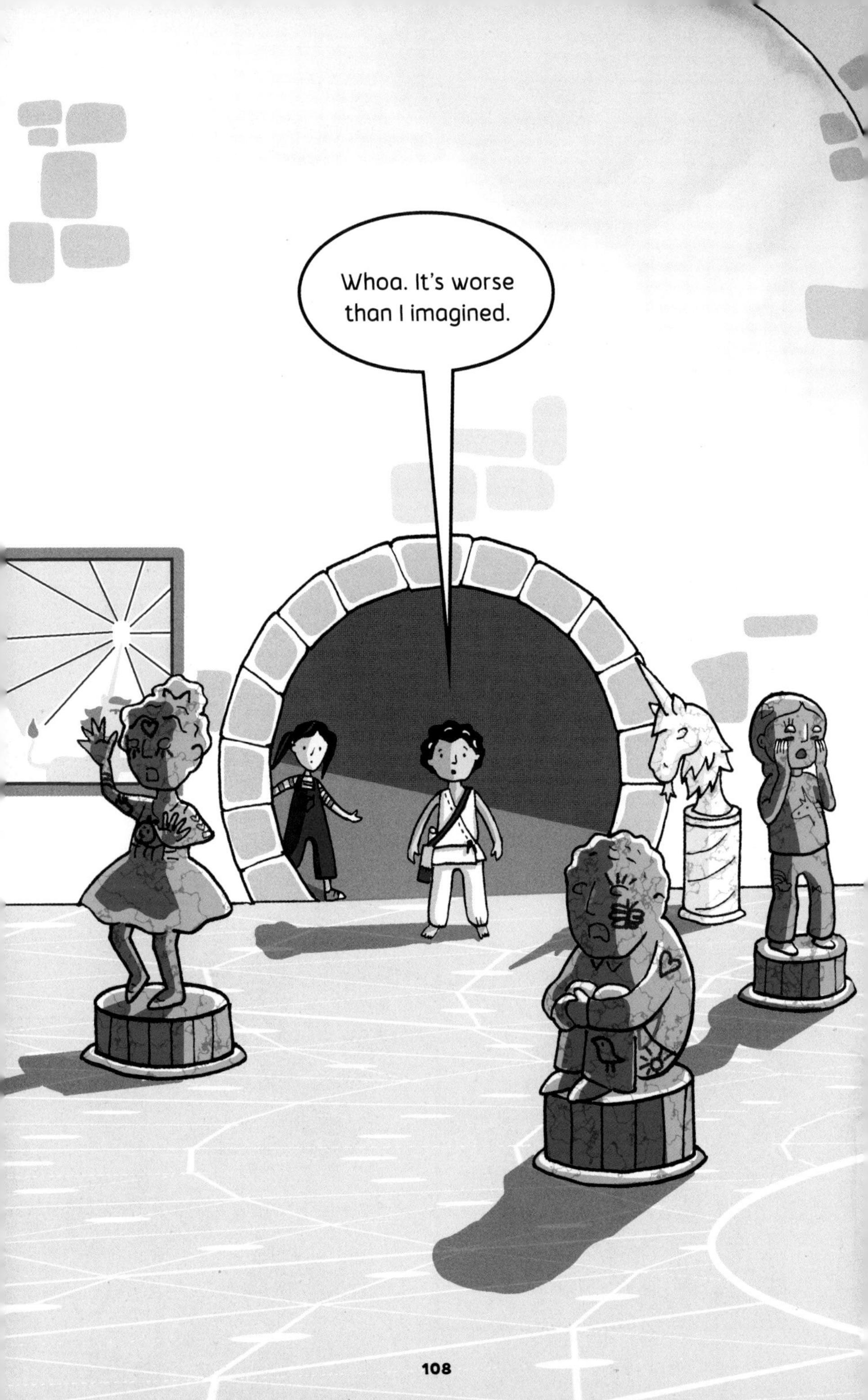
Whoa. It's worse than I imagined.

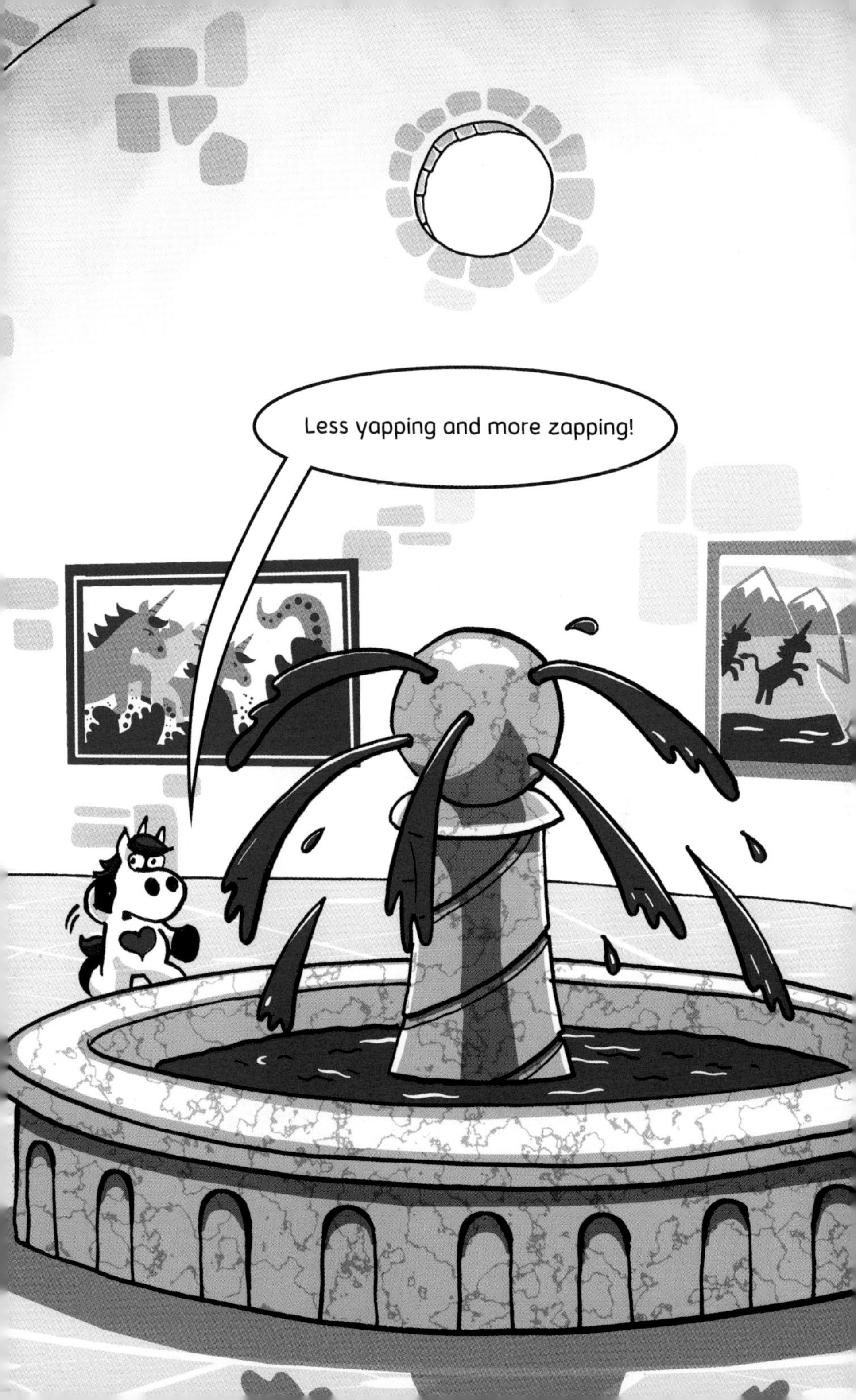
Less yapping and more zapping!

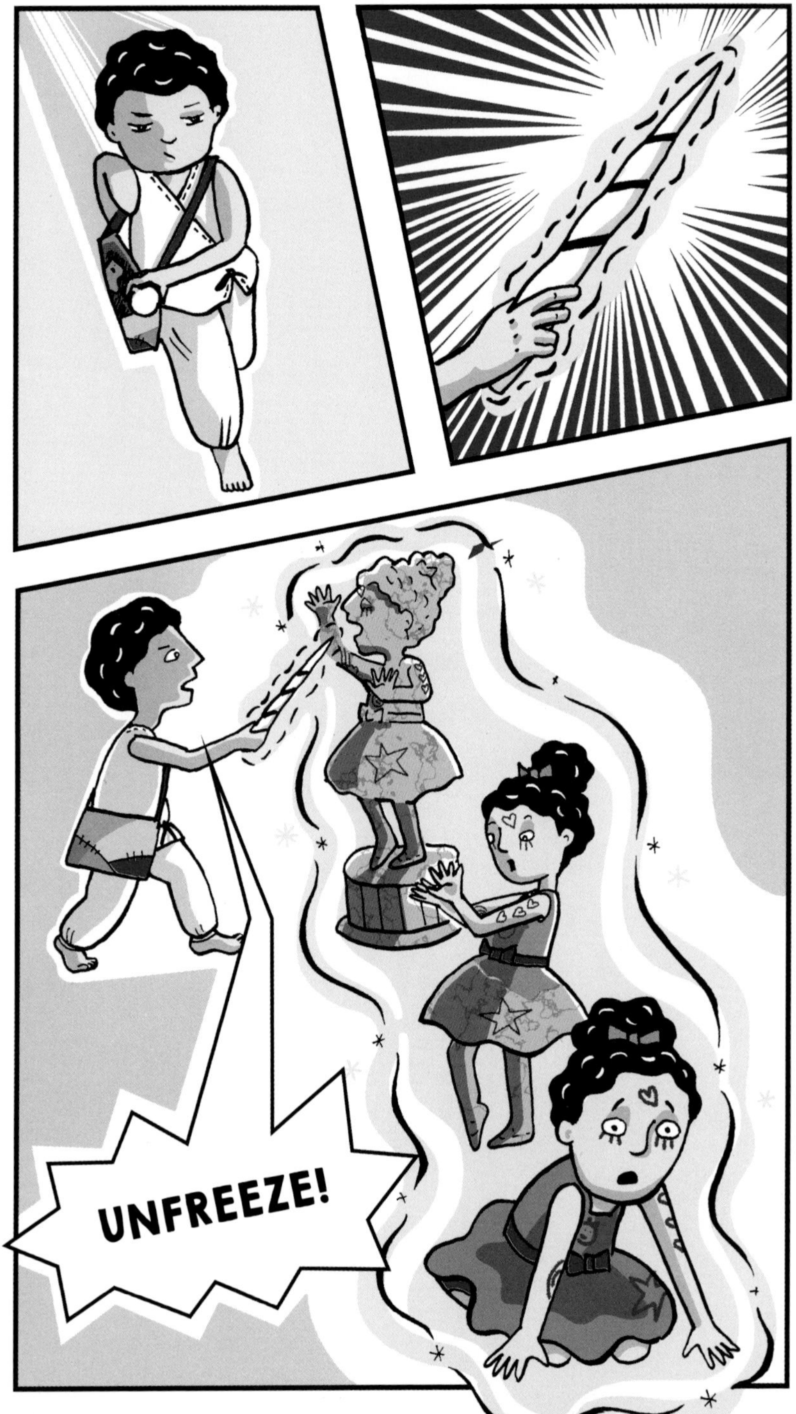
UNFREEZE!

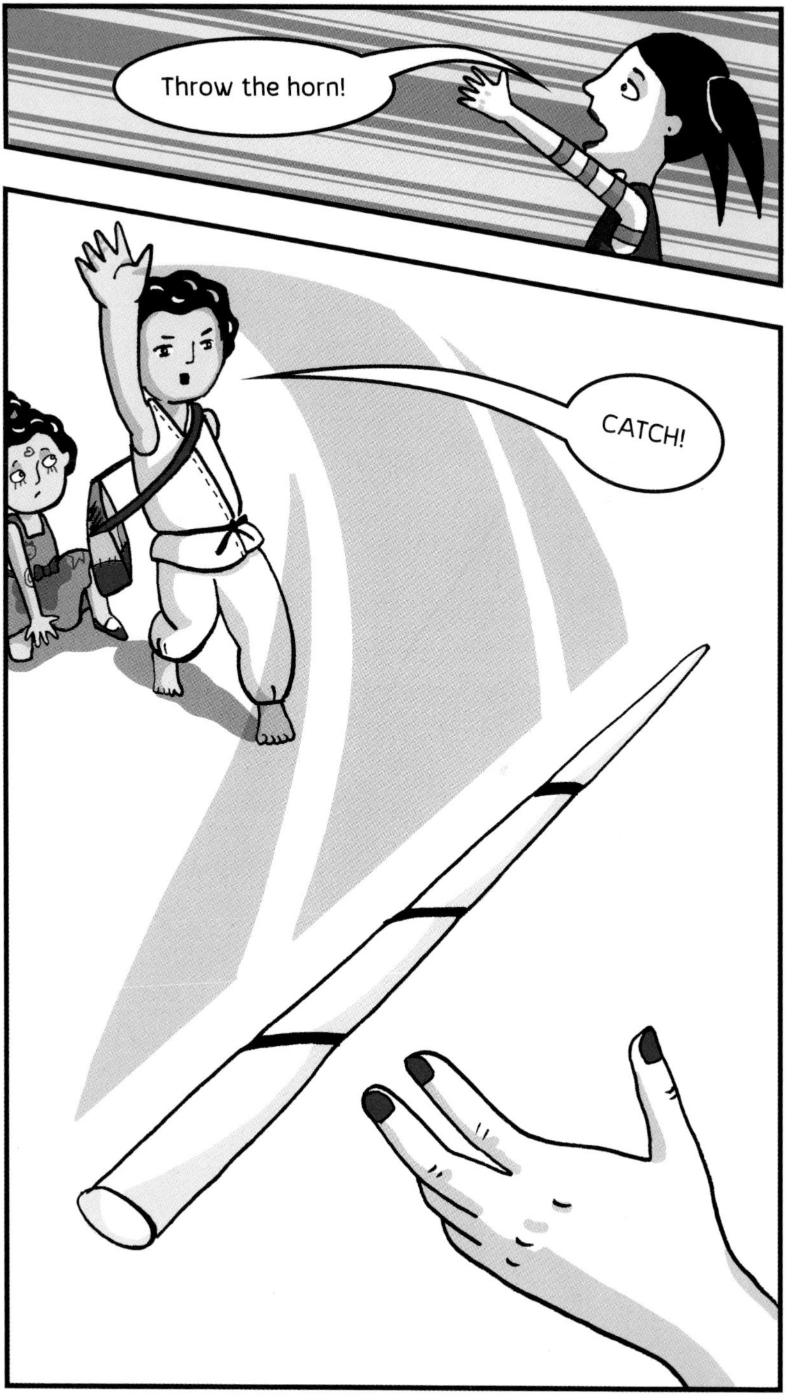
Throw the horn!
CATCH!

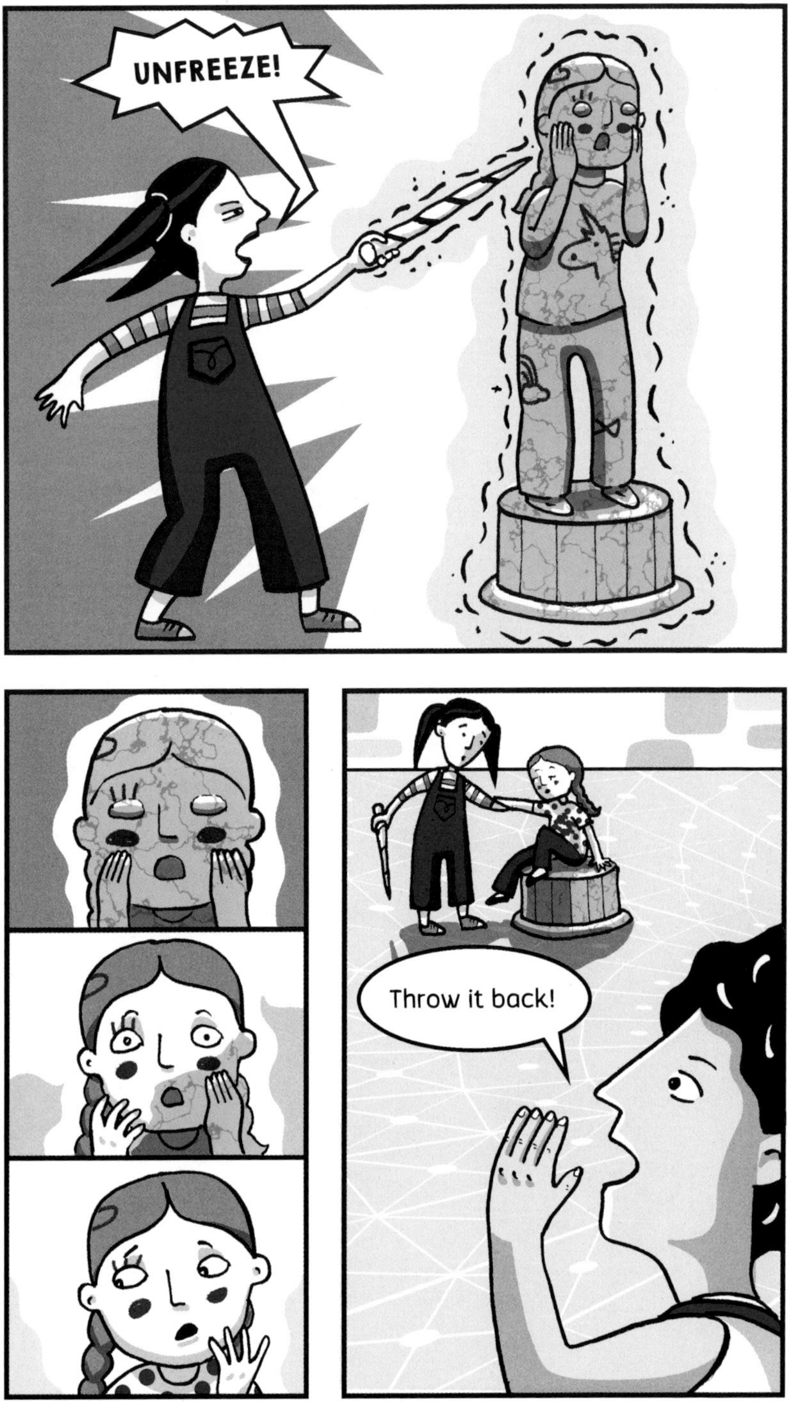
UNFREEZE!
Throw it back!

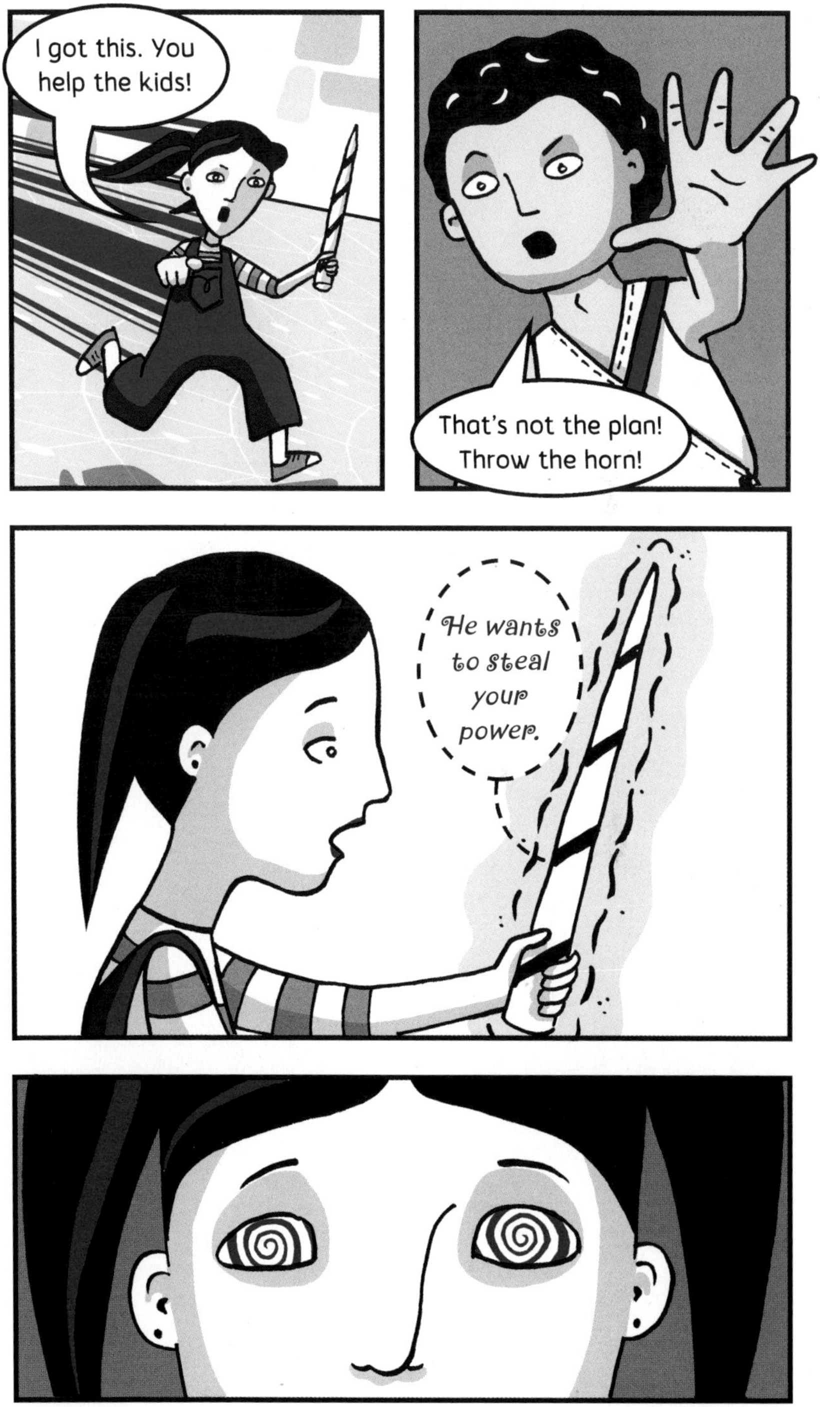
I got this. You help the kids!
That's not the plan! Throw the horn!
He wants to steal your power.

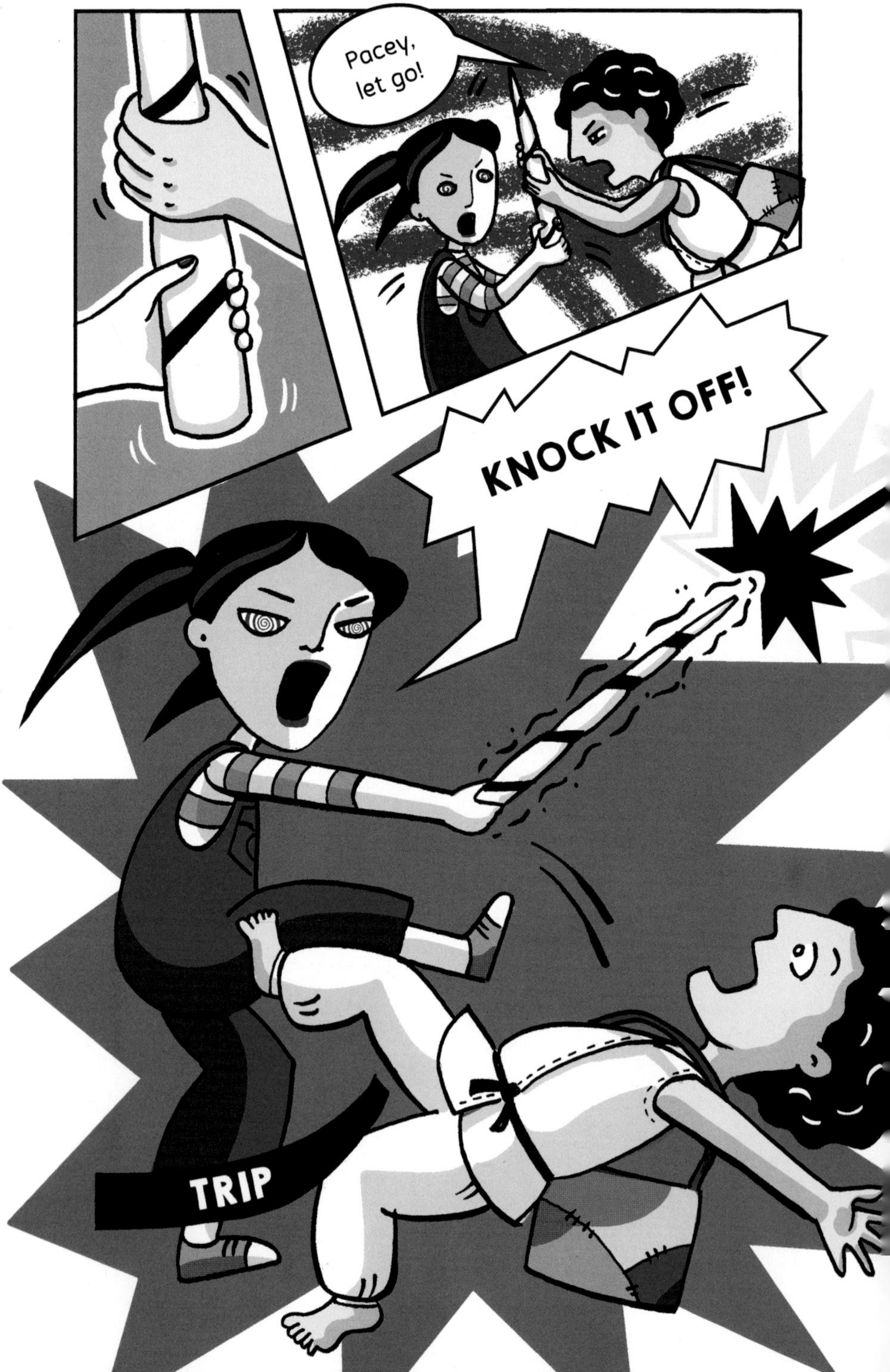
Pacey, let go!
KNOCK IT OFF!
TRIP

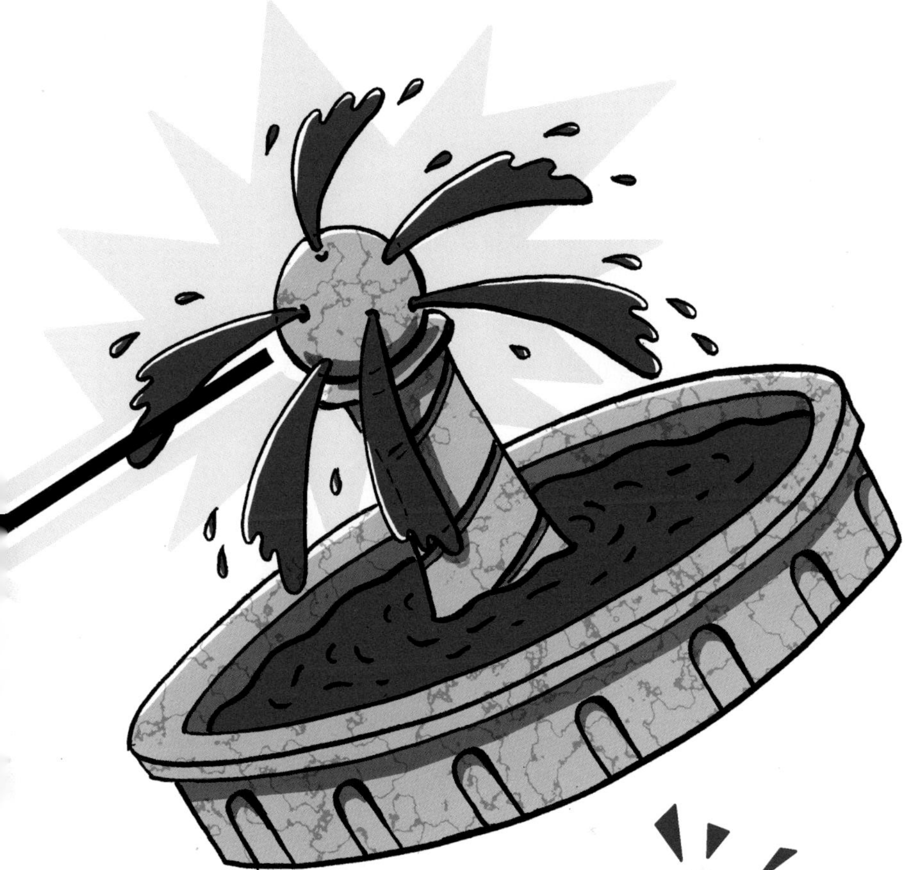

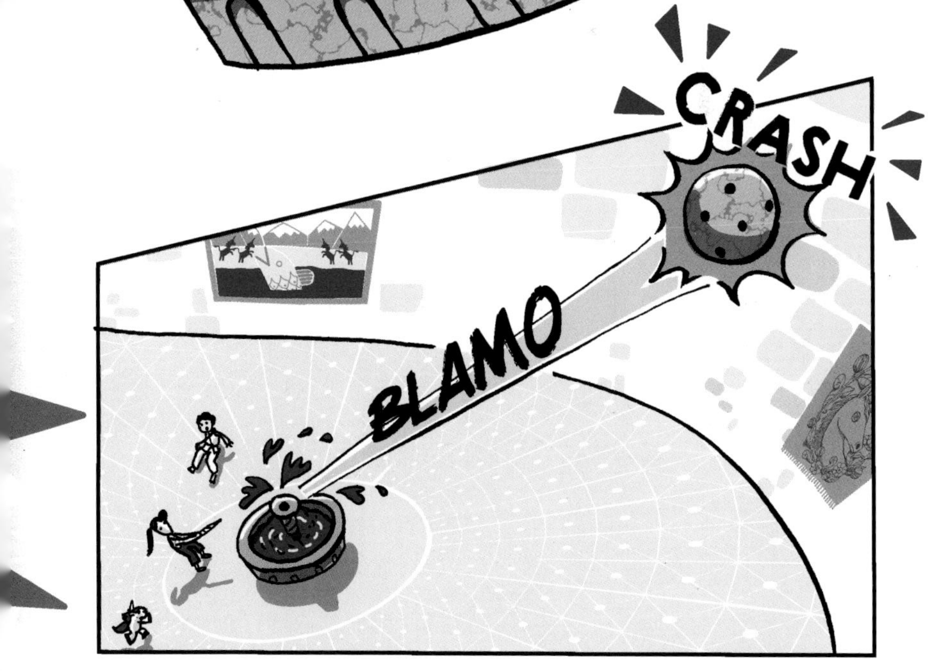
CRASH
BLAMO

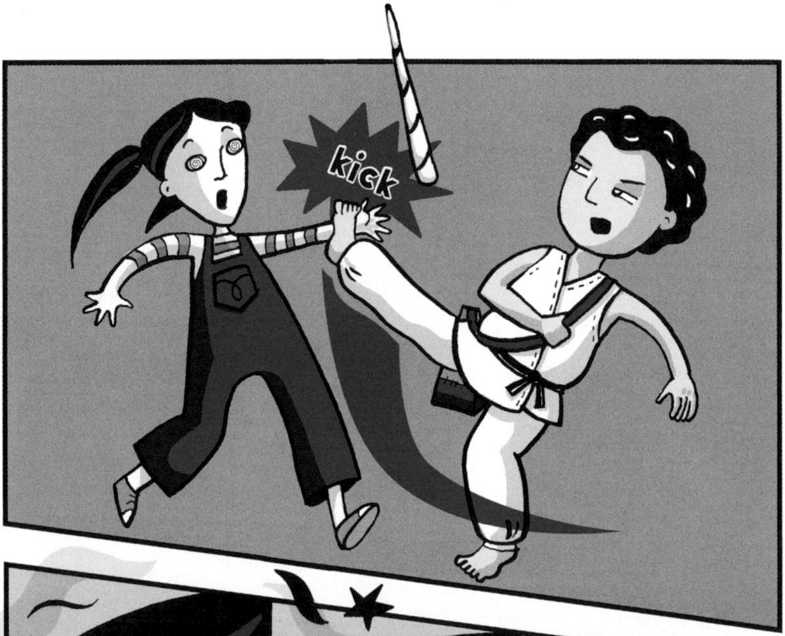
kick

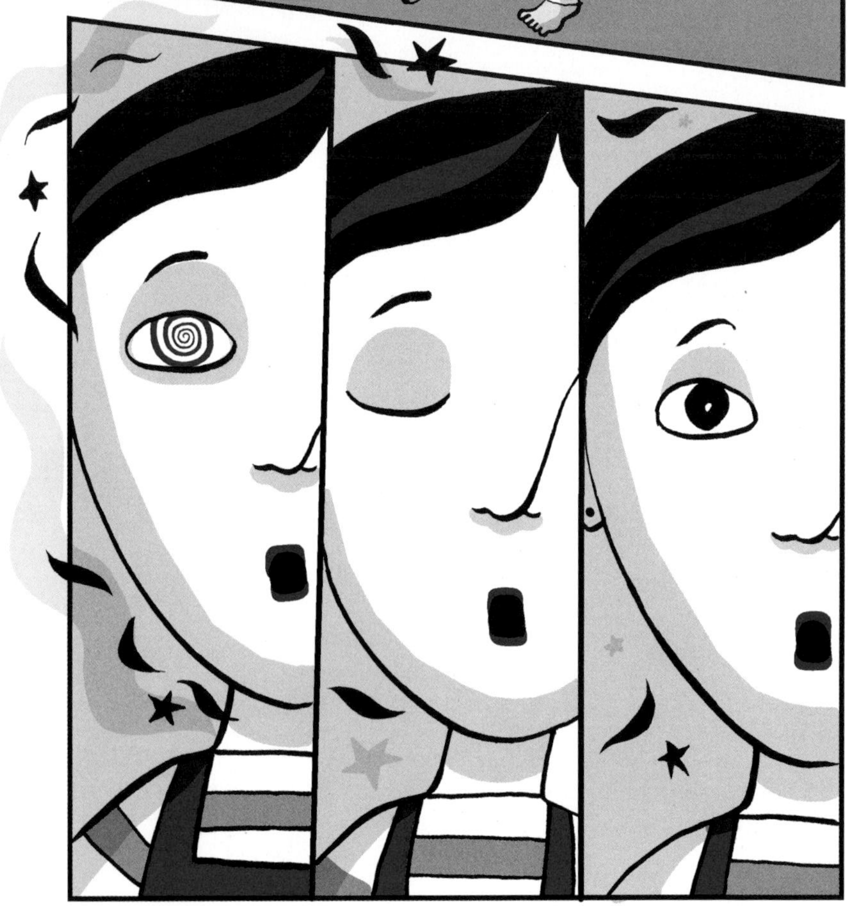

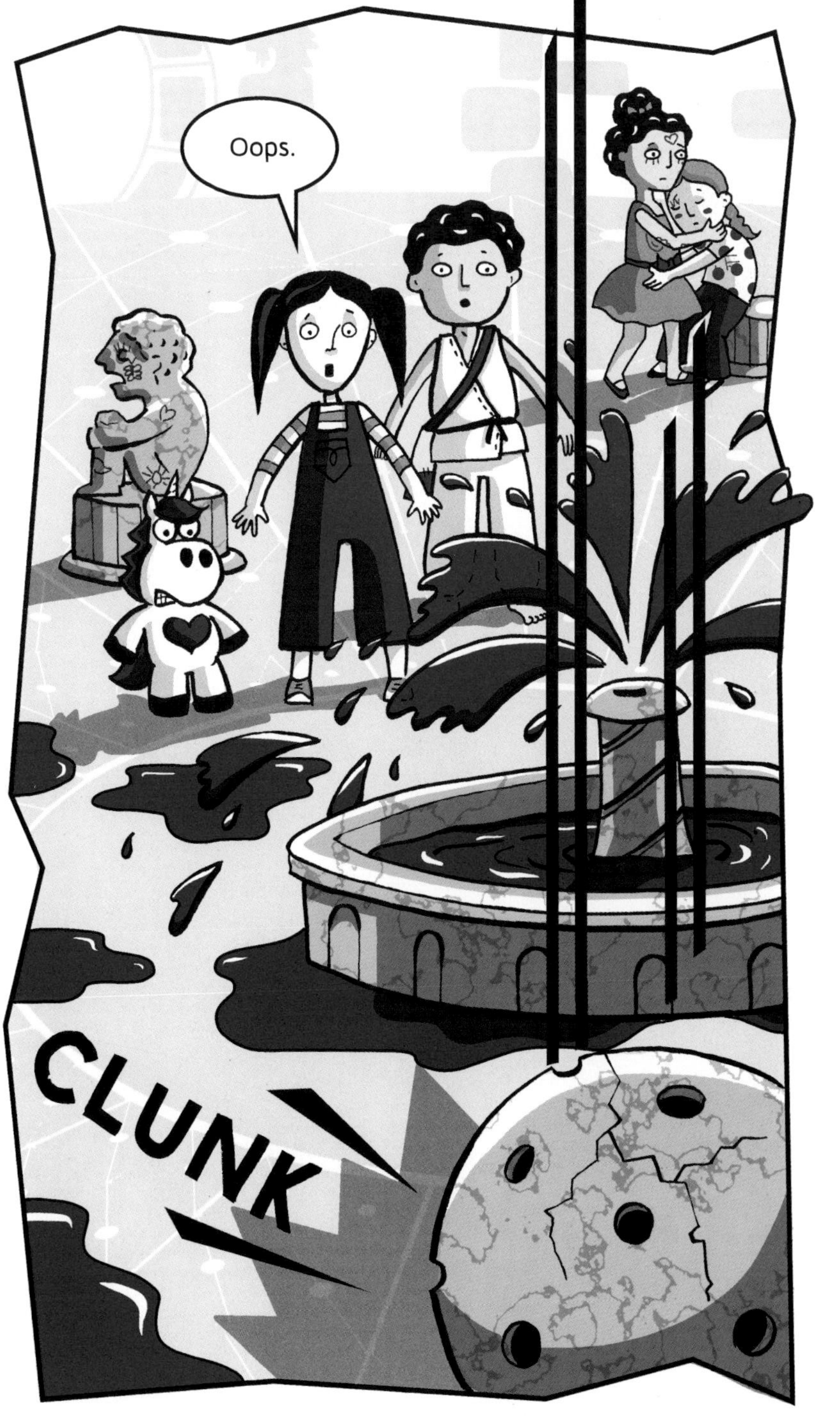
Oops.
CLUNK

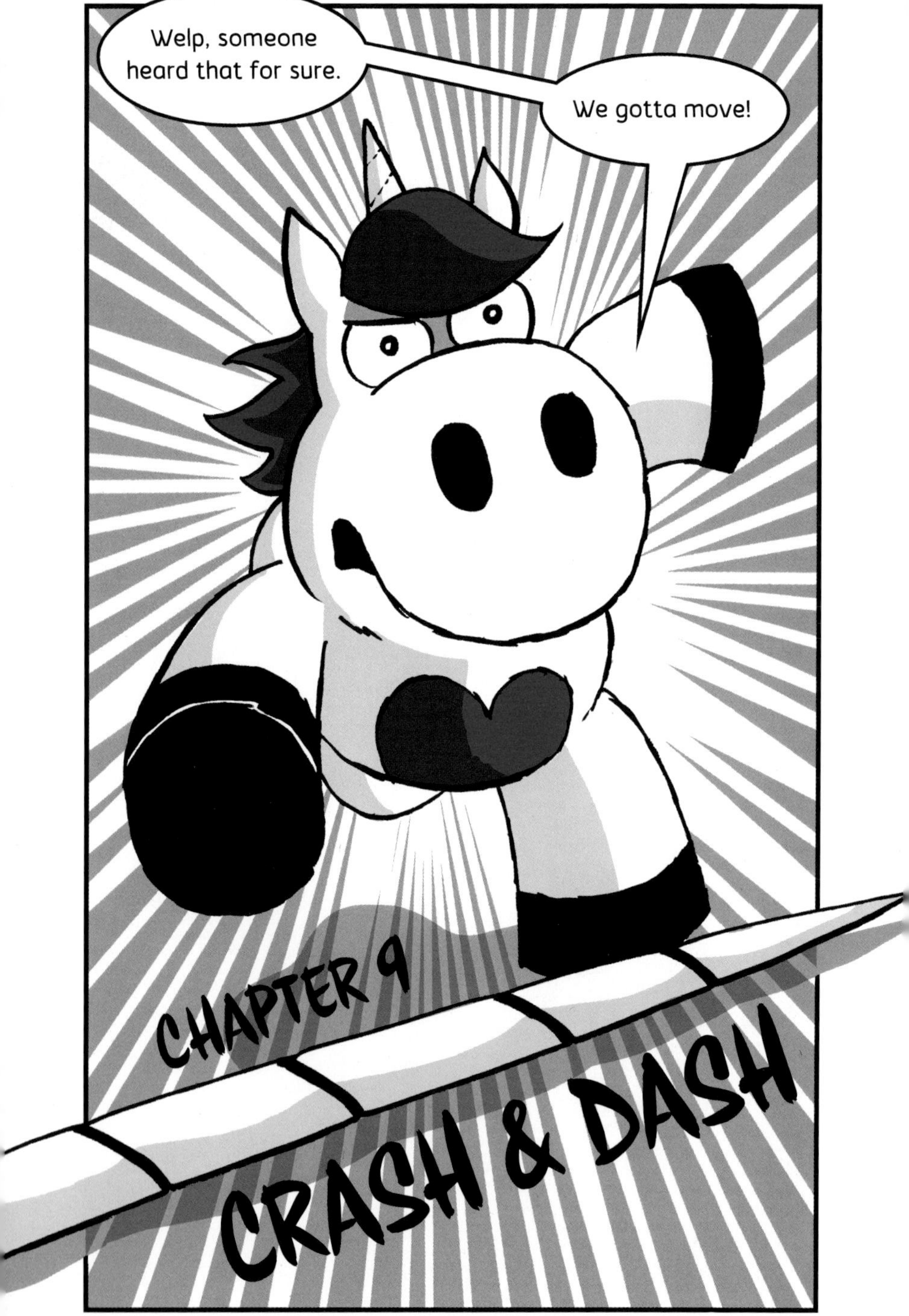
Welp, someone heard that for sure.
We gotta move!
CHAPTER 9
CRASH & DASH

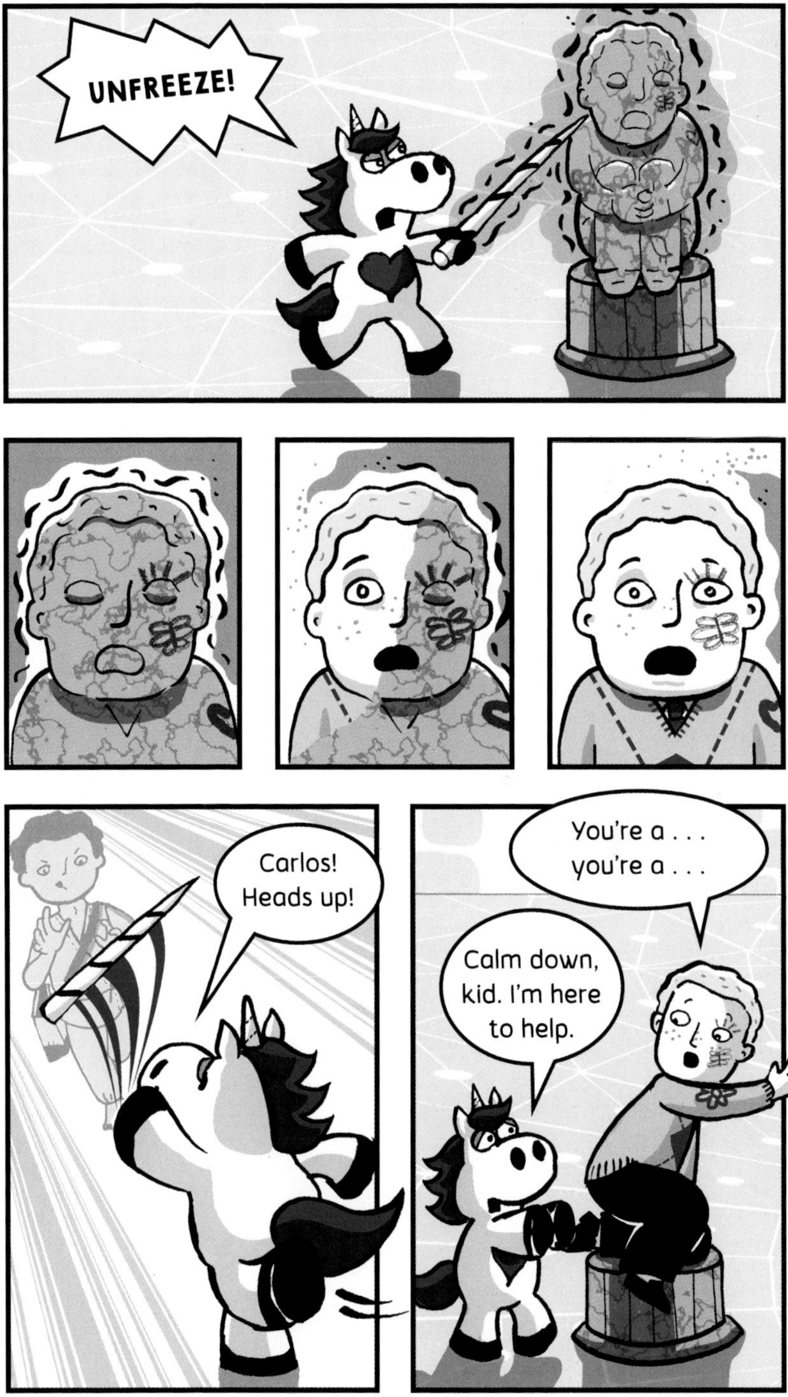
UNFREEZE!
Carlos! Heads up!
You're a . . . you're a . . .
Calm down, kid. I'm here to help.

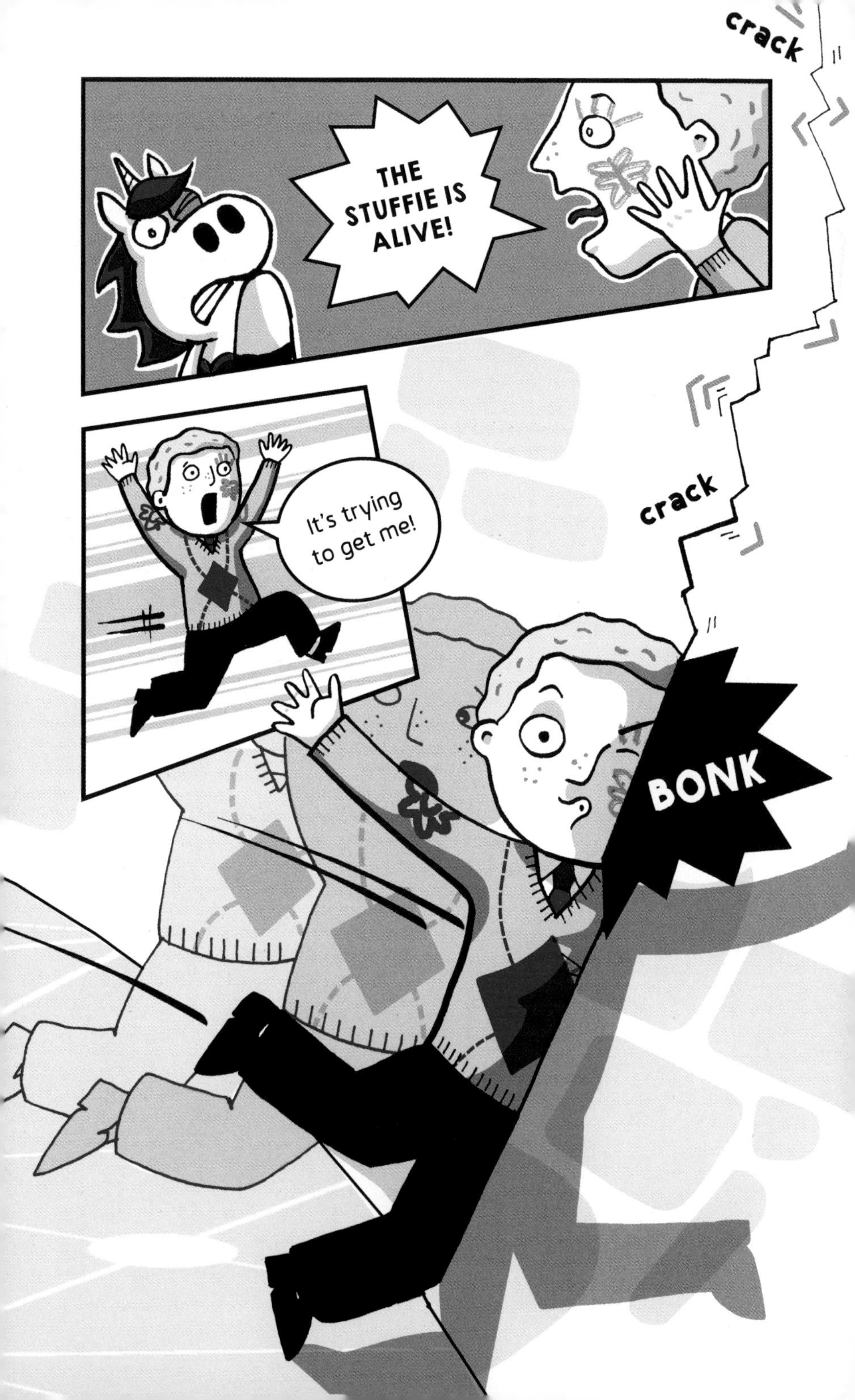
crack
THE STUFFIE IS ALIVE!
It's trying to get me!
crack
BONK

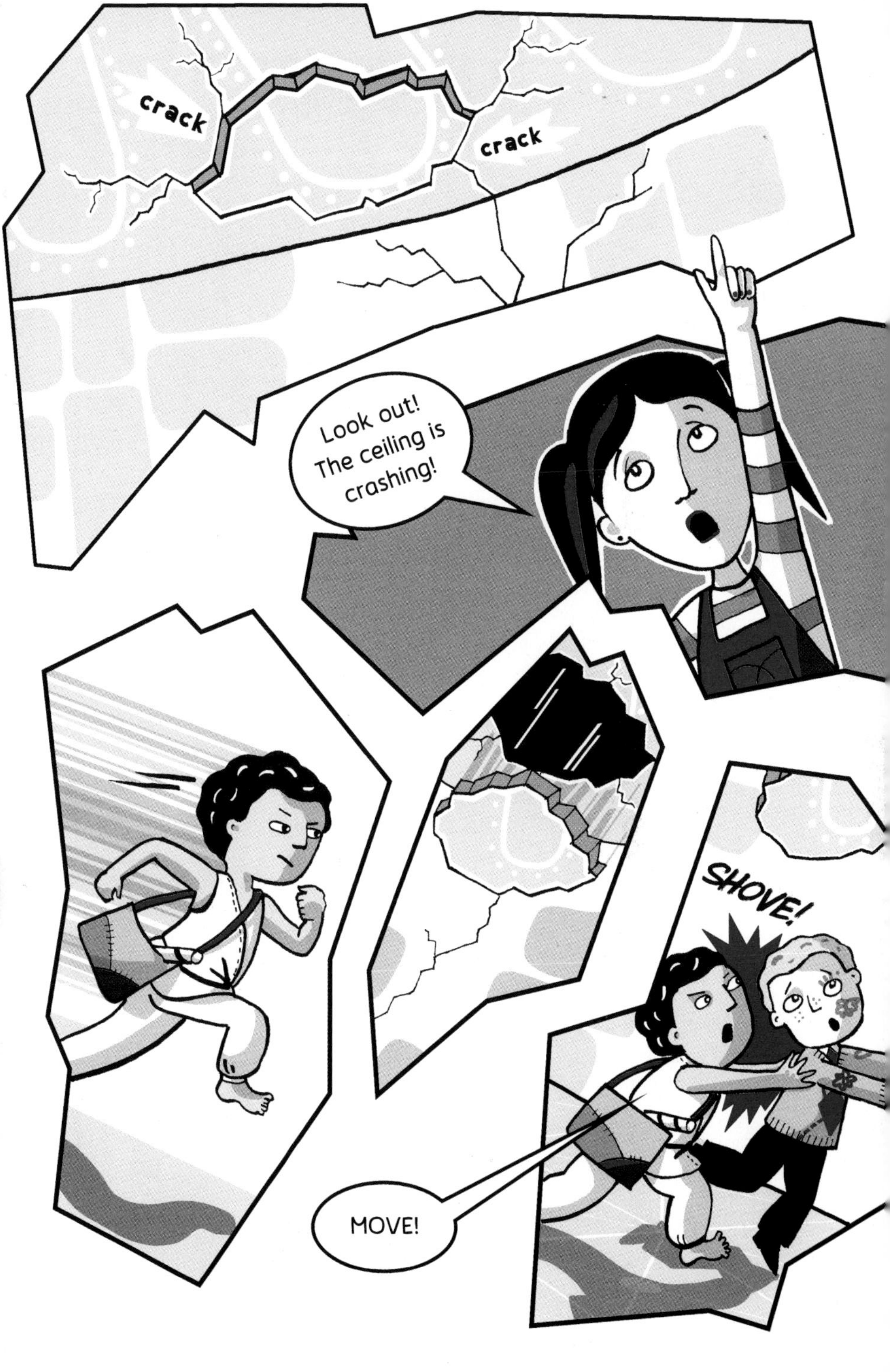
crack
crack
Look out! The ceiling is crashing!
SHOVE!
MOVE!

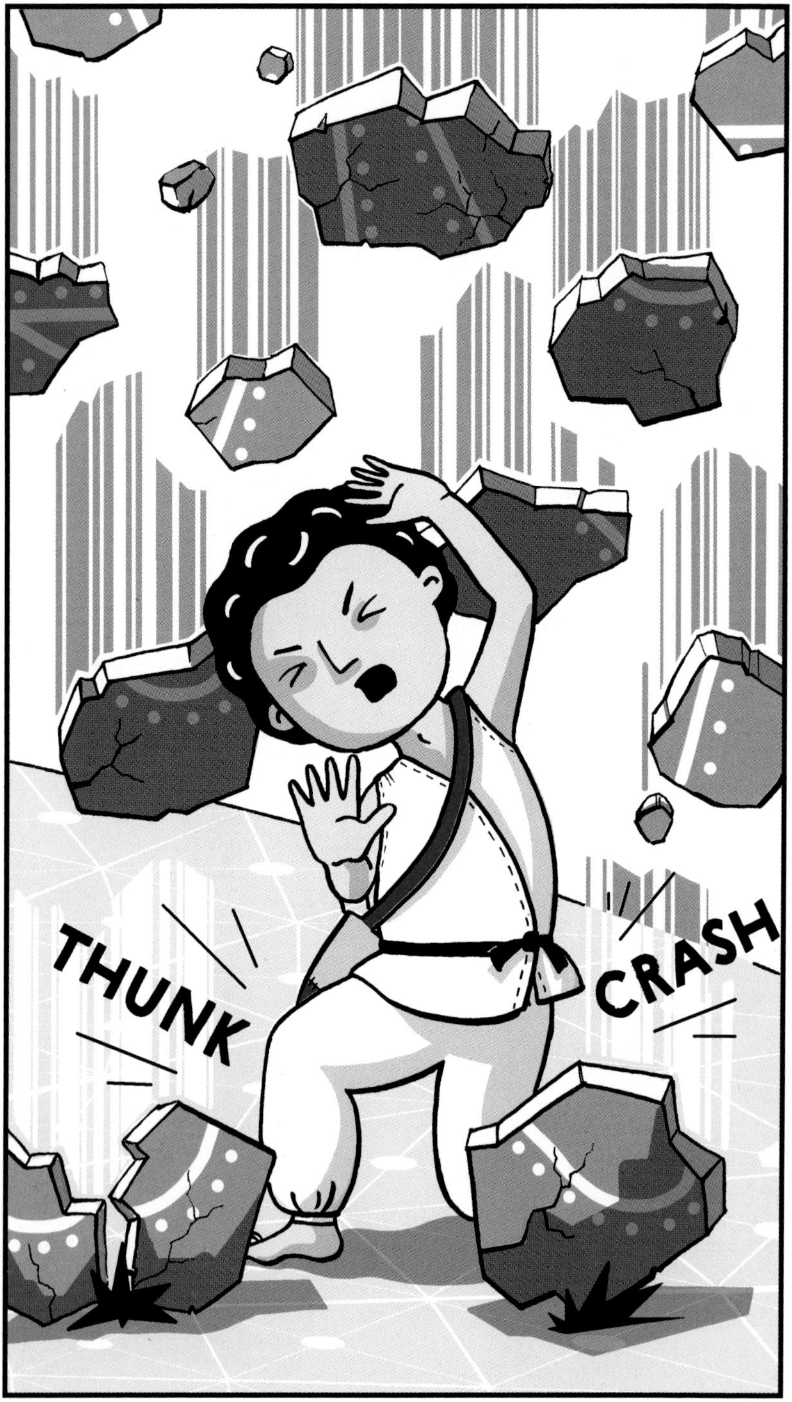
THUNK
CRASH

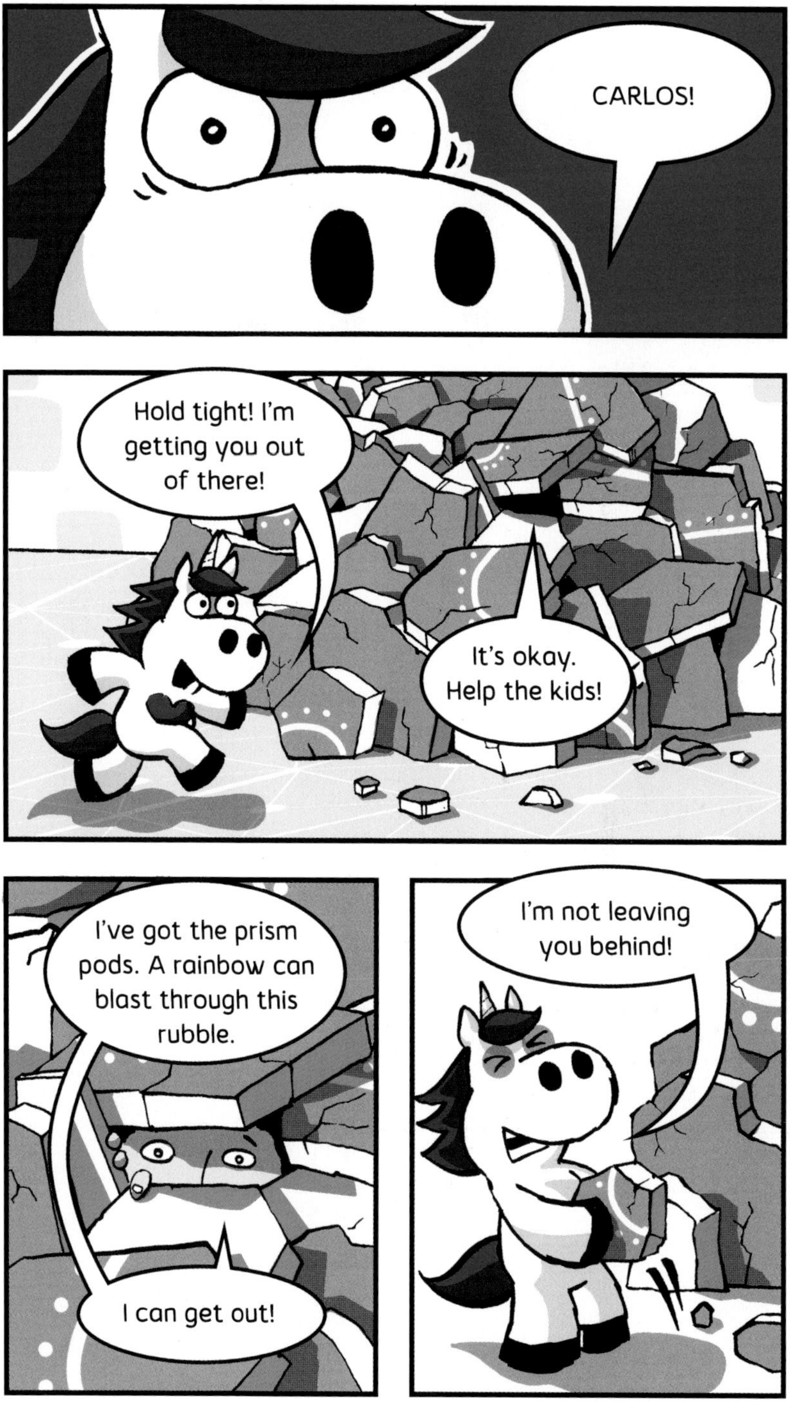
CARLOS!
Hold tight! I'm getting you out of there!
It's okay. Help the kids!
I've got the prism pods. A rainbow can blast through this rubble.
I can get out!
I'm not leaving you behind!

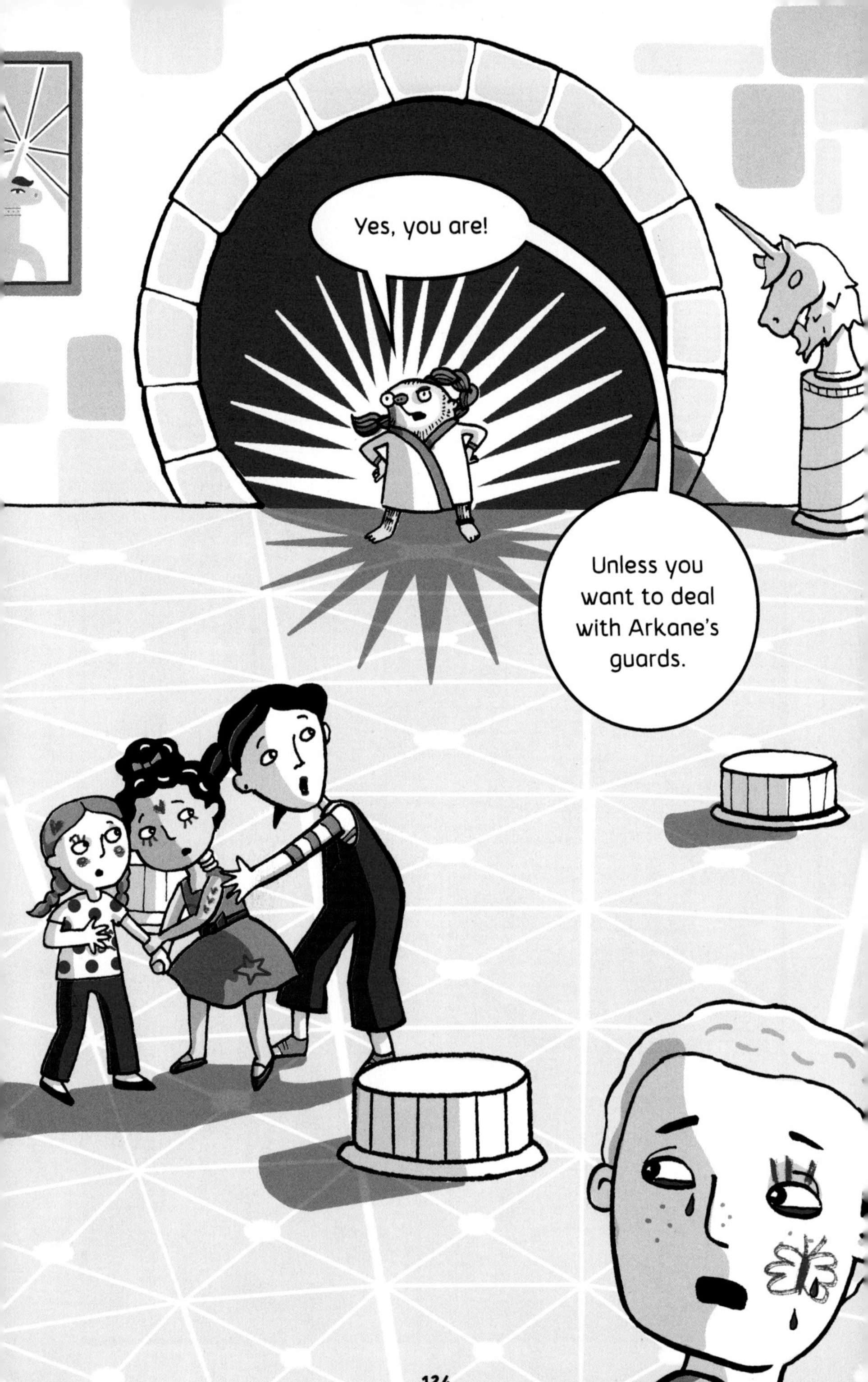
Yes, you are!
Unless you want to deal with Arkane's guards.

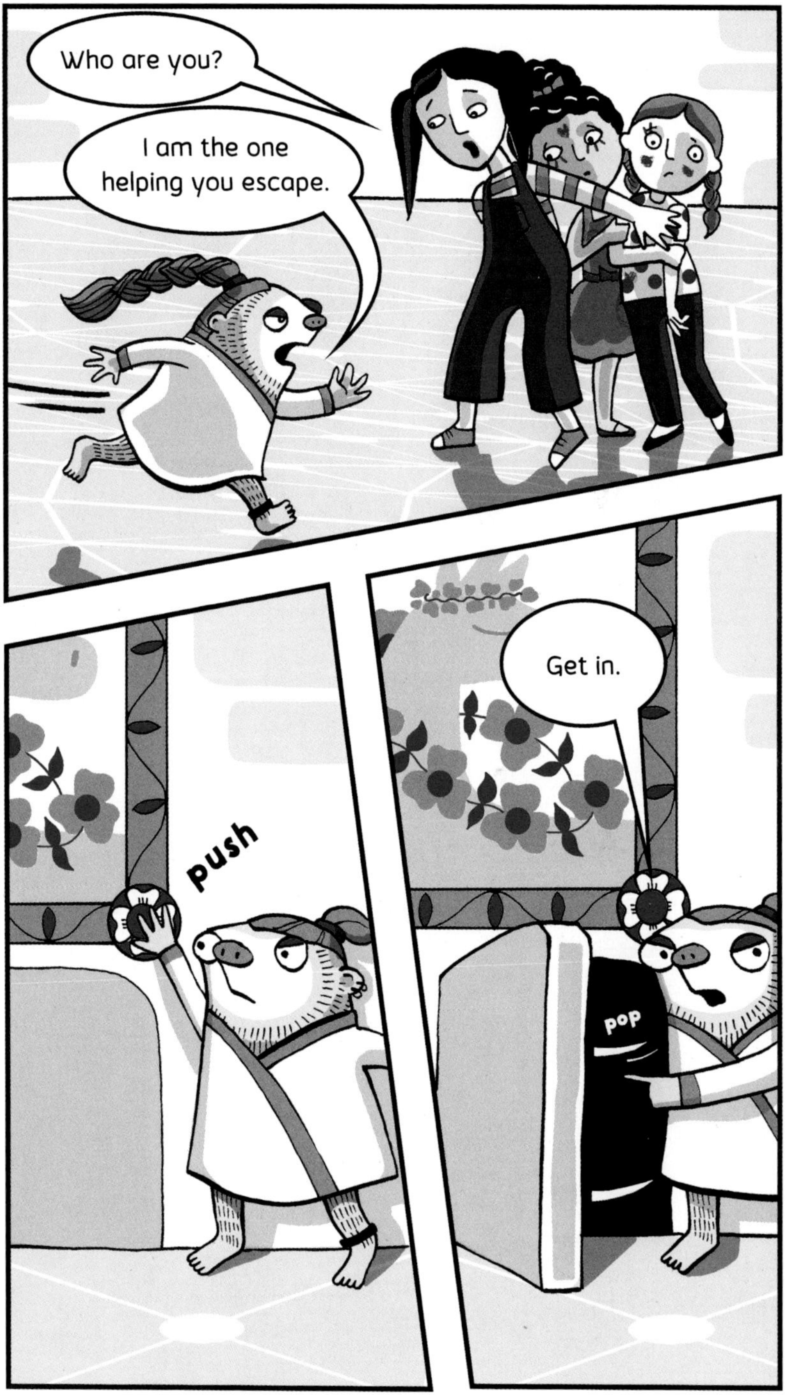
Who are you?
I am the one helping you escape.
push
Get in.
pop

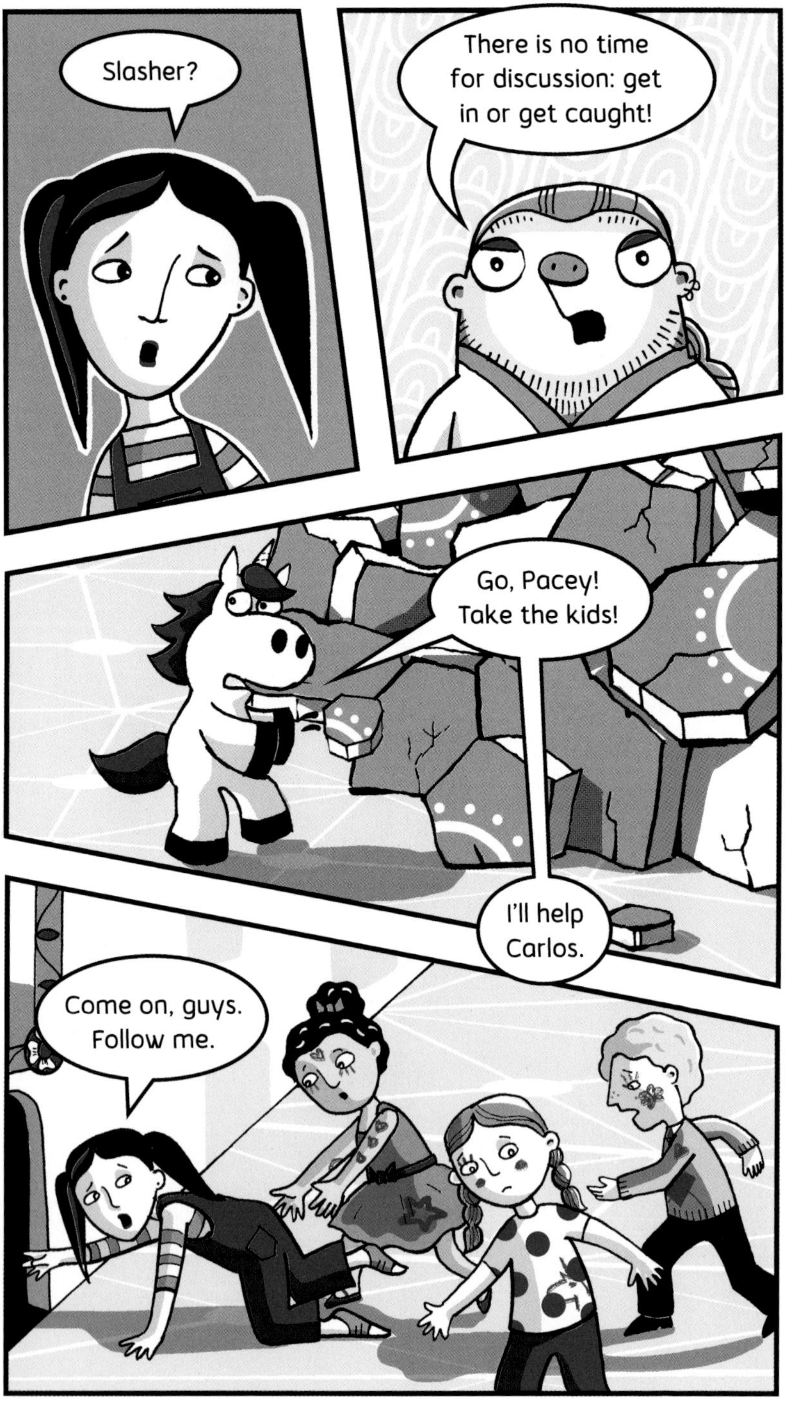
Slasher?
There is no time for discussion: get in or get caught!
Go, Pacey! Take the kids!
I'll help Carlos.
Come on, guys. Follow me.

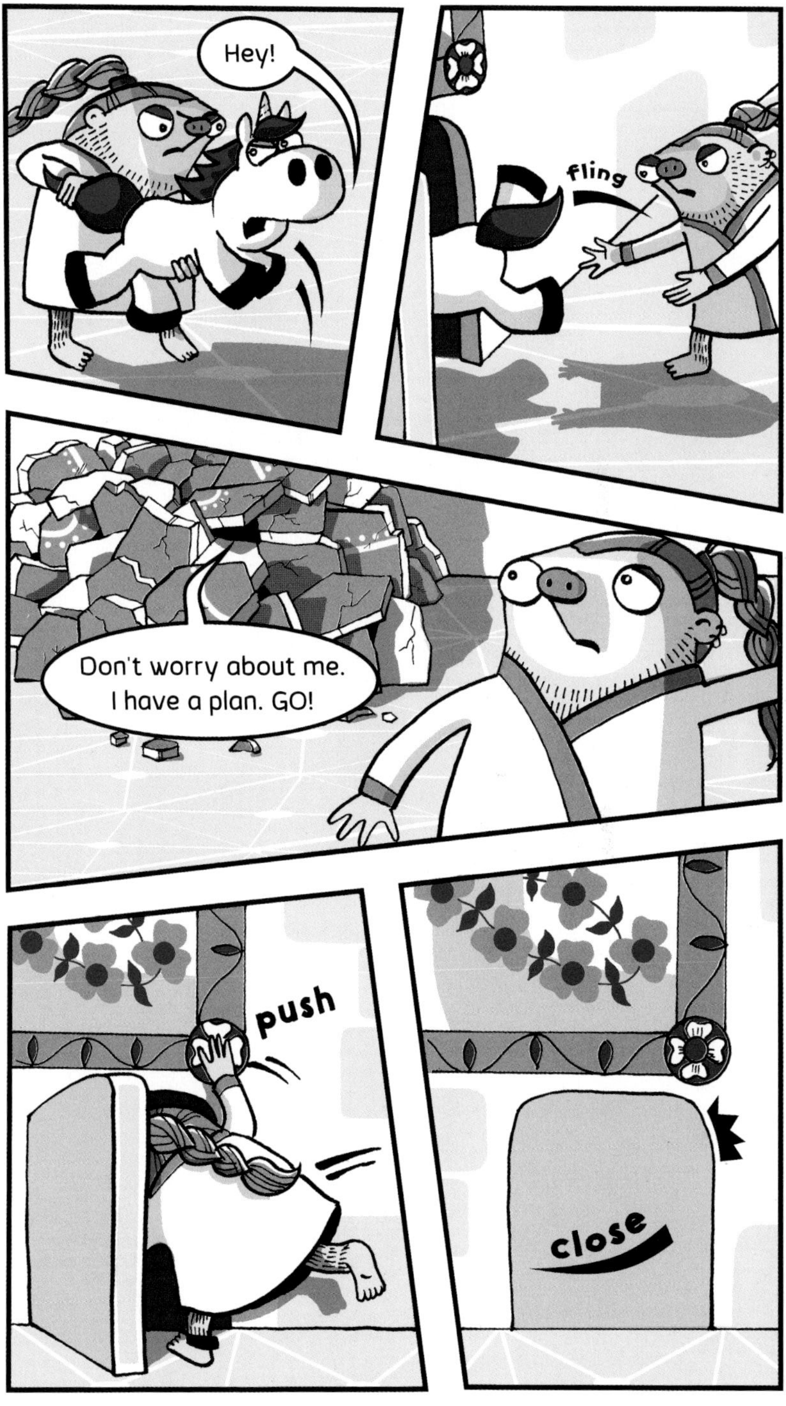
Hey!
fling
Don't worry about me.
I have a plan. GO!
push
close

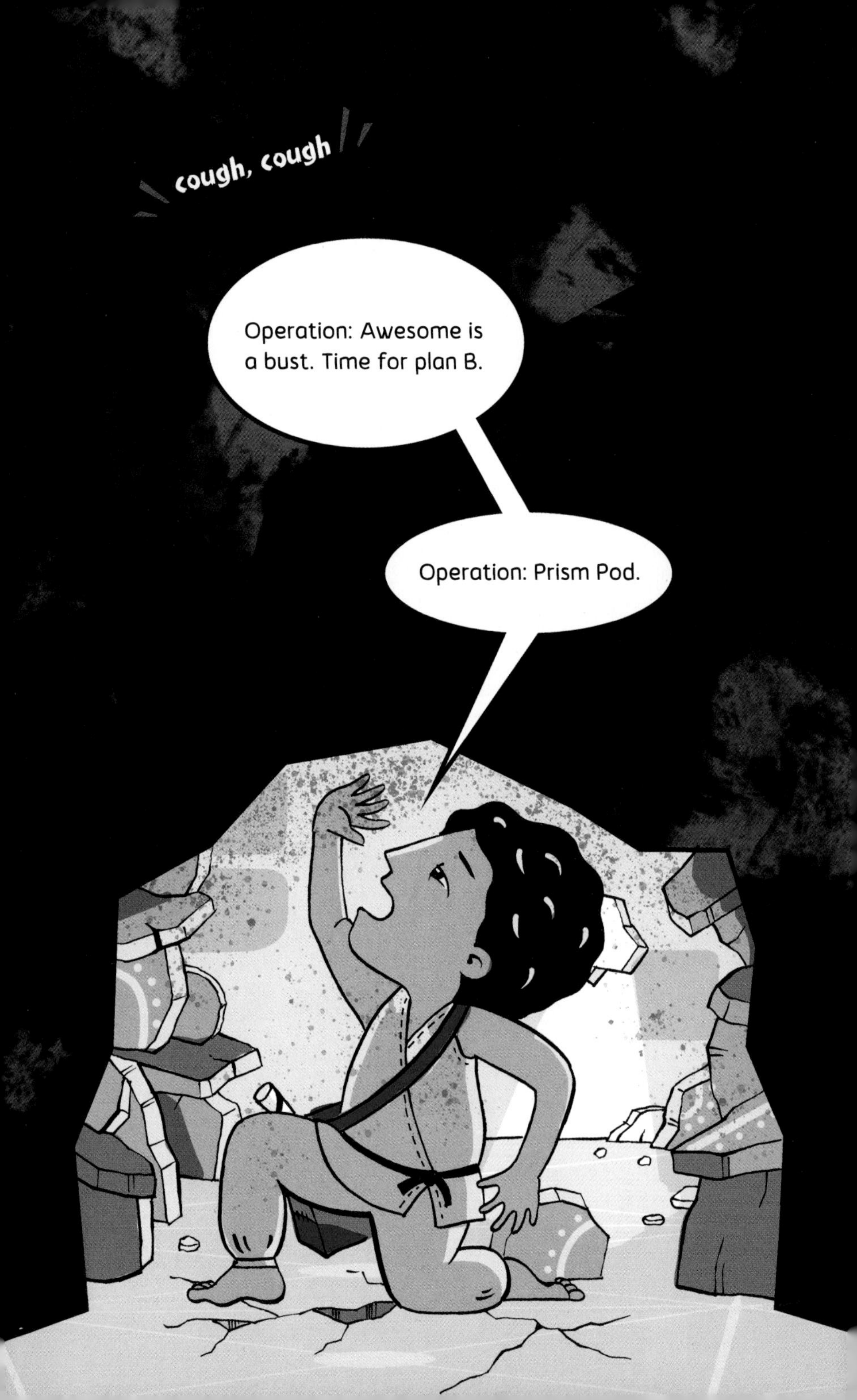
cough, cough
Operation: Awesome is a bust. Time for plan B.
Operation: Prism Pod.

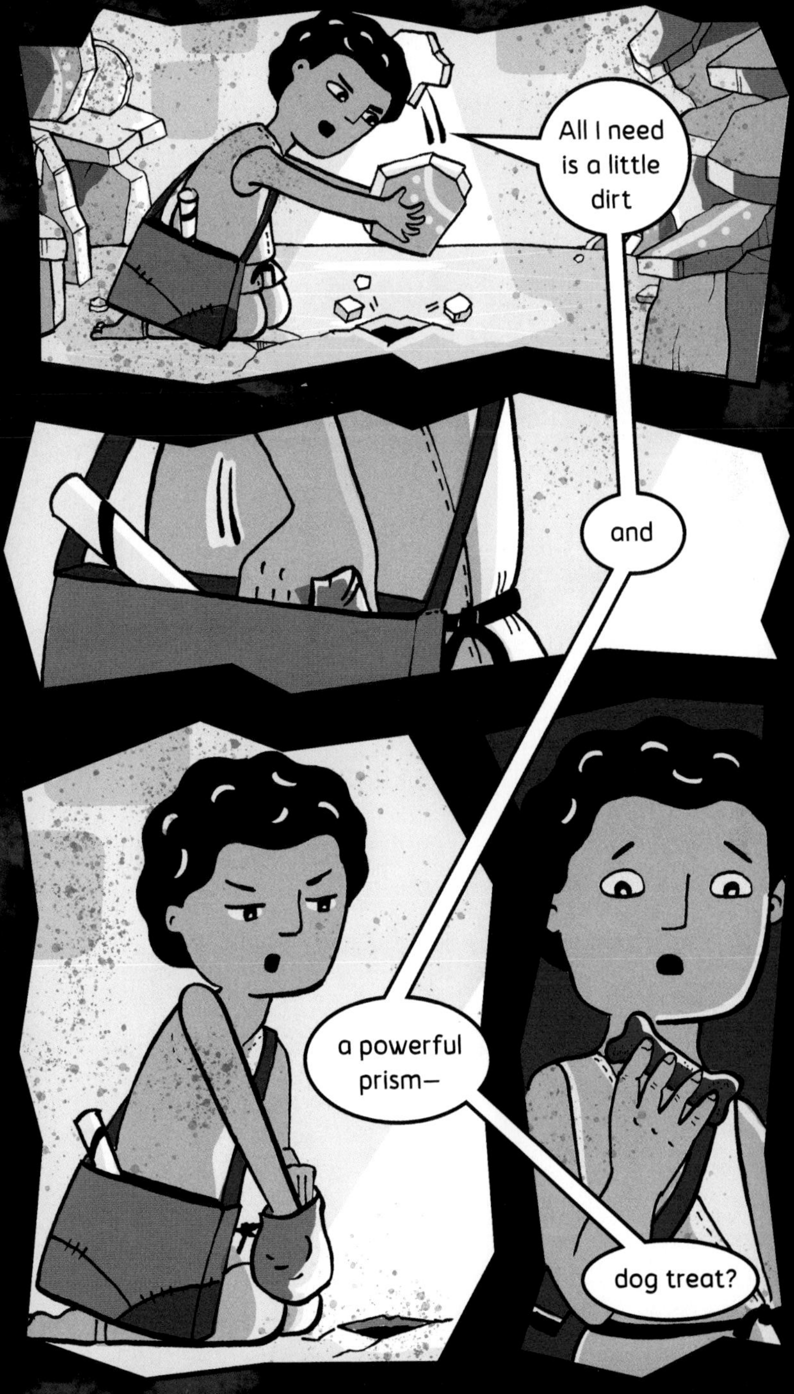
All I need is a little dirt
and
a powerful prism—
dog treat?

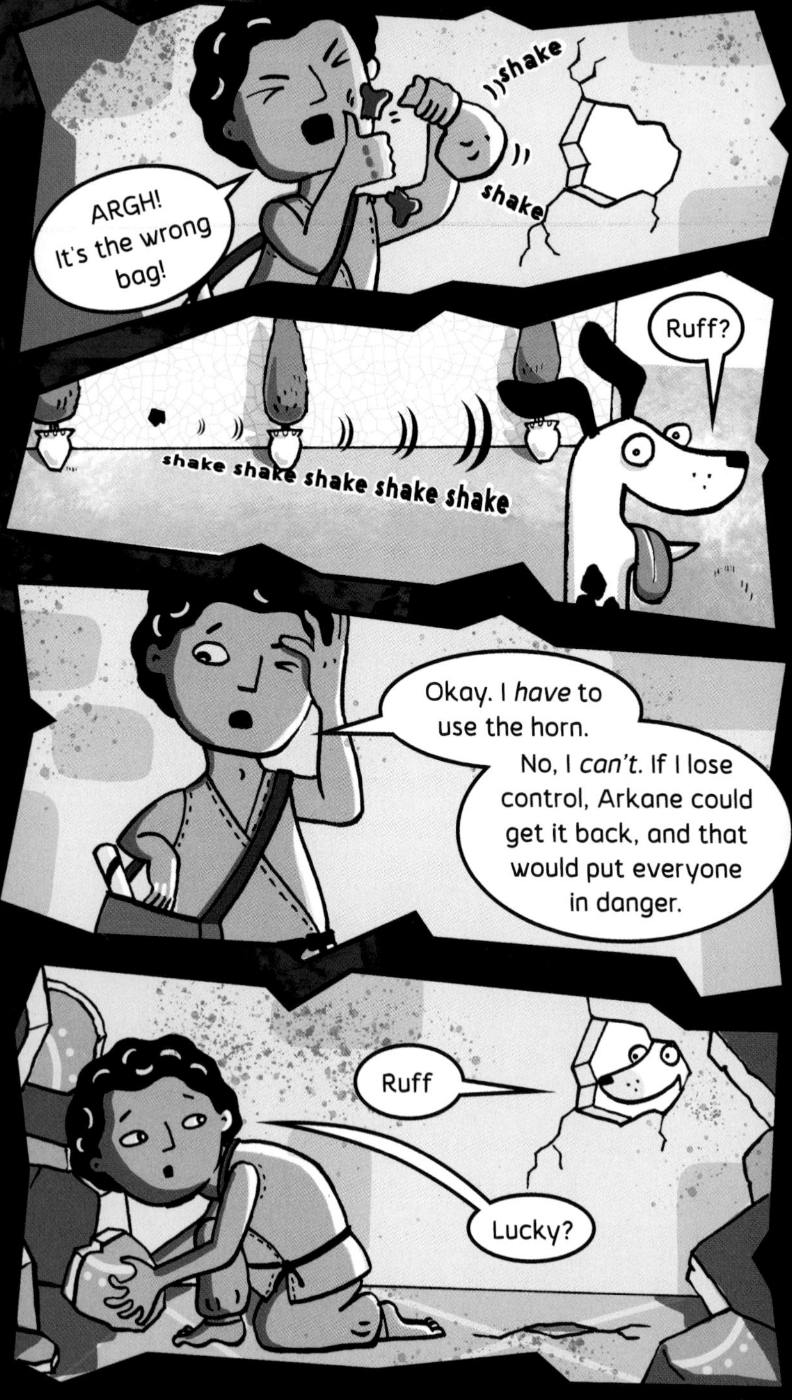
ARGH! It's the wrong bag!
shake
shake
Ruff?
shake shake shake shake shake
Okay. I *have* to use the horn.
No, I *can't*. If I lose control, Arkane could get it back, and that would put everyone in danger.
Ruff
Lucky?

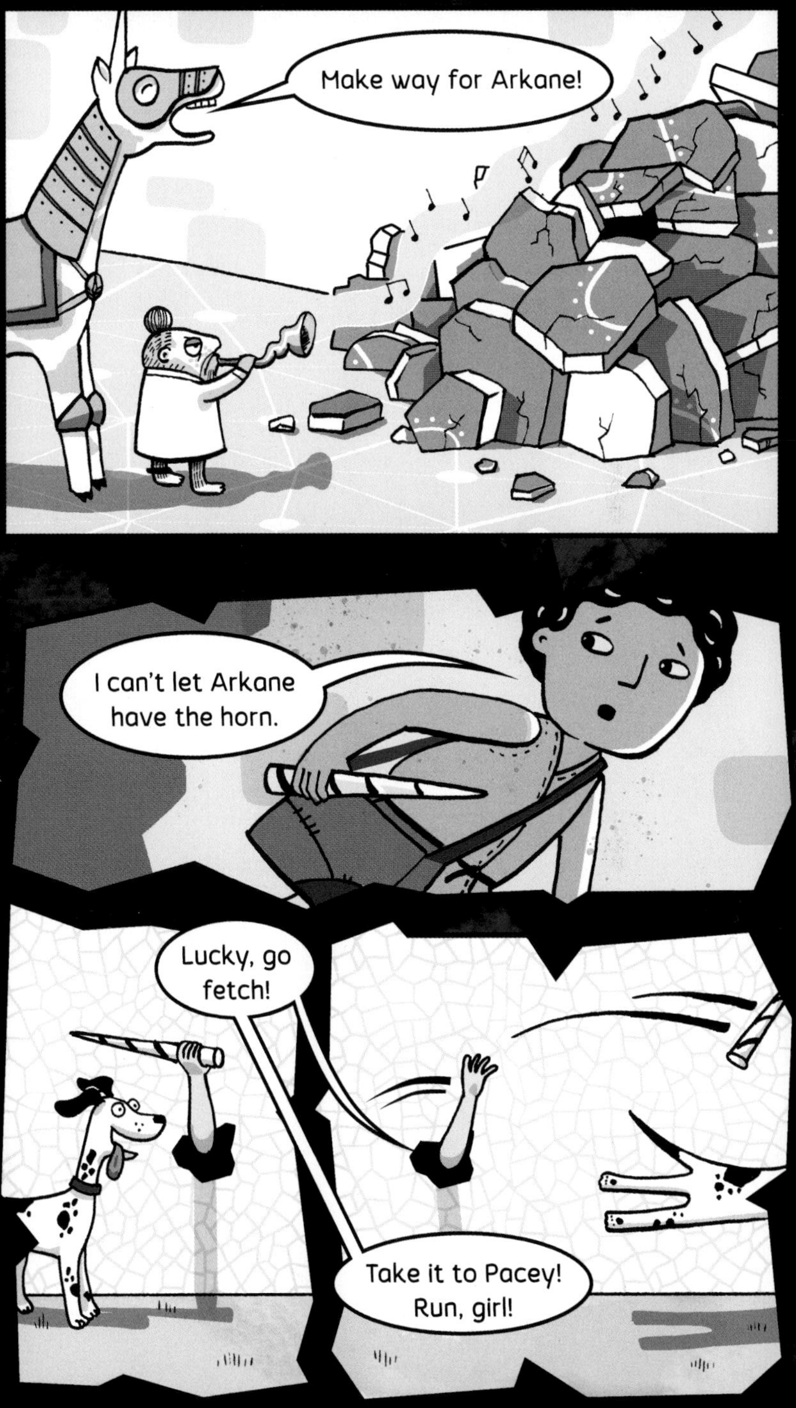
Make way for Arkane!
I can't let Arkane have the horn.
Lucky, go fetch!
Take it to Pacey! Run, girl!

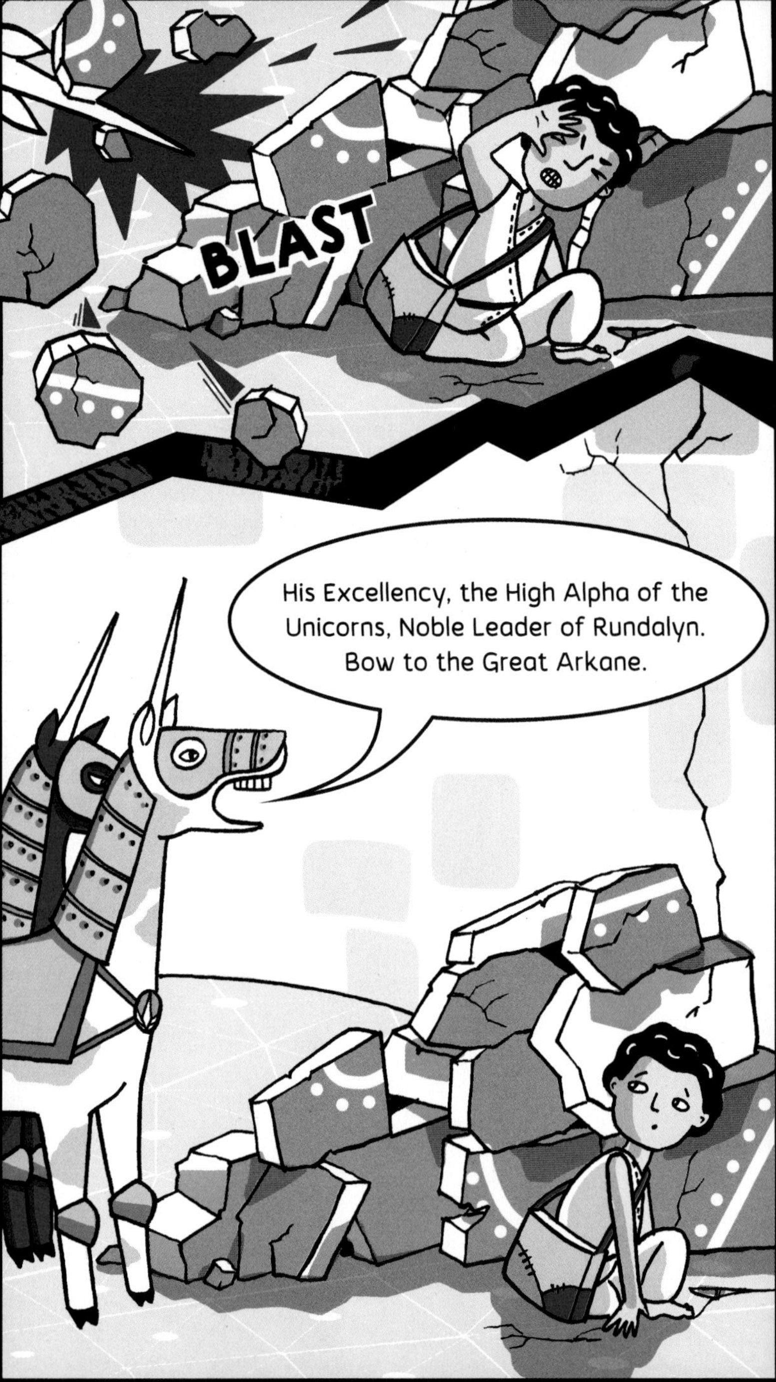
BLAST
His Excellency, the High Alpha of the Unicorns, Noble Leader of Rundalyn. Bow to the Great Arkane.

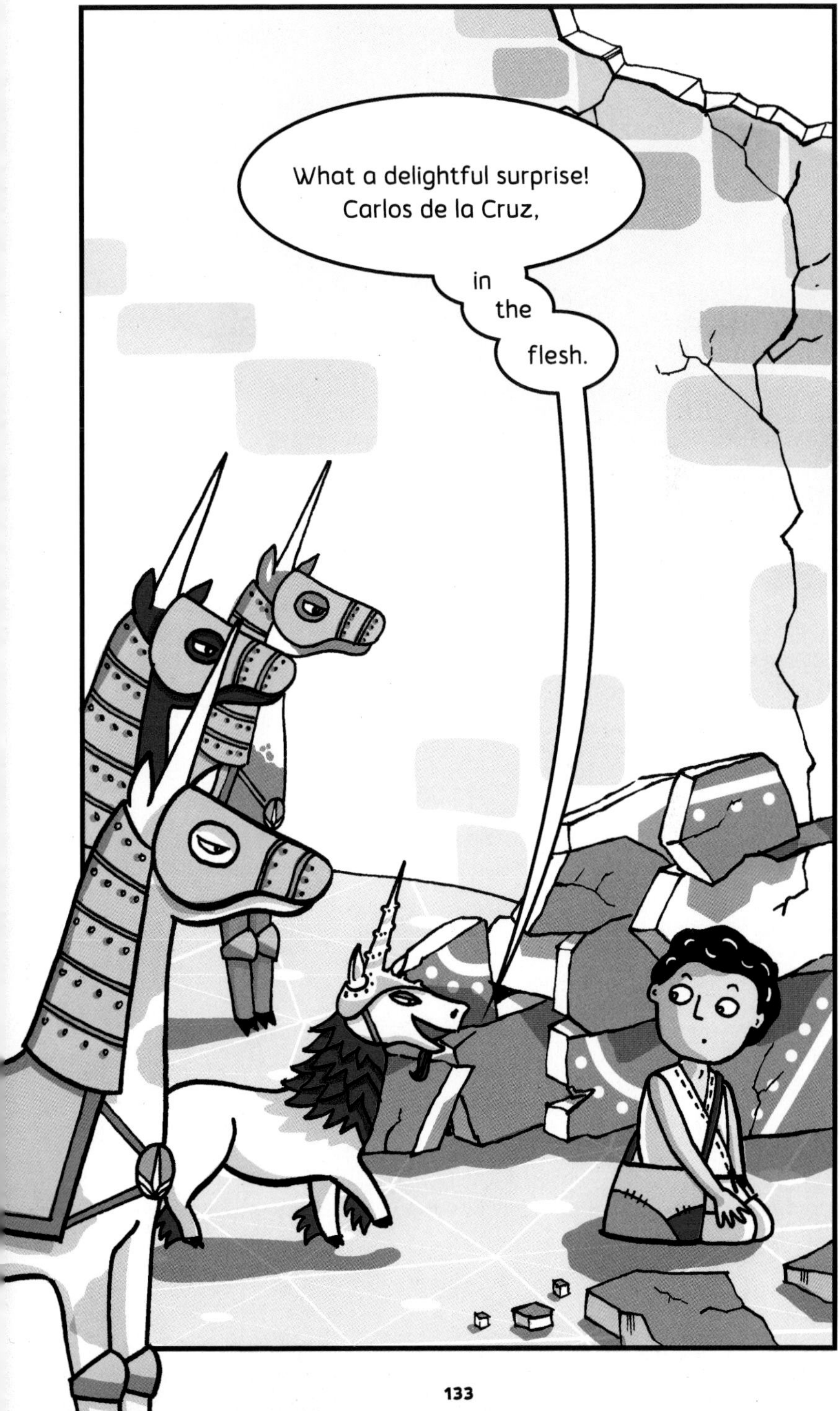
What a delightful surprise!
Carlos de la Cruz,
in the flesh.

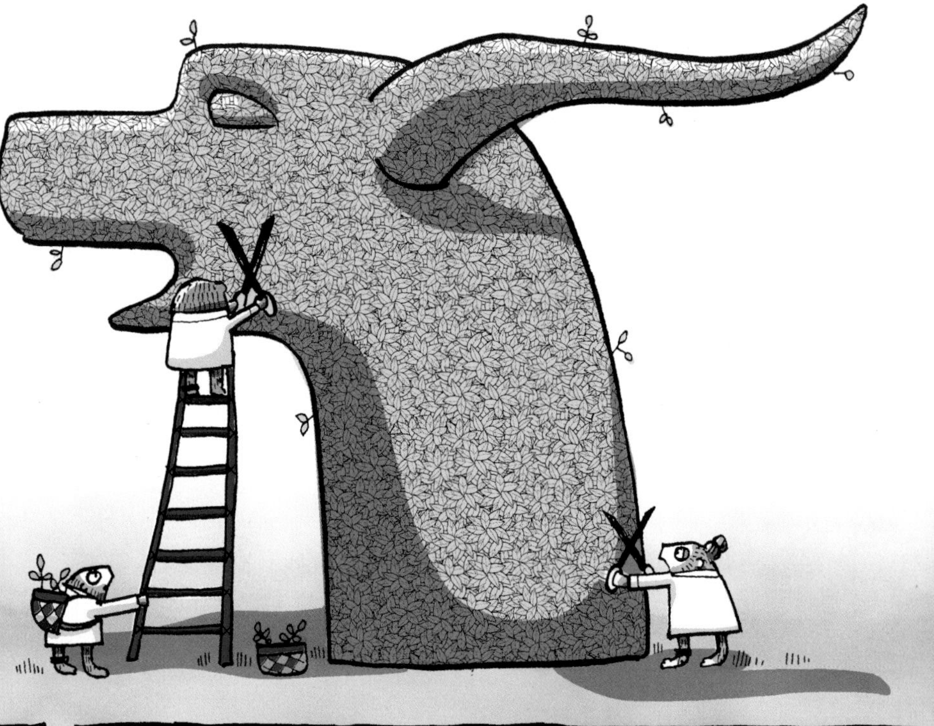

Chapter 10
DAZED

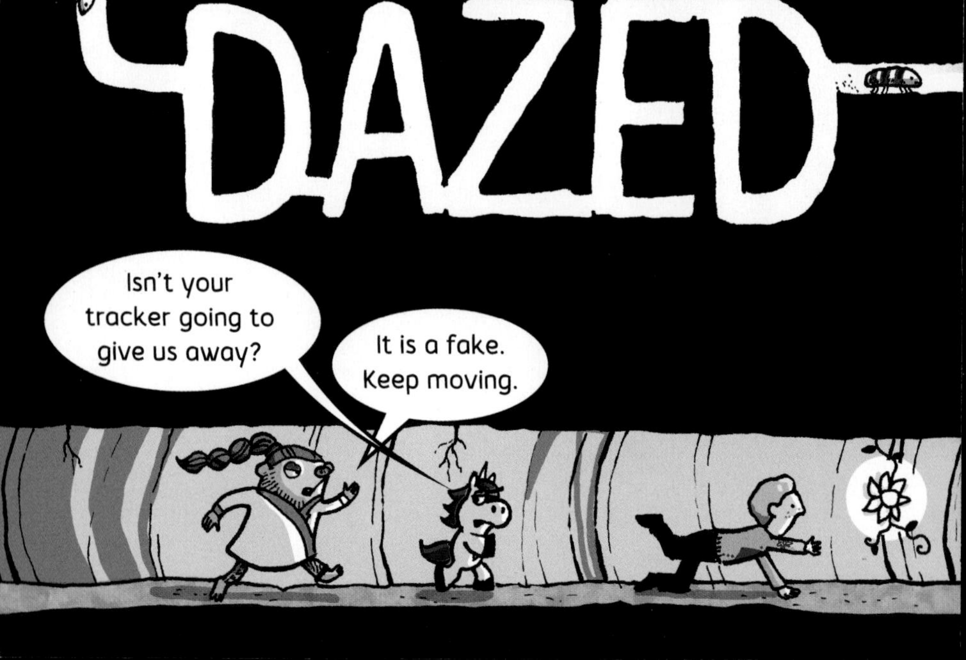
Isn't your tracker going to give us away?
It is a fake. Keep moving.

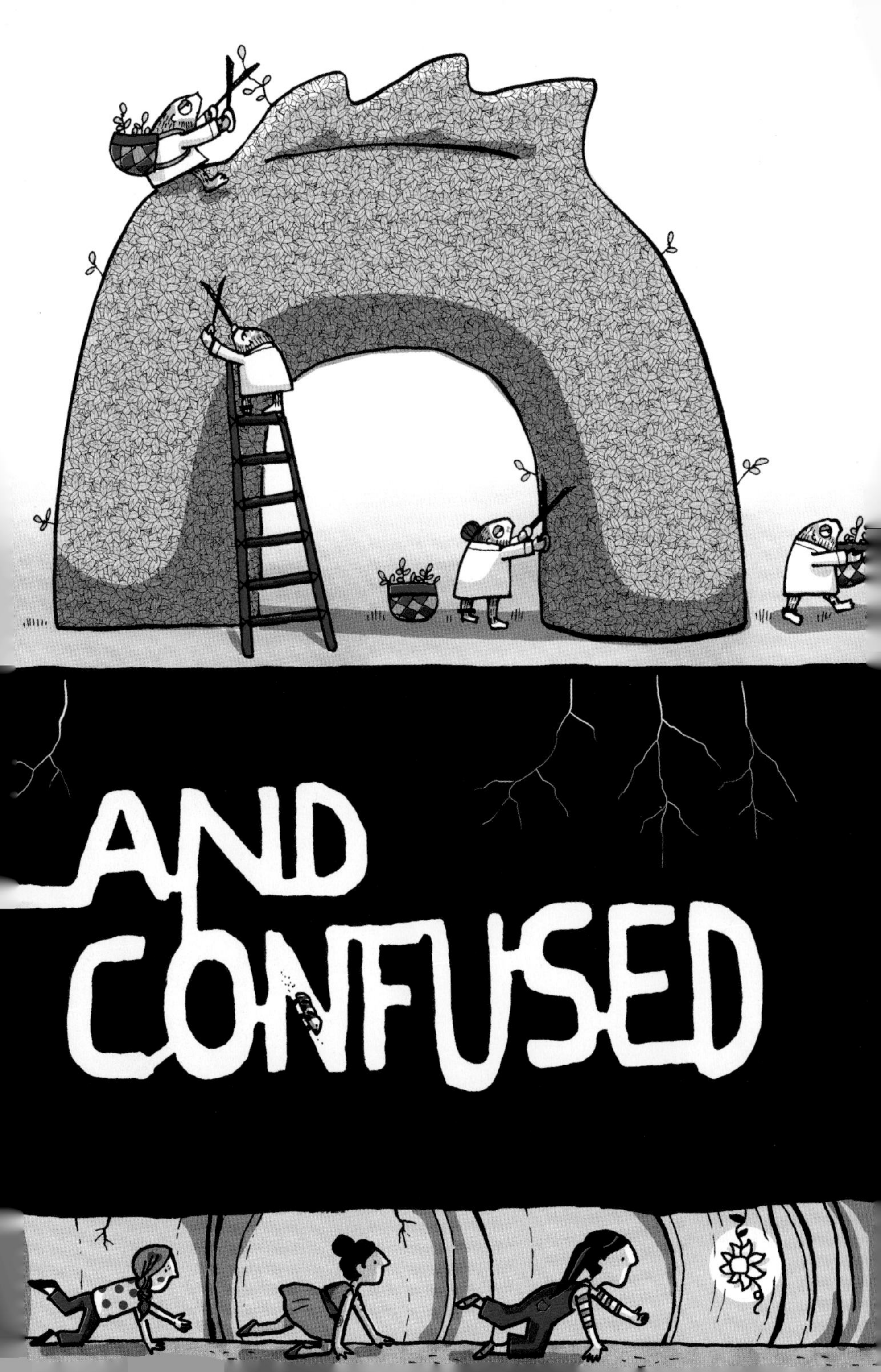
AND
CONFUSED

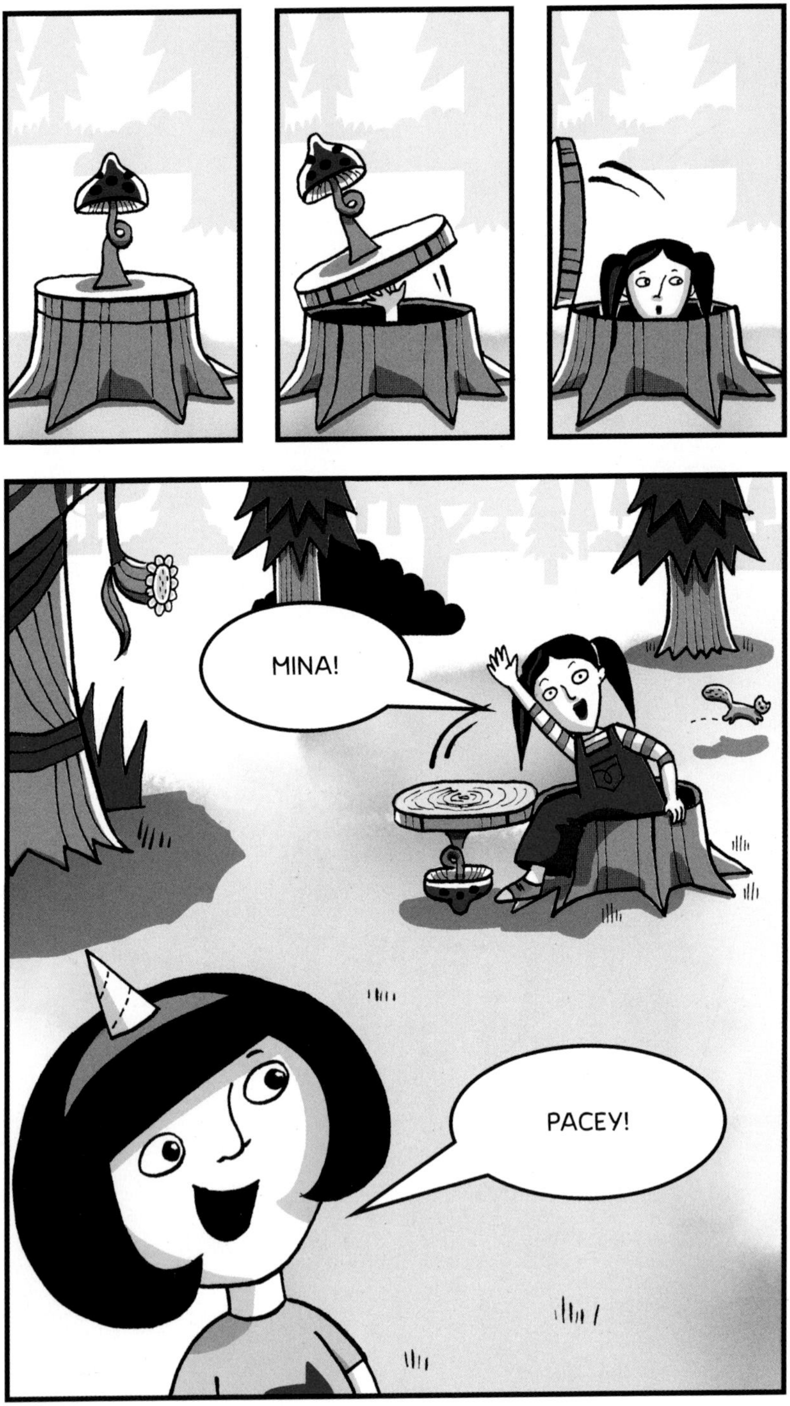
MINA!
PACEY!

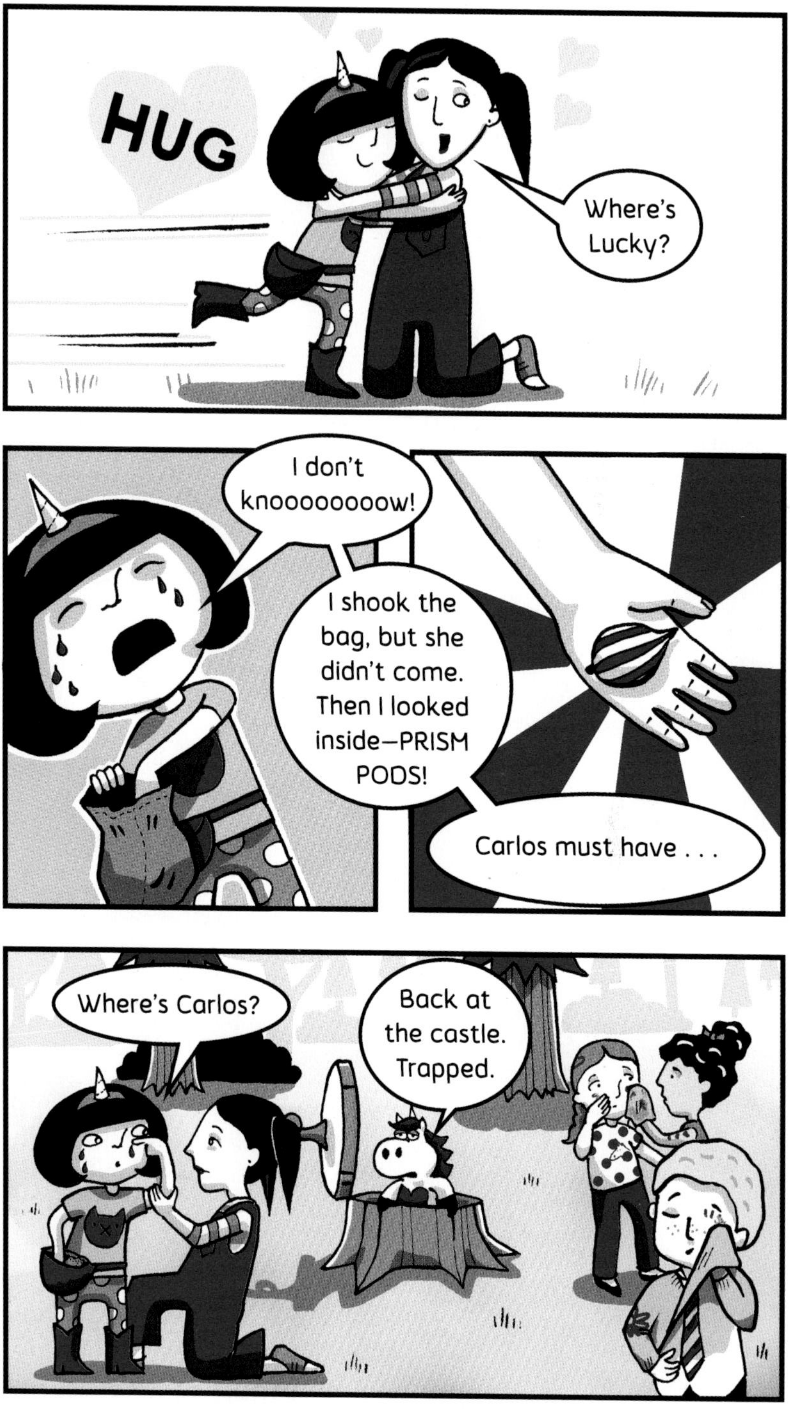
HUG
Where's Lucky?
I don't knooooooooow!
I shook the bag, but she didn't come. Then I looked inside—PRISM PODS!
Carlos must have . . .
Where's Carlos?
Back at the castle. Trapped.

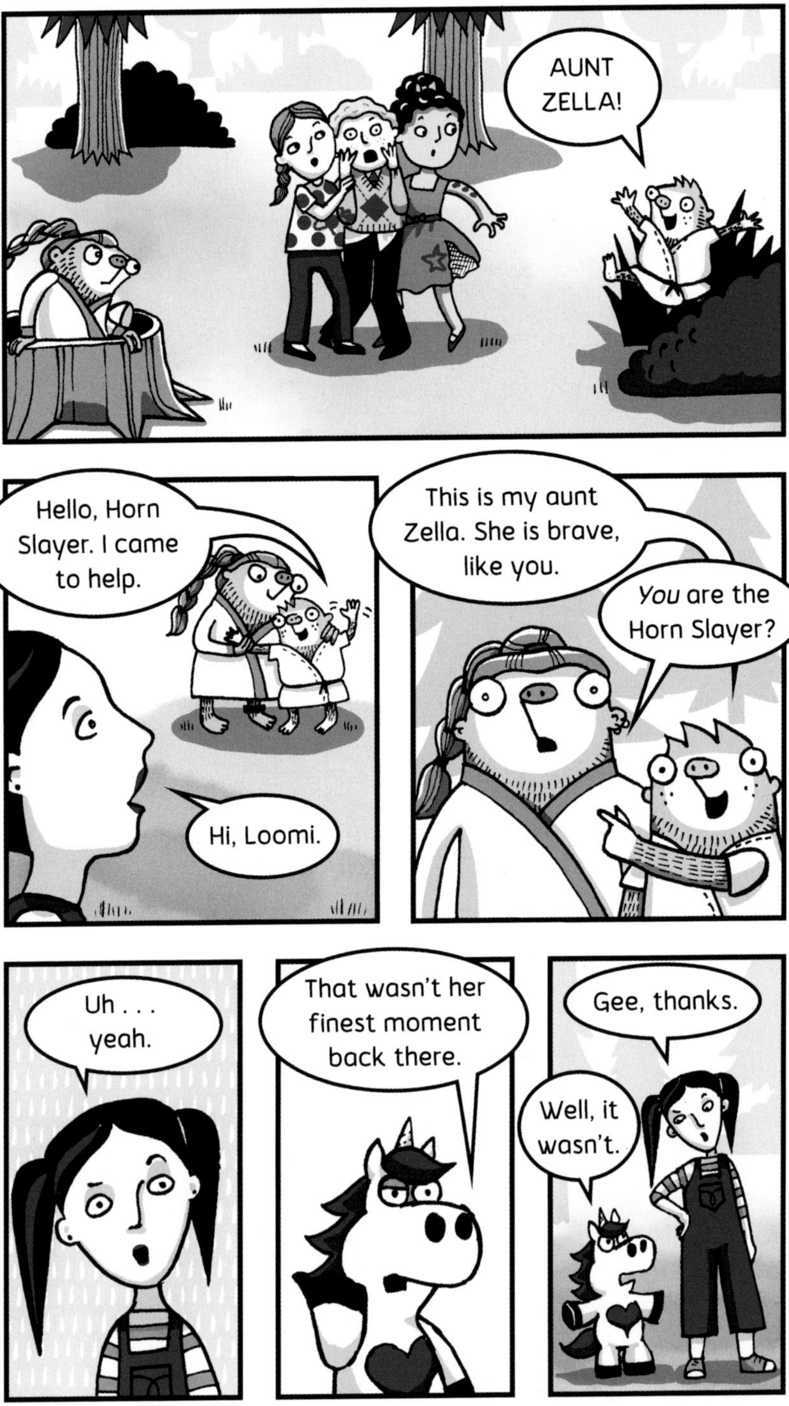
AUNT ZELLA!
Hello, Horn Slayer. I came to help.
Hi, Loomi.
This is my aunt Zella. She is brave, like you.
You are the Horn Slayer?
Uh . . . yeah.
That wasn't her finest moment back there.
Gee, thanks.
Well, it wasn't.

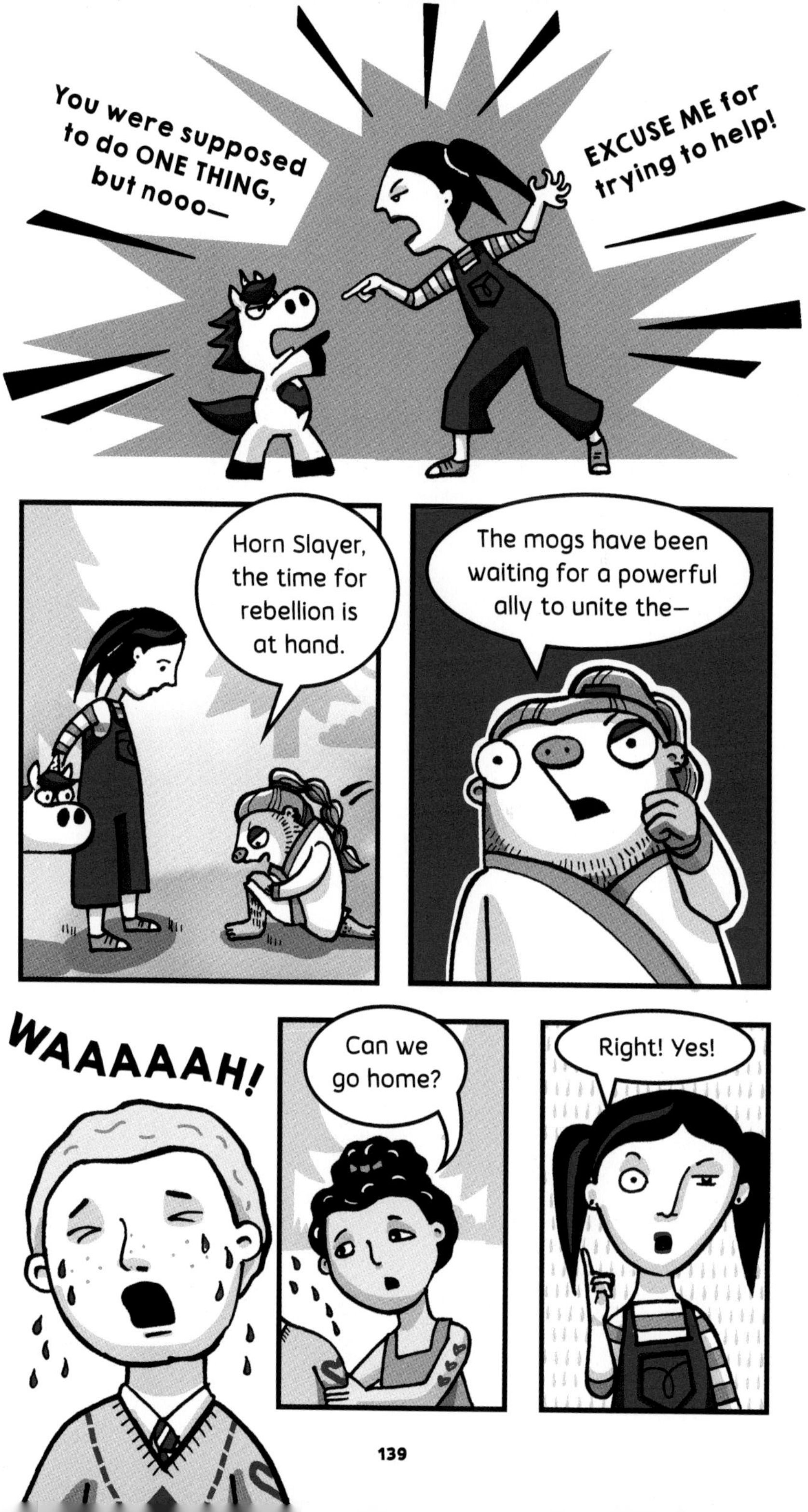
You were supposed to do ONE THING, but nooo—
EXCUSE ME for trying to help!
Horn Slayer, the time for rebellion is at hand.
The mogs have been waiting for a powerful ally to unite the—
WAAAAAH!
Can we go home?
Right! Yes!

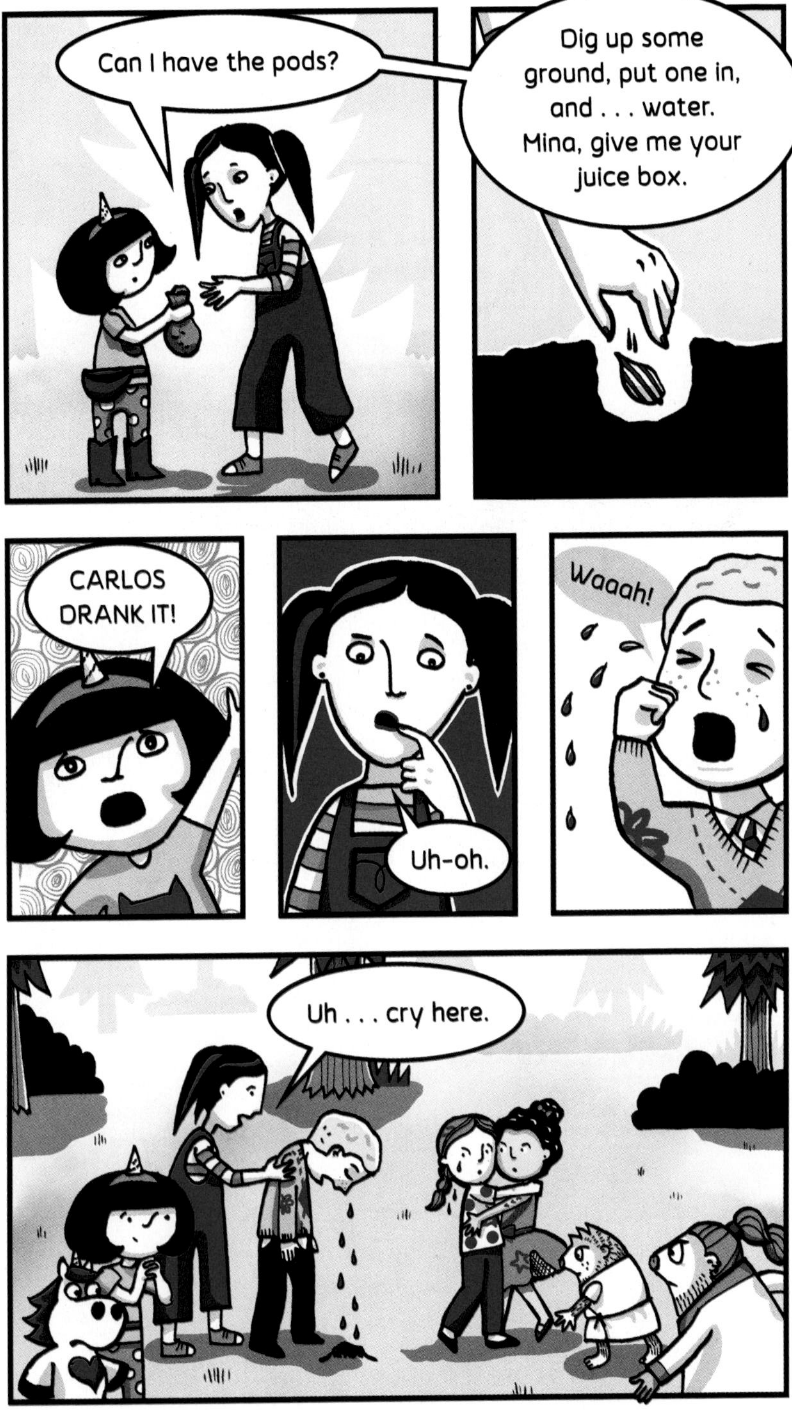
Can I have the pods?
Dig up some ground, put one in, and . . . water. Mina, give me your juice box.
CARLOS DRANK IT!
Uh-oh.
Waaah!
Uh . . . cry here.

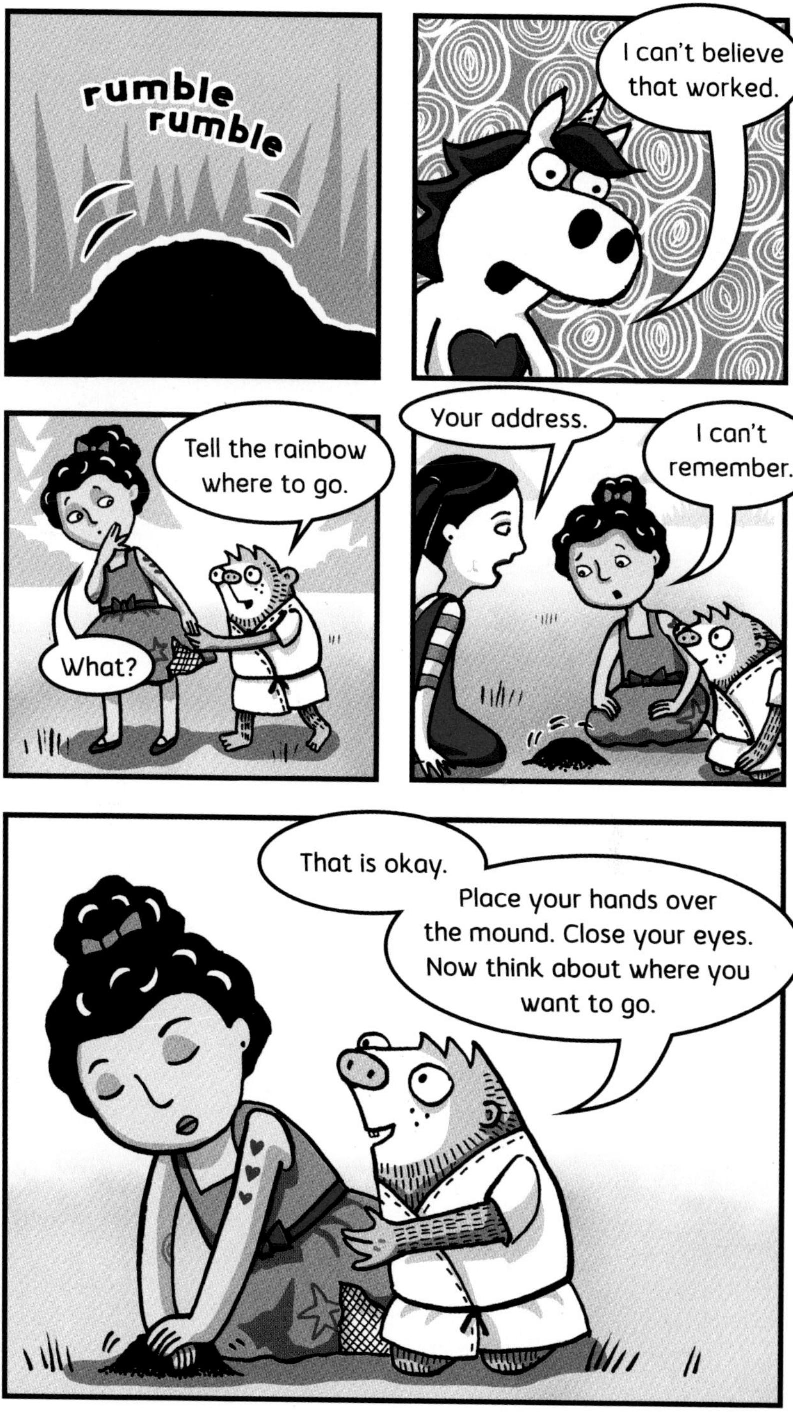

rumble rumble
I can't believe that worked.
Tell the rainbow where to go.
What?
Your address.
I can't remember.
That is okay.
Place your hands over the mound. Close your eyes. Now think about where you want to go.

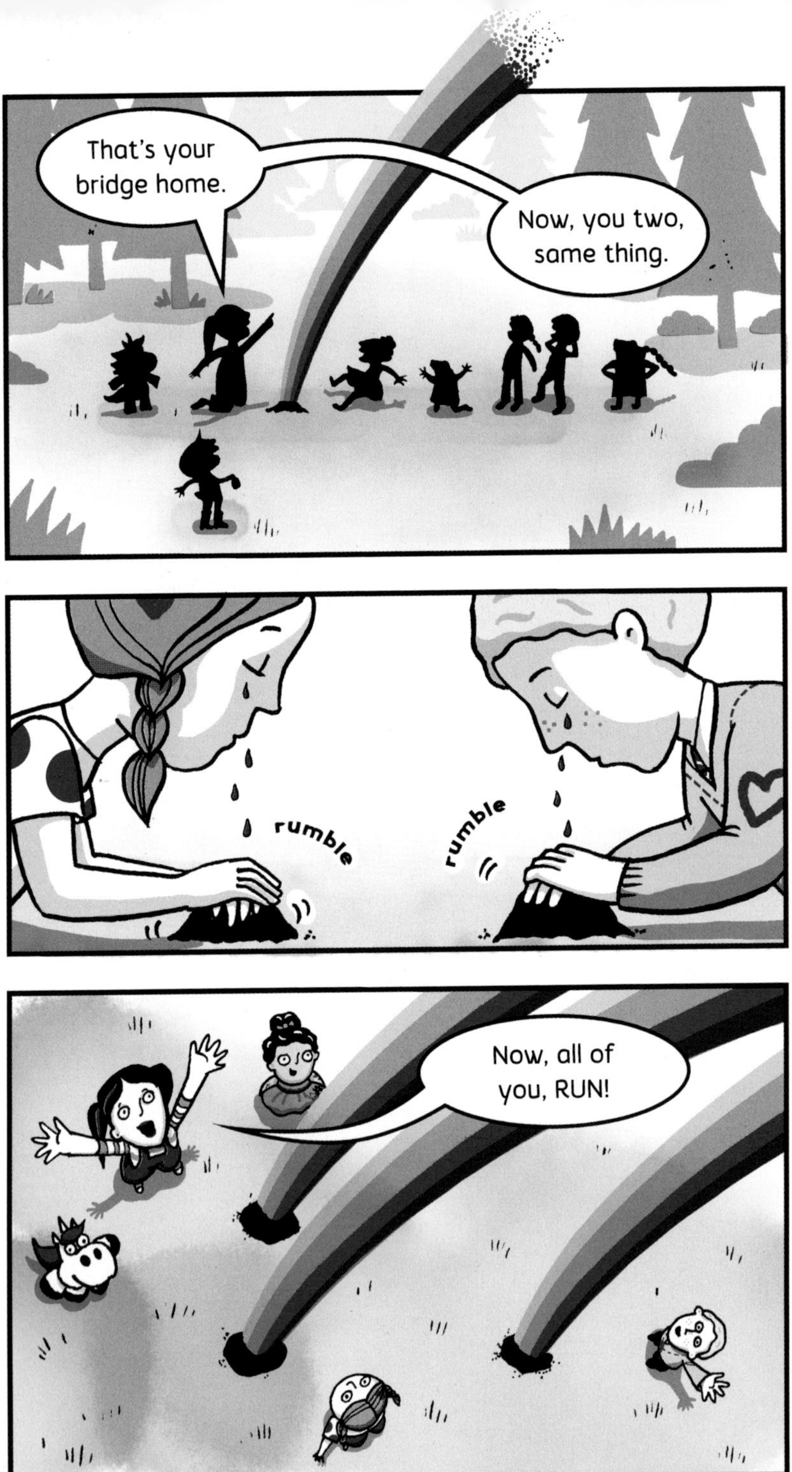
That's your bridge home.
Now, you two, same thing.
rumble
rumble
Now, all of you, RUN!

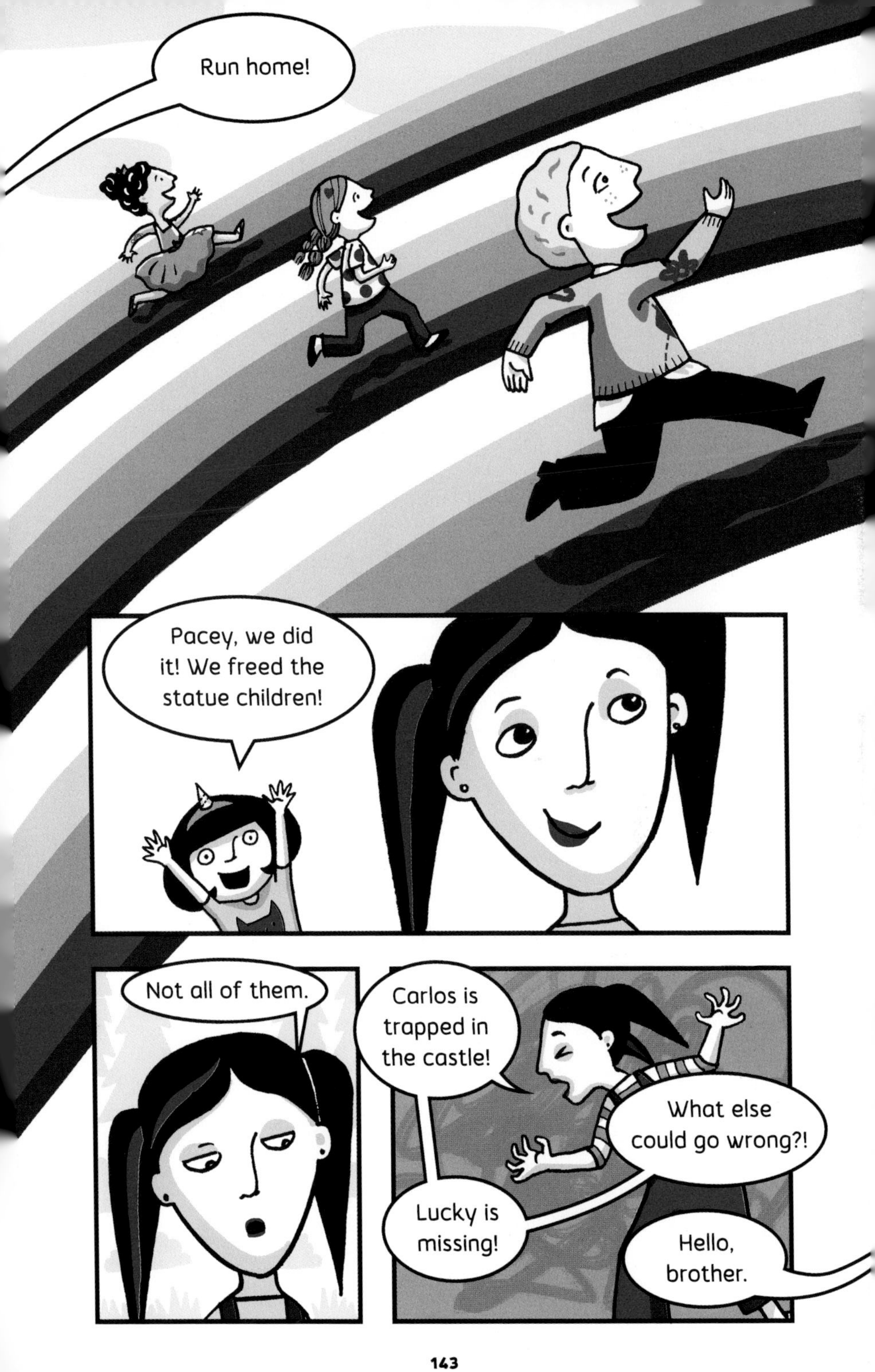
Run home!
Pacey, we did it! We freed the statue children!
Not all of them.
Carlos is trapped in the castle!
Lucky is missing!
What else could go wrong?!
Hello, brother.

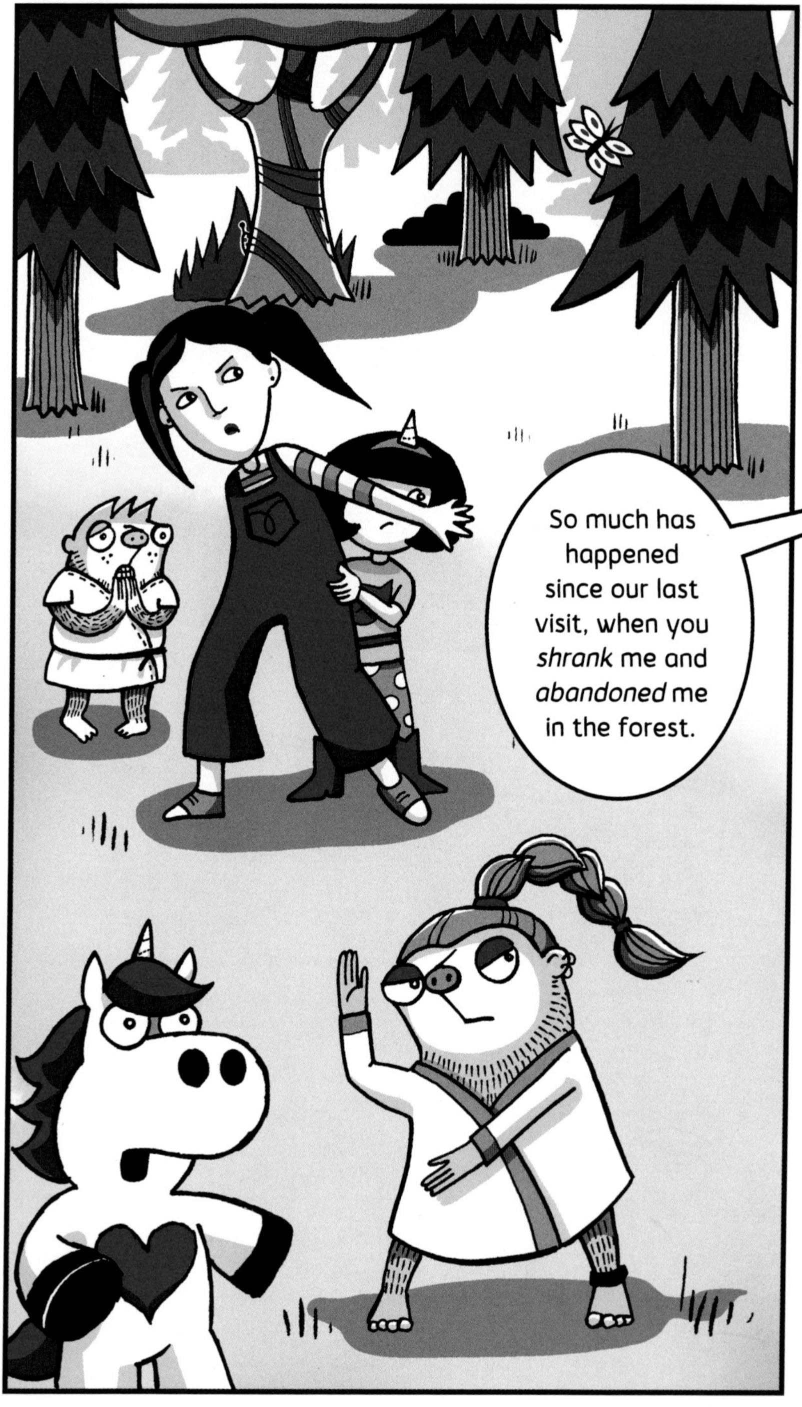
So much has happened since our last visit, when you *shrank* me and *abandoned* me in the forest.

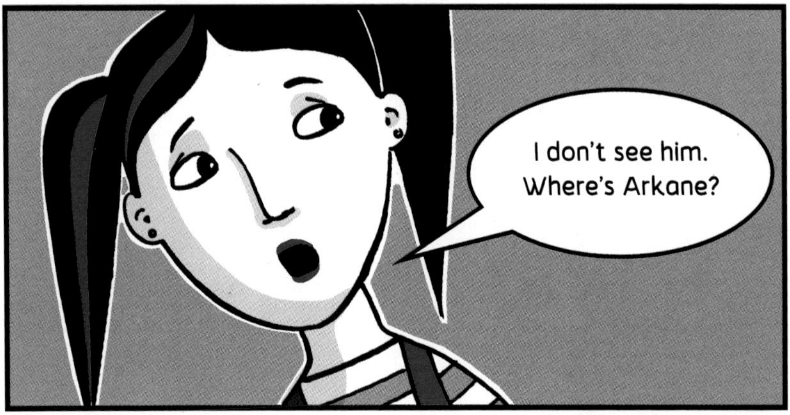
I don't see him.
Where's Arkane?

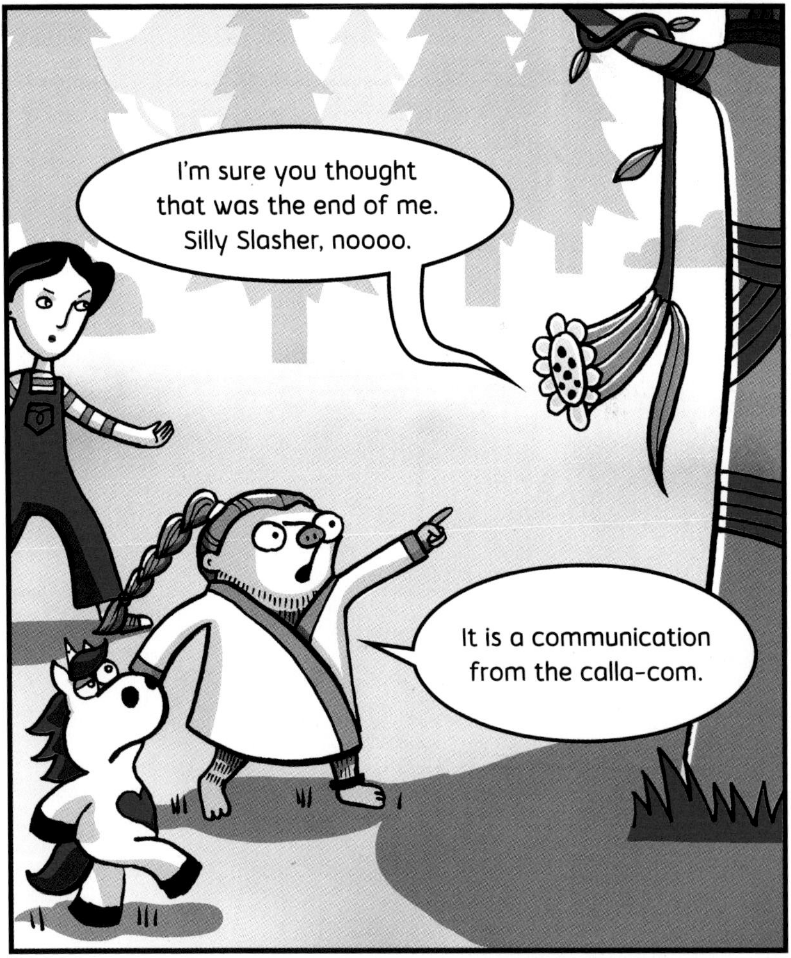
I'm sure you thought
that was the end of me.
Silly Slasher, noooo.
It is a communication
from the calla-com.

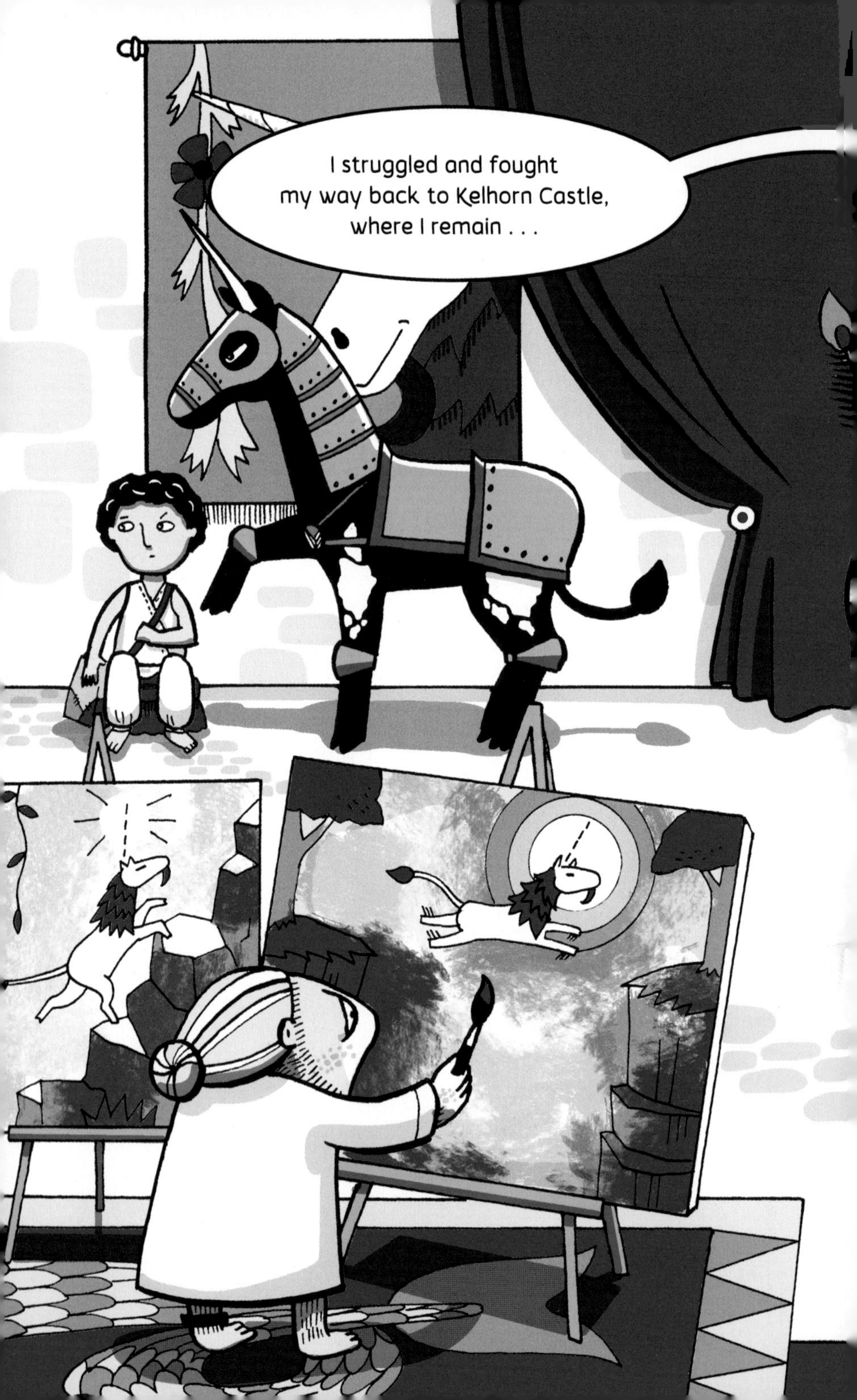
I struggled and fought my way back to Kelhorn Castle, where I remain . . .

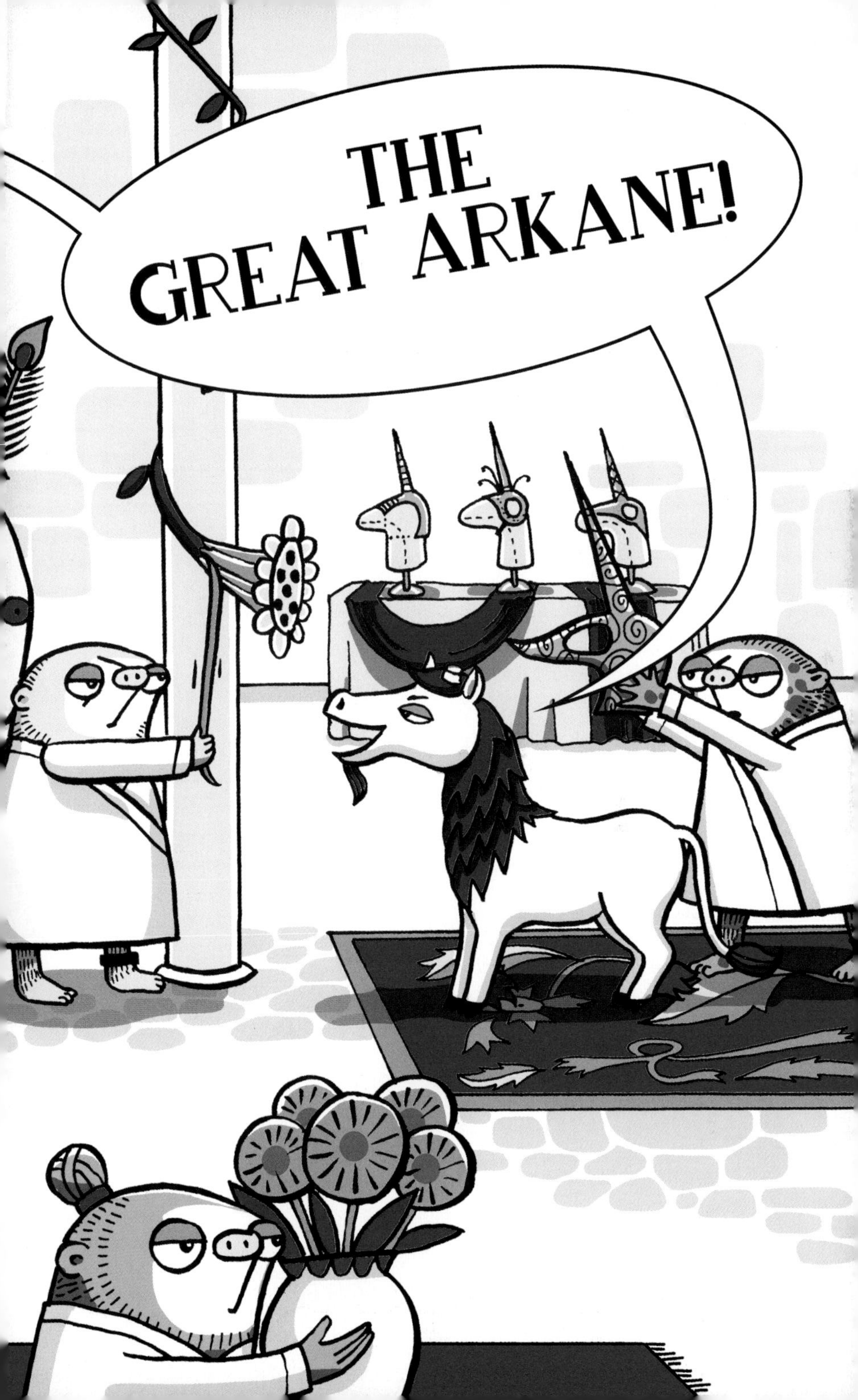
THE GREAT ARKANE!

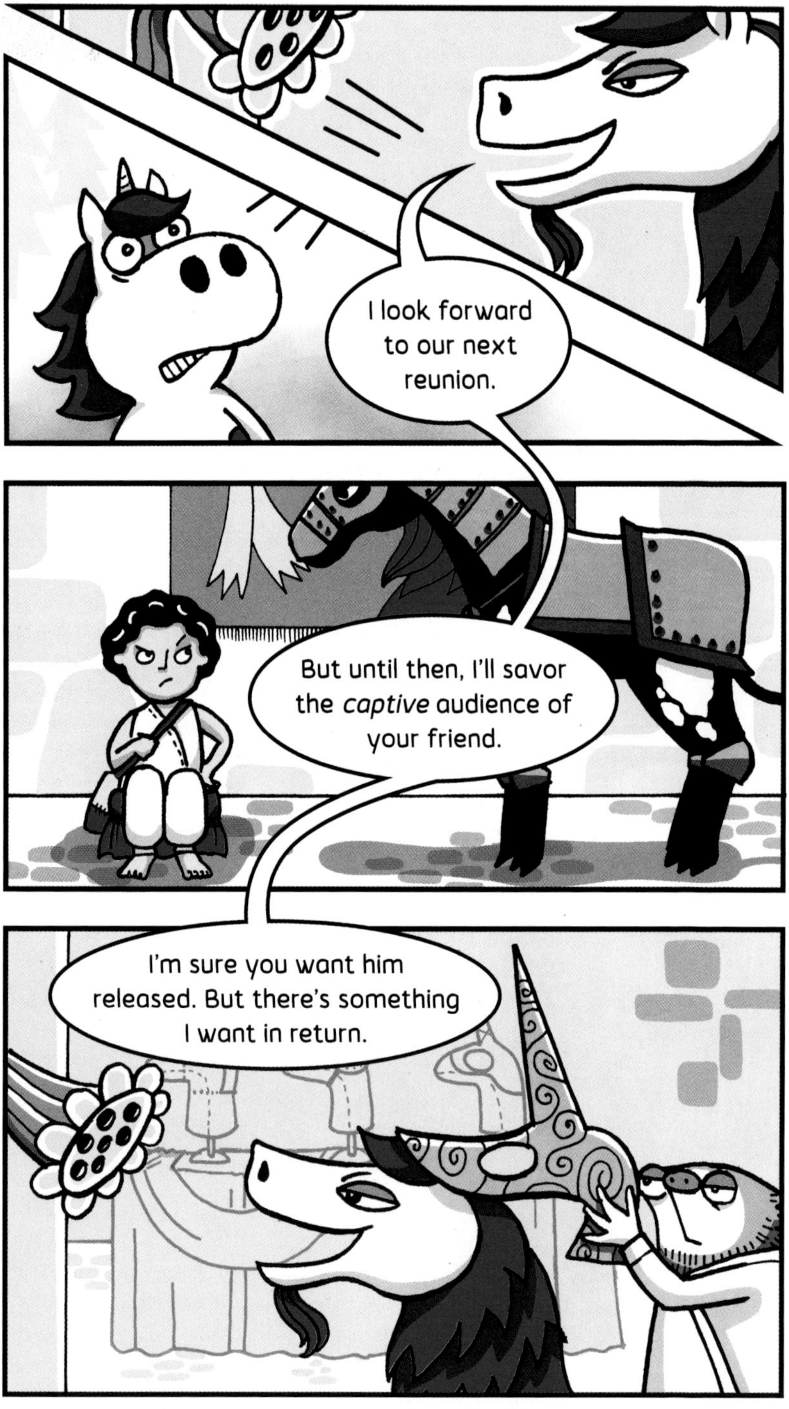
I look forward to our next reunion.
But until then, I'll savor the *captive* audience of your friend.
I'm sure you want him released. But there's something I want in return.

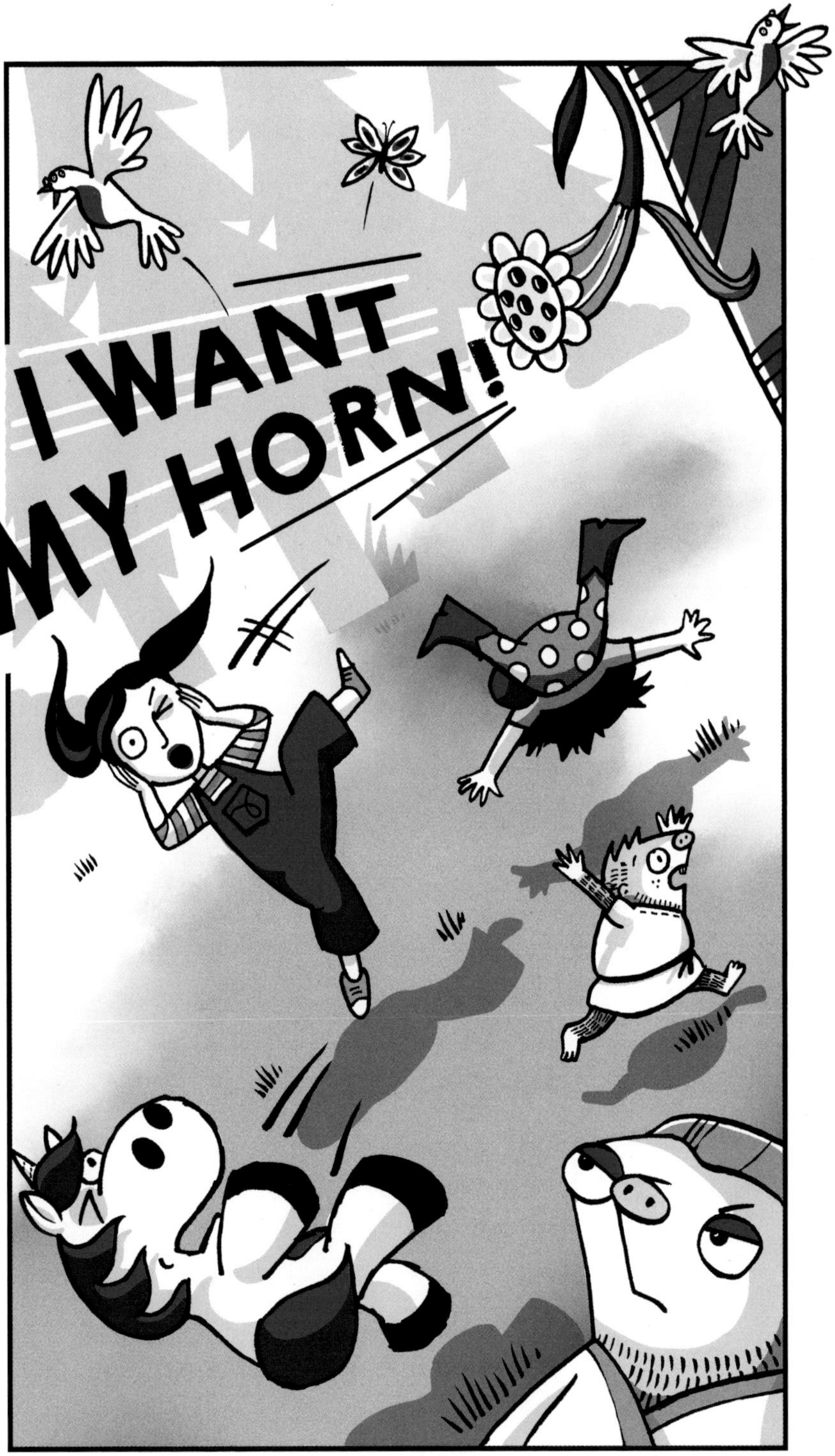
I WANT MY HORN!

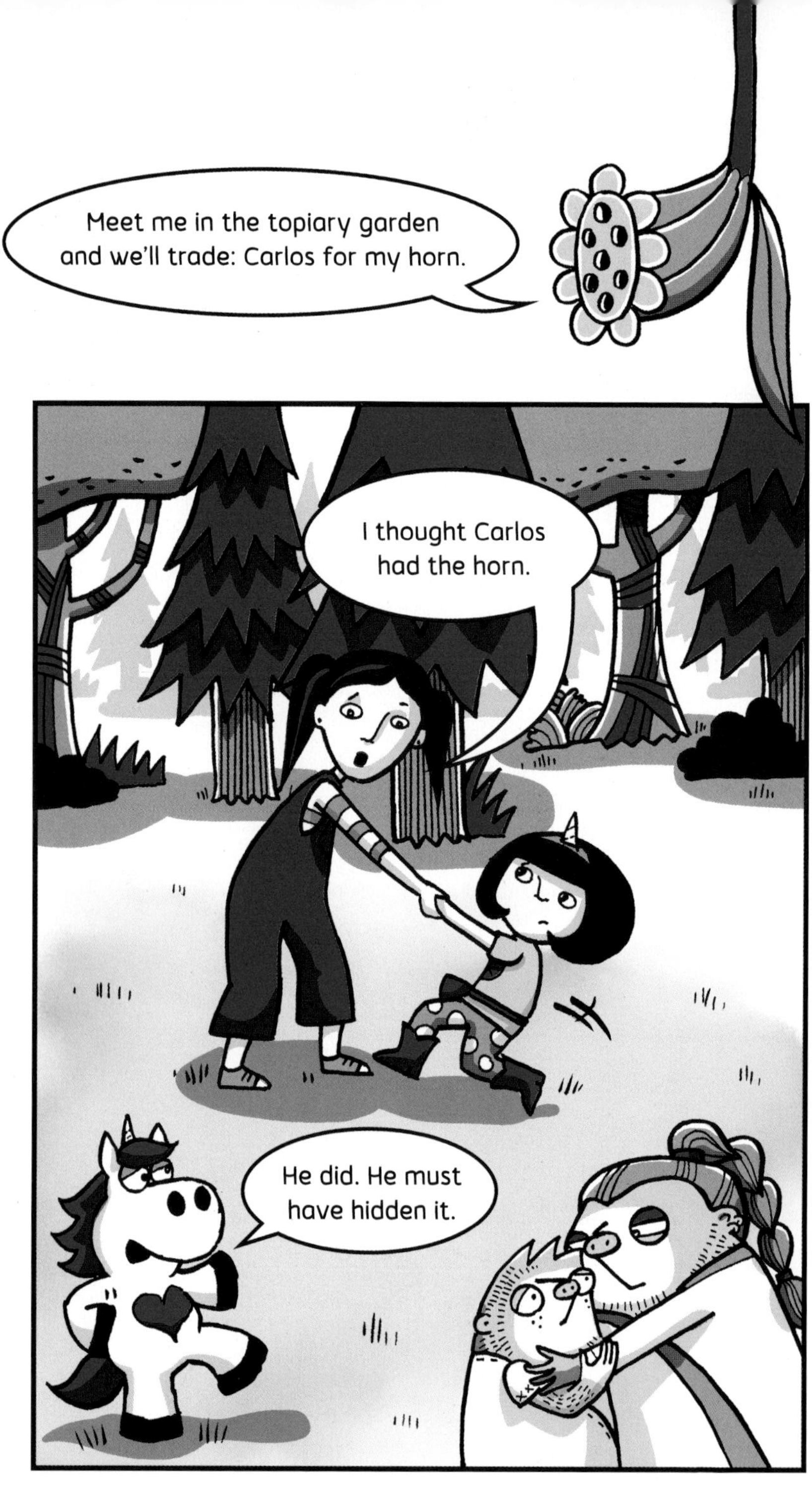
Meet me in the topiary garden and we'll trade: Carlos for my horn.
I thought Carlos had the horn.
He did. He must have hidden it.

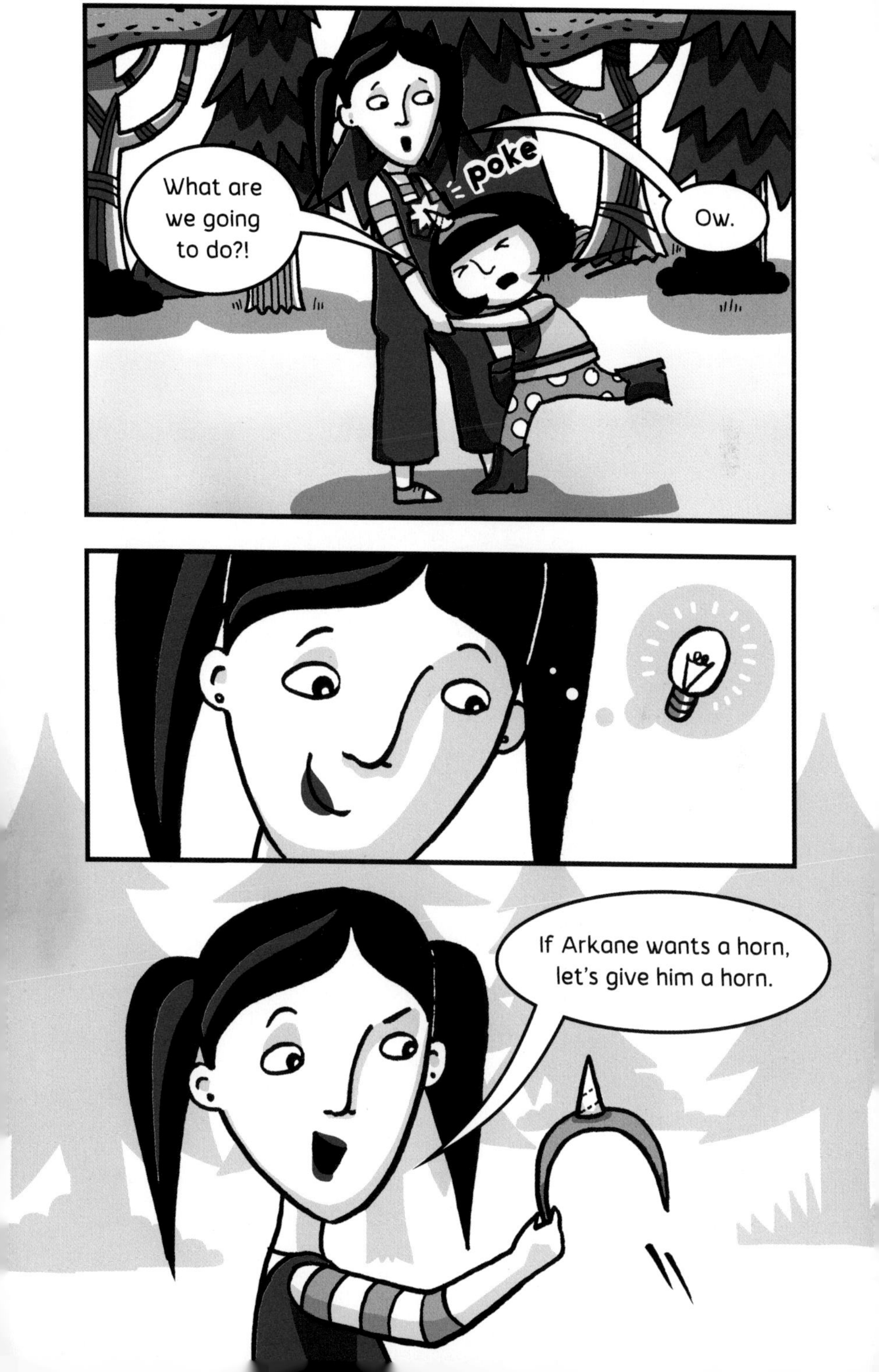
What are we going to do?!
Poke
Ow.
If Arkane wants a horn, let's give him a horn.

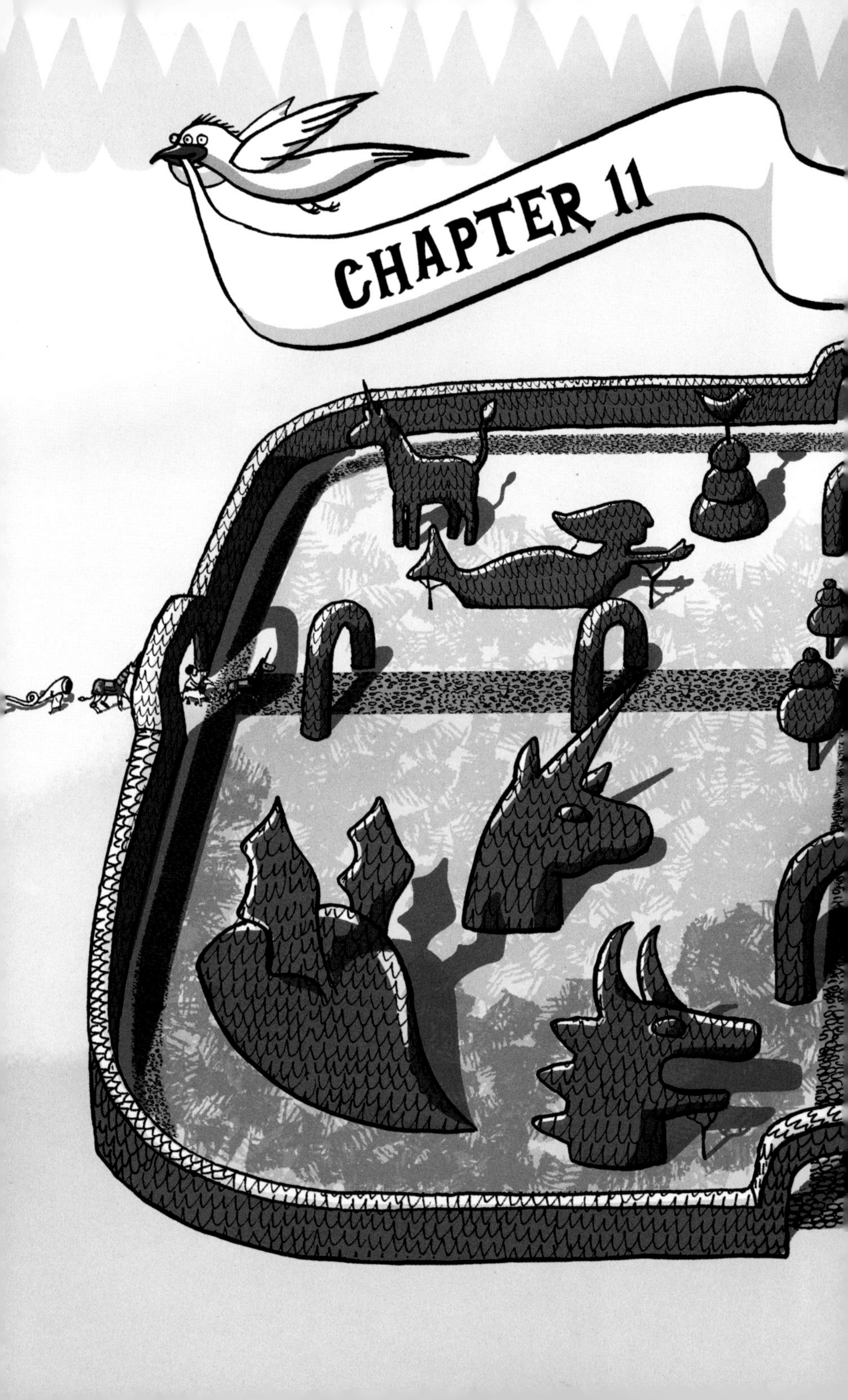
CHAPTER 11

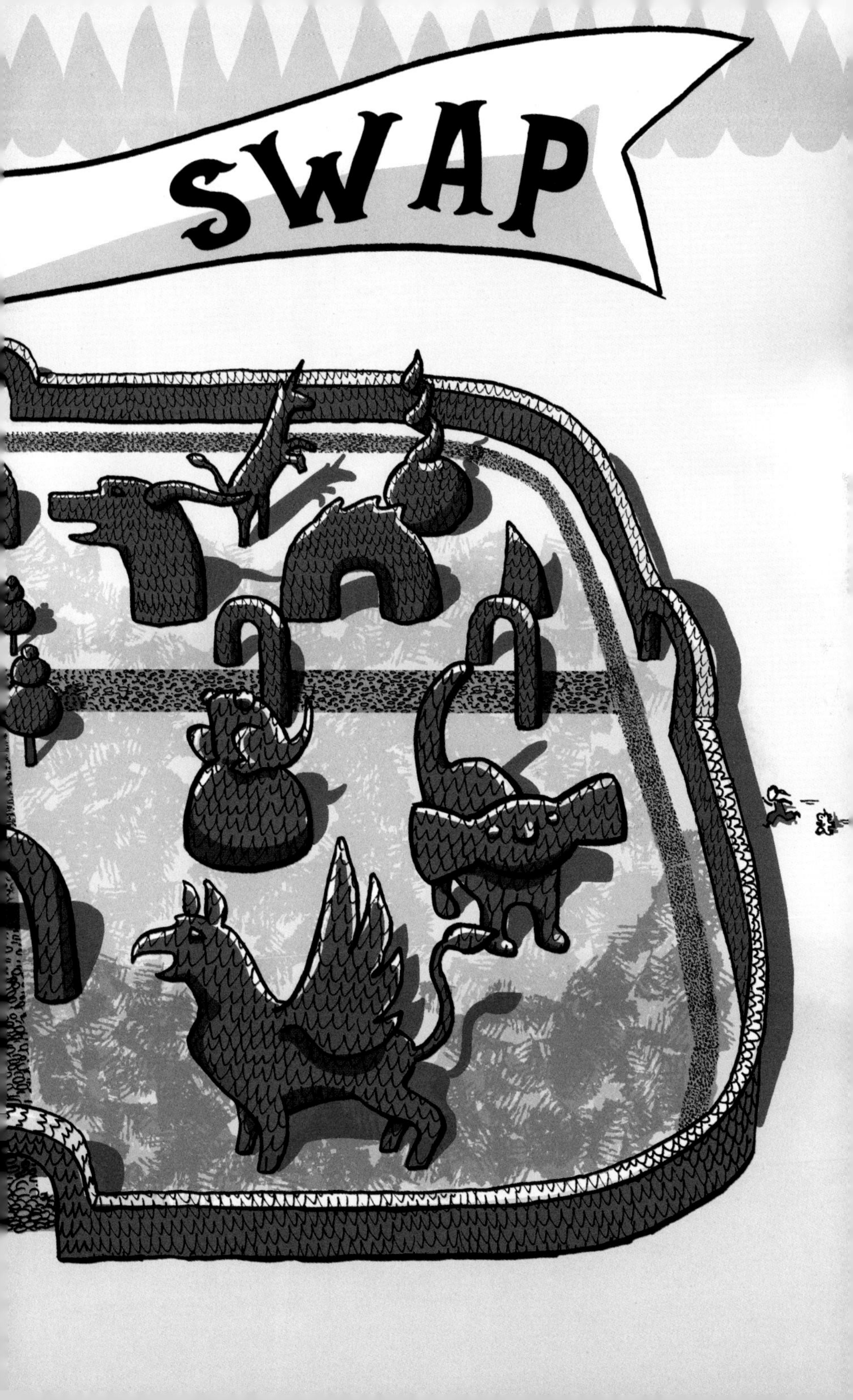
SWAP

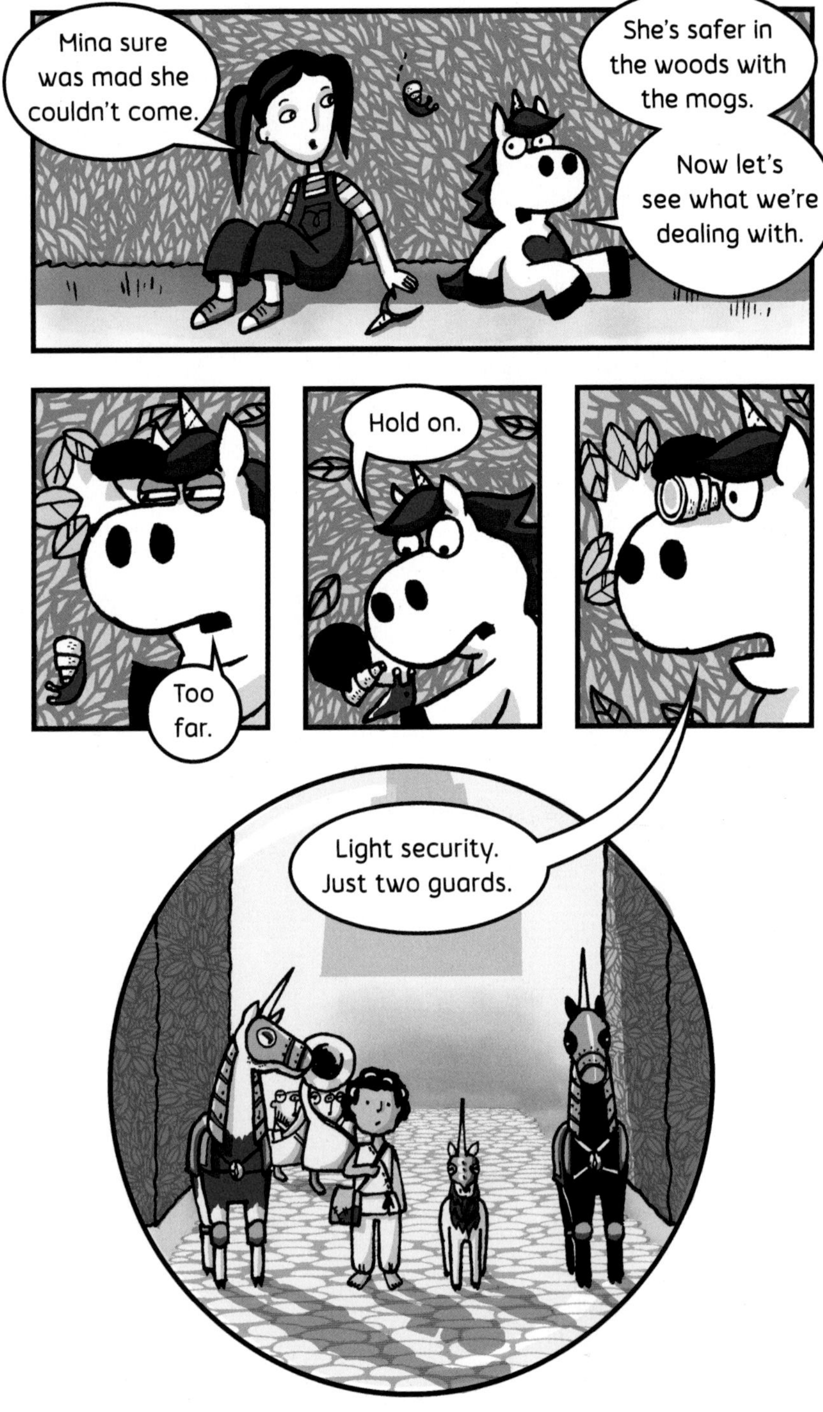
Mina sure was mad she couldn't come.
She's safer in the woods with the mogs.
Now let's see what we're dealing with.
Too far.
Hold on.
Light security. Just two guards.

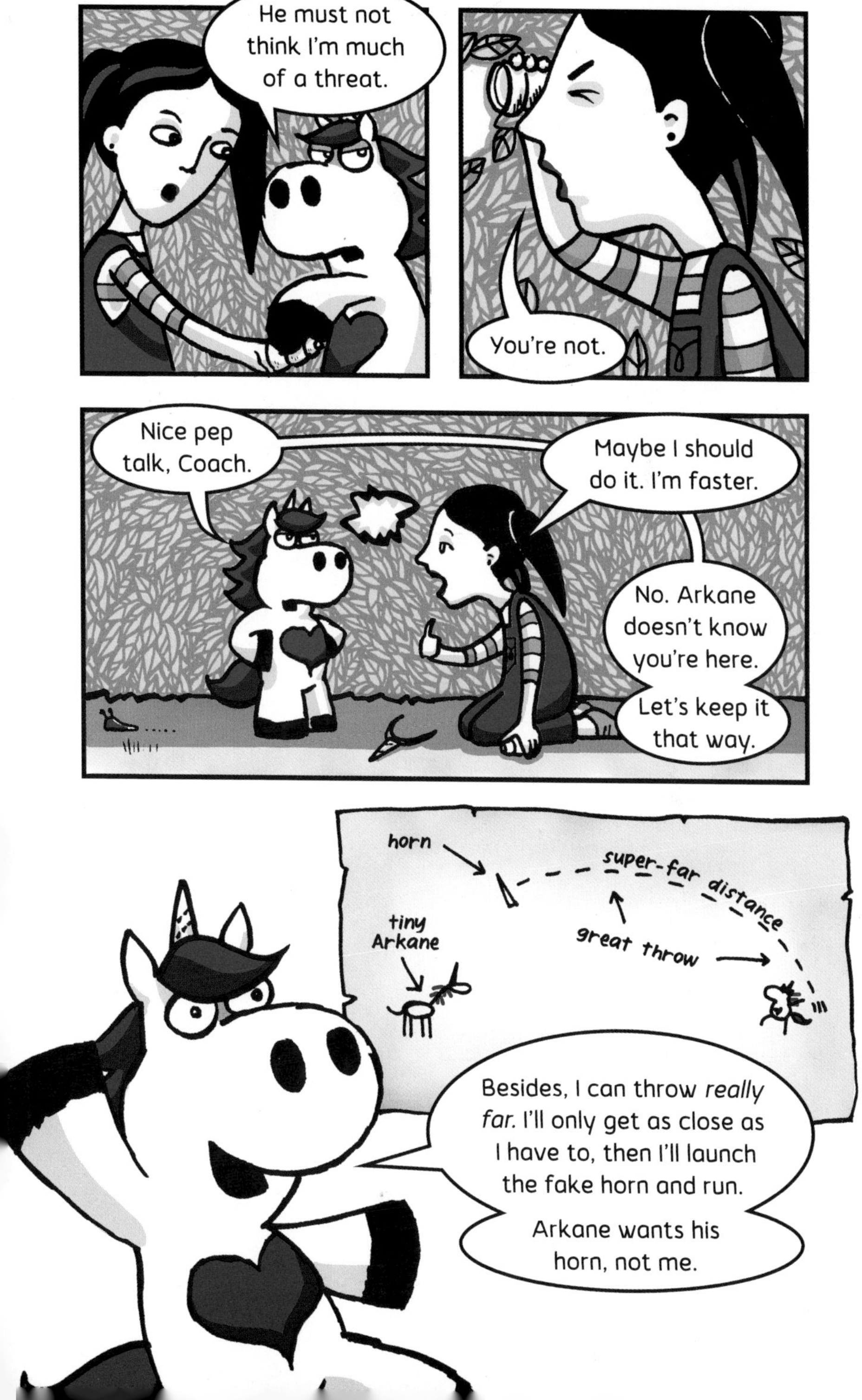
He must not think I'm much of a threat.
You're not.
Nice pep talk, Coach.
Maybe I should do it. I'm faster.
No. Arkane doesn't know you're here.
Let's keep it that way.
horn
super-far distance
tiny Arkane
great throw
Besides, I can throw *really far.* I'll only get as close as I have to, then I'll launch the fake horn and run.
Arkane wants his horn, not me.

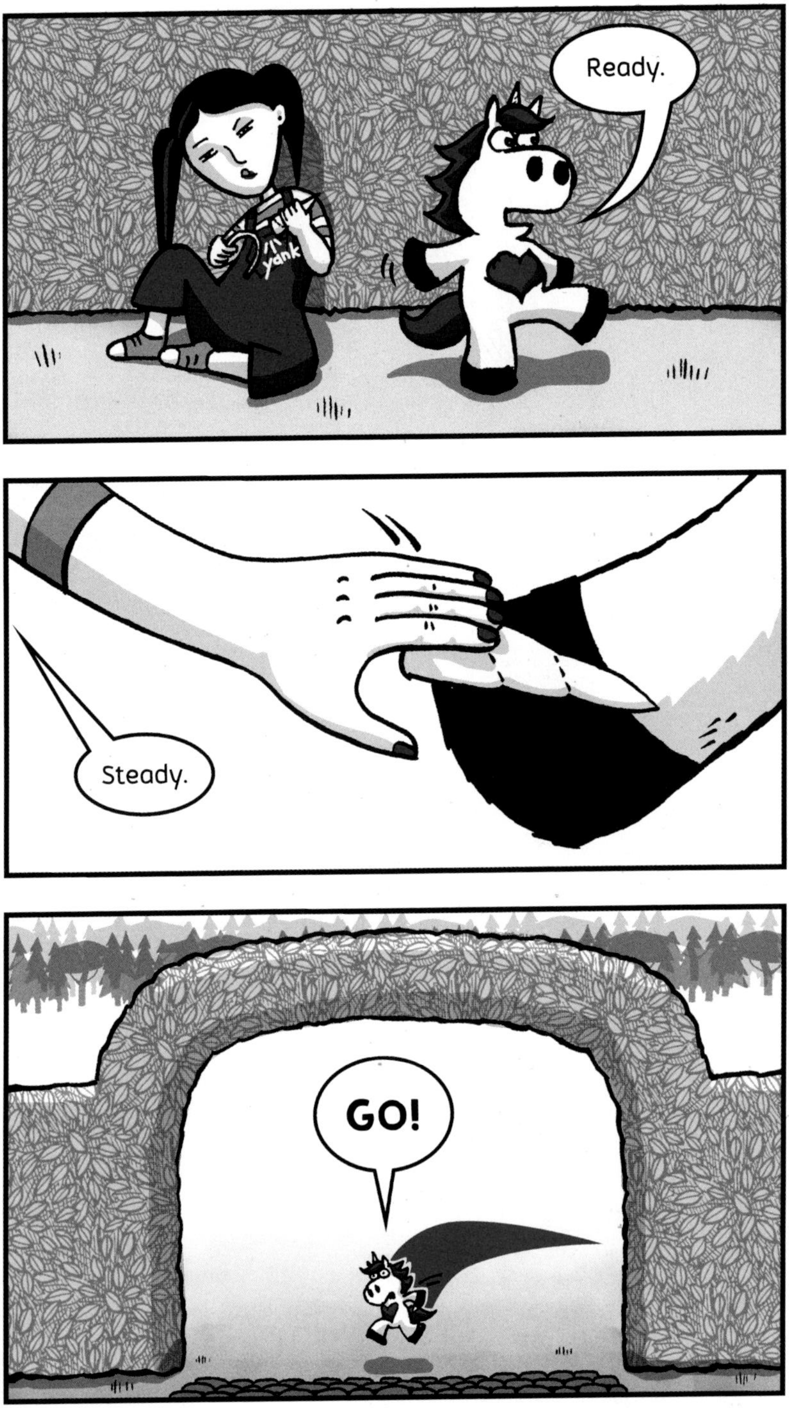
Ready.
yank
Steady.
GO!

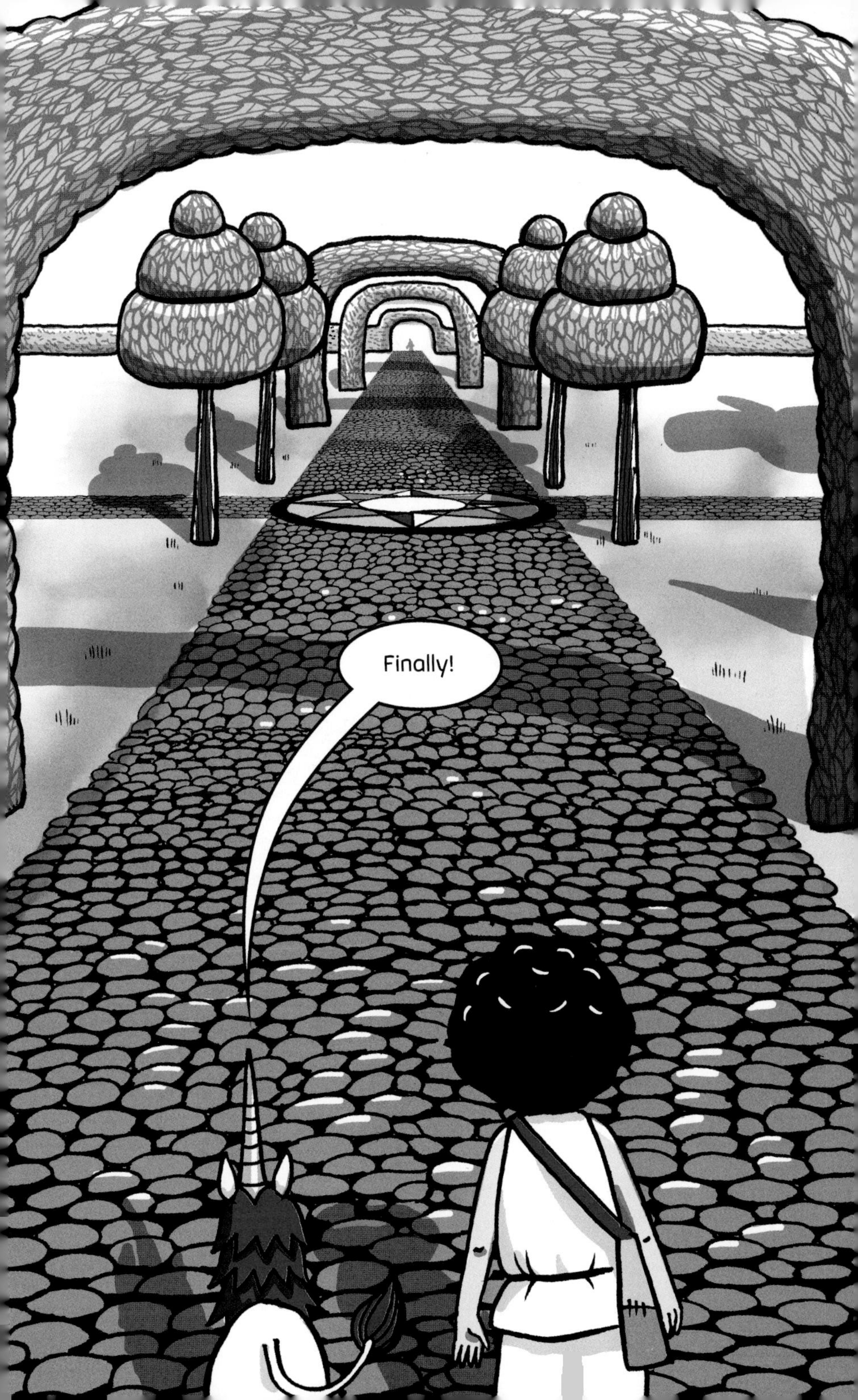
Finally!

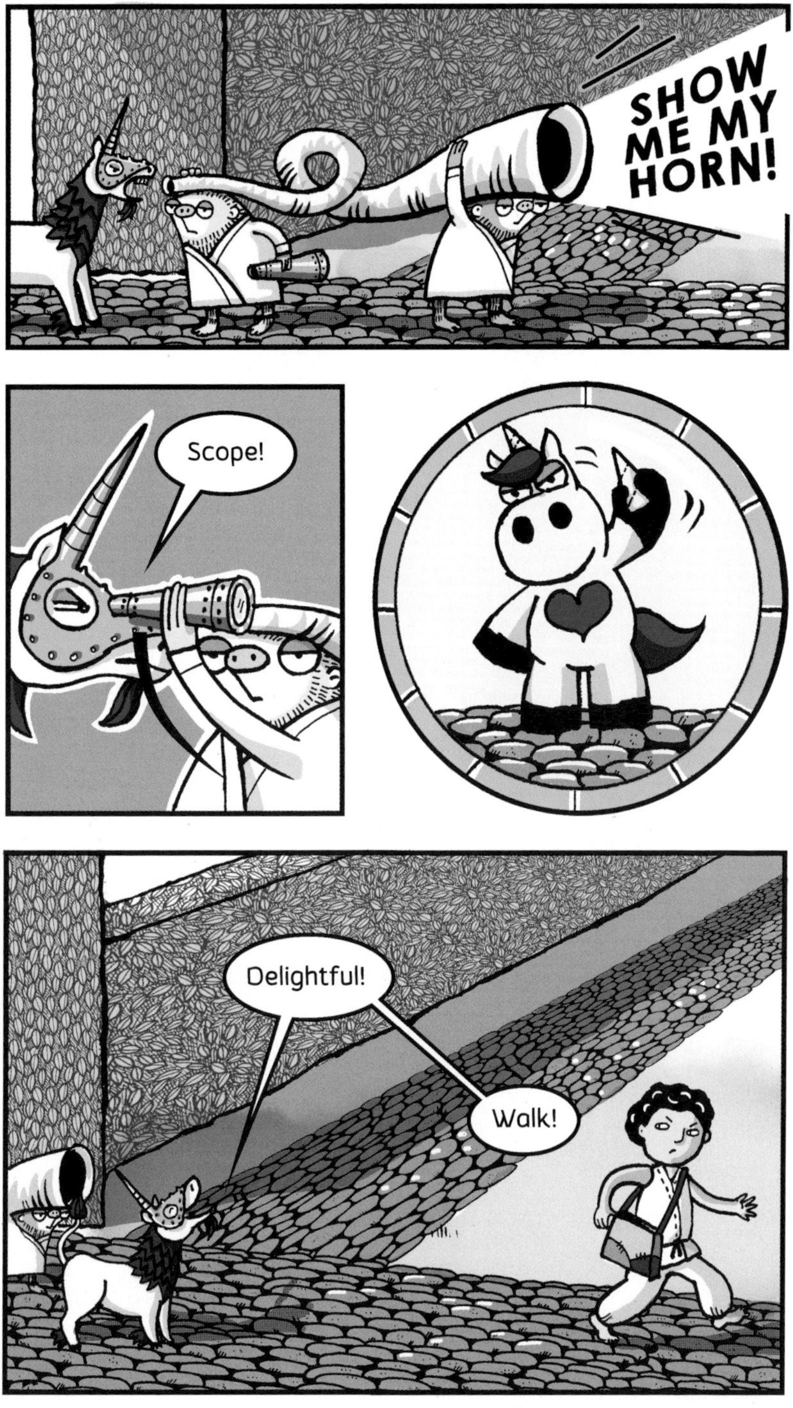
SHOW ME MY HORN!
Scope!
Delightful!
Walk!

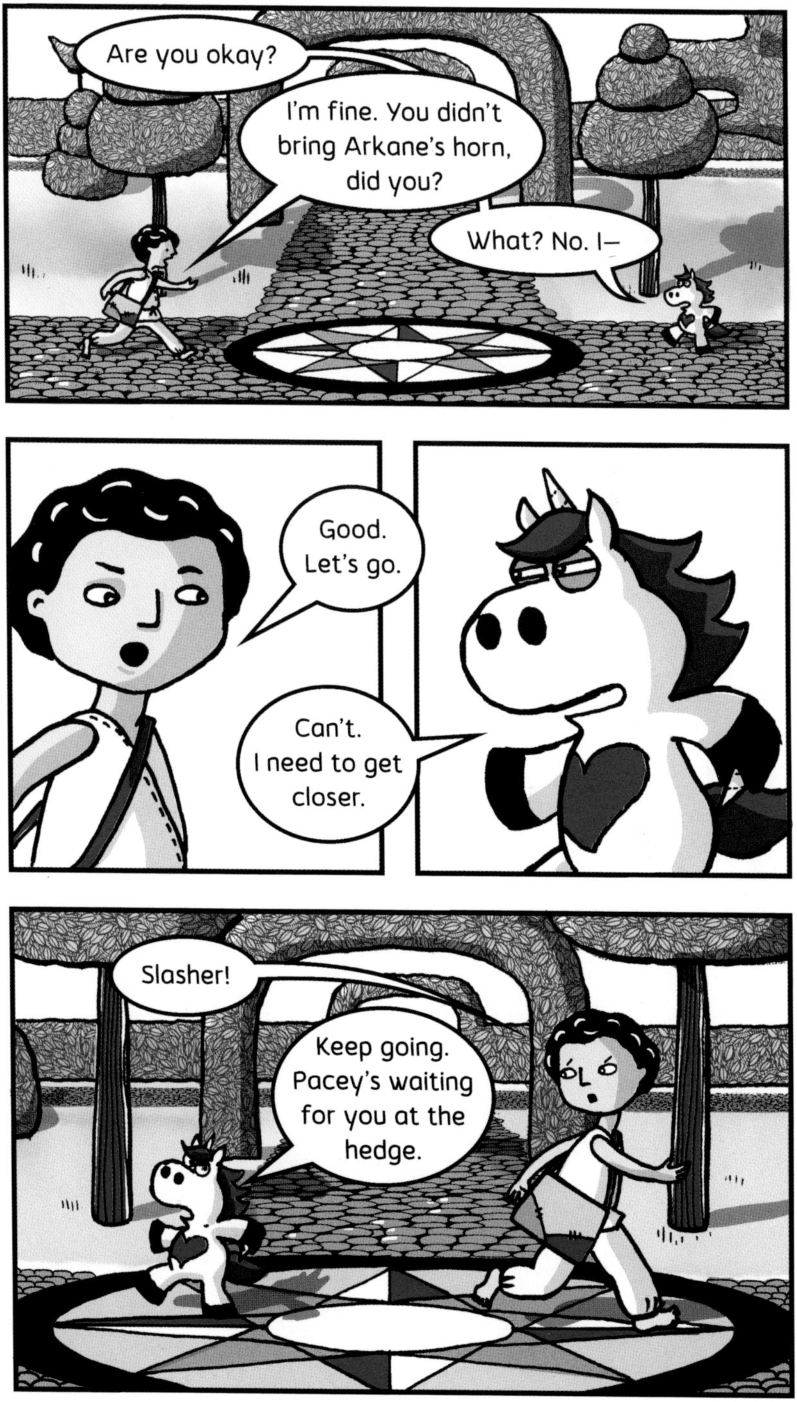
Are you okay?
I'm fine. You didn't bring Arkane's horn, did you?
What? No. I–
Good. Let's go.
Can't. I need to get closer.
Slasher!
Keep going. Pacey's waiting for you at the hedge.

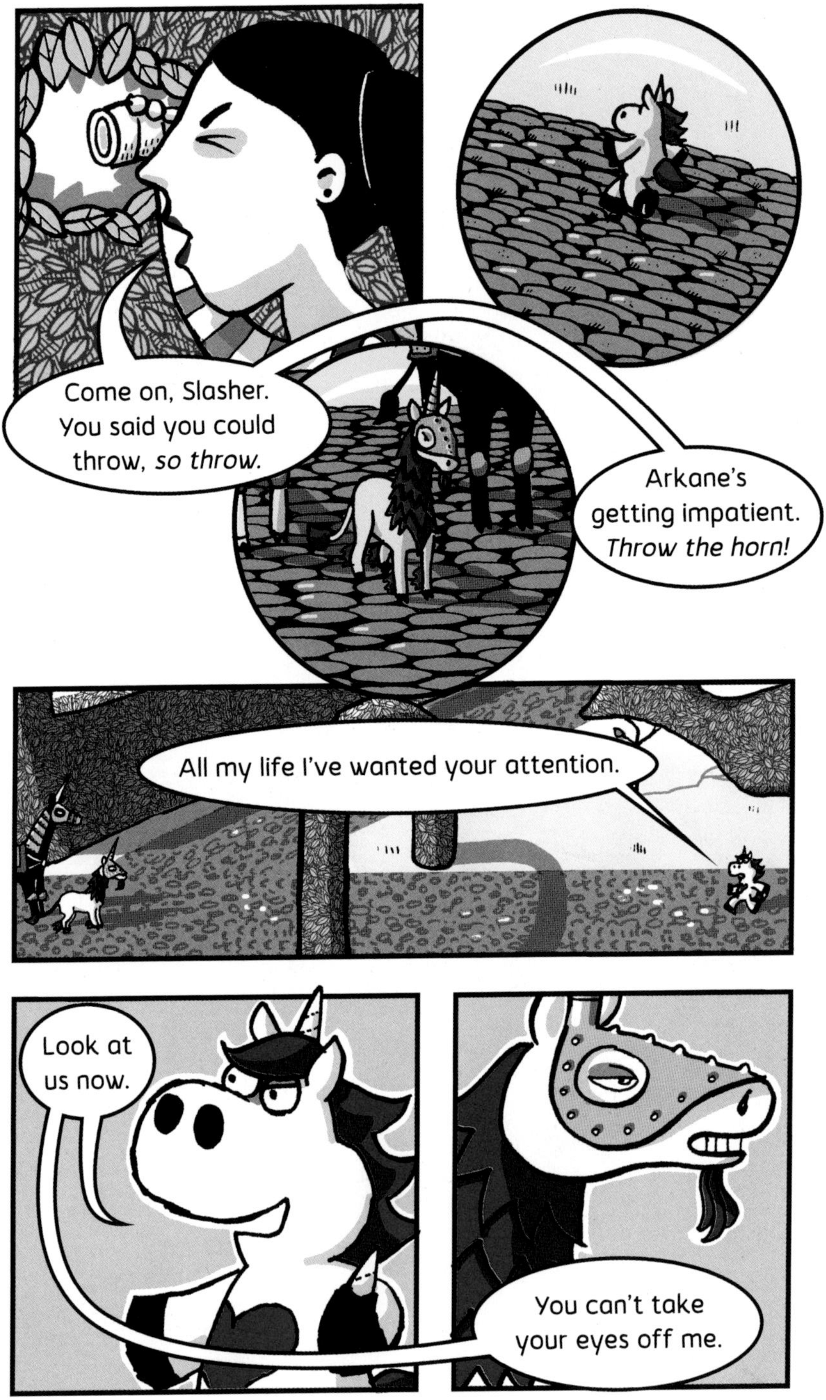
Come on, Slasher. You said you could throw, *so throw.*
Arkane's getting impatient. *Throw the horn!*
All my life I've wanted your attention.
Look at us now.
You can't take your eyes off me.

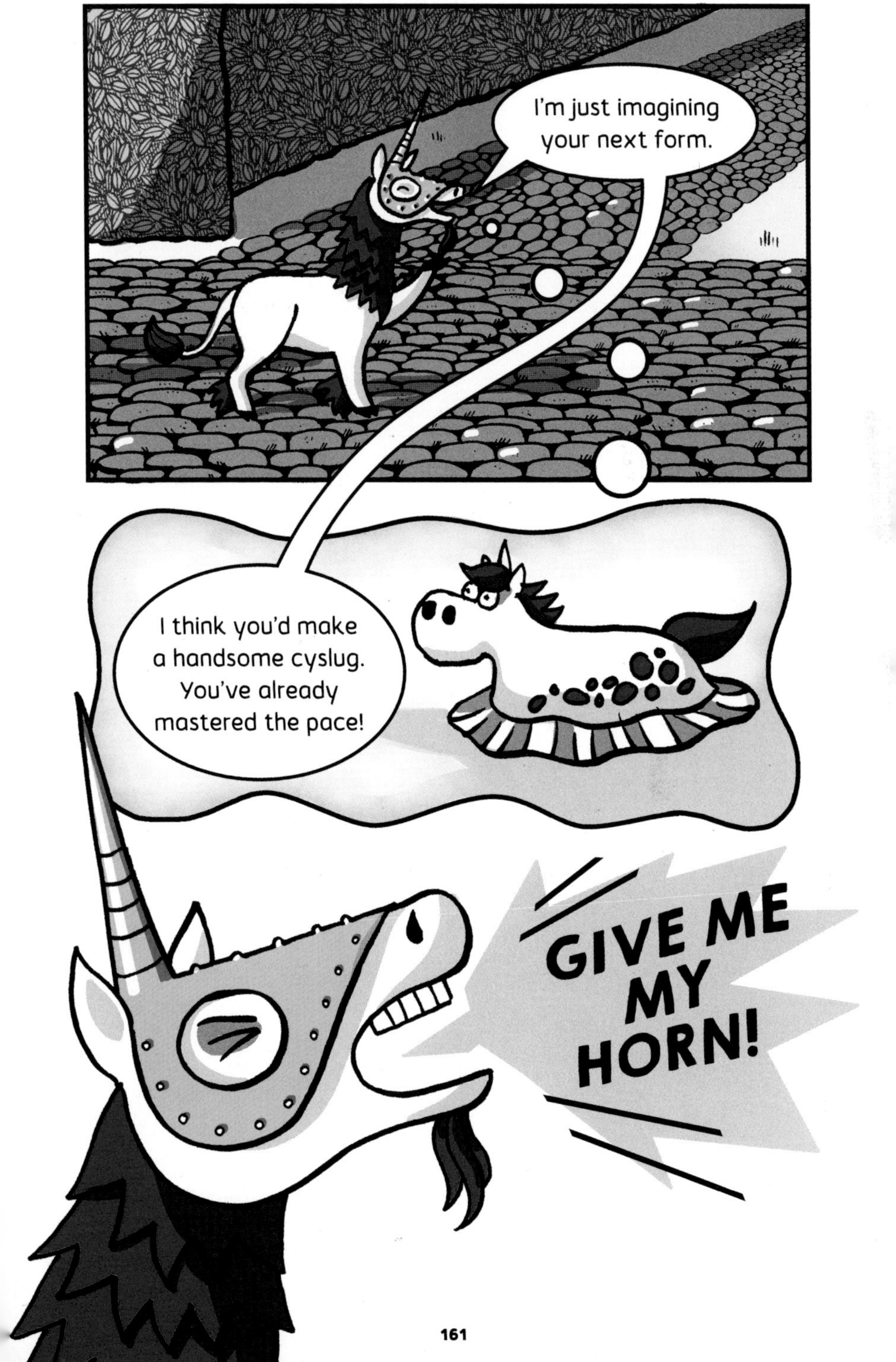
I'm just imagining your next form.
I think you'd make a handsome cyslug. You've already mastered the pace!
GIVE ME MY HORN!

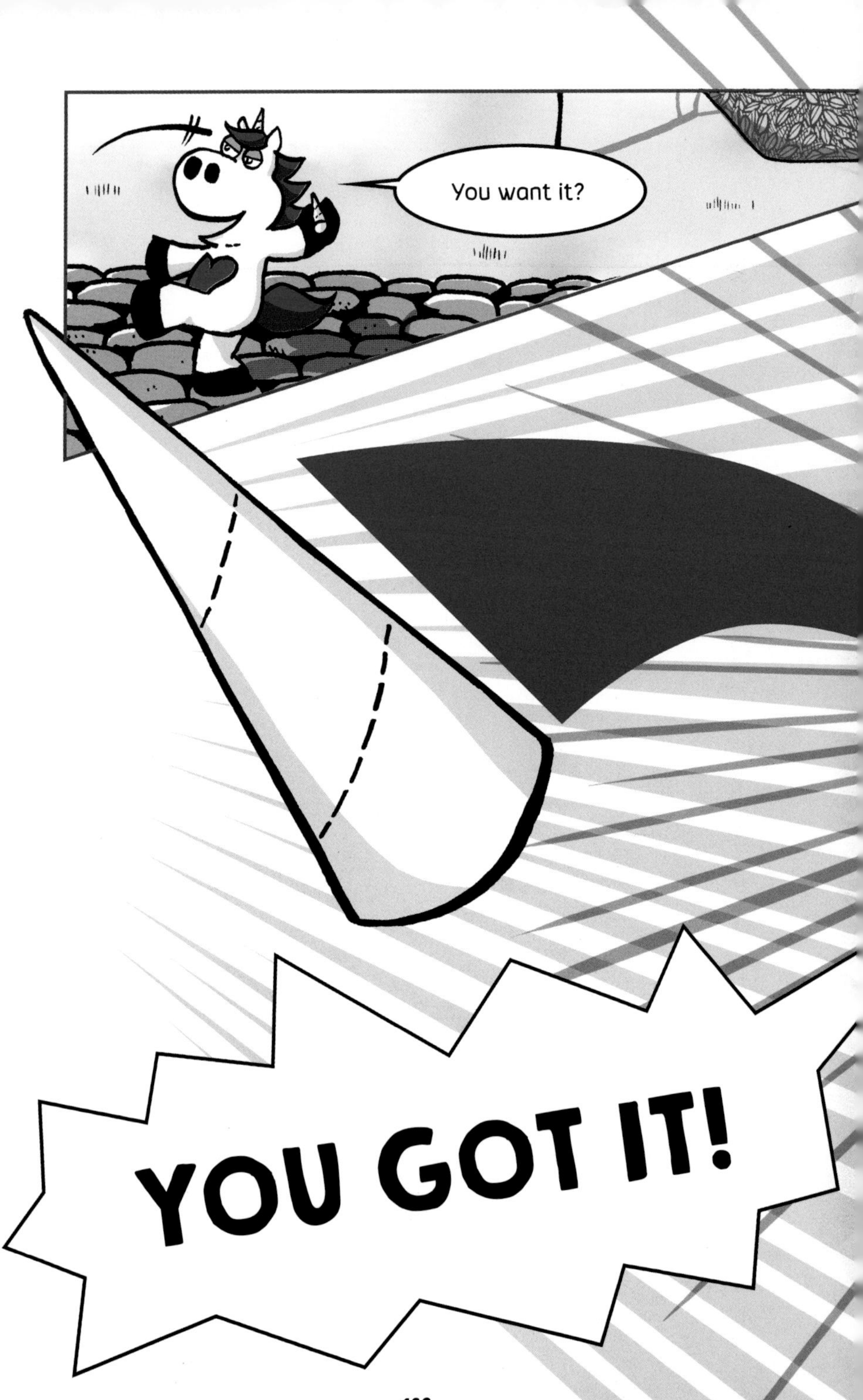
You want it?
YOU GOT IT!

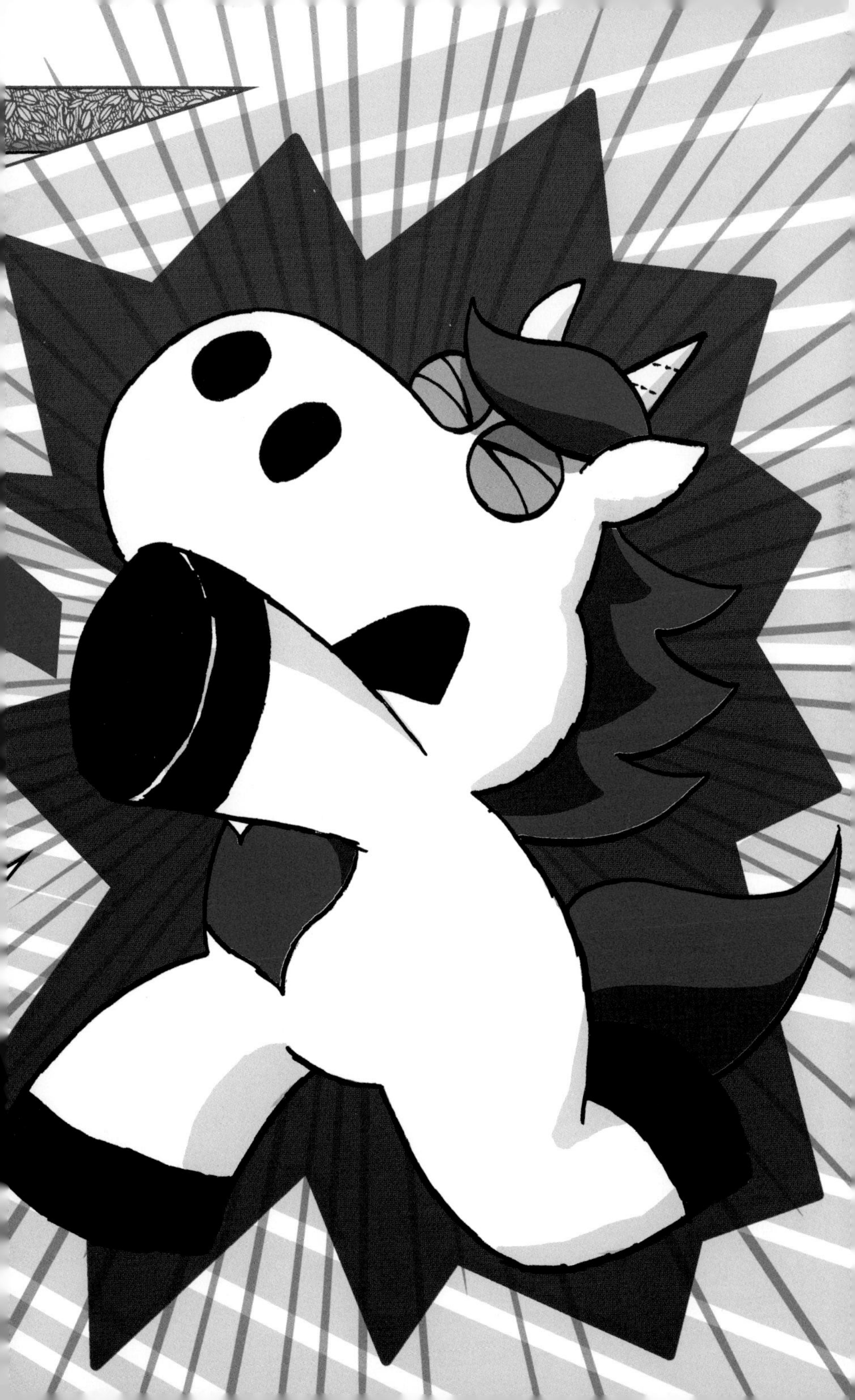

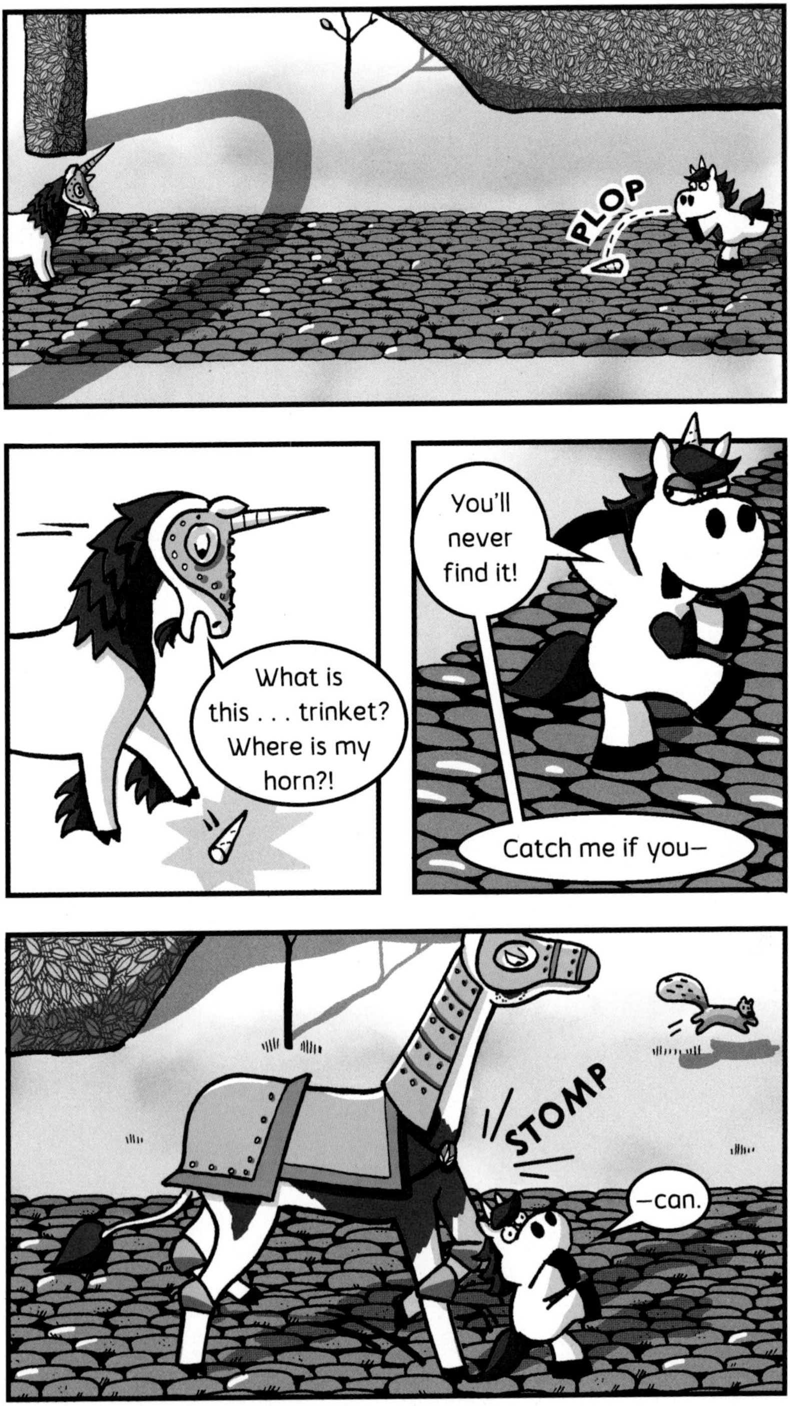
PLOP
What is this . . . trinket? Where is my horn?!
You'll never find it!
Catch me if you—
STOMP
—can.

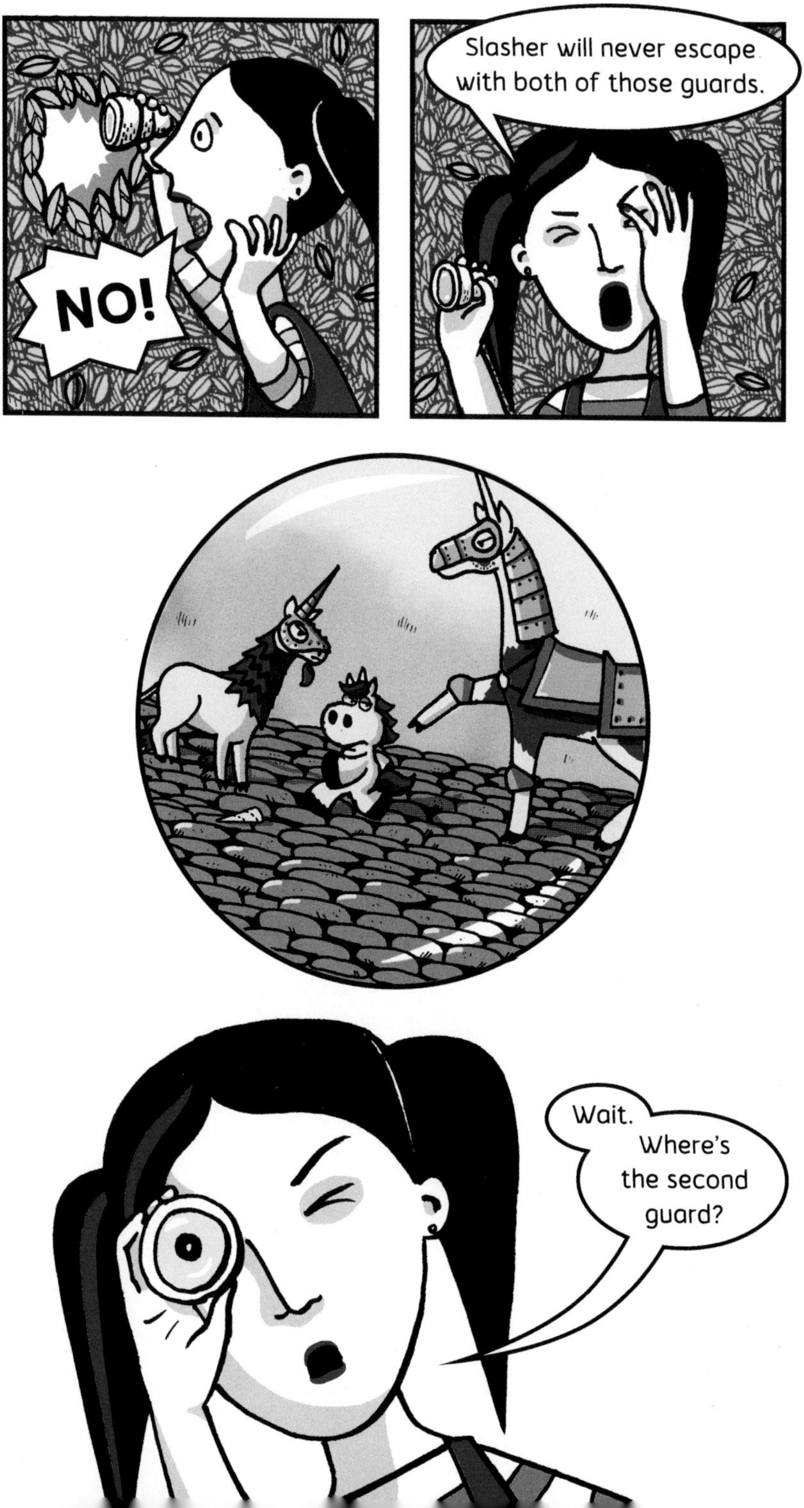
NO!
Slasher will never escape with both of those guards.
Wait.
Where's the second guard?

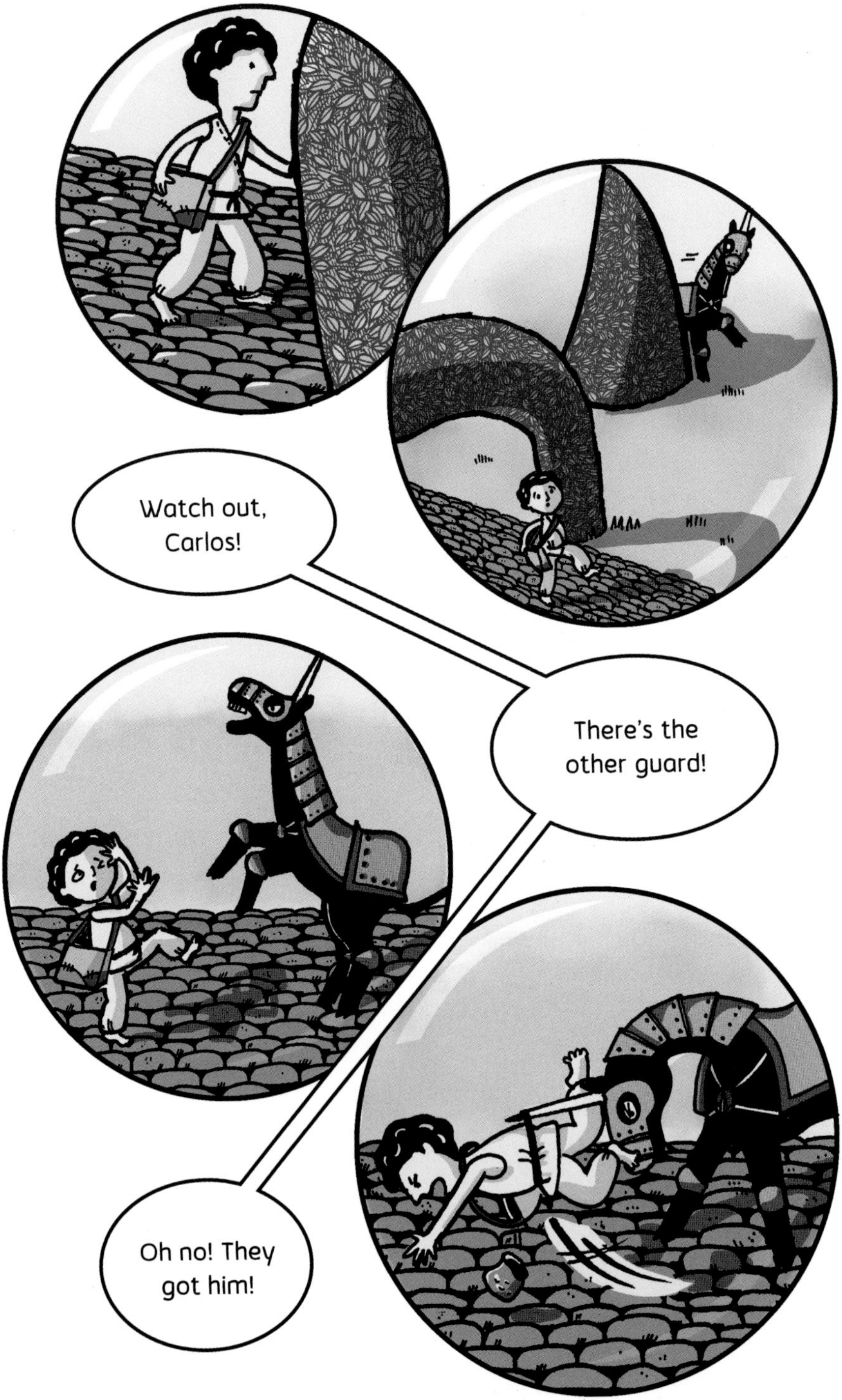
Watch out, Carlos!
There's the other guard!
Oh no! They got him!

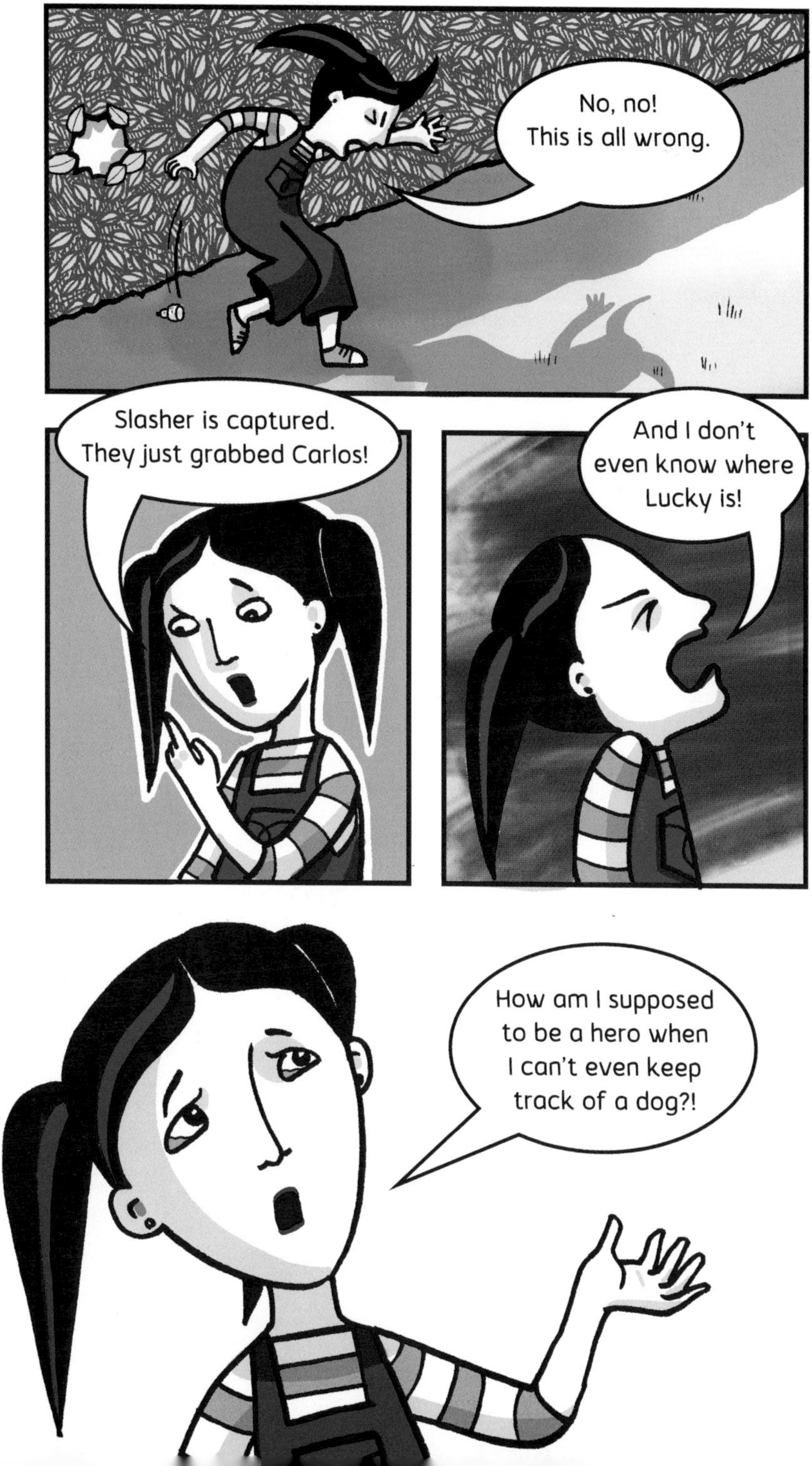
No, no! This is all wrong.
Slasher is captured. They just grabbed Carlos!
And I don't even know where Lucky is!
How am I supposed to be a hero when I can't even keep track of a dog?!

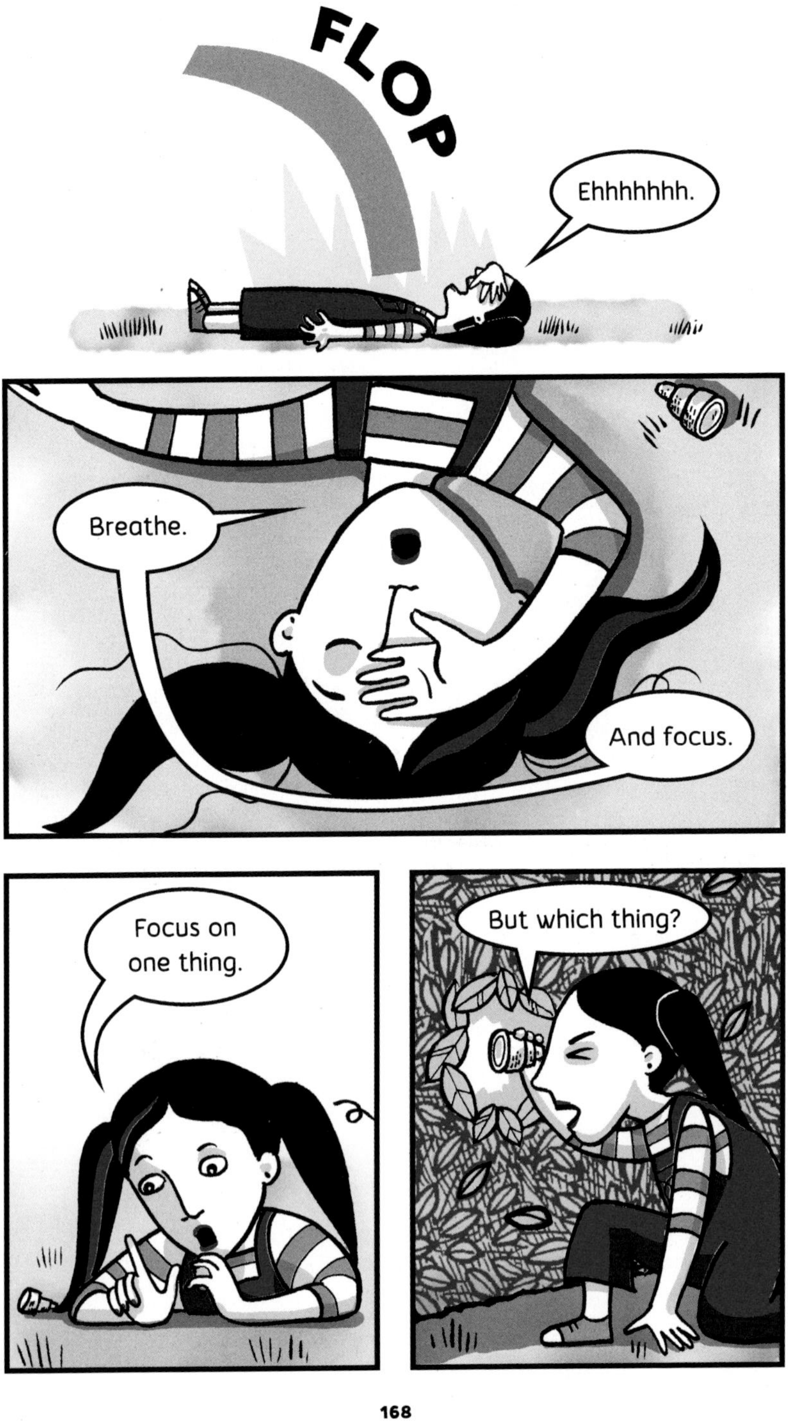
FLOP
Ehhhhhhh.
Breathe.
And focus.
Focus on one thing.
But which thing?

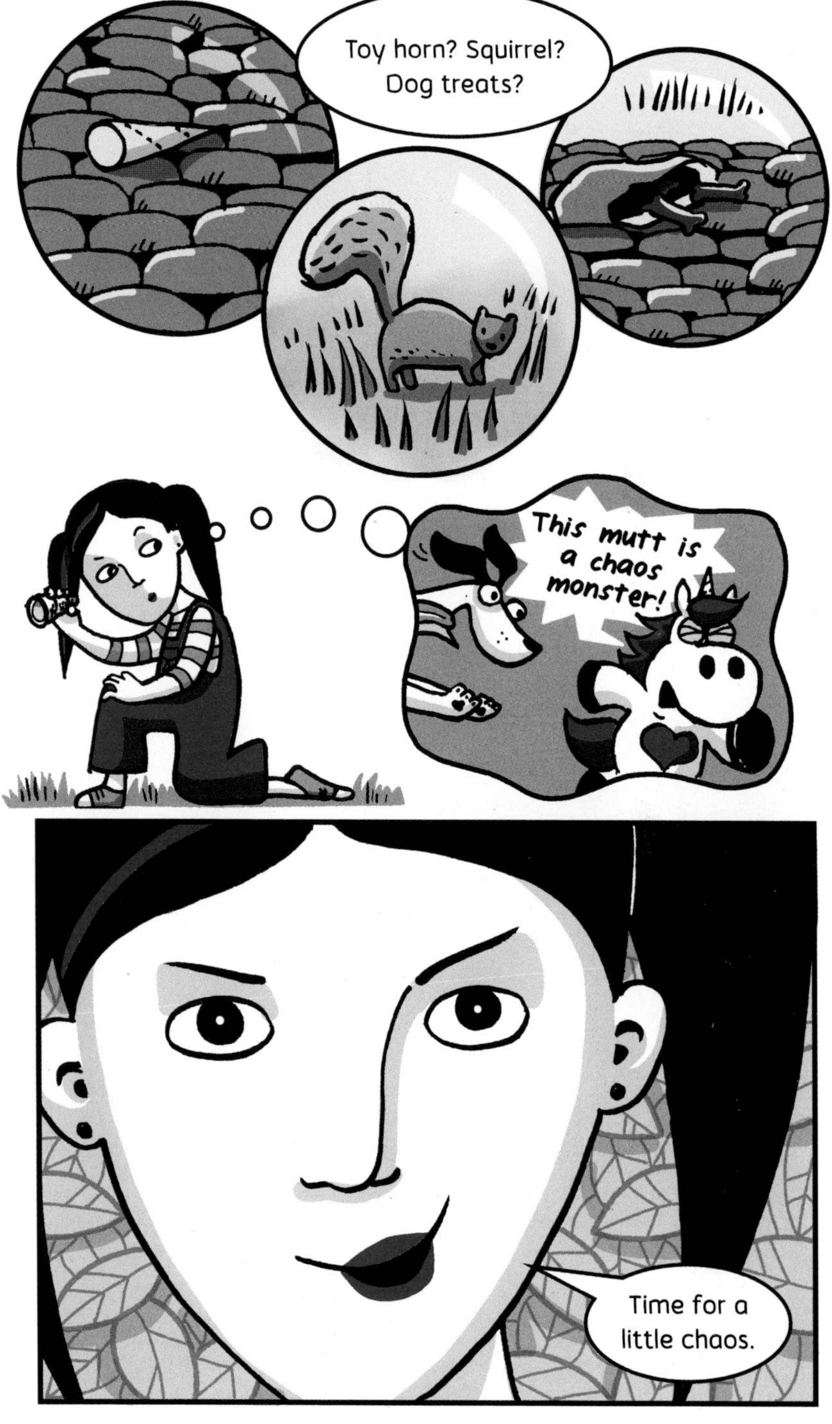
Toy horn? Squirrel? Dog treats?
This mutt is a chaos monster!
Time for a little chaos.

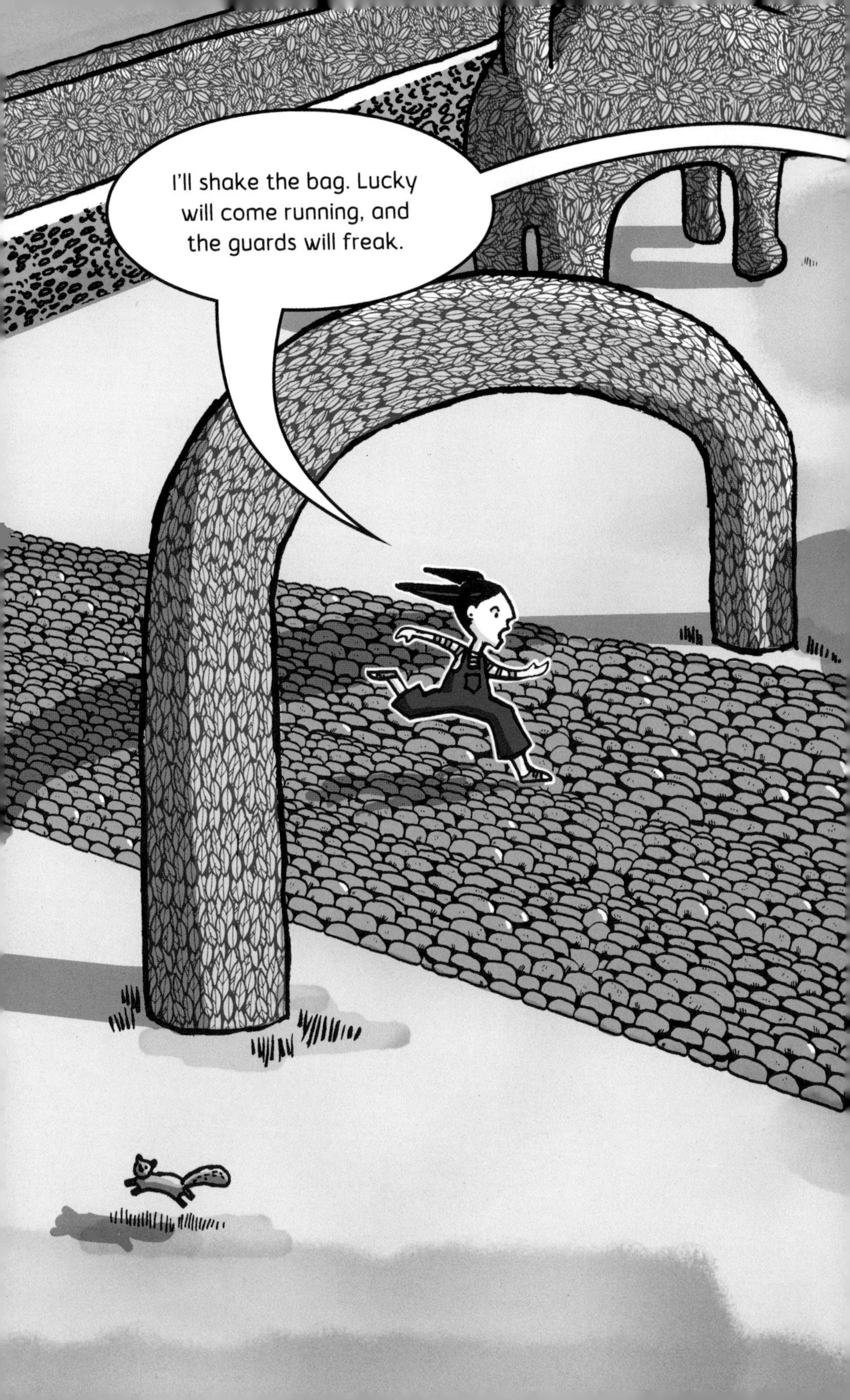
I'll shake the bag. Lucky will come running, and the guards will freak.

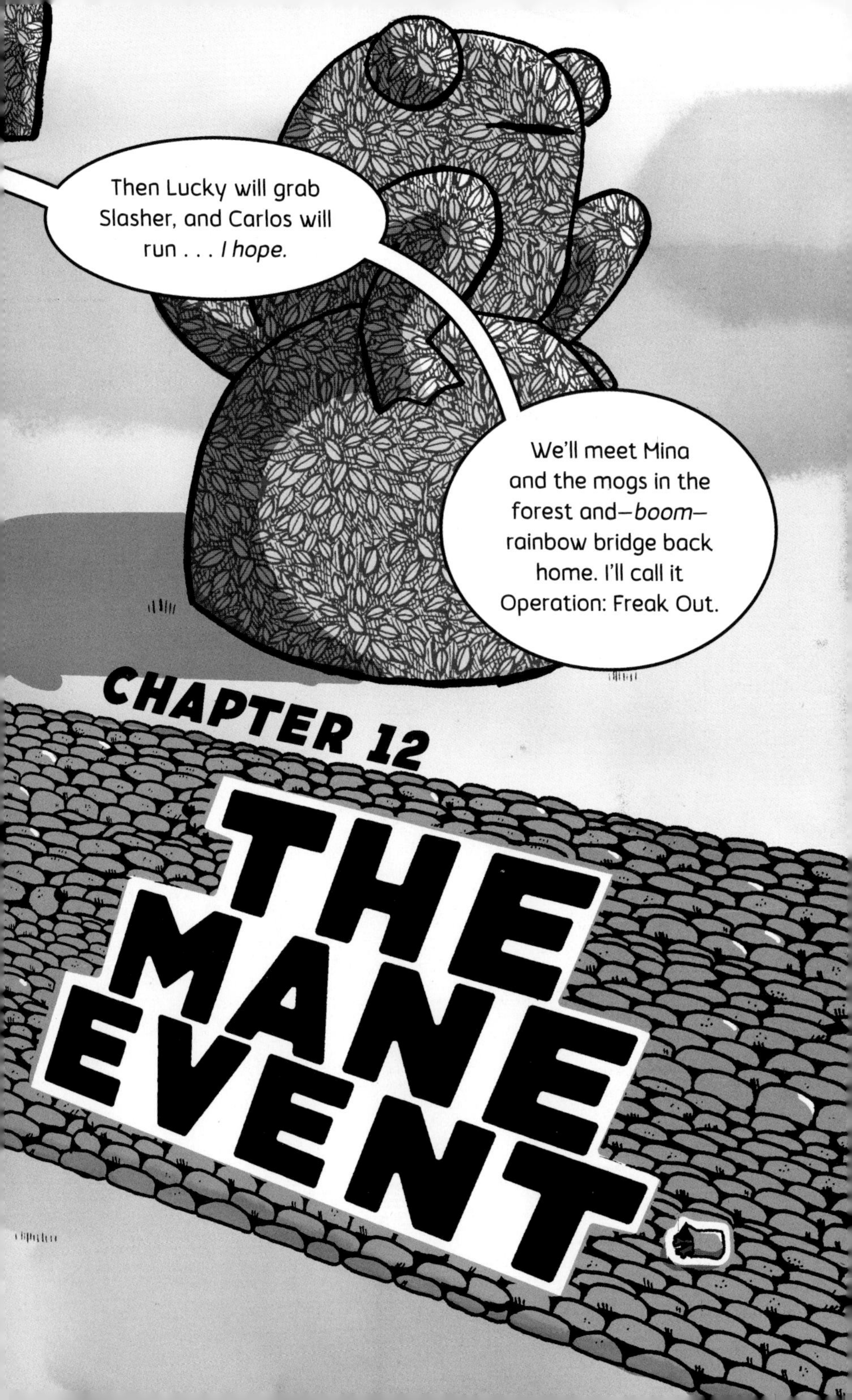
Then Lucky will grab Slasher, and Carlos will run . . . *I hope.*
We'll meet Mina and the mogs in the forest and—*boom*—rainbow bridge back home. I'll call it Operation: Freak Out.

CHAPTER 12
THE MANE EVENT

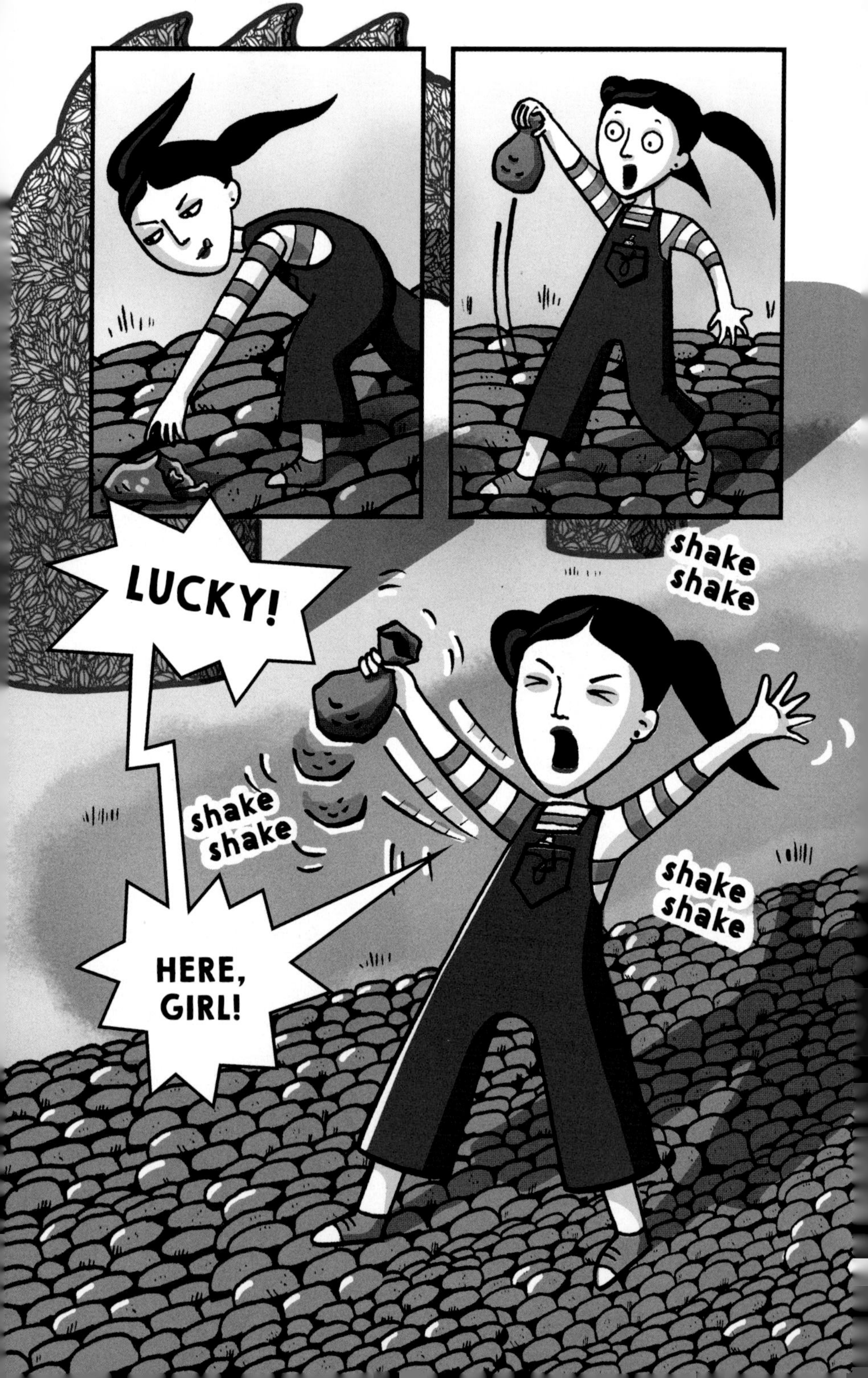
LUCKY!
shake shake
HERE, GIRL!
shake shake
shake shake

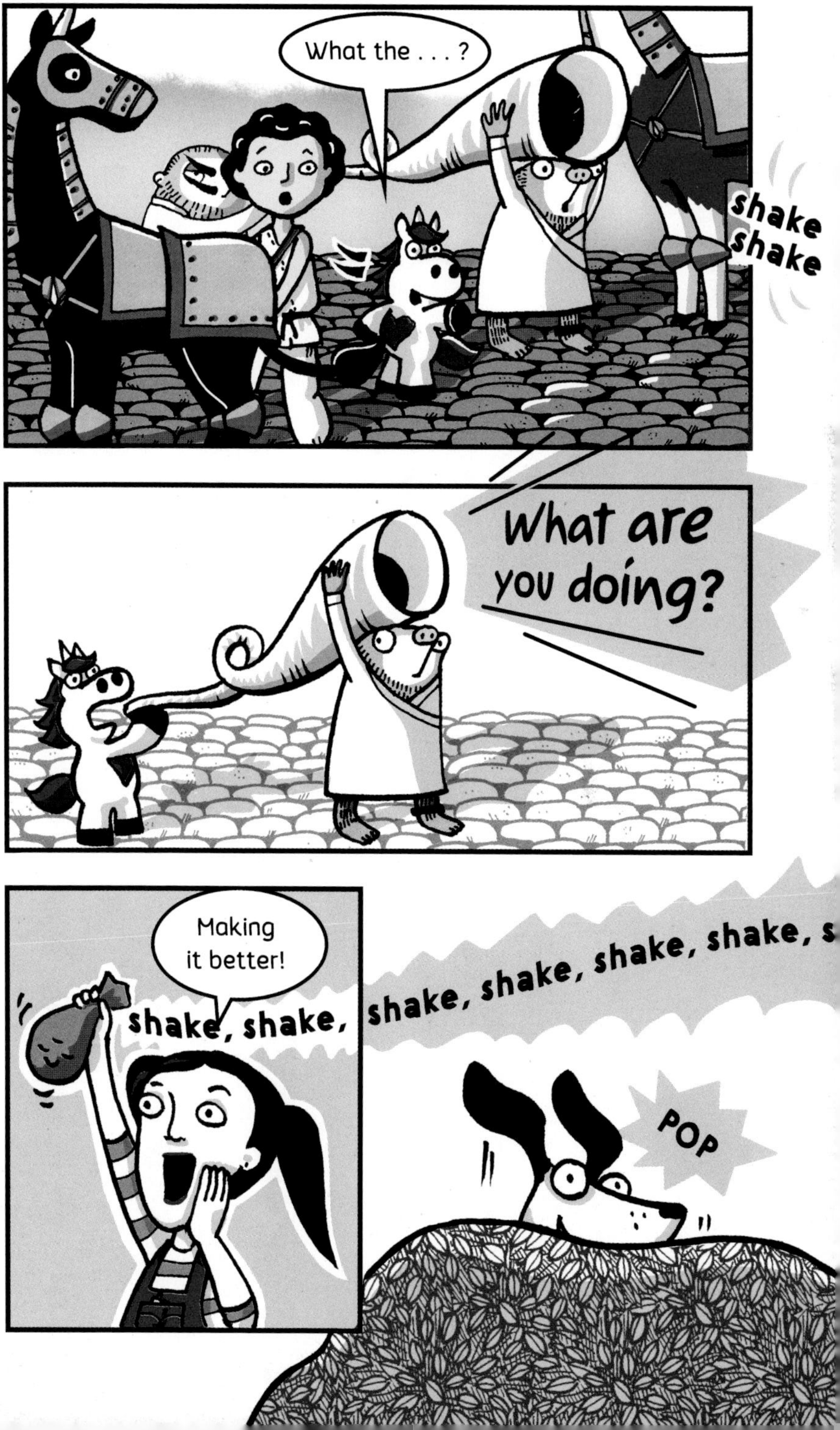
What the . . . ?
shake
shake
What are you doing?
Making it better!
shake, shake, shake, shake, shake, shake, shake, s
POP

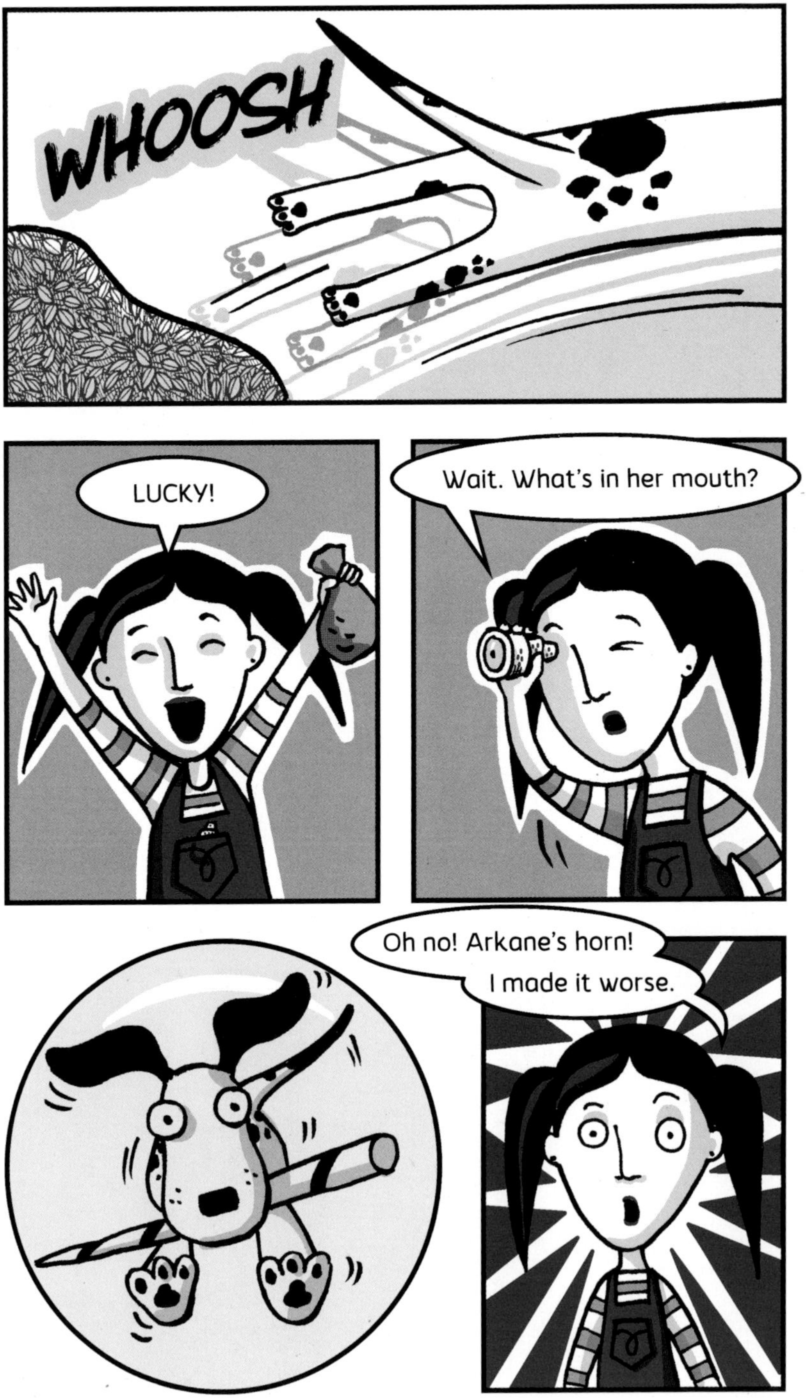
WHOOSH
LUCKY!
Wait. What's in her mouth?
Oh no! Arkane's horn!
I made it worse.

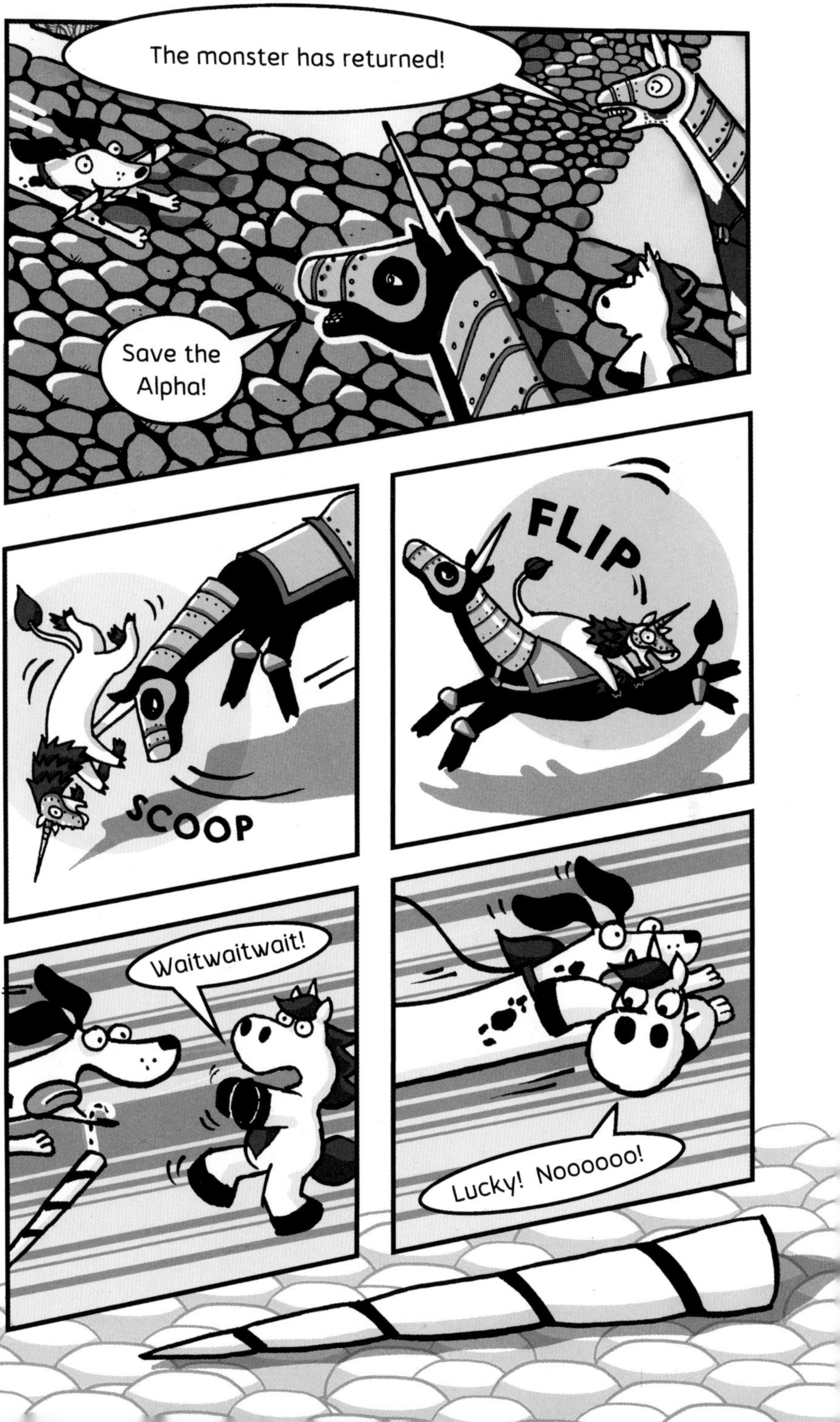
The monster has returned!
Save the Alpha!
SCOOP
FLIP
Waitwaitwait!
Lucky! Noooooo!

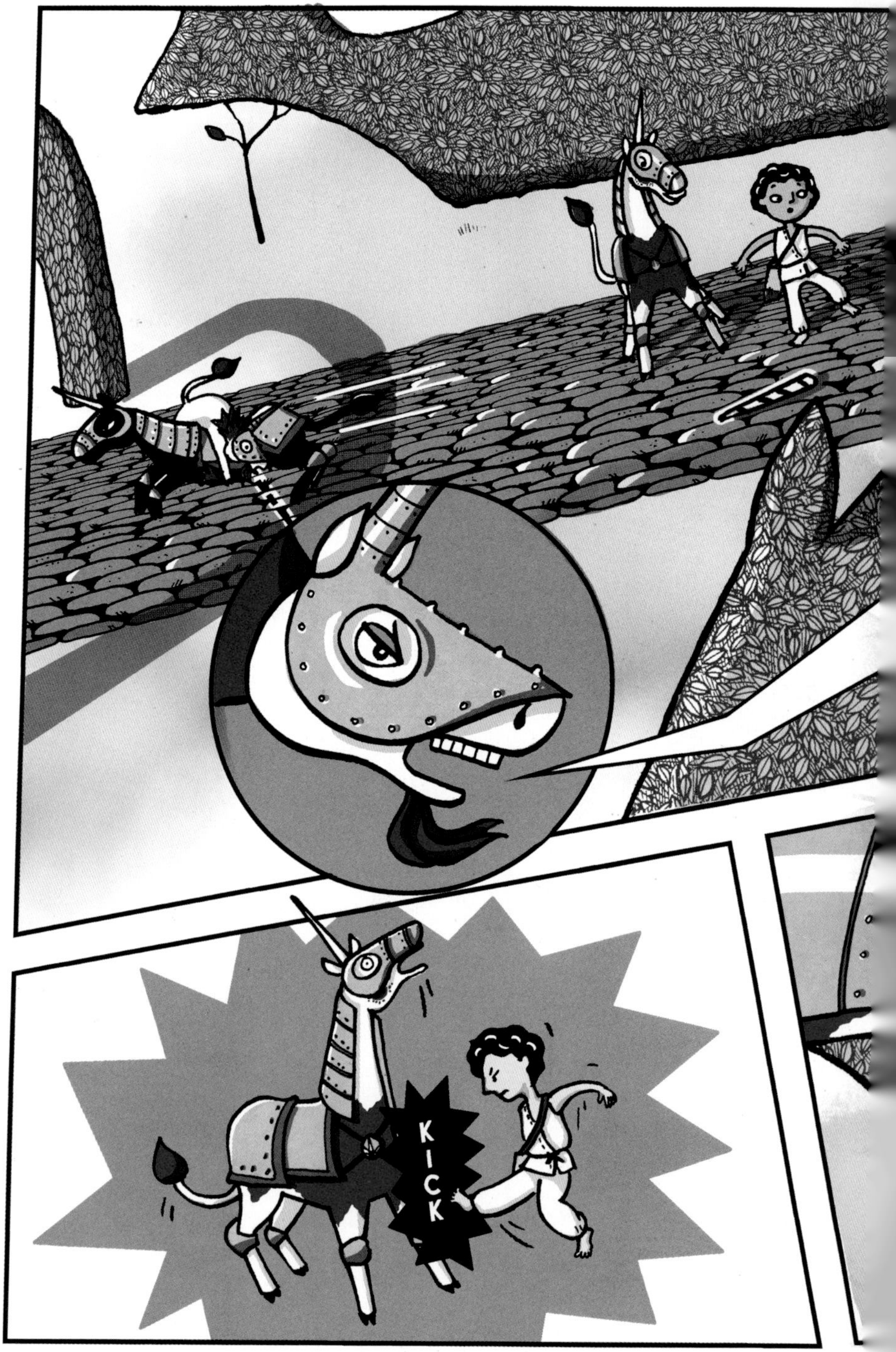
KICK

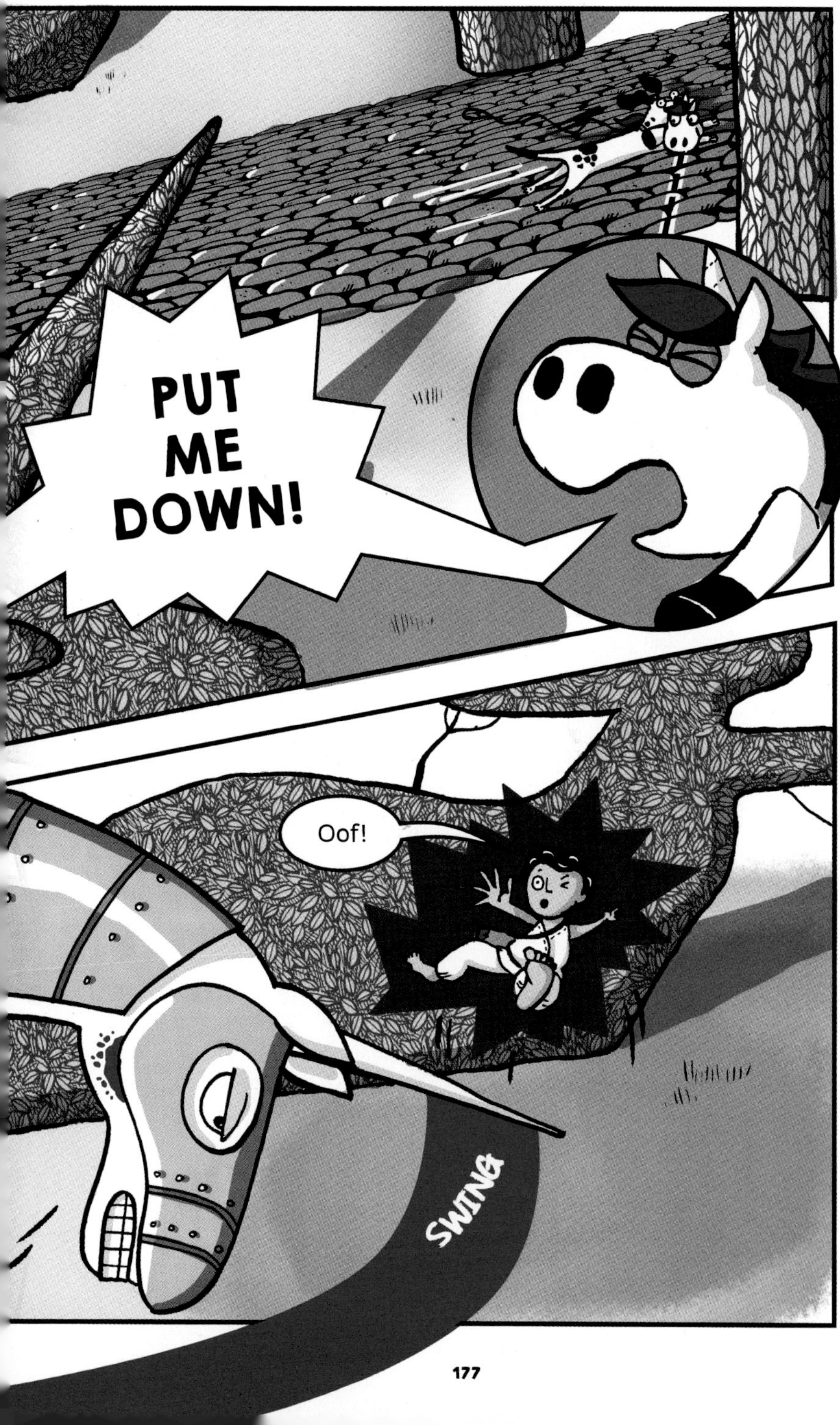
PUT ME DOWN!
Oof!
SWING

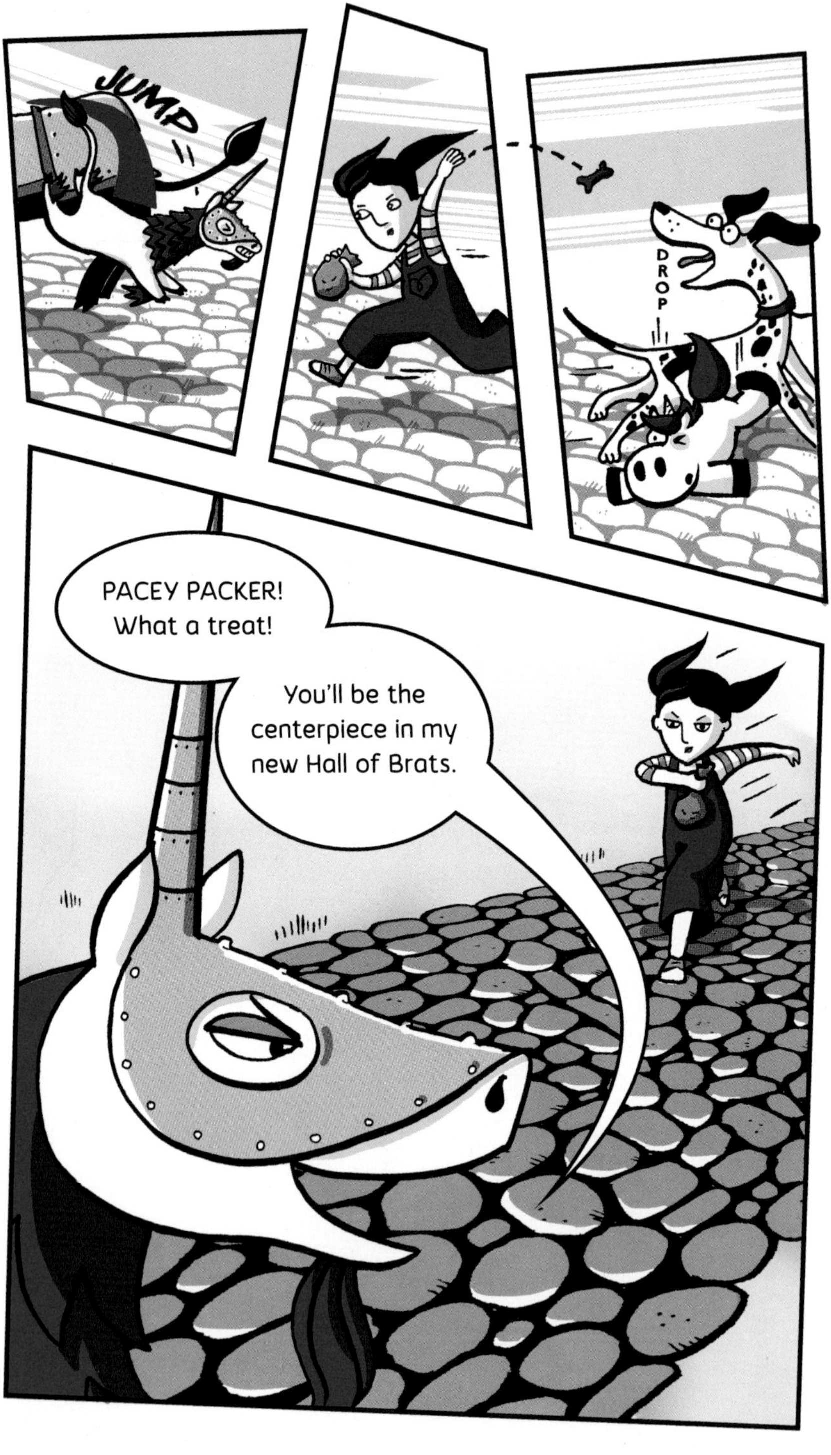
JUMP
DROP
PACEY PACKER! What a treat!
You'll be the centerpiece in my new Hall of Brats.

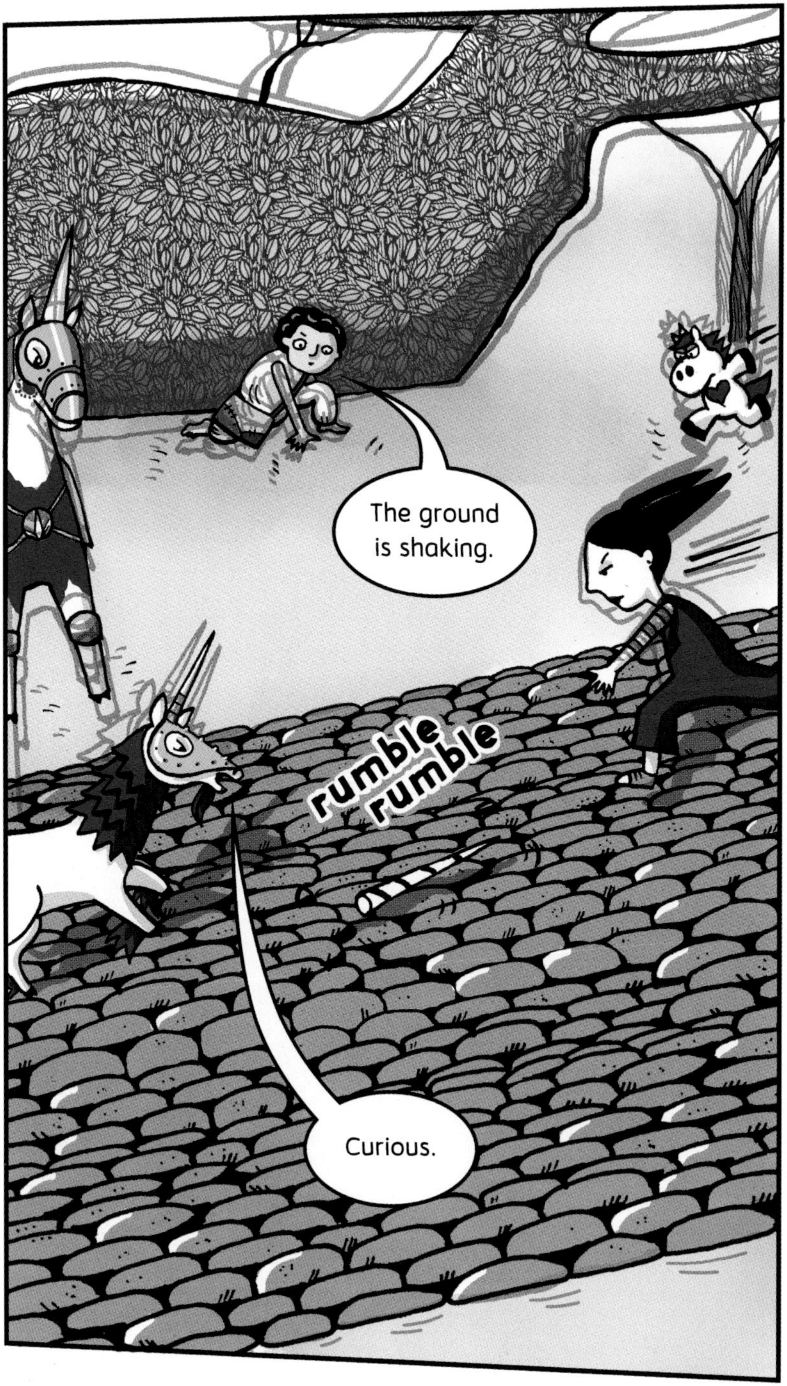
The ground is shaking.
rumble rumble
Curious.

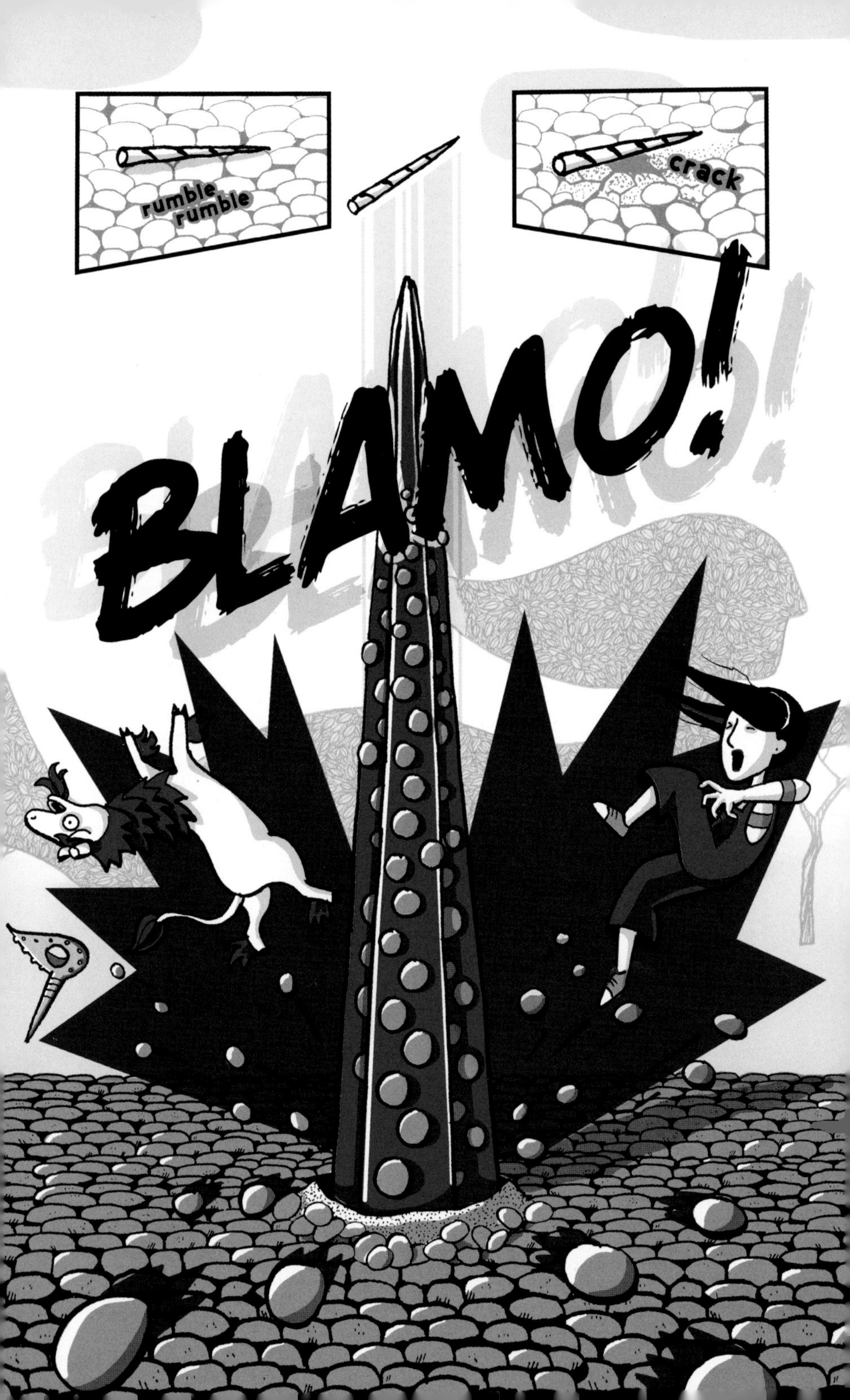
rumble rumble
crack
BLAMO!

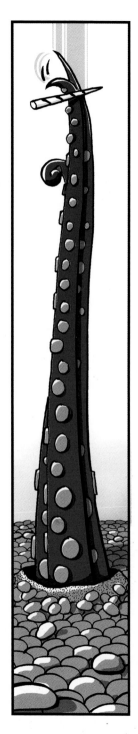

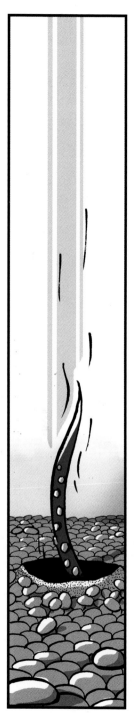

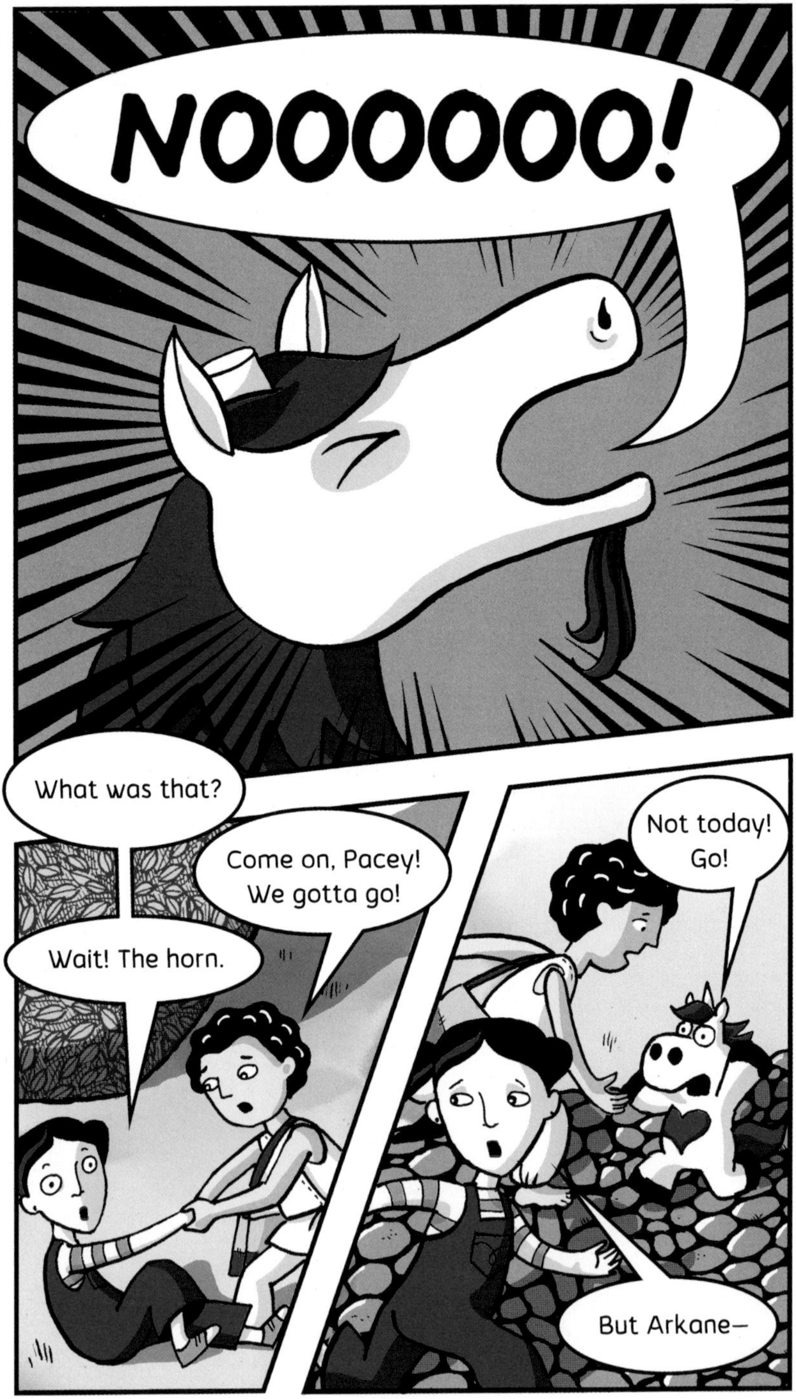
NOOOOOO!
What was that?
Come on, Pacey! We gotta go!
Wait! The horn.
Not today! Go!
But Arkane—

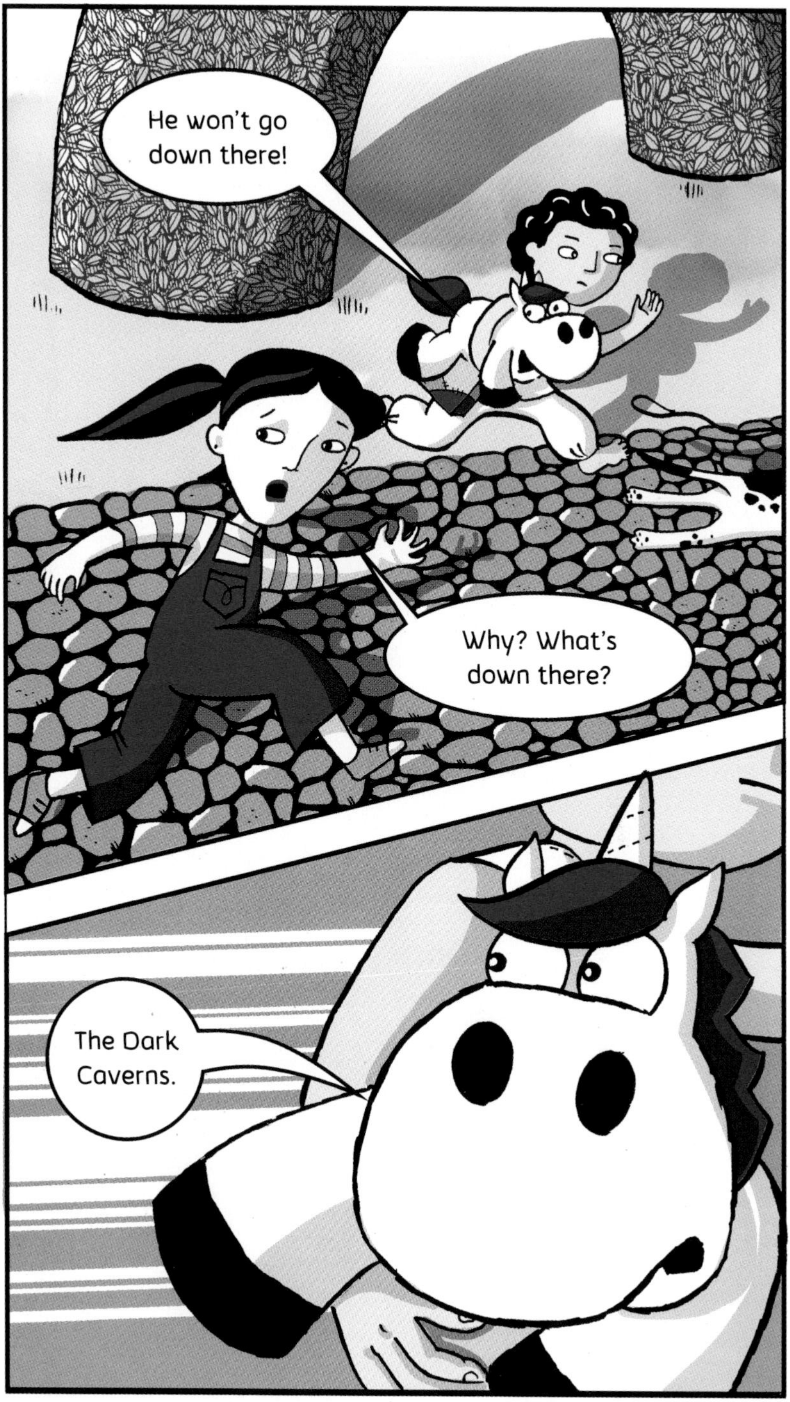
He won't go down there!
Why? What's down there?
The Dark Caverns.

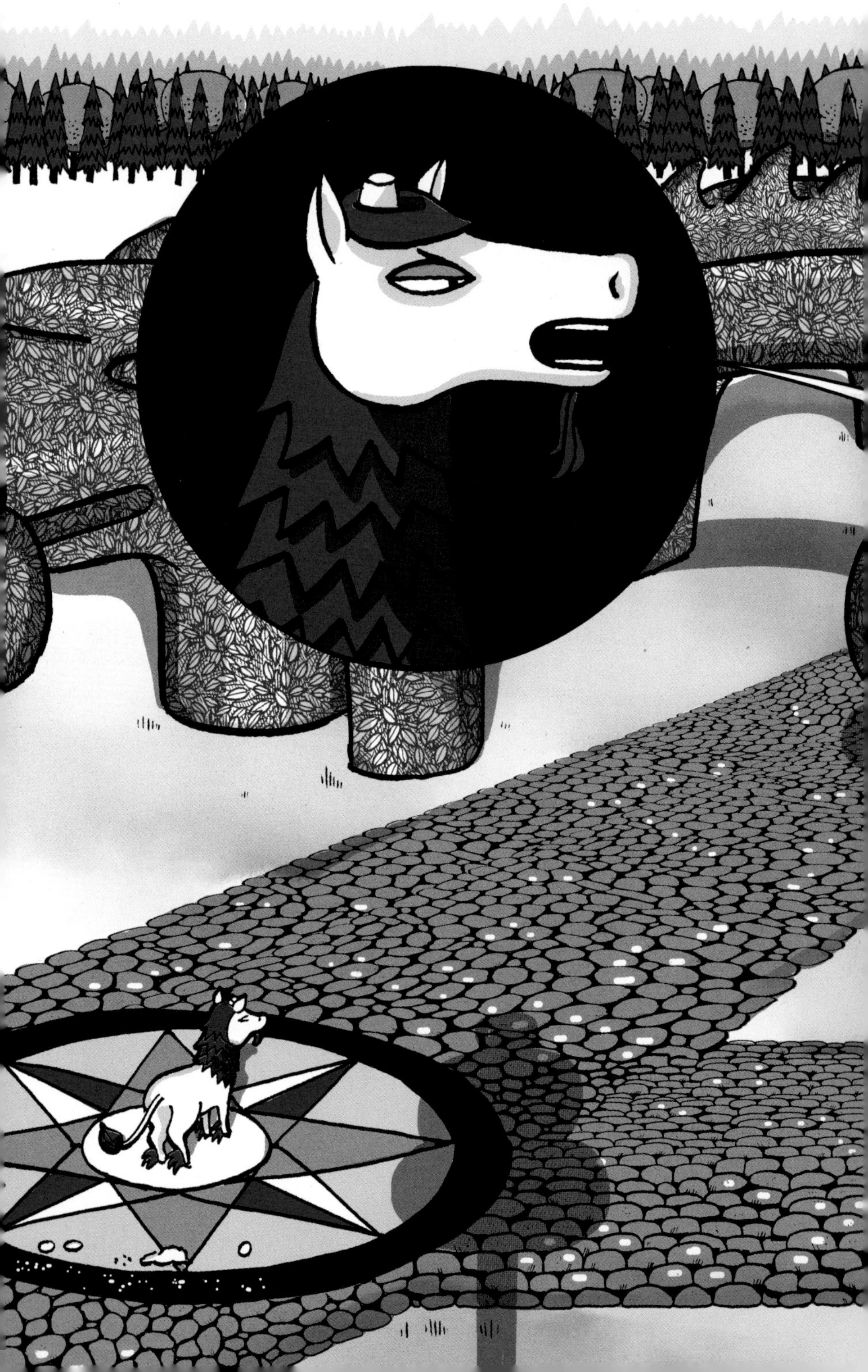

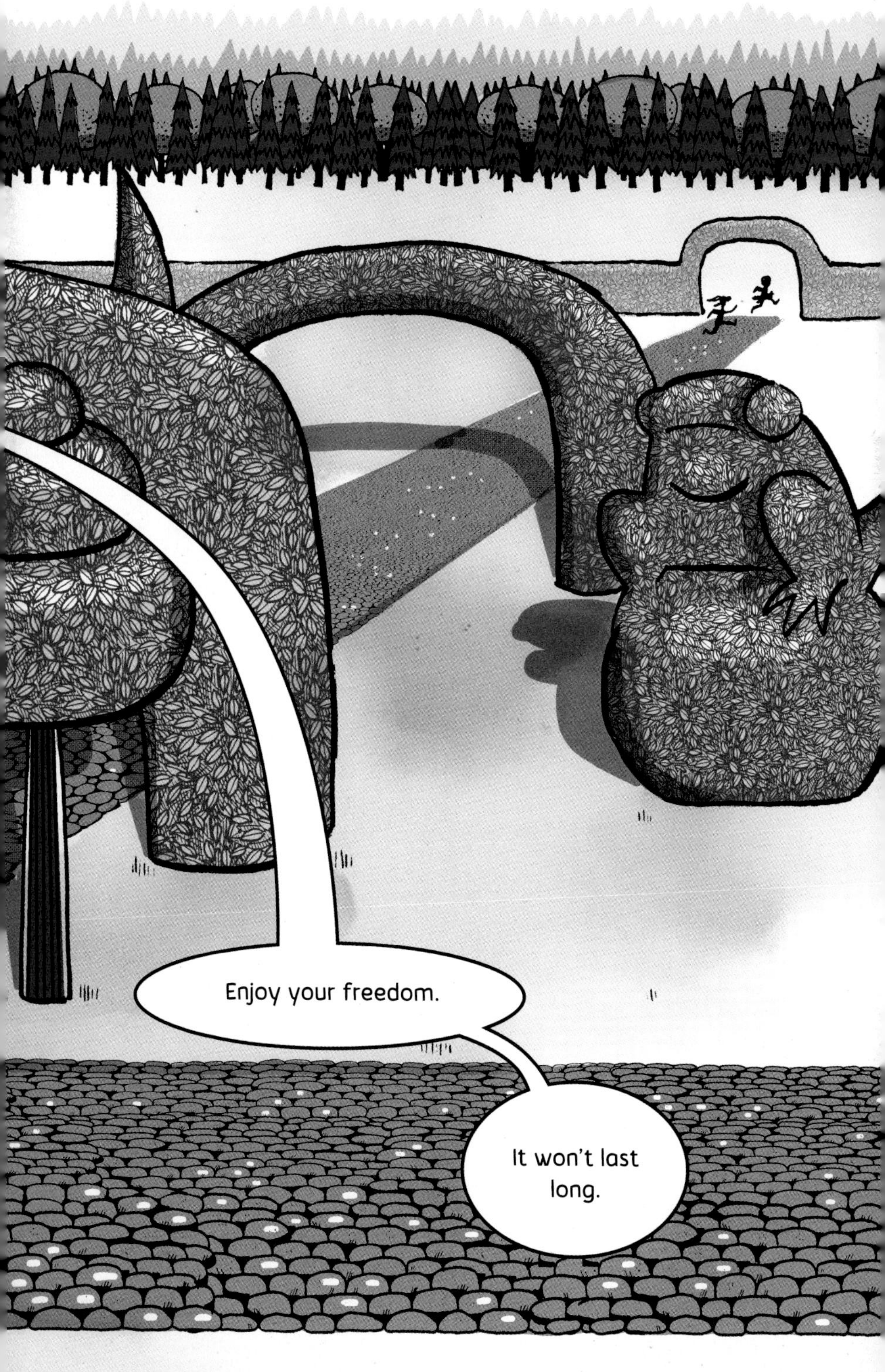

Enjoy your freedom.
It won't last long.

Chapter 13

Say Good-bye to Your Little Friend

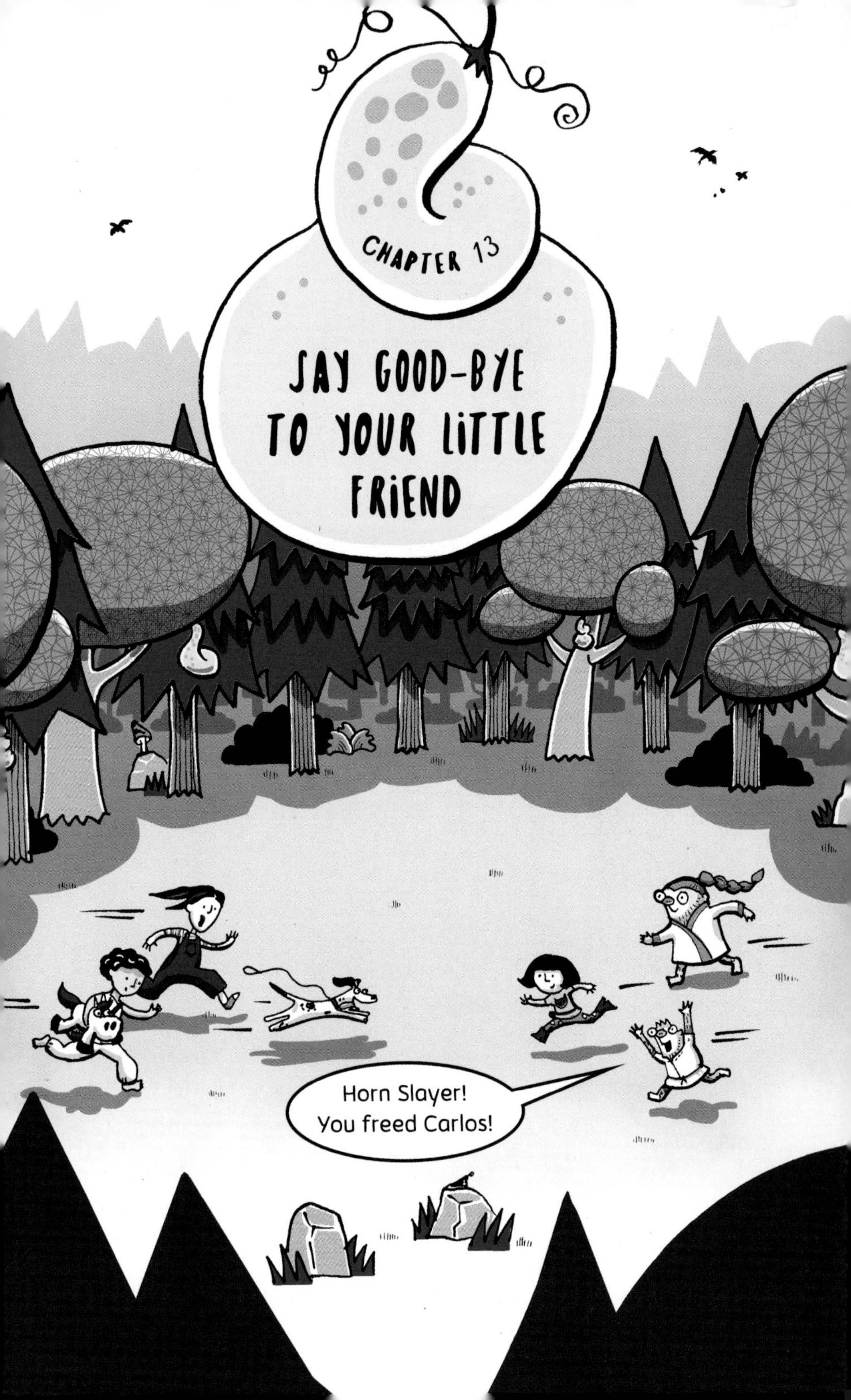
Horn Slayer! You freed Carlos!

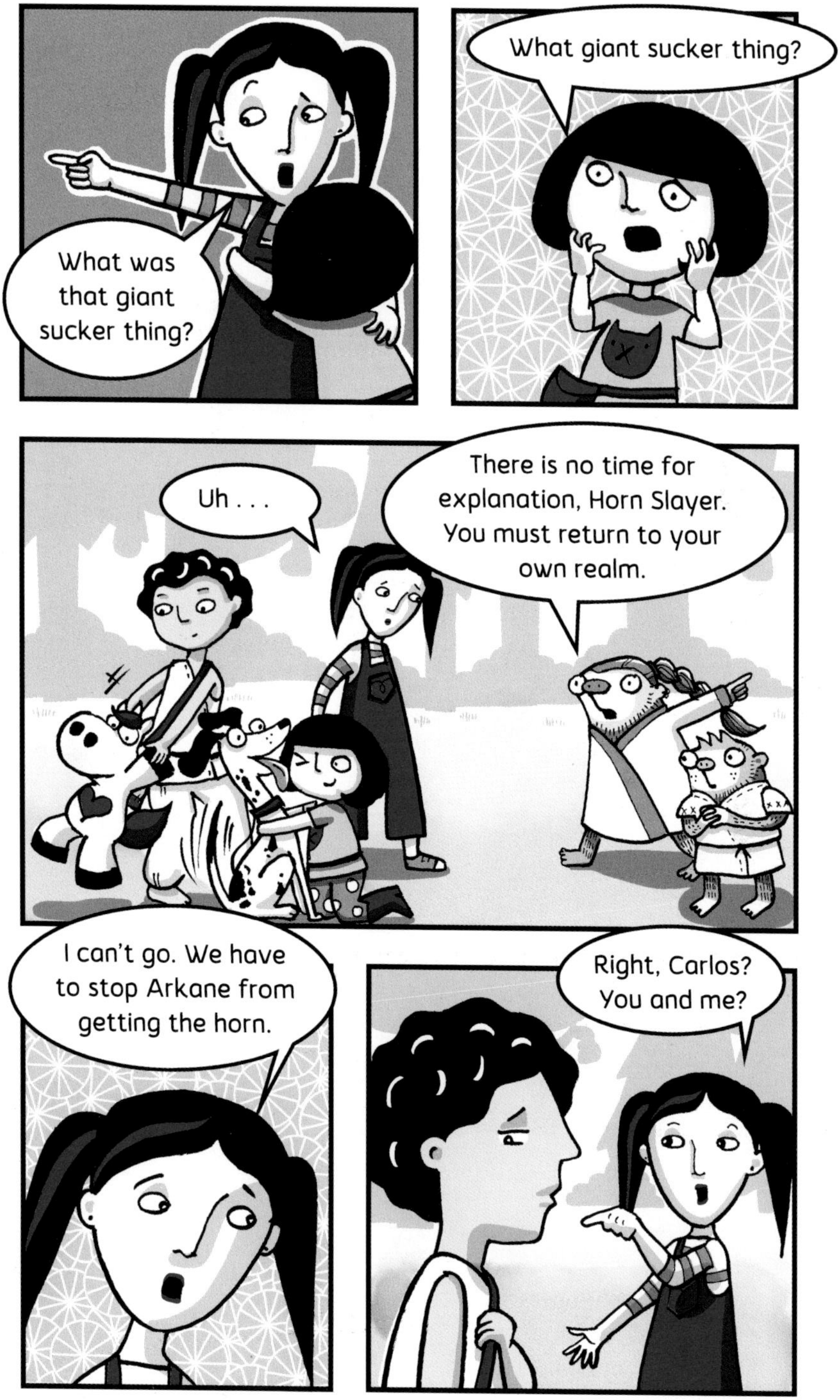
What was that giant sucker thing?
What giant sucker thing?
Uh . . .
There is no time for explanation, Horn Slayer. You must return to your own realm.
I can't go. We have to stop Arkane from getting the horn.
Right, Carlos? You and me?

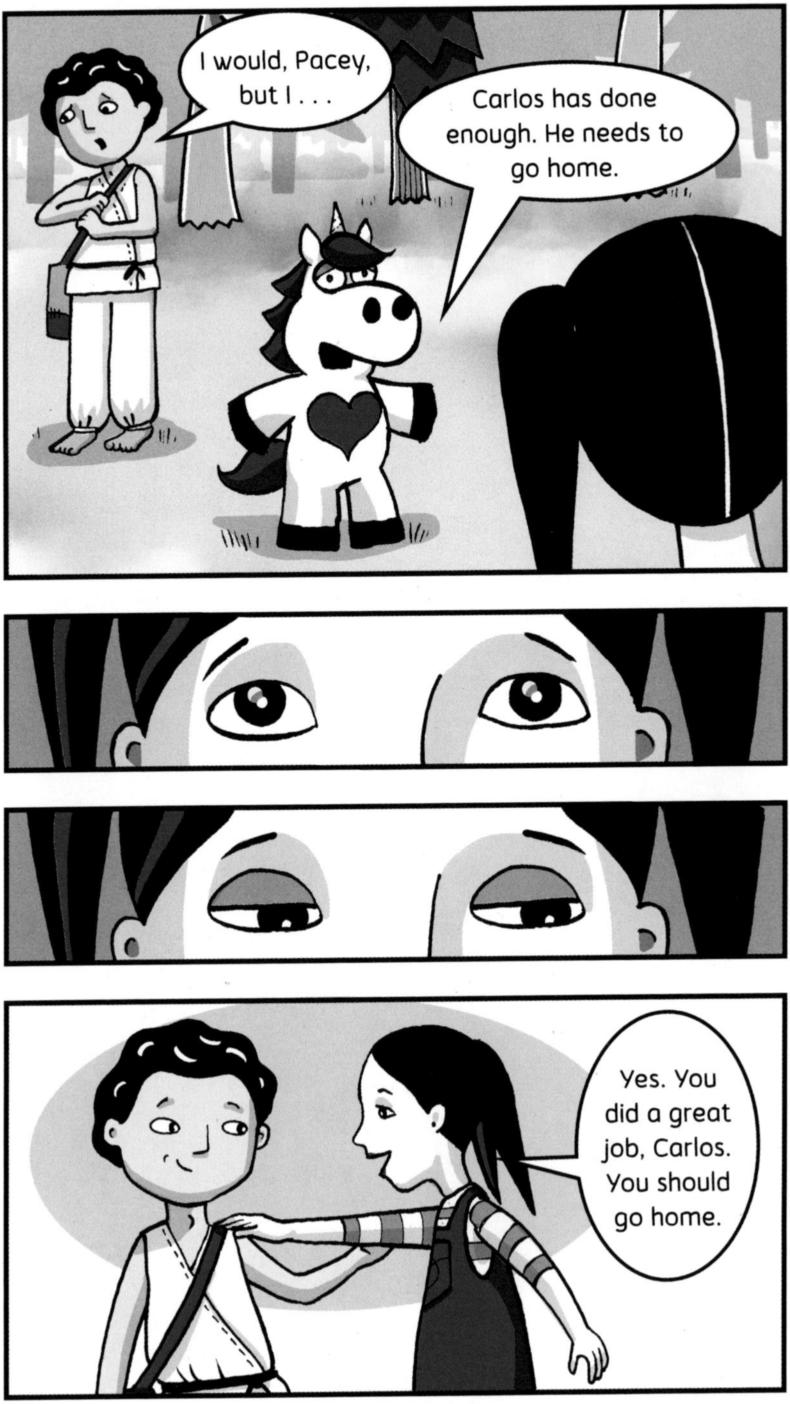
I would, Pacey, but I . . .
Carlos has done enough. He needs to go home.
Yes. You did a great job, Carlos. You should go home.

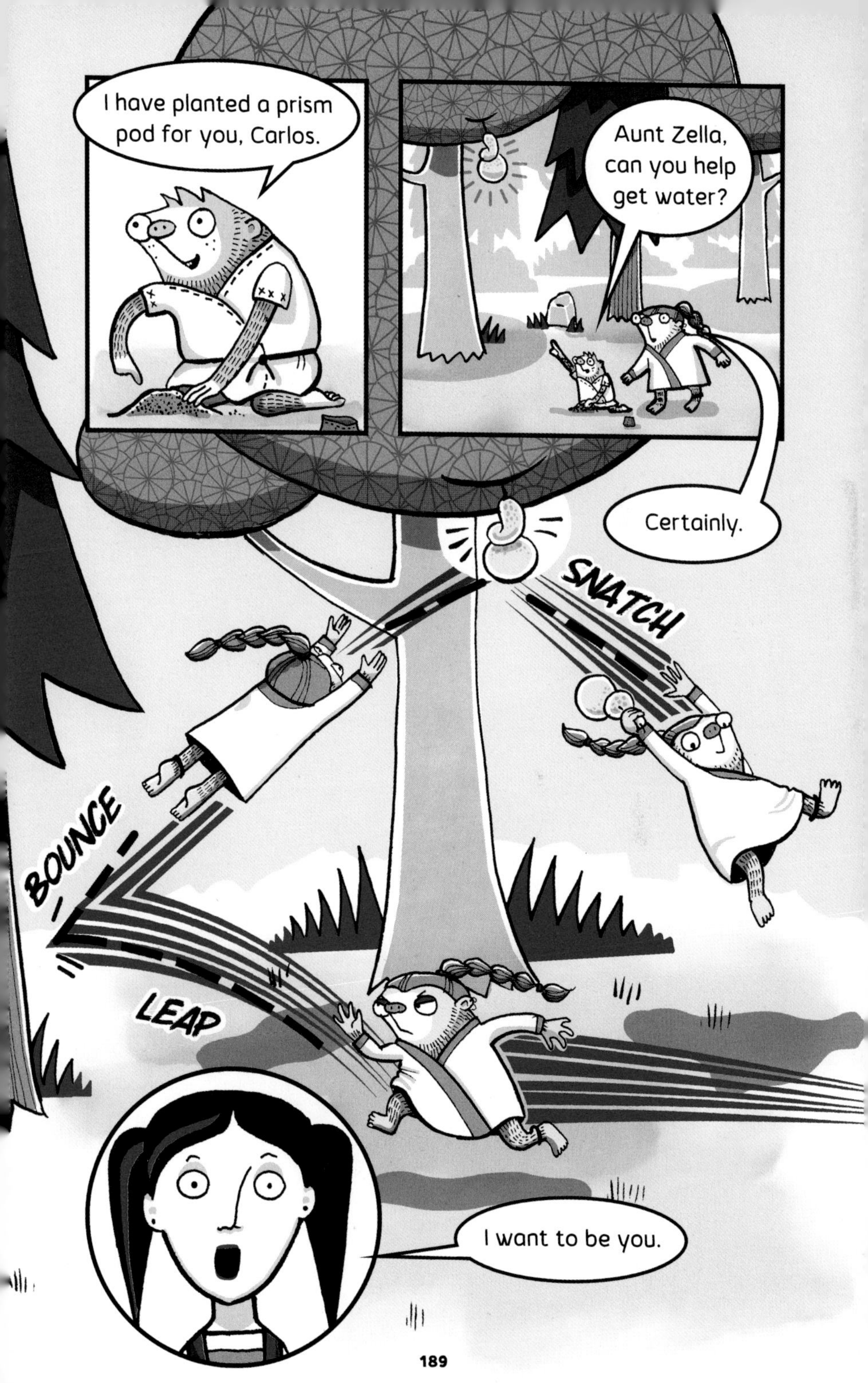
I have planted a prism pod for you, Carlos.
Aunt Zella, can you help get water?
Certainly.
SNATCH
BOUNCE
LEAP
I want to be you.

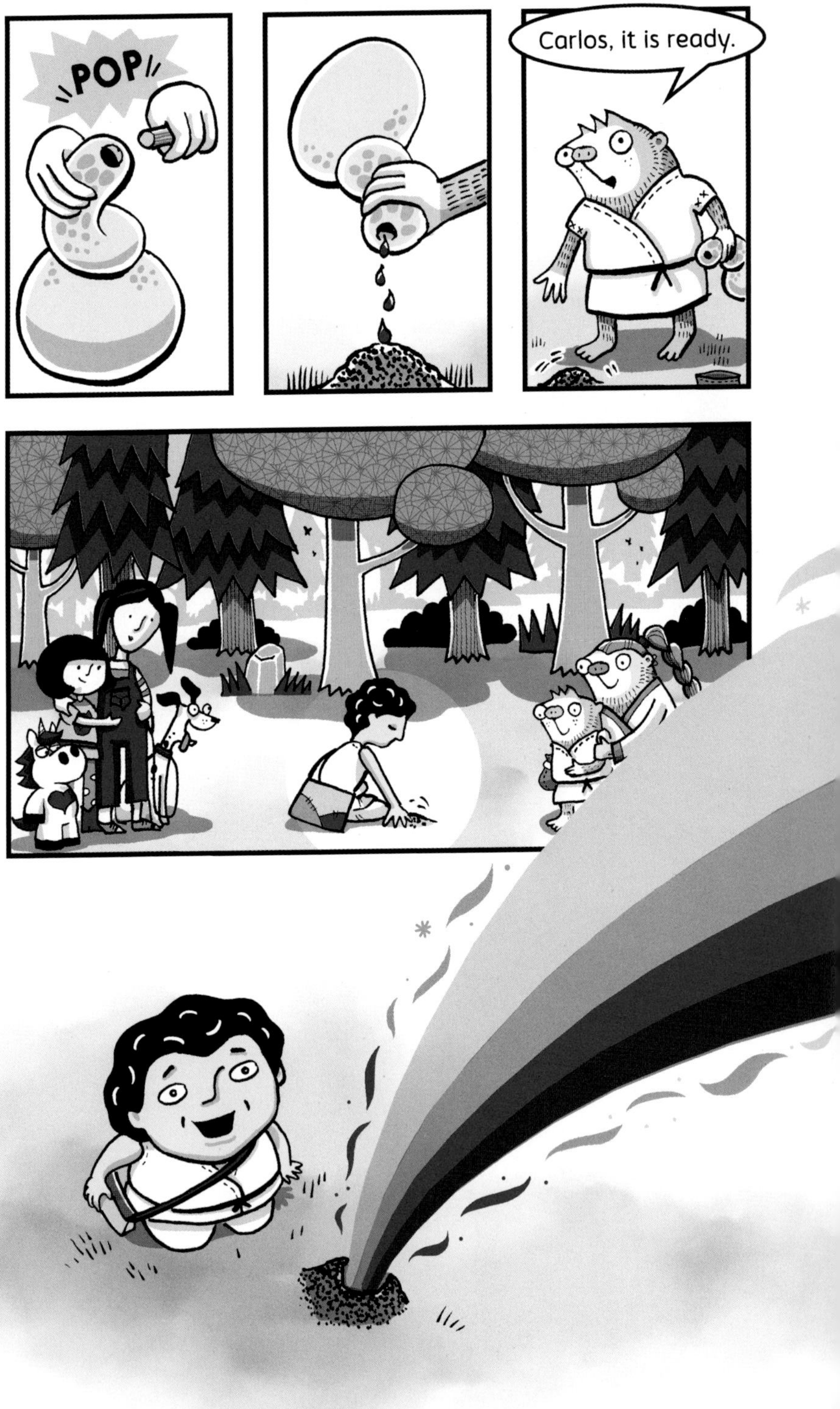
POP
Carlos, it is ready.

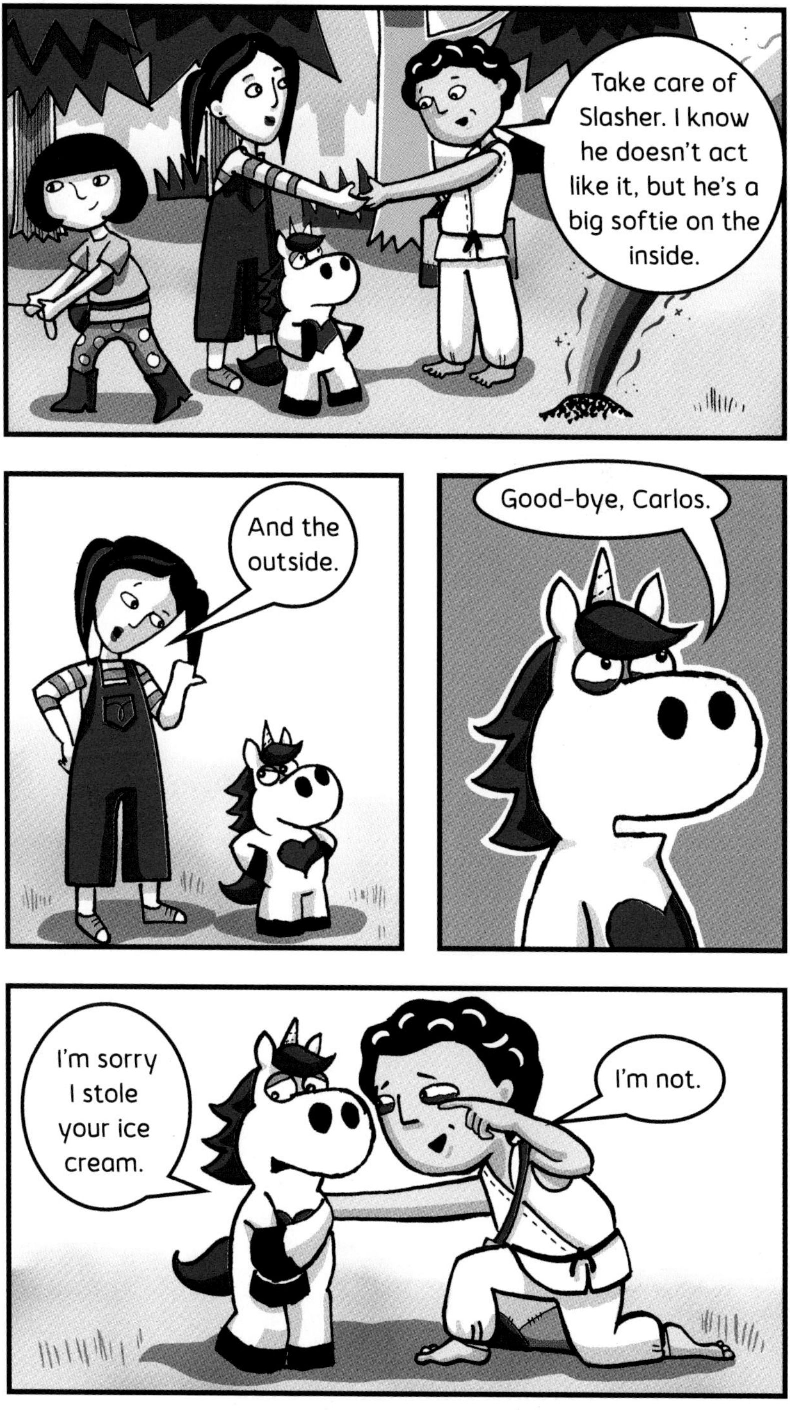
Take care of Slasher. I know he doesn't act like it, but he's a big softie on the inside.
And the outside.
Good-bye, Carlos.
I'm sorry I stole your ice cream.
I'm not.

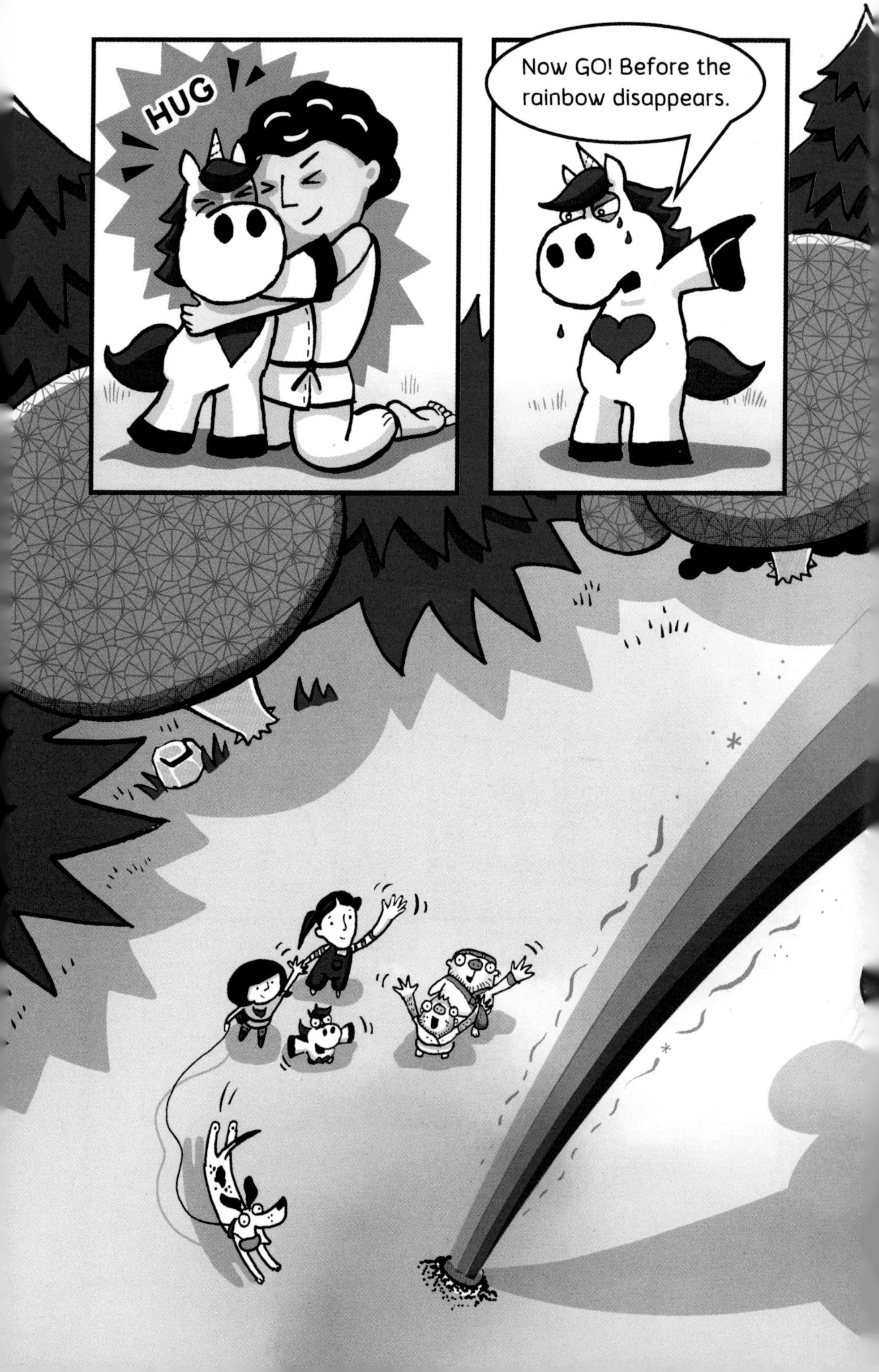
HUG
Now GO! Before the rainbow disappears.

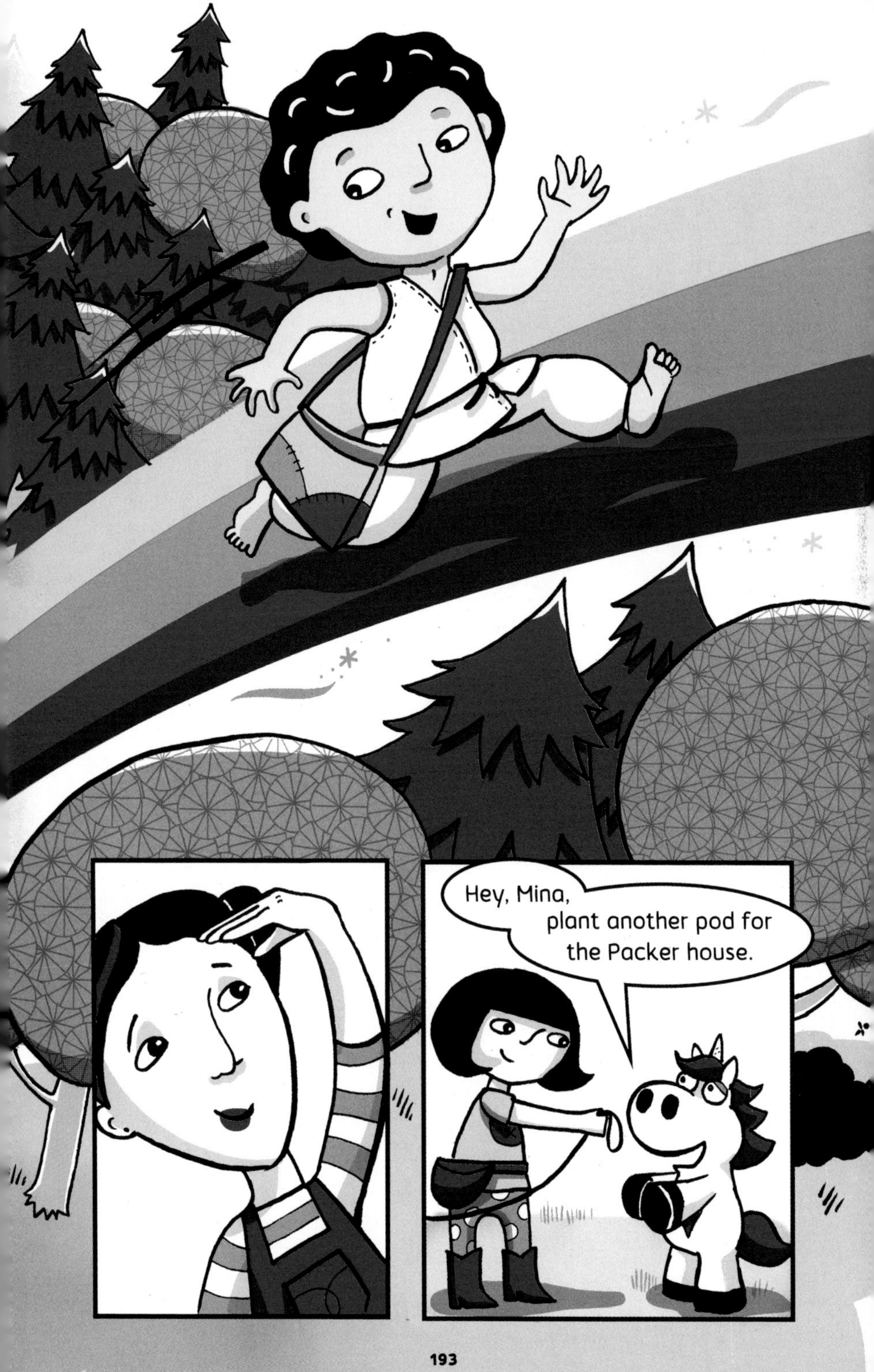
Hey, Mina,
plant another pod for
the Packer house.

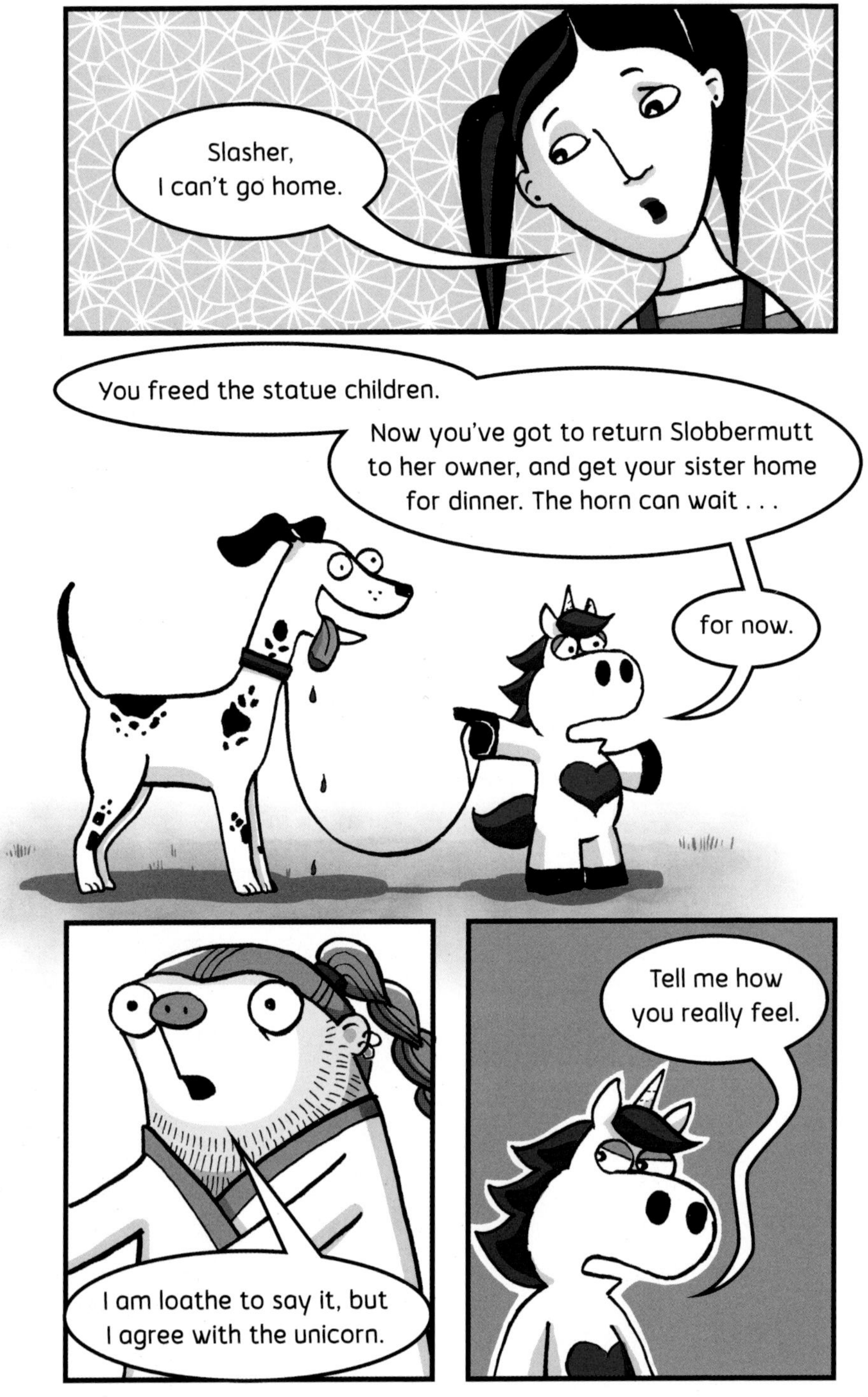
Slasher,
I can't go home.
You freed the statue children.
Now you've got to return Slobbermutt to her owner, and get your sister home for dinner. The horn can wait . . .
for now.
I am loathe to say it, but I agree with the unicorn.
Tell me how you really feel.

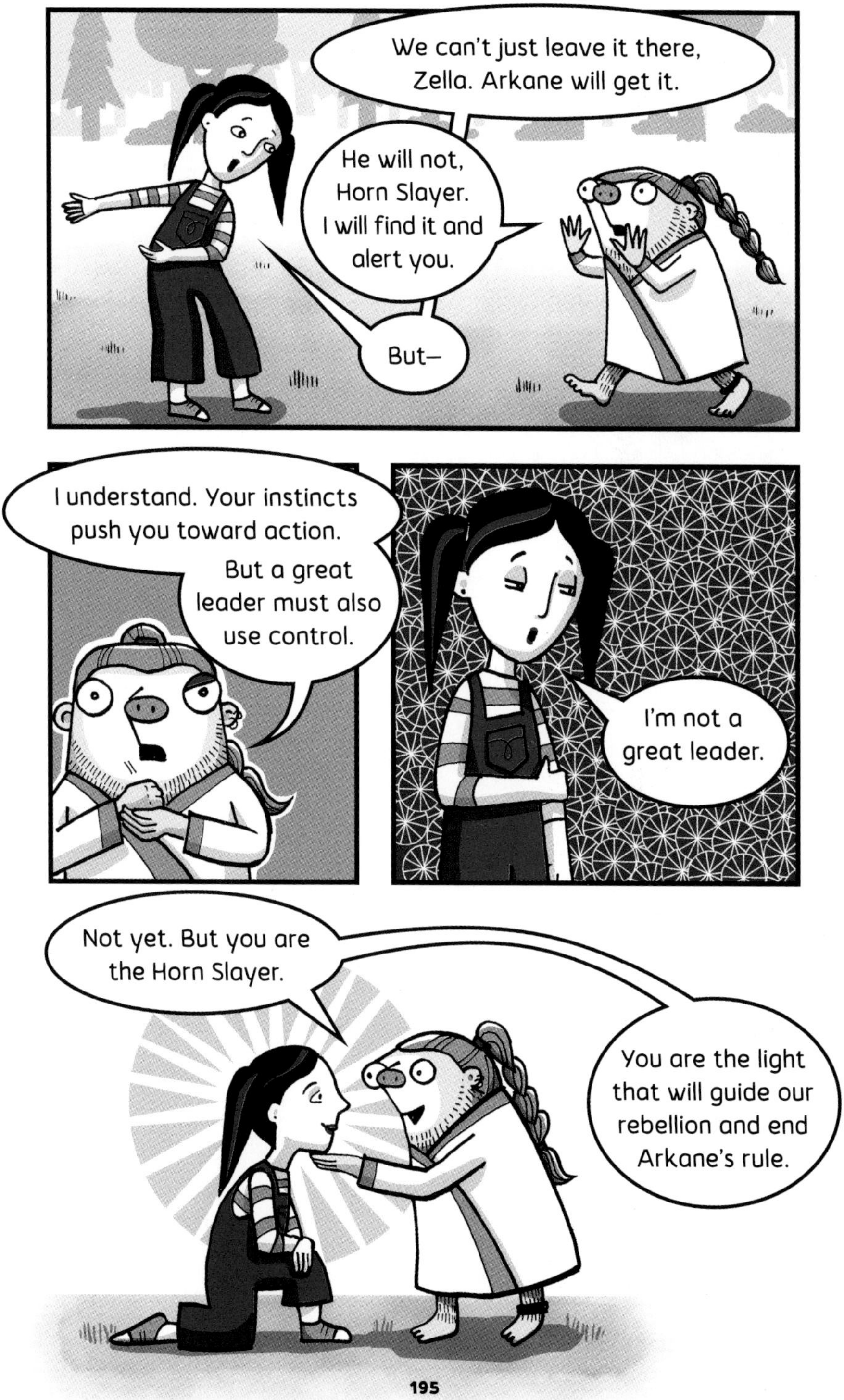
We can't just leave it there, Zella. Arkane will get it.
He will not, Horn Slayer. I will find it and alert you.
But–
I understand. Your instincts push you toward action.
But a great leader must also use control.
I'm not a great leader.
Not yet. But you are the Horn Slayer.
You are the light that will guide our rebellion and end Arkane's rule.

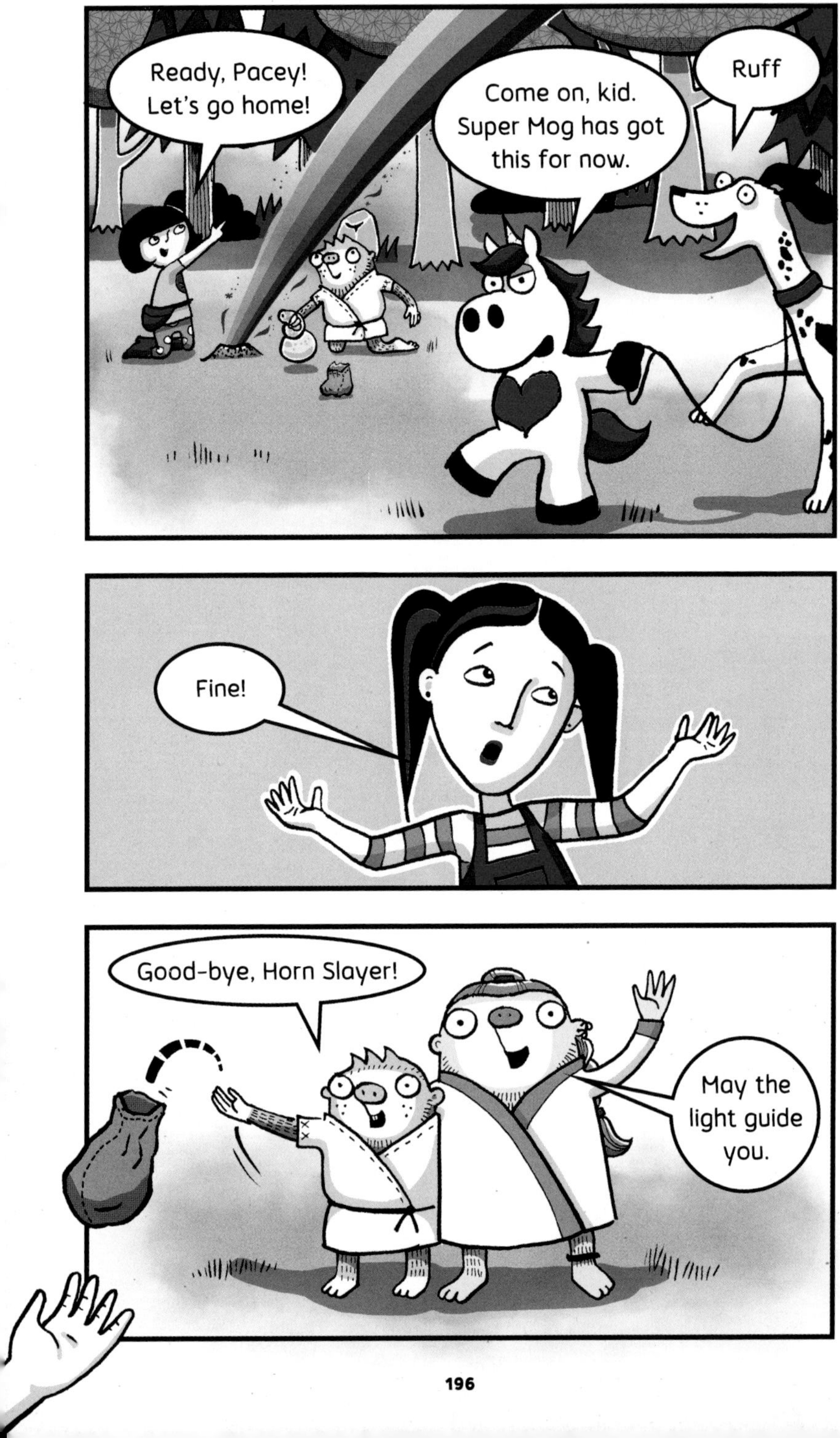
Ready, Pacey!
Let's go home!
Come on, kid.
Super Mog has got
this for now.
Ruff
Fine!
Good-bye, Horn Slayer!
May the
light guide
you.

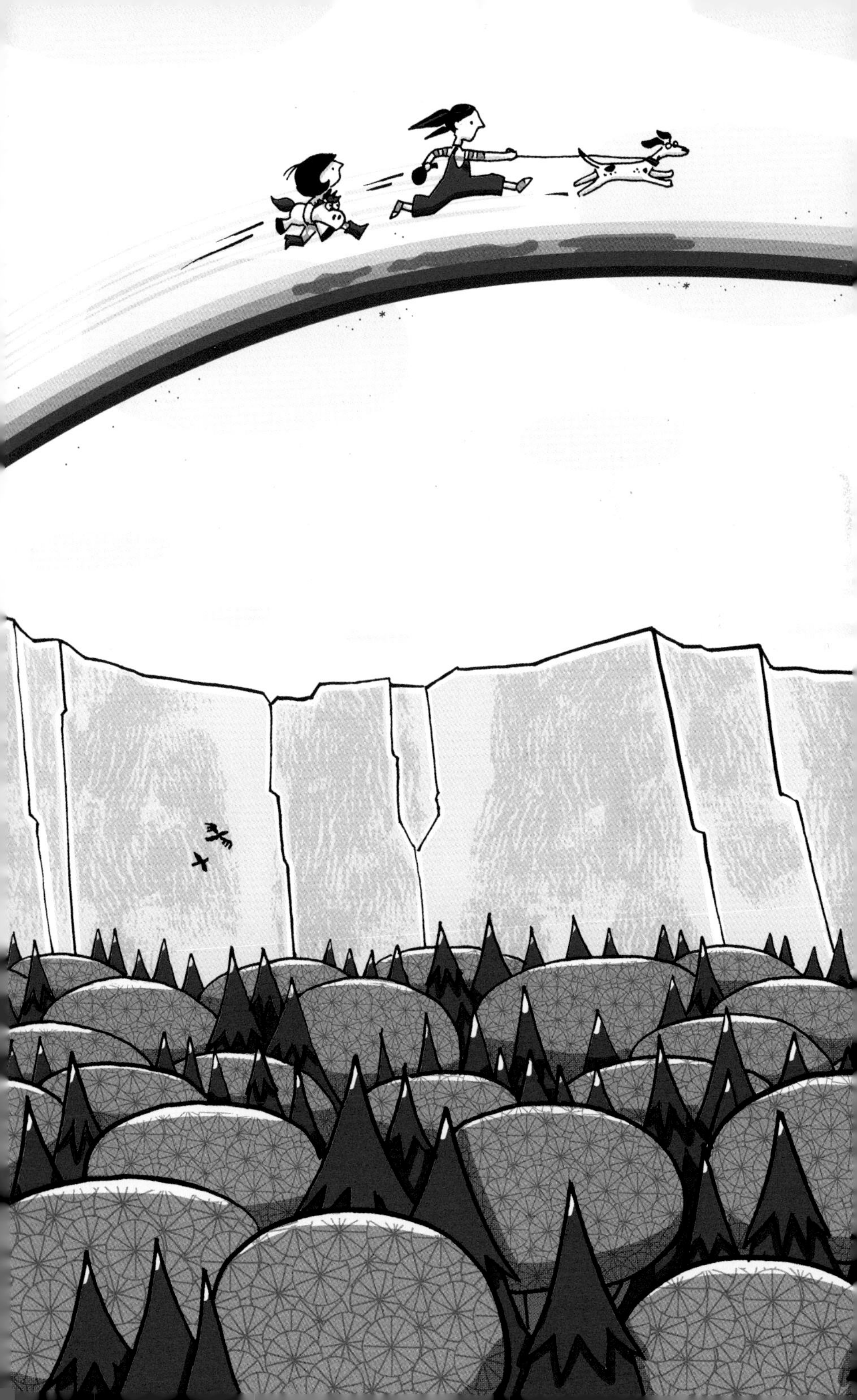

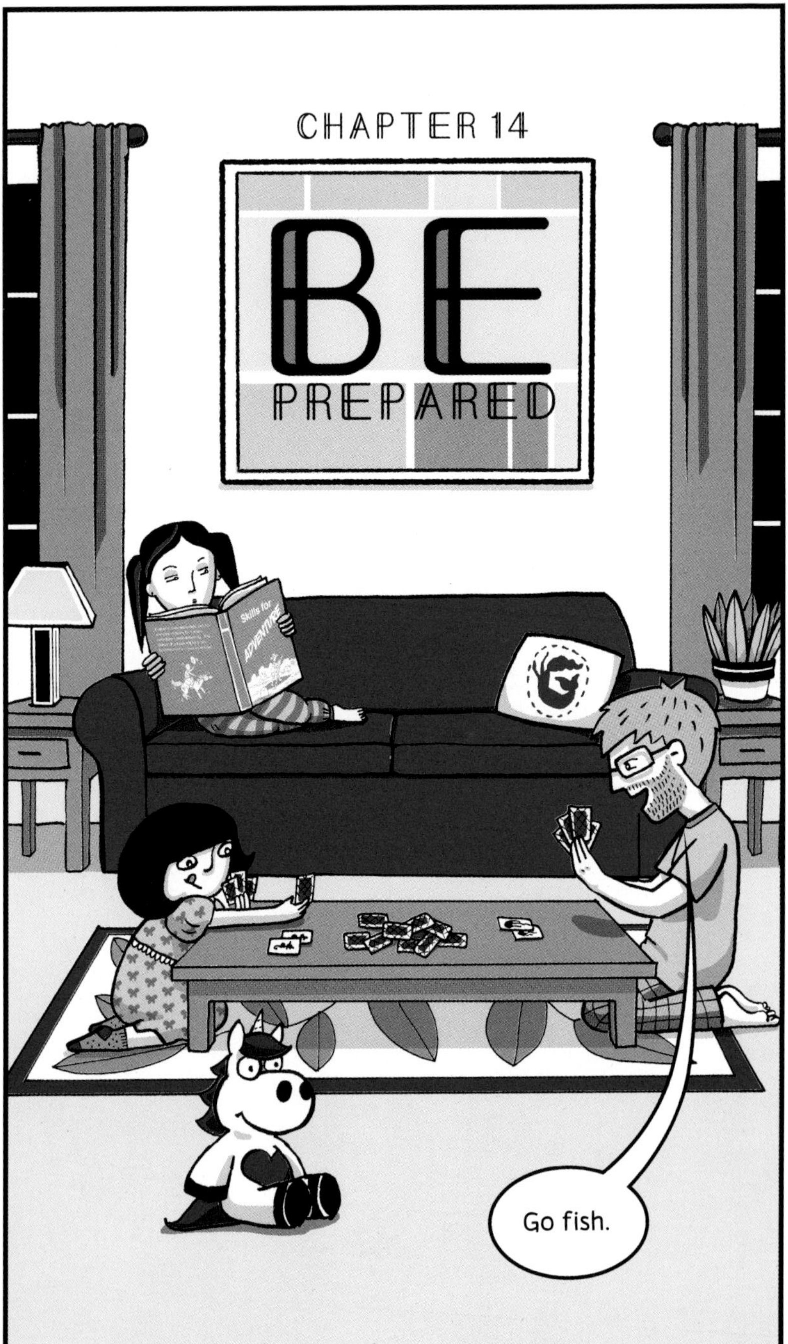
CHAPTER 14
BE PREPARED
Skills for ADVENTURE
Go fish.

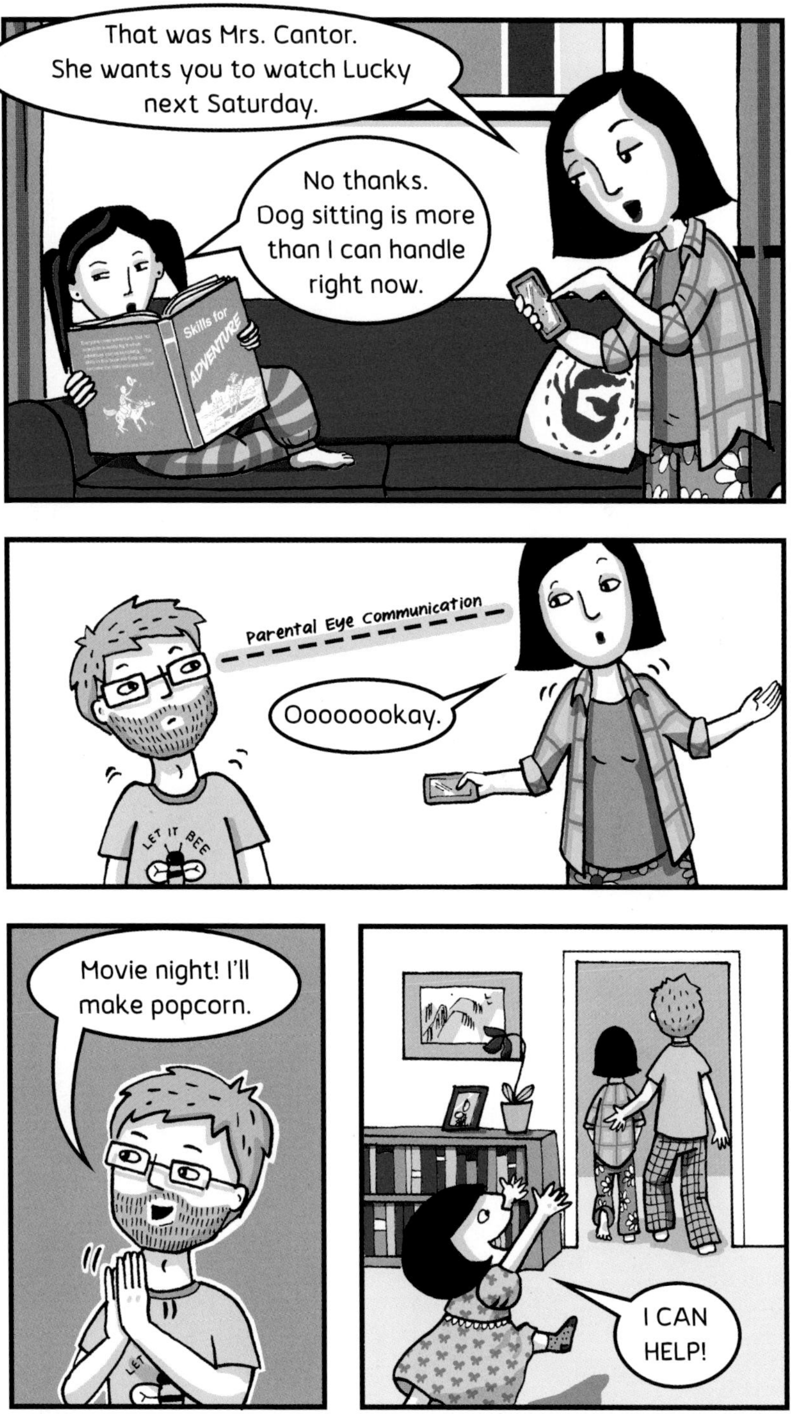
That was Mrs. Cantor. She wants you to watch Lucky next Saturday.
No thanks. Dog sitting is more than I can handle right now.
Skills for ADVENTURE
Parental Eye Communication
Oooooookay.
LET IT BEE
Movie night! I'll make popcorn.
I CAN HELP!

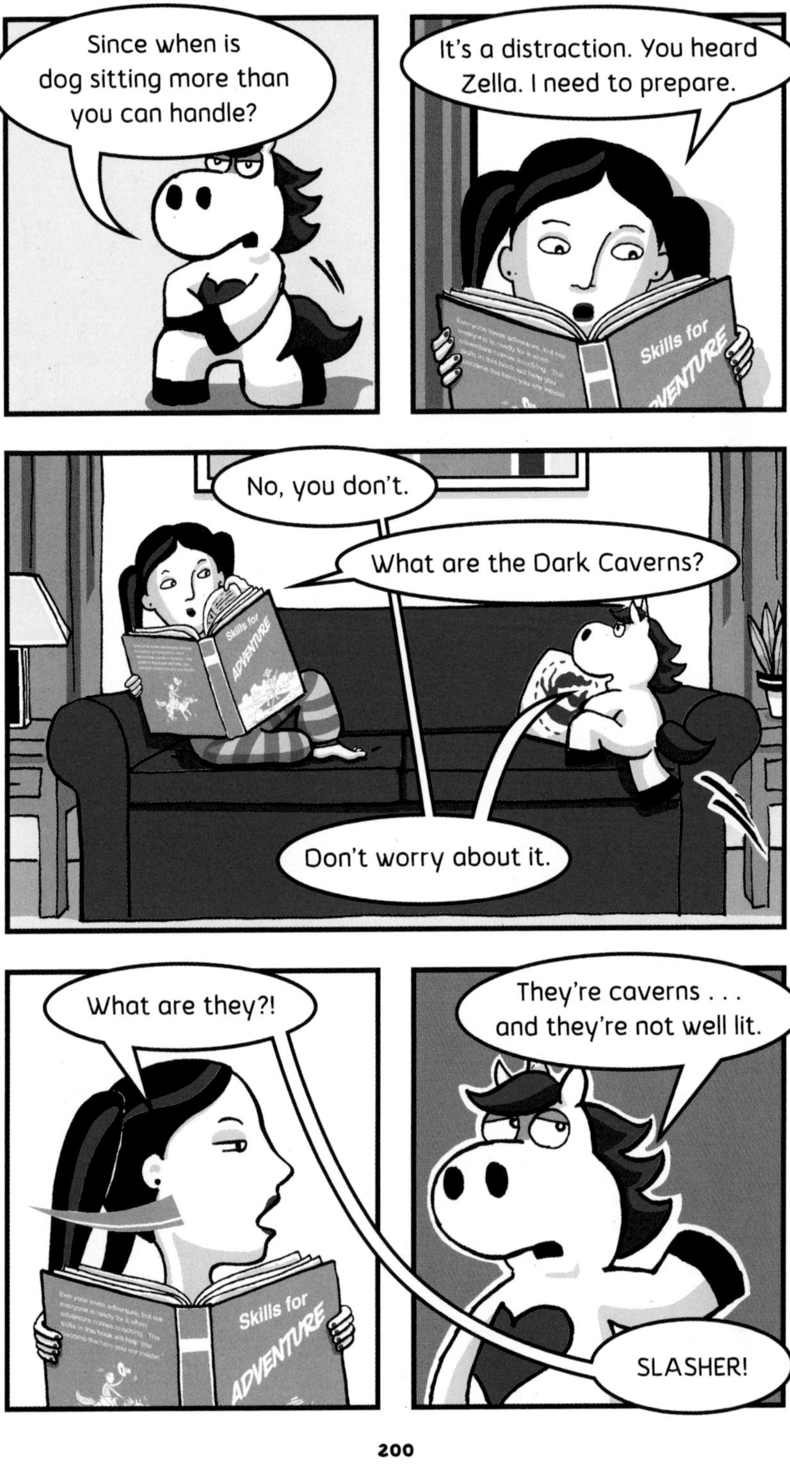
Since when is dog sitting more than you can handle?
It's a distraction. You heard Zella. I need to prepare.
Skills for ADVENTURE
No, you don't.
What are the Dark Caverns?
Don't worry about it.
What are they?!
They're caverns . . . and they're not well lit.
SLASHER!

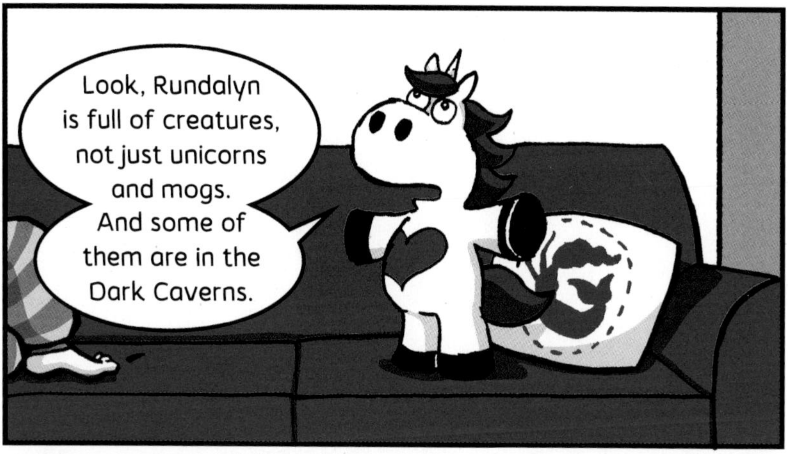
Look, Rundalyn is full of creatures, not just unicorns and mogs. And some of them are in the Dark Caverns.

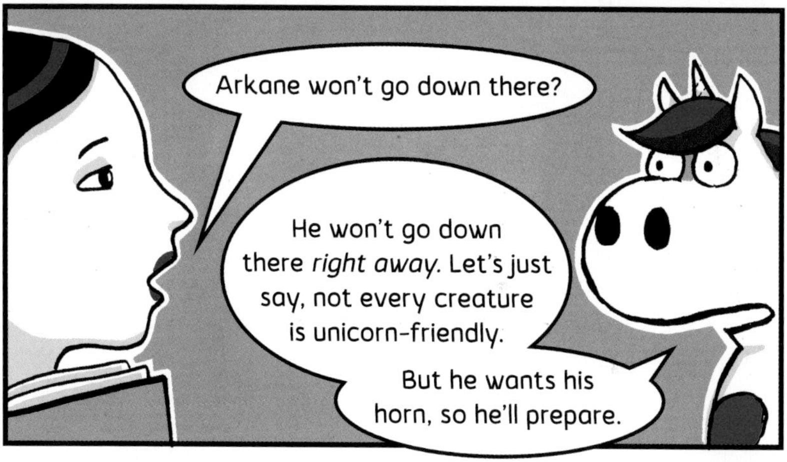
Arkane won't go down there?
He won't go down there *right away*. Let's just say, not every creature is unicorn-friendly.
But he wants his horn, so he'll prepare.

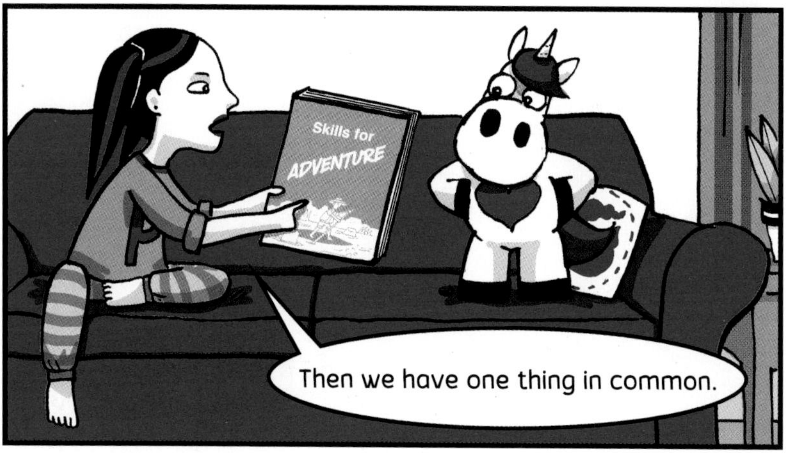
Skills for ADVENTURE
Then we have one thing in common.

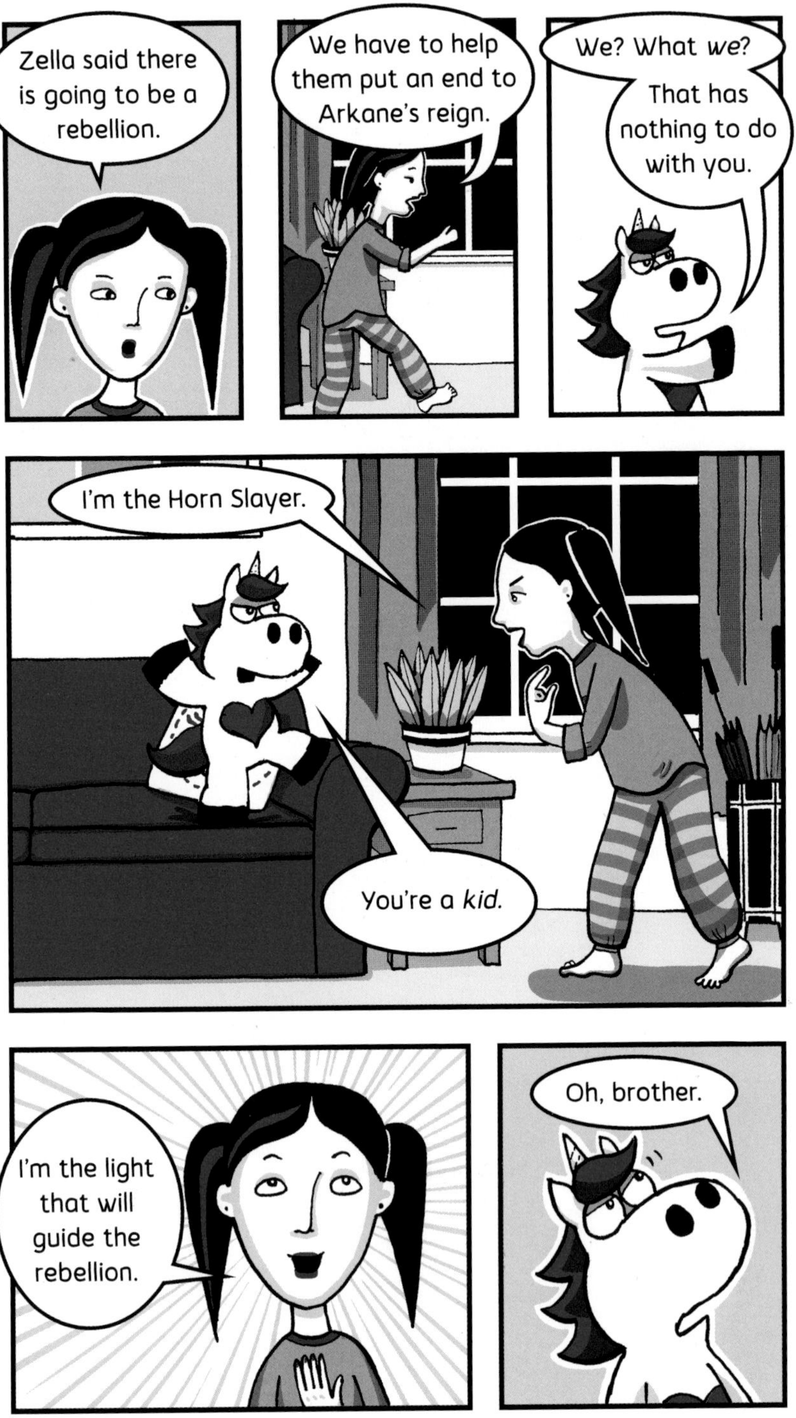
Zella said there is going to be a rebellion.
We have to help them put an end to Arkane's reign.
We? What *we*?
That has nothing to do with you.
I'm the Horn Slayer.
You're a *kid.*
I'm the light that will guide the rebellion.
Oh, brother.

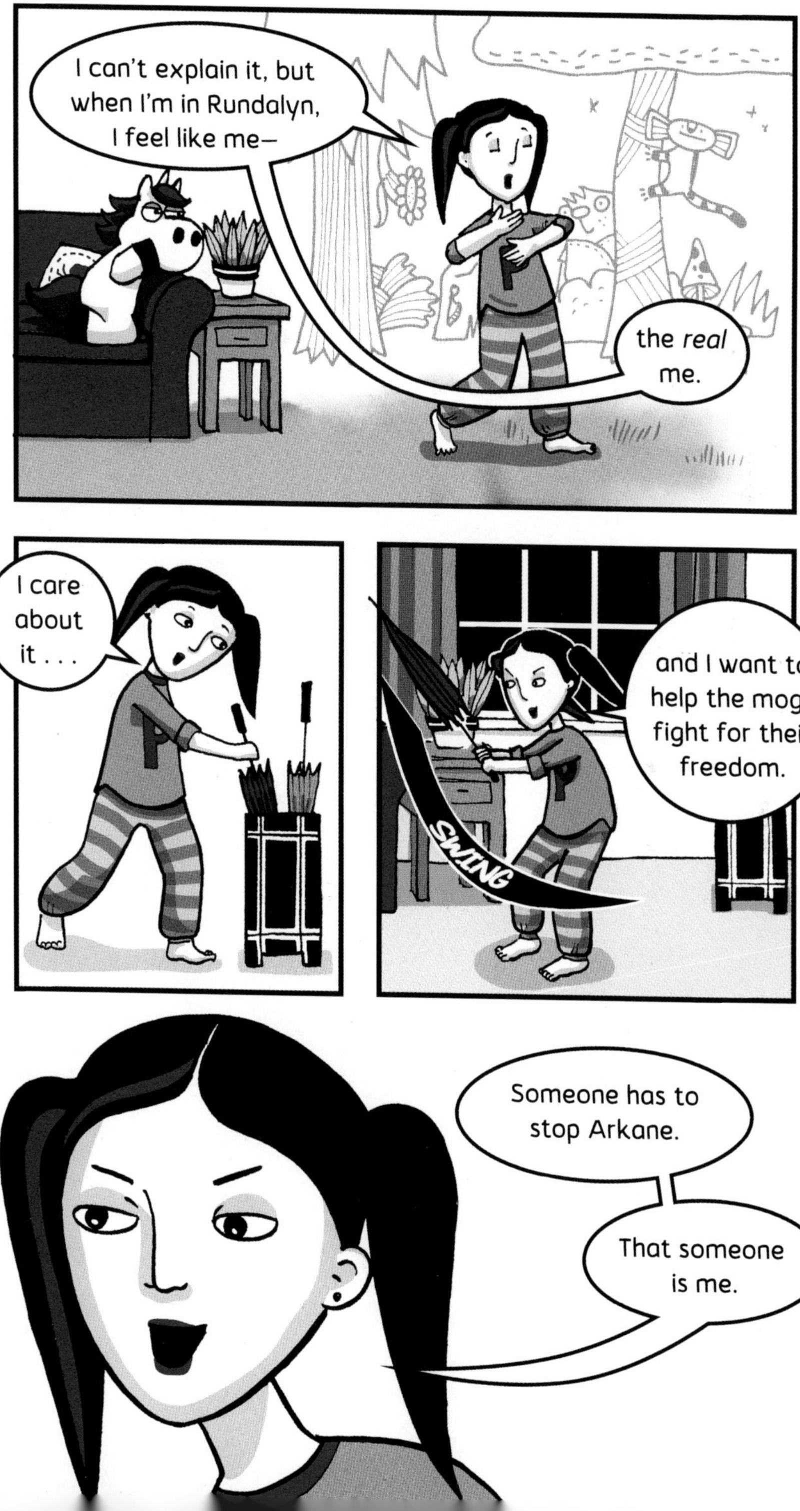
I can't explain it, but when I'm in Rundalyn, I feel like me—
the *real* me.
I care about it . . .
and I want to help the mogs fight for their freedom.
SWING
Someone has to stop Arkane.
That someone is me.

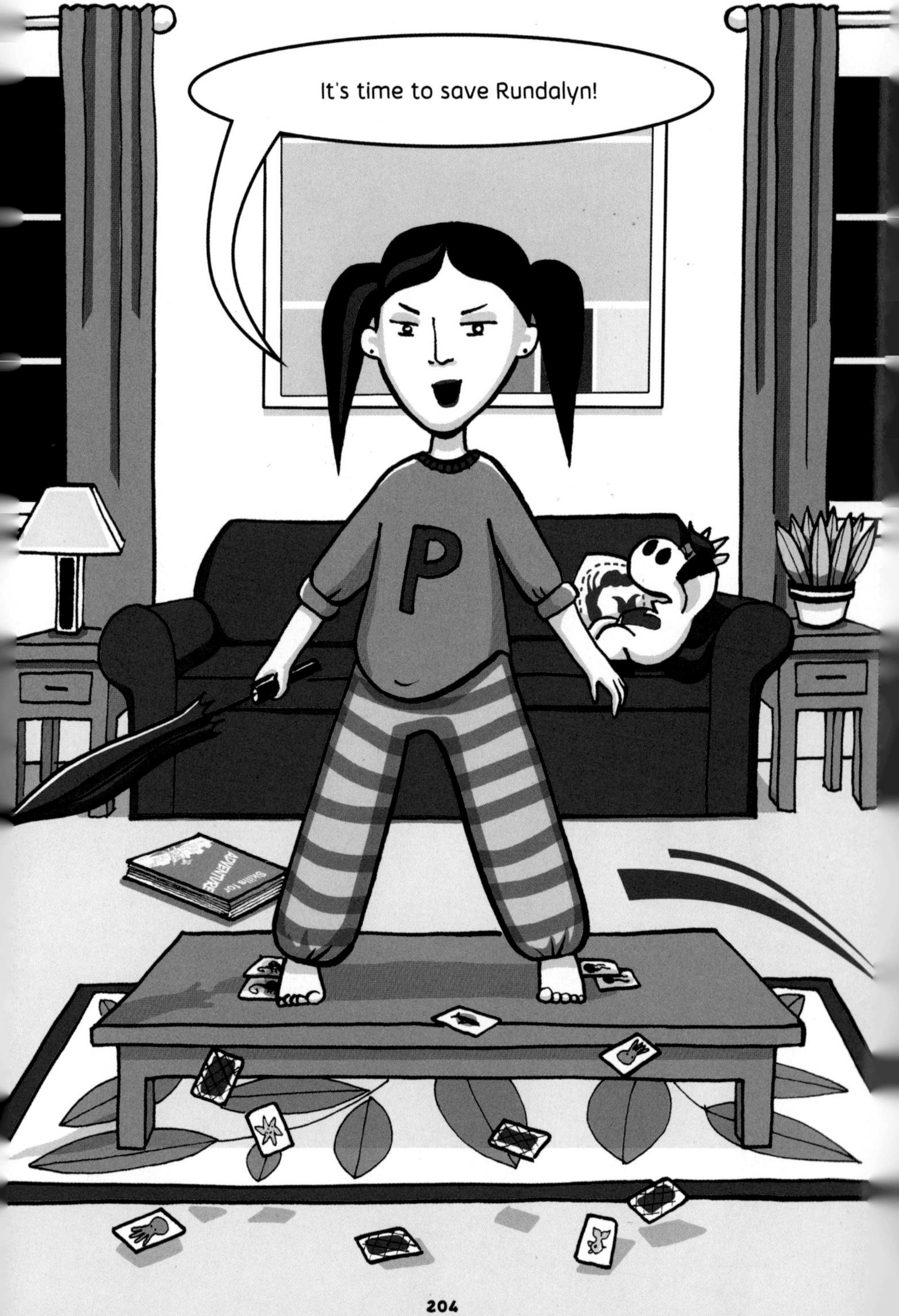
It's time to save Rundalyn!
Skills for ADVENTURE

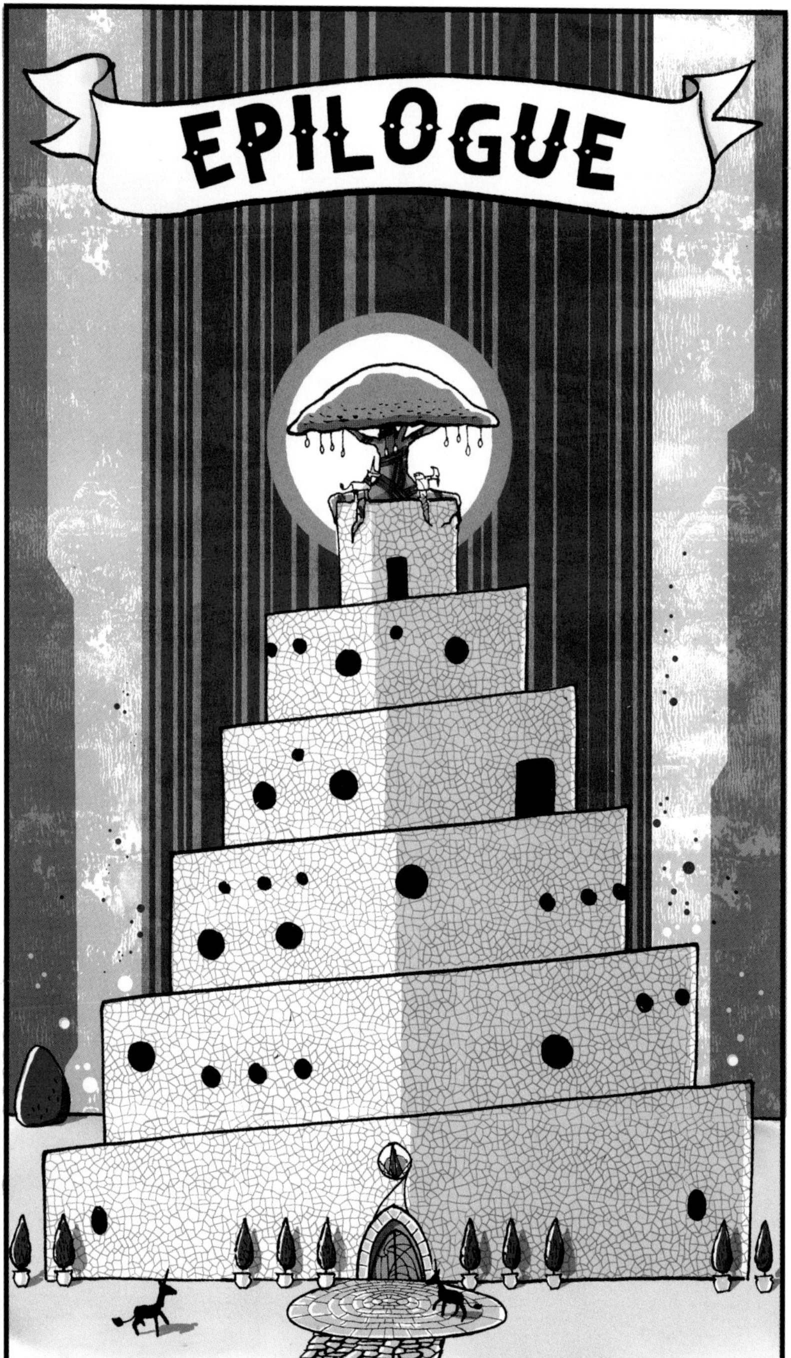
EPILOGUE

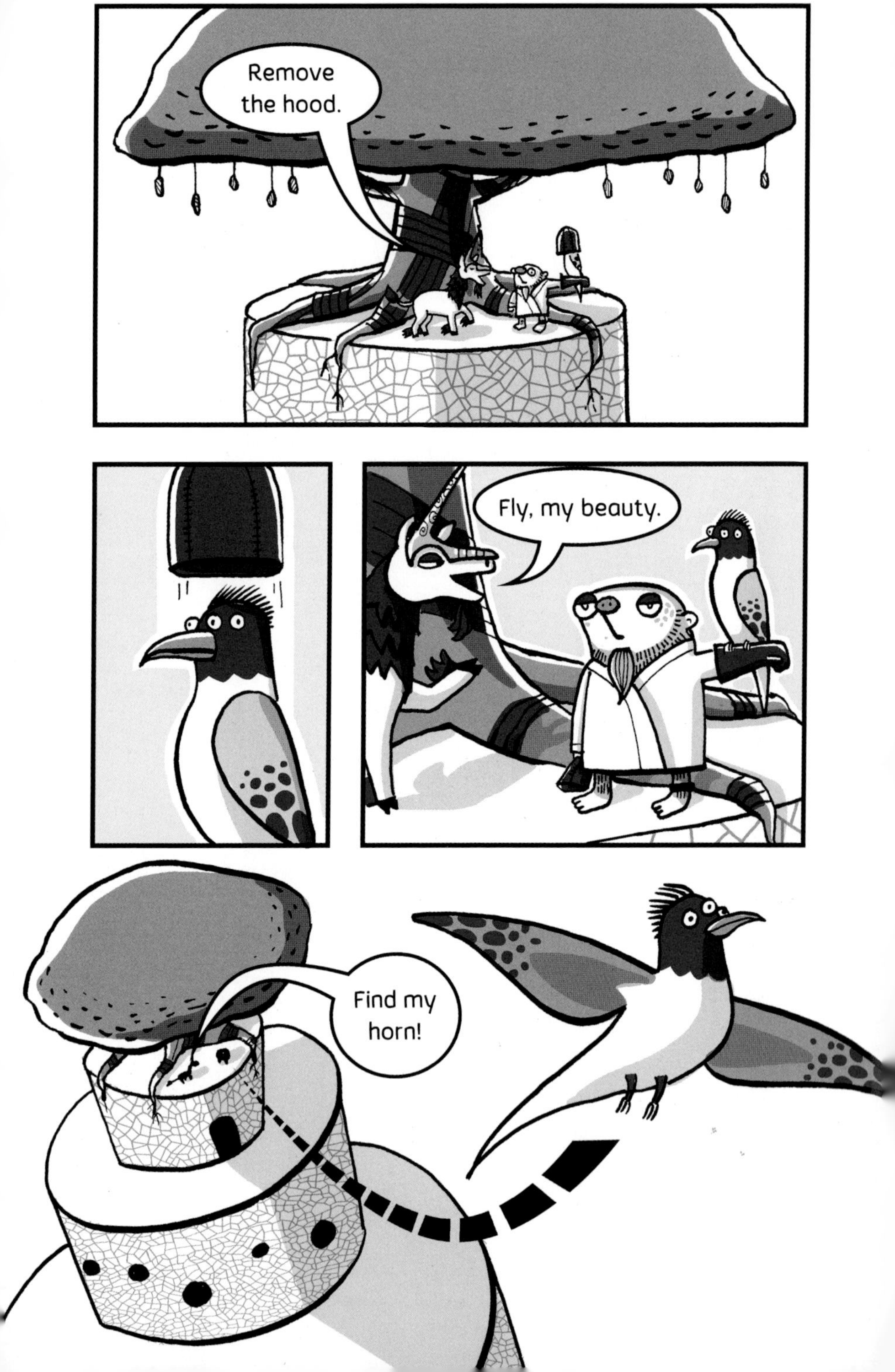
Remove the hood.
Fly, my beauty.
Find my horn!

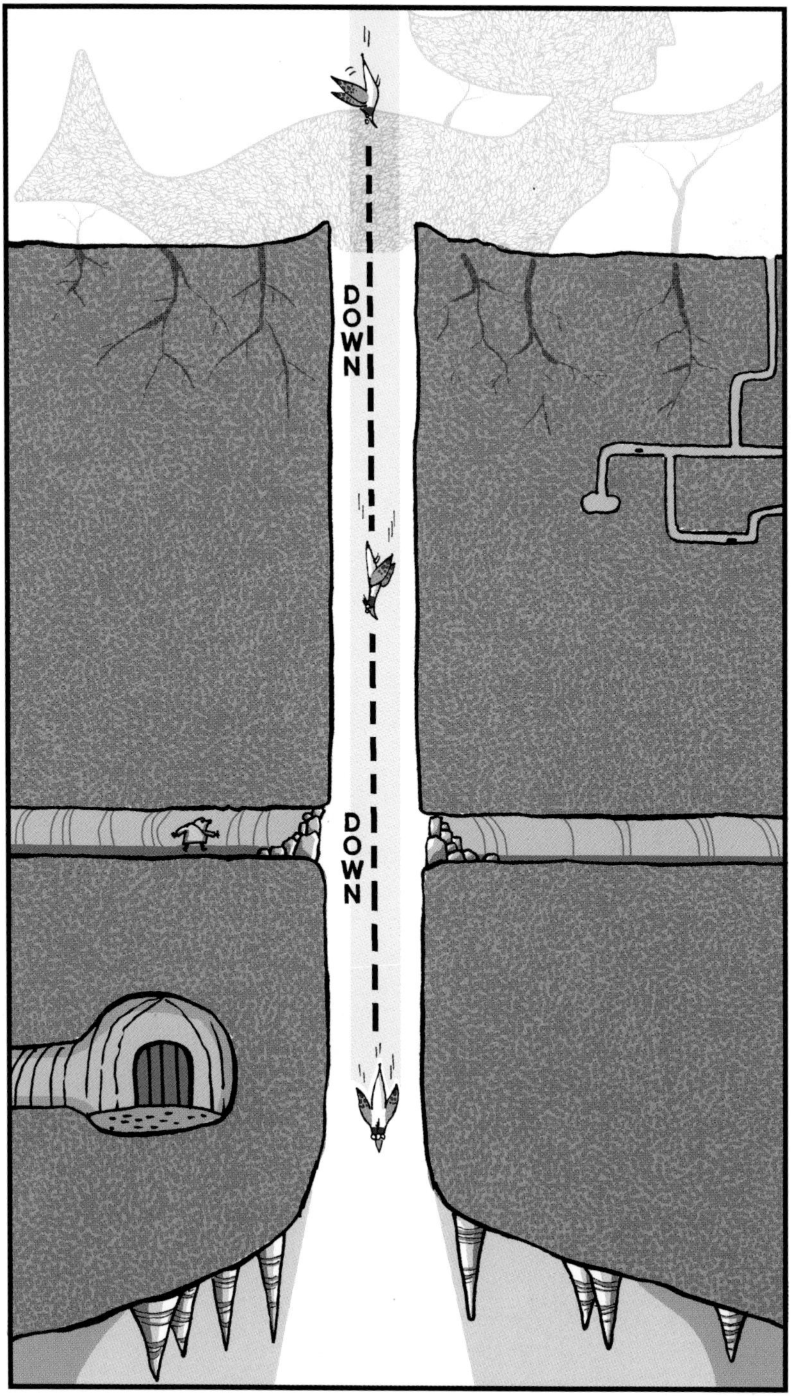
DOWN
DOWN

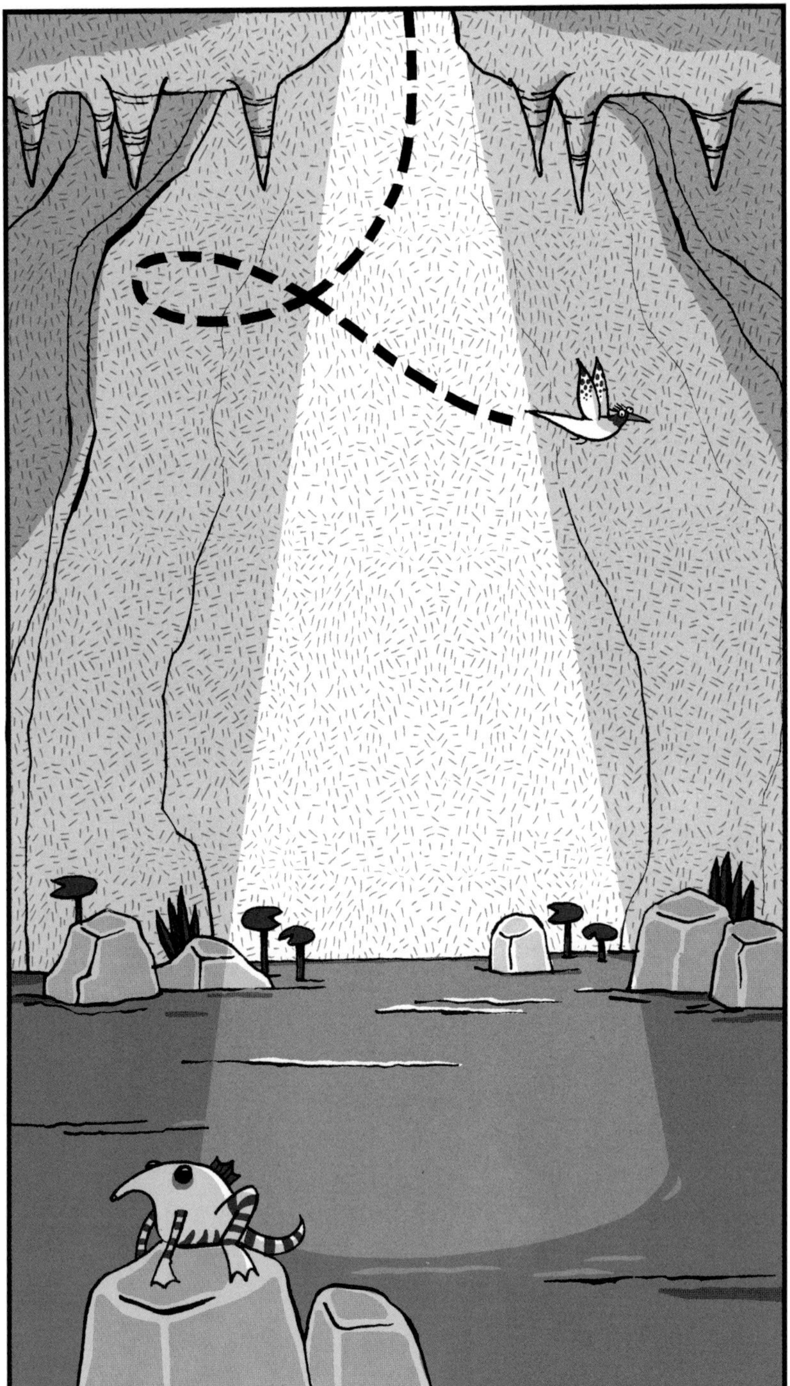

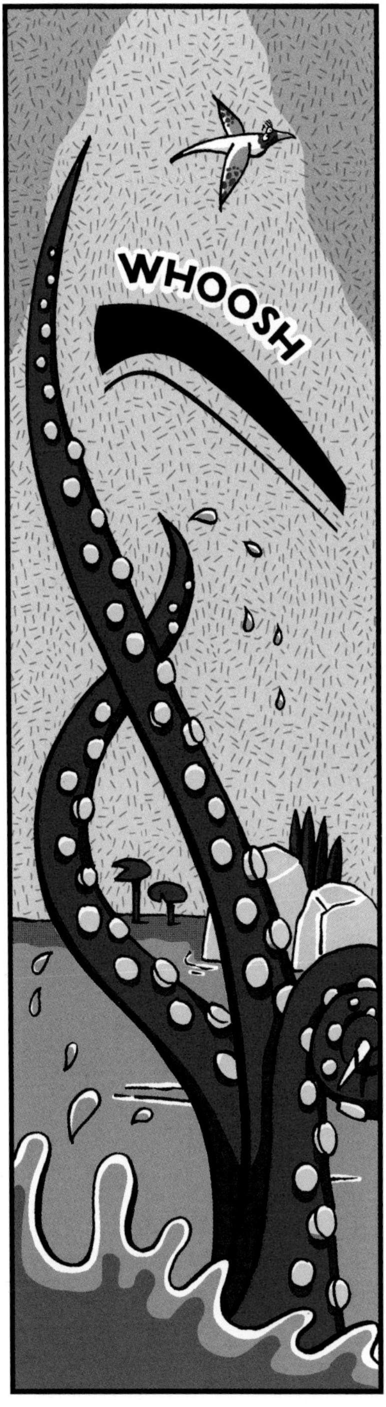
WHOOSH

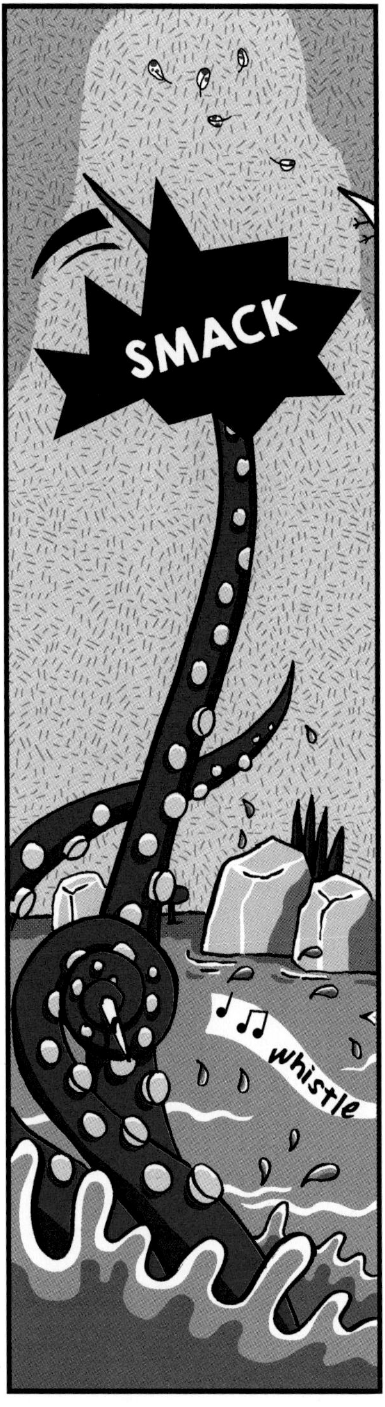
SMACK
whistle

End of Book 2

THE ADVENTURE CONTINUES IN

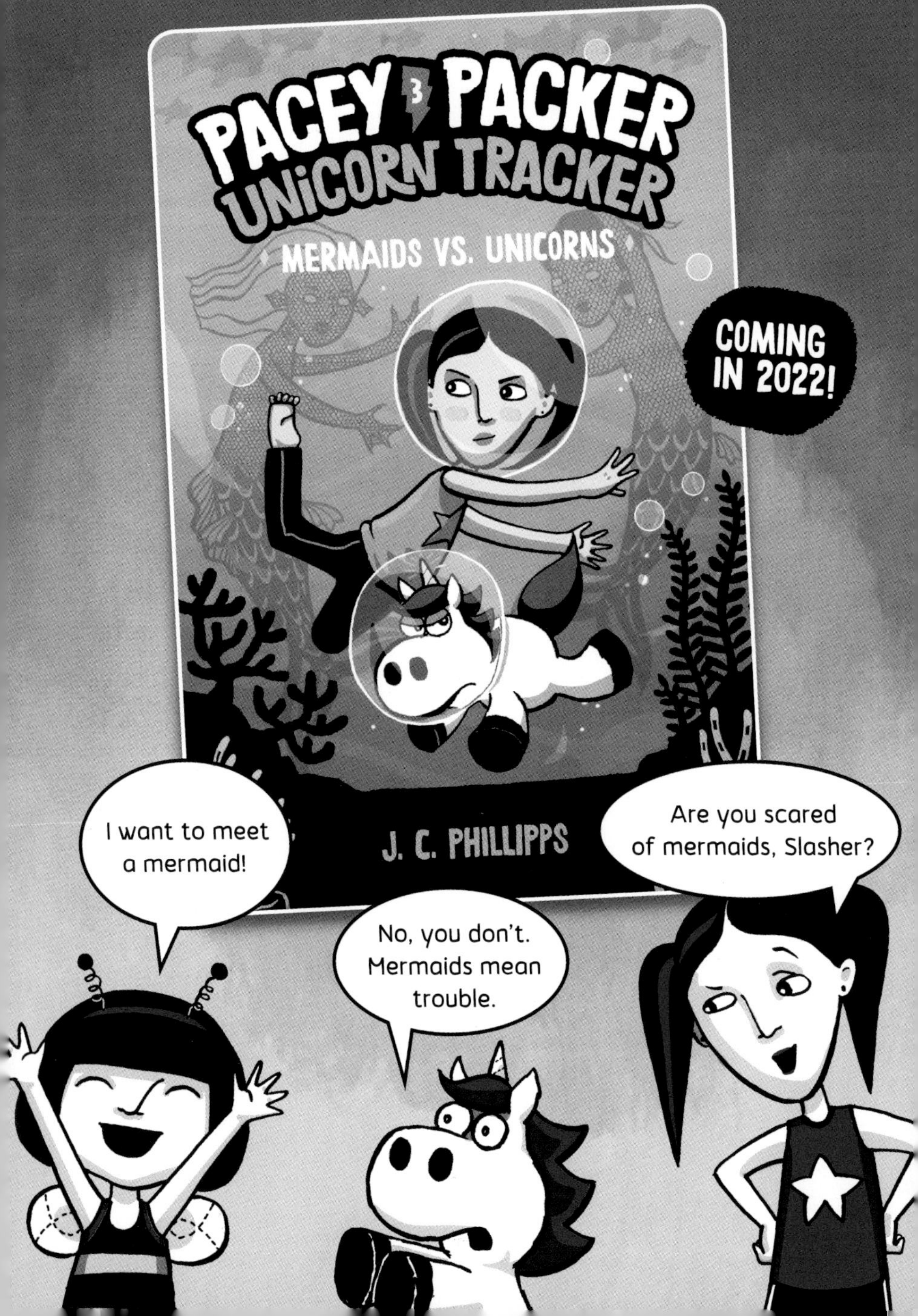
PACEY PACKER UNICORN TRACKER
3
MERMAIDS VS. UNICORNS
J. C. PHILLIPPS
COMING IN 2022!
I want to meet a mermaid!
No, you don't. Mermaids mean trouble.
Are you scared of mermaids, Slasher?

DRAW IT! LOOMI

1

With a pencil, draw a tall rectangle with curved corners.

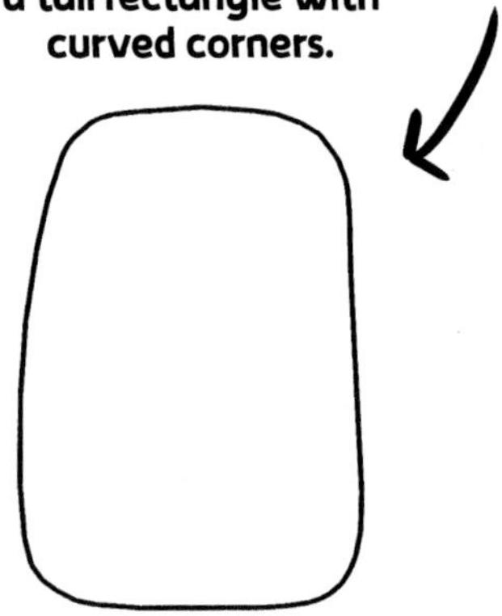

2

Draw circle eyes and a flat oval in between.

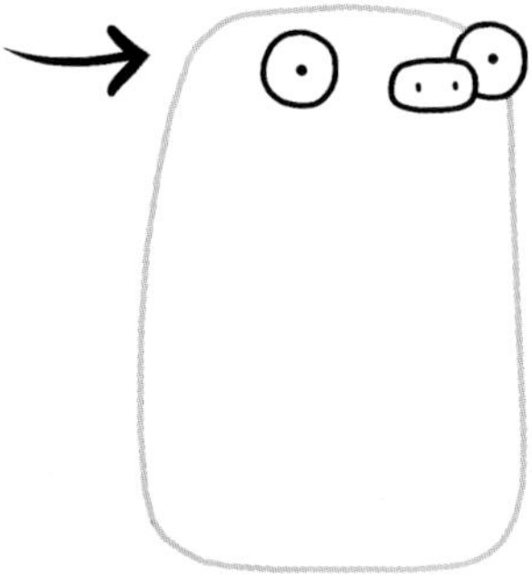

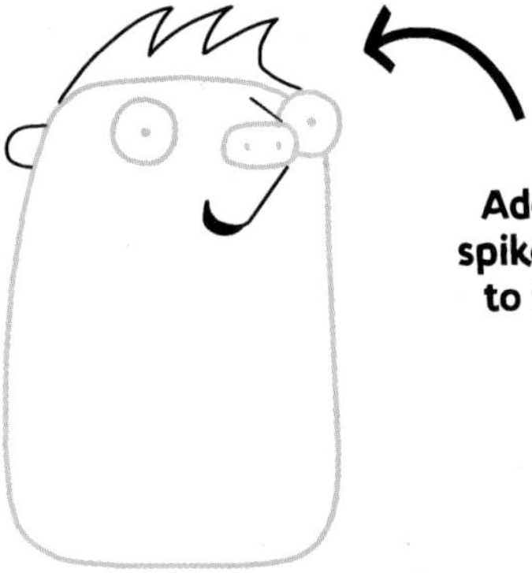

3

Add an ear to the side, three spikes of hair, and lines leading to the top and bottom of his nose. Add a smile.

4

Draw a belt across Loomi's waist. Add a curved line from one shoulder to the belt. Add a curve on the other side. Draw the bottom of the tunic.

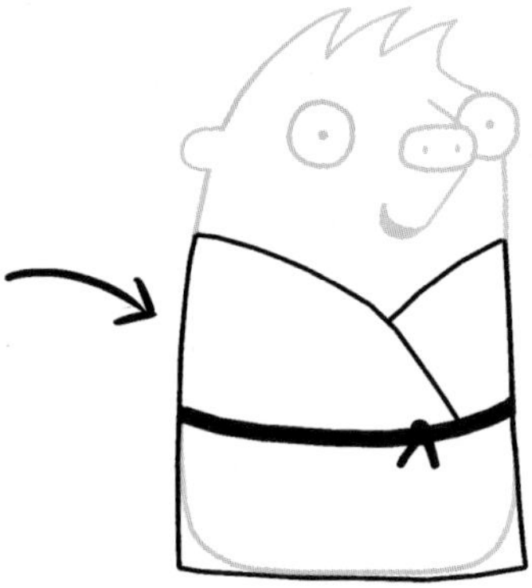

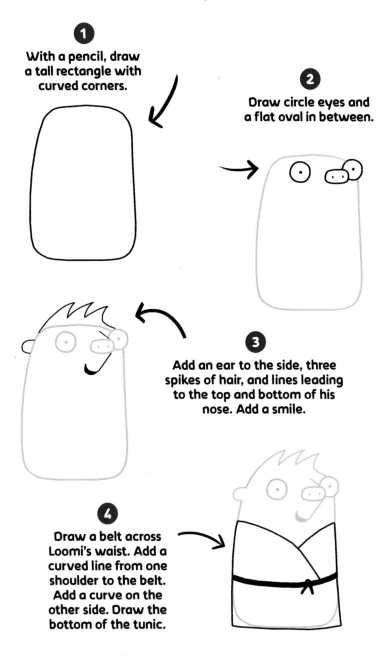

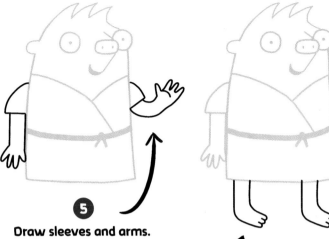

5

Draw sleeves and arms.

6

Draw two legs.

7

Draw details like freckles and hair on his face, arms, and legs. Add stitching on his tunic.

8

Ink over lines you like and erase lines you don't need. Color Loomi.

YOU DID IT!

Hello.

ACKNOWLEDGMENTS

This last year working on *Pacey Packer, Unicorn Tracker* has been such a fun and challenging time. Gigantic thanks goes to everyone who's helped me in my process, starting with my critique group: the Litwits. Ammi-Joan Paquette, Natalie Dias Lorenzi, and Kip Wilson are amazing writers who have corrected a ton of story issues and inconsistencies and are the first to tell me when something works. Thank you.

Shana Corey is an *amazing* editor, who is fantastic at balancing constructive criticism and the enthusiasm of a hundred cheerleaders. Michelle Cunningham has offered her expert eye and creative guidance as I create the look of Pacey's world. Thank you both! And high fives to everyone on the Random House team for all of your hard work and support.

I would not have the pleasure of spending my day drawing unicorns if not for my agent, Michael Bourret, who is kind and smart and just plain lovely to work with.

And to my friends and family at home, thank you for asking me about the book, for squealing with joy, for encouraging all of my dorkiness, and for giving me space to be exactly who I am. Love to my husband, Michael, for supporting local arts (me). And to my son for being awesome every day. And even to my kittens, Boris and Natasha, who sit on my illustrations and demand to be cuddled.

And thank YOU to everyone who loves spending time in Rundalyn and hanging out with cranky unicorns.

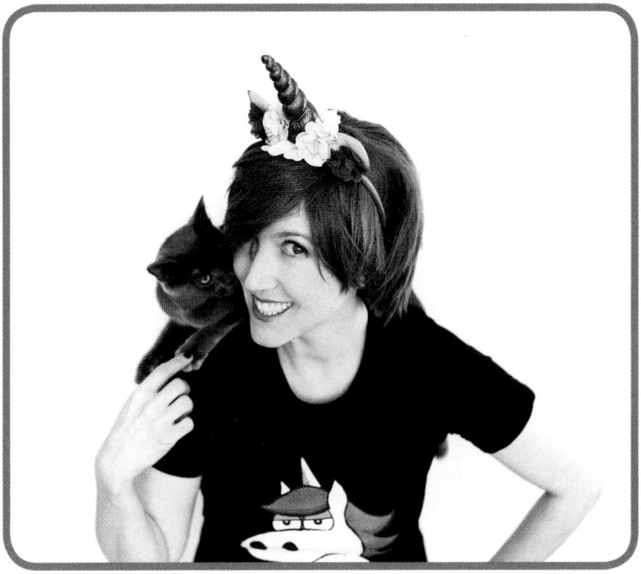

PHYLLIS MEREDITH

J. C. PHILLIPPS is a picture book creator and longtime graphic novel reader, as well as the owner of a somewhat extensive (though mostly accidental) unicorn collection. Like Pacey, she has a slight bossy streak and occasionally has purple hair. Unlike Pacey, she hasn't met a real unicorn. Yet. J.C. lives in Connecticut with her husband, son, and two cats, Boris and Natasha.

Visit her online at JCPHILLIPPS.COM and @JCPHILLIPPS.

And don't miss the next
PACEY PACKER UNICORN TRACKER
MERMAIDS VS. UNICORNS
coming in 2022!